The Maltese Defence

January – May 1941

A Misfit Squadron Novel

Simon Brading

First published 2019

This edition published 2024

ISBN: 978-1-917470-04-9

*For the James who inspired me to become what I am
and the one who brightens my future.*

PROLOGUE

11th January 1941

When the air raid siren wailed, the pilots were just finishing their breakfasts in one of the underground ready rooms of RAC Hal Far, near the southernmost point of the island of Malta. As one, they checked the chronographs attached to the wrists of their blue Royal Aviator Corps flightsuits before lifting their heads and grinning at each other. There was a heartbeat's pause, then twelve voices called out *buon giorno, Italia!* with the same cadence - that of the woman from the Imperial Italian radio station who took over at seven in the morning, precisely the same time as the Italian Air Force, the recently renamed *Legione Aerea*, launched their first raid of the day. A week earlier, that wireless station had been the only one they could get, but then, to everyone's relief, a technician at RAC Luqa had cobbled together a more powerful receiver, capable of receiving the Global Service from the repeating station at Gibraltar. The signal was intermittent and was often lost altogether if the weather was bad, or even just if the wind was in the wrong direction, but it was better than the propaganda and patriotism spouted by the state-controlled Italian station.

'This is the KBC Global Service, speaking to you from London. Here is the news at the top of the hour...'

The pilots continued with what they were doing, ignoring the siren and barely listening to the static-laden voice coming from the tannoy speaker in the corner of the room, knowing that nothing would be said that could possibly affect them, isolated as they were from the rest of the world not only by distance, but also by design of the enemy.

After three cycles of the siren, it faded to nothing, like an aircraft flying into the distance, and still the men and women didn't stir.

On any other British fighter base the siren would have prompted the pilots to leap out of their seats and race for the door, spilling their tea, tossing newspapers and bacon sandwiches aside, and scaring nearby pets, and it would have done on Malta, where the enemy bases were only sixty miles and twenty minutes of flying time away, if it weren't for the fact that the Italians insisted on still using airships. The antiquated and obsolete machines took almost an hour and a half to make the crossing from Sicily and the Italians liked their entire raid to arrive together, which meant that the British pilots had plenty of time after the enemy aircraft were spotted before they needed to take off.

The pilots weren't able to sit idly for long with the prospect of a hard fight so near, though, and they soon began to finish up and drift out of the room.

Eventually, there were only two left - a handsome young man with light brown hair and a striking blonde woman with a gap in her ready smile - the same two who lingered every day and who had learnt through extreme hardship to appreciate any chance they had to be alone together.

As Drake considered his next move, he reached across the chess board to take Tanya's calloused hand in his. He ran his thumb across the simple Duralumin band on her finger that he'd had one of the fitters fashion for them, feeling the weight of the identical one on his own.

There was no need for them to say anything. After two weeks of three sorties a day everything had already been said too many times. They knew they were pushing their luck, that one day, perhaps *that* day, one, or both of them, wouldn't come back, but neither of them were going to shirk their duty; they had long since reconciled themselves to the possibility of meeting the Dark Scythesman and had cheated him with a smile on several occasions. All that remained, then, was to appreciate the moment, take their fill of each other, then make sure they did what they had to do, to the best of their abilities, no matter what it cost them.

Drake frowned at the board. He'd taught Tanya to play chess soon after they'd arrived on Malta as a way to pass the time between sorties. She had proved to be a very quick study and, although she knew nothing about any of the openings which had been developed over centuries, she managed to improvise her own. They didn't always work, but when they did, they worked spectacularly well.

It seemed that morning's game was going to be one of those occasions when she wiped the floor with him and he had to accept that defeat was inevitable. He laid his king down and looked up from the board to give Tanya a wry smile. 'Congratulations. Again.'

He stood and offered her his hand. 'Shall we?'

She allowed him to pull her to her feet, but then surged forwards to take him into her arms and pushed him into a few dance steps.

He looked at her in surprise. 'I didn't know you could dance.'

'Of course! I taught ballroom dancing in Moscow and when we get to London you're going to take me to plenty of balls so that we can show off together.' She winked. 'I might even let you lead every so often.'

Drake found himself twirled round before he even knew what was happening and laughed as she tugged him towards the door.

Lord Rudyard Sebastian Augustus Cholmondeley Drake, Rudy to his friends, had only arrived on Malta recently, in the early hours of the 26th day of December, what had previously been called Boxing Day, under extremely unusual circumstances - he had escaped from "Bertha", the airship which was home to the elite Prussian squadron "The Crimson Barons", but which also served as a prisoner of war camp for captured pilots, by jumping through a hole in its hull created by jettisoning one of its enormous springs and using powered glidewings to fly to the island.

A ragtag bunch of escaped prisoners of war had made the perilous journey with him, including his fiancée, Tatiana Guseva, a pilot from the infamous Muscovite "Wolfpack Squadron". The rest - a Norwegian, a Pole and three other Muscovites - had since been ferried to a Muscovite port in the Black Sea by undersea boat, wanting to rejoin the fight against Kaiser Wilhelm III in their own countries, but Drake and Tanya had volunteered to join the fighter squadron defending the island, the so-called "Hal Far Fighter Force".

Sky Commodore Lloyd Hughes, the commanding officer of the RAC forces on the island, which included not only the fighter squadron, but also four bomber squadrons based at RAC Luqa and RAC Ta'Kali, had sent their request to London, along with Drake's report on the airship, Bertha, and the Prussian plans for Malta.

It would take a while for a reply to come from London - the message had to be taken by undersea boat as far as Gibraltar where it would then be transmitted - but the two pilots were desperately needed, so they immediately began flying with the squadron.

An undersea boat brought back an answer from Sir Douglas Pewtall, the Commander of the Royal Aviator Corps a week later. It not only assigned them to the squadron, but also granted Tanya a commission as an aerial officer and informed Drake that he was promoted to squadron leader, placing him in command of it. When Drake protested that he had only just arrived, Hughes explained that, not only was he already the highest-ranking pilot, but he was by far the most combat experienced, the others having been mostly transport or Naval flying boat pilots before the Italian offensive began.

Drake's new command comprised of six MK1 Hawking Harridans, four Cheltnam Sea Centurions - ageing biplanes on "permanent loan" from the Navy - and two curious, hand-crafted aircraft, built and flown by local aviation enthusiasts. Originally there had been twelve Harridans, delivered by the HMS Arturo in August, just before the carrier had headed north to take the Misfits to Muscovy, but three had been destroyed outright and three more had been cannibalised just to keep the remaining aircraft in the air.

It was a pitiful force when compared to what had defended Britain against the might of Die Fliegertruppe so recently, but it had managed to hold back the Italian assault for six months.

It wouldn't be able to do so for much longer, though, because the aircraft were on their last legs.

Due to the difficulty of getting convoys safely to the island, stocks of everything were running out. The only supplies actually coming to the island were smuggled in by fishermen or brought by the occasional undersea boat that had had occasion to visit Alexandria or Gibraltar, but they were paltry at best. Food stocks were getting low and luxuries (including tea, to the horror of every Brit on the island) were non-existent, but more importantly ammunition had almost run out and there was nothing left with which to repair the aircraft and there wasn't a single one that didn't have some damage or other. That didn't stop the pilots flying, though; the bombed-out ruins of the houses they flew over each day was a testament to how important their job was, even beyond any strategic considerations King George VI and his government might have.

Drake stood on the airfield, shading his eyes against the bright morning sun to inspect his squadron. It was not a particularly impressive sight.

The Centurions were in decent shape, but had been outdated even before the start of the war. They were slow and armed with only four .303 machine guns, but they did, however, have extremely tight turning circles and their pilots had learnt to use that to full advantage and had made a good few kills. They had wooden frames, covered by coated or "doped" linen, which meant that it was easy enough to get them back into the air after sustaining damage, but they'd been repaired so many times that the stocks of fabric had run out and most of them now had patches of red and white checks, betraying the fact that they had been mended using tablecloths, bought in bulk from a local manufacturer.

The Harridans weren't nearly as well off. They had been designed for ease of repair, and they were, but it didn't matter how easy it was if there was nothing to repair them with. Spares, including those provided by sacrificing three of them, had run out weeks ago and they were worn out. They looked it, too, with dozens of patches to show where damage to the Duralumin skin had been hastily covered with salvaged metal.

As for the two Maltese aircraft...

Drake wandered over to the colourful machines.

Like the Misfit Squadron aircraft, the pilots of the Maltese aircraft had designed and constructed their own machines, but unlike the Misfit aircraft, the Maltese ones weren't exactly state of the art.

Without access to the latest materials or construction methods the pilots had drawn on the traditions of their people for the designs and used whatever they had at hand to create machines that were best described as *unique*. That didn't mean that they weren't ingenious or effective, though, and the pilots had shot down their fair share of Italian aircraft.

The aircraft piloted by Spiru Felice, a small man with round spectacles and a permanent smile, resembled nothing more than a Luzzu, the Maltese fishing boats that could be seen off of the coast each day, although it was much narrower, designed as it was to slip through the air and not water. The fuselage was wood and ribbed like a boat, the front flat and beaked like the prows of the local vessels. The wings and tailplanes were canvas over a wooden frame and shaped like triangular lateen sails. The canopy was glass and metal and it stuck up from the fuselage, giving Felice impressive all-round vision. It was brightly painted, like the fishing boats, with blue on the bottom and yellow on top and there were two eyes on the prow, just behind the airscrew. All in all it was a strange creation that was more likely to provoke laughter than admiration, but Drake had seen it more than hold its own against the aircraft the Italians were throwing against them, especially since Felice was one of the most talented pilots he'd ever seen.

The aircraft belonging to Anton Baldacchino, a dark-haired and intense man with movie star good looks, was also nautically themed, but his at least looked like it belonged in the air and not bobbing up and down in the gentle waves of the Mediterranean Sea. It was triple-hulled, like a trimaran, making it look vaguely like Kitty Wright's *Hawk*, except that the central hull, where the cockpit and two large-calibre machine guns were situated, was the longest of the three and the others were just large enough to hold springs with their corresponding airscrews. The single tailplane on the central hull, much smaller than the one on Hawk, made it far less manoeuvrable than the American's aircraft, but with its twin springs and lightweight construction, also of wood and canvas, it more than made up for that deficit with sheer speed. It too sported eyes on its nose and was also brightly painted, although in red and blue, with a line of green dividing the colours.

Both machines had originally been powered by antique A.74 FIAM springs, imported from Italy before the war, but they had been replaced with much more modern Fischer-Berg FB601's, salvaged from enemy aircraft that had crashed on the island, improving their performance considerably.

Despite having sustained just as much damage in the hard fighting as the British aircraft, the two machines were spotless and freshly painted. That was because, while the British had limited resources and only a small team of fitters who had trouble just doing enough to keep their machines in the air, the Maltese had a small army of volunteers, mostly fishermen and their families from all around the island, who appeared from nowhere after every sortie. Proud that their countrymen were fighting for the freedom of their island alongside the British, the men, women and sometimes children, not only donated their time, but often brought along the materials that were needed, all of them readily available. They used the techniques they used on their boats, techniques that had been handed down over generations, to extremely quickly repair the aircraft, turning them around in minutes - even faster than they could be rewound and reloaded.

Usually Drake had no reason to speak to any of his pilots before takeoff; he could trust them to take care of themselves and their machines, just like those of any more conventional squadron, but that day there was something very different about the two Maltese aircraft and he felt he just had to ask about it.

The two pilots were standing together between their machines with a group of locals. They looked tired, but happy, and turned to grin at Drake when he approached.

Felice and Baldacchino snapped smartly to attention and saluted. Drake returned it out of habit, even though he liked to keep things more informal, especially among those pilots who weren't strictly under RAC discipline.

'As you were, gentlemen.'

Once the men had relaxed he nodded in the direction of Felice's aircraft and raised an eyebrow. 'Interesting modification.'

The grins on the faces of the Maltese pilots just widened as Felice replied. 'Well, my Lord, we've been thinking about our airship problem.' The Maltese pilots insisted on addressing Drake by his title, no matter how much he tried to get them not to. 'And we thought we would try to do a little fishing.'

Baldacchino nodded enthusiastically. 'It is what we do best, after all.'

The Italian airships were relics left over from the First Great War. They were nigh on indestructible, requiring an inordinately large amount of concentrated fire to bring down and the British squadron just didn't have the ammunition to spare. It wasn't really worth the trouble anyway, because they carried quite a small payload compared to a modern bomber, so Drake had ordered his pilots to ignore them and go for juicier targets, such as the medium bombers. That didn't mean he wasn't keen to knock them out of the sky, though, and he was ready to listen to any idea as to how to do so.

Drake wandered over to the colourful fighter and bent down to peer underneath it. A ten foot length of metal with a sharp point and serrated edges ran along the keel of the aircraft. It was attached to a winch that had been embedded in the fuselage, just in front of the spring, so that it could be lowered in flight.

Drake looked up at his pilots. 'A harpoon?'

'A whale harpoon.'

Drake chuckled. 'Appropriate.' He stood up and brushed his hands off on his flightsuit. 'I take it this is supposed to rip through the gas bags?'

Both pilots nodded, their grins firmly in place.

'What happens if it gets caught in something?'

Baldacchino bent down and pointed to a complicated looking series of knots just above the ring of the harpoon. 'If it doesn't cut through and come away, we've rigged it so that a sudden jerk will detach it.'

Drake contemplated the contraption. It was a pretty harebrained scheme, even by the standards of the Royal Aviator Corps, but it had its merits; the antique Italian airships were more akin to balloons than the more modern, rigid-hulled Zeppelins, so the blade should be able to cut through them, releasing their gas. It was going to be extremely risky, though, because they would have to get well within the range of the ring of defensive guns the airships mounted. He was doubtful that it would work, but, even so, after a few seconds he nodded and forced a smile. 'Good work! I'm looking forward to seeing what you can do, but only once you've carried out your runs on the bombers. Understood?'

Both men nodded again, enthusiastically, almost like children.

'Yes, Lord Drake!'

'Of course, my Lord!'

'Thank you,' Drake said, grateful that, just like with the Misfits, the Maltese pilots' individuality and eccentricity was backed up by discipline in the air and a good deal of common sense. 'Happy hunting and I hope the fish are biting today!'

'Thank you, sir! Happy hunting, sir!' The two men returned the traditional RAC encouragement and saluted again, parroted by their entire group of helpers.

Drake laughed and returned the salute to them all, giving them a last nod and grin before turning away.

A quick glance at his chronograph told him that it was nearing time for takeoff, so he hurried his steps slightly, waving to his other pilots as he went past, heading for his Harridan at the end of the flight line.

The twelve Harridans had been unmarked when they had been delivered and, in the absence of a proper squadron designation to give them, Sky Commodore Lloyd Hughes had just had letters stencilled on them to distinguish one from the other, from A to L. Only C, D, F, G, H and J survived, with F being Drake's and H Tanya's.

'Morning, sir.'

'And a very good morning to you, Sergeant Forrester! How does she look?' Drake gave his chief fitter, Gertrude Forrester, a nod and a smile, receiving only a scowl in return as usual.

Forrester was in her mid-twenties, but her permanent frown and the way her hair was pulled back severely under her uniform cap made her look a lot older. Drake had confessed to Tanya one of the first nights that they had been there that he felt intimidated by her, not only because of her forbidding nature, but also because she reminded him of one of the nuns he'd been unfortunate enough to make the acquaintance of in his youth.

The woman shook her head. 'If it was up to me she wouldn't be flying, sir.'

Drake grinned. 'If it was up to me I wouldn't be flying either; I'd be at home with my feet up, drinking tea, eating biscuits and reading a good book. Unfortunately it's not up to me, it's up to the Italians, so we'll just have to make do.'

'Hrumph.' Forrester grunted, her frown deepening, but she made no further comment and just ducked under the wing of the Harridan.

Drake shared an amused look with Giuseppe, the young Maltese recruit who served as Forrester's second, before crouching to follow her.

He squatted beside the undercarriage with her, using the strut to support himself and looked up at the wing where the day before he had been hit by a cannon shell from a heavy bomber. He was surprised to see that the hole was still there and he could see the clear blue Mediterranean winter sky through it. 'Um...'

'Before you say anything, *sir*, let me just tell you that my crew and I were up all night repairing the rest of the damage you brought my bird home with yesterday and we didn't have time to make her all pretty for your approval.'

It was Drake's turn to frown; he wasn't so much worried about the hole making the aircraft look less pretty as whether she could fly, and more importantly *stay together*, with a bloody great gap in the wing root.

She saw his expression and squinted at him - her ultimate expression of disapproval. 'Do you think I would let her take you up if I didn't think she would bring you back down?' She didn't wait for his answer but just looked back up at the hole, sticking one of her gloved hands into it. 'Having said that, you were damn lucky yesterday. This cannon round not only punched a hole through the frame *here*,' she tapped one of the slats that supported the wing's skin and he saw that it had been roughly welded and reinforced with pieces of metal of an unknown origin, 'but it also damaged the aileron control wires and they were hanging on by a thread.'

She pointed out the thick control wires and Drake saw that they had been replaced... with what looked like fishing line.

Once again she reacted to his sour expression. 'It'll hold.' She jerked her head in the direction of the group of fisherfolk loudly wishing the two Maltese pilots well as they climbed into their machines. 'I got it from them and they assure me it'll hold.'

Drake was doubtful, but he had no choice but to accept the woman's word, and that of the fishermen. He just hoped that if the line did break, it didn't do so while he was in combat.

'Alright, then, Sergeant. What else should I know about?'

Forrester quickly walked him through the rest of the imperfections of the aircraft, most of which he already knew about, having flown with them for a while, like that he only had five working .303 Whiting machine guns instead of eight, that the spring tension gauge was broken, and that there was a crack on the left side glass panel of his canopy. The last was especially annoying because it kept catching his attention and made his scans for enemy fighters far less efficient.

Drake signed the log book, accepting the status of the Harridan and taking responsibility for it, then handed it back to Forrester with a wide smile. He got only a disdainful sniff in return, as he had every sortie since he'd started flying F, but he'd promised himself that he would get her to crack a smile one day and he wasn't going to stop trying.

With only a couple of minutes left, Drake climbed into the cockpit and strapped himself in, thanking the fates for the umpteenth time that there were enough glidewings for the pilots, even if he, Tanya and a few of the others were using the ones they had borrowed from the Prussians.

He did final checks, paying special attention to the ailerons, moving the stick from side to side in an effort to see if he could feel any difference with the new control wire and was relieved when he couldn't.

When he was ready he gave Forrester a thumbs up, which she returned before backing away to the front of the aircraft and putting her hand in the air. She waited, looking down the line of aircraft, and when she saw that all of the chief fitters had their hands in the air, she blew her whistle.

The Centurions were first to go, accelerating smoothly and taking off after an incredibly short run. Less than a minute later it was the turn of the Maltese machines, which lumbered down the runway almost comically, pursued by the laughing children of the fisherfolk, before lurching deceptively heavily into the air. Finally, the Harridans, led by Drake, took to the air. He waggled his wings, knowing that the Maltese families would be watching, along with everybody else nearby, wanting to give them heart.

The Hal Far Fighter Force climbed away from the dusty fields, stone houses, sleepy fishing villages and bustling towns of Malta, which had remained almost unchanged for hundreds of years. They passed almost directly over the capital, Valletta, with its fortresses and the impressive Grand Harbour, which had sheltered ships for thousands of years, and headed north, out over the sea. They reached their operating height, ten thousand feet above the Italian bombers, with plenty of time to organise themselves into the pairs in which they fought and form a long line abreast.

As usual, the Italians were formed into three groups, with a dozen or so airships lowest of all, at fifteen thousand feet, one hundred plus medium and heavy bombers at twenty thousand, and the fighter cover, a single squadron of sixteen aircraft, above them all at twenty-five thousand feet.

The Italians had always decorated their aircraft as flamboyantly and individually as the Muscovites and during the First Great War the British had gotten used to the sight of gaily-coloured machines going into battle with them against the Prussians. That had changed with the advent of the Second Great War, though. After seeing the easy conquests the Prussians were making, the Italian king had decided he'd really quite like to have an empire of his own and had joined the Prussians in what had become known as the "Coalition" (although most people, the British press included, tended to refer to the Coalition as just "the Prussians", whether they were or not - indeed, most people were completely unaware that a good few of the machines that had flown in the battle over Britain had been Italian). The newly-crowned emperor of the Italian Empire had immediately commanded that everything possible should be done to bring back the glory days of the Roman Empire. He had begun an ambitious construction programme to rival that of Kaiser Wilhelm III's in Berlin and had invaded a few countries in North Africa as a start towards growing his empire. He had also made sweeping, but largely cosmetic, changes to his armed forces, renaming the army, navy and air forces as "legions" of the ground, sea and air respectively, changing their ranking system accordingly and giving them new uniforms and new liveries for their vehicles. Consequently, the aircraft that dropped bombs on Malta several times a day weren't the garish hotchpotch that they had been, but were rather impressively painted a blood red a few shades darker than that of the Crimson Barons, with gleaming gold markings and highlights. Even the bombs had been given a coating of gold paint for some reason - there was an unexploded and defused bomb on display in the town square of Valletta, which attracted plenty of visitors.

The snazzy new paint jobs did nothing to improve the performance of the aircraft, though. Like the Centurions, the fighters and bombers dated from before the war and aerial technology had evolved considerably in a year and a bit of hard fighting. They were easy pickings for the Harridans and the only thing stopping the British from destroying the whole lot of them was a lack of ammunition.

'All Falcon aircraft, this is Falcon Leader. You know what to do. Happy hunting.'

Drake waited for the acknowledgements to finish before switching to the frequency he shared only with Tanya as his wingmate. 'Falcon Two, this is Falcon Leader, what's your status?'

Drake winced as vehement swearing in Russian filled his ears and he glanced over at Tanya who was gesticulating widely at her aircraft.

He waited for her to run out of steam, knowing that it was useless to try to get a word in edgewise, then grinned at her. 'That good, eh?'

'Sorry, but this bucket of bolts is really annoying me today. How am I supposed to concentrate on killing Italians when my aircraft is trying to kill *me*?'

Drake frowned. 'If it's that bad, then return to base and get repairs - you'll have plenty more chances to shoot down some Eyeties later.'

'Not a chance, Leader, I'm not leaving you on your own.'

'But if...'

'On second thoughts, it's not too bad after all. I was wrong. I'm fine, Leader, ready to go. Thank you. No need to worry.'

She gave him a thumbs up and a cheery smile, before turning her full attention back to the struggle with her machine.

Drake grimaced, concerned, but there was no time to say anything more or order her home because they were on top of the Italians.

Ignoring the fighters angling to attack - the Centurions were assigned to deal with them - he picked out a flight of medium bombers at the front of the formation, squarely in the middle, and grinned; it was time to put the cat amongst the pigeons.

'Diving now.'

Trusting Tanya to stay on his wing, he pushed his stick forward and lined up on the lead bomber. He didn't aim to pounce on it from above, though, but rather come down in front of it then take it head on.

It was a tactic they'd used dozens of times and it worked just as well as it always did. The Italian pilots panicked at the sight of the Harridan fighters closing with them at them at more than six hundred miles per hour and broke in all directions. Unfortunately none of them crashed into each other - something that had happened before - but their neat formation was broken up, meaning that their guns no longer created a deadly crossfire. It also meant they would be delayed slightly and the raid would no longer arrive over the island together, giving the anti-aircraft guns a better chance to shoot them down.

Drake put a half-second burst into the belly of the lead bomber, then ducked under it and did the same to the next in line. In a flash he was through the bomber formation and he put the Harridan on its wing and pulled hard, bringing the fighter round for another run. He felt rather than saw Tanya separate from him, her aircraft evidently unable to sustain the turn. It didn't worry him too much, though; she could easily take care of herself. He just hoped her Harridan would be agile enough to evade the fighters when they finally came down for them.

The bombers came back into Drake's sights and now there were streams of tracers reaching out towards him from them. He kept his Harridan moving unpredictably with quick movements on his stick and rudder pedals as he closed the gap and grinned as he saw at least half a dozen of the bombers drop their payloads and dive away, heading back to Sicily.

The next pass took longer to complete, now that he was going in the same direction as the bombers, but it was also far more successful and two bombers turned for home with smoking engines, while one began a lazy dive towards the sea.

Once he was through he pulled the nose up and took a few seconds to check on the rest of his squadron. Tanya was racing to get back on his wing after having completed her own second pass through the formation of bombers, but the other Harridans, along with the Maltese machines were still making their second runs and, even as he watched, three more of the large red and gold machines dropped away.

Satisfied that the fight was going well, Drake turned his attention skywards towards the fighters.

He fully expected to find chaos, as the highly manoeuvrable Centurions spun and banked, taking what shots they could at the faster, but more sluggish Italian fighters, however what he saw made his blood turn cold.

Two of the Centurions were tumbling from the sky, broken and battered, wings snapped and flapping uselessly. A third was on fire and plummeting straight down towards the sea. The fourth was in a shallow dive, the pilot obviously dead, Italian machines swarming around it, still taking potshots.

For a moment he couldn't understand what had happened, but then he saw them - a squadron of Muhlenberg MU9's, already screaming down towards the fighters attacking the bombers.

The Prussians had sent fighters to help their allies gain air superiority over Malta.

'Break! Break! Bandits coming down!'

There was nothing more Drake could do to help his men and women because he suddenly had his hands full trying to survive himself as four of the MU9's had chosen him and Tanya as their targets.

The Prussians had the advantage of height and speed, so all the two of them could do was try to make life at least a little bit more difficult for them by turning into them and returning fire.

Drake banked hard towards the attack and squeezed off a quick burst, knowing full well it would go wide, but only wanting to put them off. There was a bang and the Harridan lurched, but then the Prussians were past. He continued banking to follow them, yelling to force blood back into his head as the G forces piled on. Dimly, he was aware that he had lost Tanya again, but he had no time to spare her a second thought as his turn took him directly back into the bomber formation.

He weaved his way in and around them, using them as cover from the pursuing MU9's, but all too soon he was in clear sky again.

A quick glance at his ammunition indicator showed him he was down to a few seconds at the most. That was barely enough to do anything worthwhile against the fighters, let alone the bombers, and in any other circumstances he would have gotten clear, but that would mean abandoning the rest of his squadron and he just wouldn't do that.

Tracers flew past his cockpit and he pushed the stick forwards to dive away from them while simultaneously rolling and kicking the rudder to perform a kind of split S which brought him back in the opposite direction. He'd sacrificed altitude for speed and he used it now to gain some distance from the MU's; he'd spotted Tanya in trouble on the other side of the melee, being pursued by an entire flight of MU9's and knew that her only chance of survival, and his, would be to work together.

'Falcon Two, I'm two miles away on your four o'clock and coming straight for you. Turn towards me on my mark and go under.'

'Roger, Leader.'

He threw his throttle wide open, pouring on emergency unwind to keep ahead of the two fighters coming up behind him and flew straight towards the Muscovite's Harridan, breaking the most important rule of combat flying in his haste to get to the woman he loved.

As he futilely urged his fighter on to greater speed, he bit his lip and watched Tanya fly, praying for her to survive the time it would take for him to close the gap.

Bombers buzzed past as Drake careened into the pack, missing some of them by only feet and sending a couple of them banking away in fright in an attempt to avoid him. A few of them passed through his sights, but he ignored all of them; he was going to need all the ammunition he had left if he and Tanya were going to get away.

Whilst they had hiked through the frozen north, trying to stay out of the clutches of the Prussians, Tanya had demonstrated that she was extremely good at everything she put her mind to, so Drake hadn't been surprised when she'd turned out to be an excellent pilot as well. He had only ever seen one other pilot with such raw skill, in fact, and that was Gwenevere Hawking, or Gwen Stone as she was now known - one of the renowned Misfit Squadron pilots. She and Drake had met as children and he had watched with amazement, and not a little envy, as the six-year-old girl had taken to the sky like a natural and surpassed him after only a couple of months of lessons, despite his two-year head start.

In the short weeks that the two of them had been on Malta, he had watched the young Muscovite woman do the same thing.

Drake had kept a close eye on her during the first sorties they'd gone on with the Maltese Squadron, knowing that she lacked experience, having been shot down in her very first mission with the Wolfpack Squadron. He needn't have worried; even though she was undisciplined in the more technical aspects and flew mainly on instinct, she still managed to carry out manoeuvres that were beyond most pilots and the weeks of constant sorties since had only served to hone those instincts. She was becoming a truly brilliant pilot and Drake, as an instructor, would have liked to say that he'd had something to do with it, but the truth was there just hadn't been time to give her lessons and, beyond a few pointers and the answer to some of her questions, he'd had no hand in her transformation.

However, this was the first time she was truly being put to the test and she was doing it in a machine that was barely functioning.

He watched, hardly able to breathe, as the four machines vied with each other for positioning behind her and every time one or other of them fired he tensed, sure that the game was up, that he would see her spinning away for the long fall to the sea below, but every time she spun or wheeled away. He was beginning to think that she was going to survive long enough for him to get to her, but then everything changed - two MU9's finished off the Harridan they'd been chasing and moved to head her off.

She had nowhere to go. He was going to be too late.

A strange calmness came over him as he realised that the day he and Tanya had feared had finally arrived and he gripped his stick tightly and prepared to do all he could to avenge her before he too was overwhelmed.

Drake hadn't counted on the rest of his squadron, though, and before the trap could be closed on the Muscovite, two extremely colourful aircraft appeared from behind a mass of bombers and pounced on the two MU9's closing in on Tanya, taking advantage of their attention being too firmly fixed on her. One of the Prussian machines broke up and tumbled from the sky and the other abandoned the chase, spinning away in a desperate attempt to avoid the incoming fire. However, in coming to her rescue, the Maltese pilots had temporarily ignored their own attackers and they paid dearly for their gallantry. Large chunks flew from Felice's machine before it went spinning away, but Baldacchino's machine burst into flames before it fell, almost instantly becoming a huge fireball that smeared a trail of black across the sky.

Drake tore his eyes from the horrific sight only just in time. 'Two! Break now!'

For a moment, he thought Tanya hadn't understood him, because her aircraft pulled up and away from him, but then, when she completed the barrel roll and ended up with her nose pointed directly towards him he understood - that had been the only way she could do a sharp enough turn for his plan to work.

Drake had timed it perfectly and, as the two Harridans closed on each other, a third aircraft, one of the largest Italian machines, a five-engined "Grand Eagle" heavy bomber, moved in between them. He pursed his lips nervously as the bomber loomed large in his windscreen, blocking out his view of the Muscovite's Harridan; if she didn't remember his instruction to go under the bomber then his plan would come to a very abrupt end.

At the very last moment he jerked his stick back, clearing the dorsal gun of the bomber by mere inches, then immediately pushed it forwards again.

The four MU9's were exactly where he expected them to be and the fire from his machine guns ripped apart the leader. A quick adjustment put a second in his sights and he squeezed off more shots, but they went wide as the Prussian pushed his stick forwards and dived away, followed by the other two - it seemed they had less appetite for the fight now that their prey were fighting back. Drake immediately forgot about them and banked hard, craning his neck to look for Tanya. He didn't find her, but what he did see was the wreckage of another Muhlenberg, presumably one of the ones that had been chasing him, tumbling towards the sea. He rotated further, putting the Harridan on its back and pulled the stick back hard, disengaging from the fight.

'Two, once you're clear, break away and head for home.'

His heart leapt into his throat when he didn't immediately hear from her, but after a few seconds his radio crackled in his ears.

'Roger. Leader.'

He frowned when he heard how strained her voice was, but forced himself to relax and concentrate on what he was doing; there were many reasons why she would have trouble speaking, not least among them pulling as many G's as he was at that moment in order to get away.

All thoughts of Tanya were momentarily put out of his mind, though, when he caught sight of what was happening almost immediately below him.

Felice's aircraft had apparently not been as damaged as it had seemed and he had used his convincing death dive not to escape, but rather to take him towards the airships. He had deployed his harpoon and, even though he had been followed down by a pair of MU's, was succeeding in wreaking havoc. Three of the airships were sinking from the air, huge tears in their gasbags flapping as they deflated, and he was already lined up on a fourth. However, as Drake watched, the Maltese pilot's luck ran out. He was bracketed by fire from several airships and when he tried to dodge he put himself squarely in the sights of the pursuing MU's. His left wing was torn off at the root, putting him into a spin which carried him squarely into the airship he'd been targeting.

The tangled wreckage of both machines dropped from the sky, tumbling wildly, and Drake knew that if the ever-smiling man hadn't already been killed in the impact, there was no way he'd be able to get free and deploy his glidewings.

There was nothing he could do for him, so Drake just continued his almost vertical dive, angling towards Malta, now only a few miles away. There was another Harridan a few thousand feet below him, heading in the same direction and he hoped it was Tanya, but he couldn't make out the letter on its fuselage because of the angle.

As he plummeted from the sky, he rotated the Harridan about its axis and slewed its tail back and forth, looking for enemy fighters, but there were none - they most likely had orders to stay with the bombers and not chase too far. What he did see, though, were puffs of deceptively pretty black smoke blooming among the bombers as the island's anti-aircraft barrage began and he took a few seconds to appreciate the sight, wishing the gunners luck, before gently beginning to pull up and turning on a course for home.

An hour later, Drake stood at the bottom of the ramp down to the underground hangar at Hal Far airfield, looking disconsolately at what was left of his command being hastily repaired - three Harridans which were completely outclassed by the Prussian MU9's, even before he took into consideration that they were so damaged they could barely get into the air in the first place.

Worse, though, was the fact that, of the twelve men and women who had taken off that morning only four had survived, and Drake was the only one who had escaped injury.

Tanya was in the infirmary having dozens of small glass splinters removed from her face and body - during their desperate last manoeuvre she had been hit by machine gun rounds from the MU's chasing Drake, one of which had shattered her canopy and narrowly missed her.

The pilot of the third and last Harridan that had made it home was a young woman called Betsy Jones, who'd been working in the typing pool until Sky Commodore Lloyd Hughes had asked for volunteers to join the Hal Far Fighter Force. Even though she'd earned her wings with London University Air Squadron before the war she'd never been in combat, but Hughes had been desperate for pilots and had given her a Harridan. Since then she'd proved to be a more than decent pilot and had even scored a few victories against the equally inexperienced Italians, but the Prussians were a whole other matter. A pair of MU9's had gotten on her tail and pumped round after round into her before she'd been able to shake them off. She'd managed to bring her badly damaged aircraft back to Hal Far and it would fly again, but she wouldn't; a cannon round had penetrated her cockpit, ripping a horrific wound in her leg and the doctors at Valletta hospital expected her to lose it.

The last survivor was Anton Baldacchino. He had managed to get out of his aircraft, but only after being badly burned over almost the entirety of his body. He had been picked up by a fishing boat a few miles off the coast and rushed to the hospital, but wasn't expected to last the day.

'So, the Prussians have finally decided to show their faces, what?'

Drake turned and saluted as Sky Commodore Lloyd Hughes appeared beside him. He was accompanied by a man dressed in a long black robe - the priest who turned up with the fisherfolk every morning to "bless" the Maltese aircraft.

'Yes, sir.'

'But no sign of the Barons, eh?'

'No, sir.'

'Hmm. I wonder what took the blighters so long.'

'I like to think they might have had their hands full for a while with Bertha, sir.'

When Drake had escaped Bertha he had been forced to leave behind hundreds of other prisoners of war. Most of them had been in no condition to make the jump anyway, but those that could have done insisted on remaining behind instead to free the other prisoners and then make an attempt to bring down the gigantic airship.

Hughes smiled sadly. 'Well, whatever the reason for the delay, this message couldn't have come at a better time.' He handed Drake a tiny scrap of paper.

TO O/C HAVEN STOP BADGERS ON THEIR WAY STOP HOLD WITH ALL YOUR MIGHT STOP CHIN UP AND BEST OF BRITISH STOP GEORGE R

Drake gave his commanding officer a scathing look. 'So, the Misfits are coming to save us all... Well, I hope they bloody get here soon, sir; we'll be lucky to last two days!'

The black-clad priest stepped forward and spoke for the first time. 'Hope is something we still have plenty of, Lord Drake.'

Drake looked him up and down. He was in his mid to late thirties, with black hair and kind features, a large wooden crucifix around his neck his only jewellery.

Priests, as leaders of the local community, were acting as liaisons between the British and the Maltese at the three airbases and the naval base at Valletta - Archbishop Caruana himself was the liaison at Luqa, the main British airbase.

'I don't think we've been properly introduced, sir.' Drake stuck out his hand and the priest took it with a smile.

'My name is Bugelli, Father Bugelli, but who I am is not important, what is important is that you continue to believe in your ability to defend this island. Like we do.'

The priest motioned to the side and Drake noticed the silent group standing in the sunshine to one side of the ramp out of the way, peering down into the darkness of the hangar. He searched their faces, looking for some sign of the belief that the man was talking about and was astounded when, instead of the sorrow he'd expected at the loss of their countrymen, he saw fierce determination.

'Why? Why do you still think we can defend you? If we couldn't do it with twelve aircraft, why do you think we can do it with only three?'

'Because we know you will never give up and also...' the priest gestured towards the Harridans. 'We have been given a sign.'

'A sign?' Drake raised an eyebrow.

The priest laughed. 'Yes! I know perfectly well you British don't believe in such things anymore, but we Maltese do.' He opened his arms and raised his voice as if preaching. '"And now abideth faith, hope, and charity..."' He smiled and winked at Drake. 'I'm paraphrasing a bit, but those were the words of St Paul after being shipwrecked on this very island.'

'And? What has that got to do with anything?' Drake had no idea what the man was talking about and he was fast losing patience; the last thing he wanted to do was stand around debating religion when Tanya was in the infirmary.

The priest pointed at the three Harridans in turn. 'F, H, and C. Faith, Hope and Charity. Christian virtues according to St Paul.'

Drake eyed the Harridans, taking in the letters painted on their side. Even though he didn't share the beliefs of the priest or the islanders he had to admit the RAC were going to need something if they were going to hold on until reinforcements arrived, call it luck or divine intervention. However, the scientist in him wasn't willing to give up to superstition without a fight and he smiled. 'Well, it's not much of a sign, is it? I mean, yes, we do have three aircraft, but we only have a couple of pilots left, so only two of them will be going up

Hughes smiled. 'That's where you're wrong, Squadron Leader; I will be joining the squadron from now on. Under your command of course.'

'But, sir...'

Hughes held up a hand to stop him. 'It's not as if there's much left to coordinate with the bombers grounded and our fighters reduced to a quarter their strength. The best way I can help this island now is by helping you take the fight to the Prussians.'

'Very well, sir.'

The three of them blinked in surprise as the air raid siren sounded and Drake checked his chronograph, puzzled. 'There shouldn't be another raid for a couple of hours, yet.'

Hughes sighed. 'Well, the Prussians are here now. You know them, they'll want to step things up a bit.'

Drake nodded. 'And they probably won't bother with the airships.'

There was a brief moment of silence as Hughes took in the implications of what Drake had said. 'We'd better hop to it, then.'

The men looked up at the sound of running boots behind them as Tanya came racing out of the emergency medical station next to the ramp. 'One hundred plus bandits, fifteen minutes out! Come on!'

She ran past them without slowing, heading for her machine and Drake grimaced slightly as his mind automatically called it *Hope*. He shook his head, then turned back to Hughes. 'Grab a helmet, sir, and let's go. You're Falcon Three, in "C".'

'In *Charity*, yes, Leader!' Hughes grinned and broke into a trot towards the third Harridan as Drake groaned. Out of the corner of his eye he caught movement and turned just in time to see the priest finish crossing himself. 'I do have faith, Father, just not your kind, I'm afraid.'

'That will be enough, young man.'

As Drake sprinted to his machine, the priest climbed the ramp to join his flock and began to lead them in prayer.

The bright blue sky to the north was filled with enemy aircraft and three Harridans climbed from RAC Hal Far to meet them.

Only three Harridans to face an invading force of more than a hundred aircraft.

They were all that was left to defend Malta's airspace, so it would have to be enough.

CHAPTER 1

26th January 1941

The two women watched Gibraltar slowly sinking below the horizon from the flight deck of the aircraft carrier, HMS Arturo. They weren't the only ones doing so - dozens of other men and women were on deck, basking in the late morning sun, such a welcome change after the freezing temperatures and snow of the winter which was still holding the British Isles firmly in its icy grip.

However, while their attention was firmly fixed on the rock which marked the last bastion of British strength before they steamed into the mainly enemy-controlled Mediterranean, that of the people around them was very much divided.

There was nothing obvious to explain why the two women were being watched surreptitiously by everyone else. It wasn't because they were sitting close and had their arms around each other; that wasn't particularly unusual. Neither was it because the taller of the two was stunningly beautiful, her long blonde hair streaming to the side in the wind over the flat deck. In fact the only thing differentiating them from the rest of the men and women was the lighter blue of their uniforms, but that provided the vital clue as to who or rather *what* they were and justified the snatched glances.

They were pilots, members of the famed *Misfit Squadron*. More importantly, though, the shorter, particularly ordinary-looking one, was Gwen Stone, who had not only attained an almost mythical status in the eyes of the British public and armed forces, but had also become something of a hero with the crew of the Arturo when she had named her new aircraft *Excalibur* in honour of their ship.

The two women were oblivious to the attention, though; they were very much in love and determined to enjoy a rare moment of peace together.

Gwen leaned her head against Kitty's shoulder with a groan. 'I'm starting to feel really stuffed after all these dinners. If this goes on much longer I'm not going to fit in my cockpit.'

Since the convoy had sailed, five days before, the Misfits had dined once with Captain Hewer, twice with the Arturo's officers and had even been transferred across to the flagship, the HMS Brunel, to dine with Admiral Myerscough, the veteran admiral commanding the small twenty-two-ship fleet, including escorts and merchant vessels, half of which would carry on to Alexandria after supplies, including a squadron of Spitsteams and the Misfits, had been delivered to Malta. Each meal had been a sumptuous affair with the best food each ship could offer in vast quantities, accompanied by as much wine, beer and spirits as the pilots could handle - which in most cases was an equally vast quantity and in some, far more than they should.

'I've seen the size of Excalibur's cockpit and I don't think you need to worry about that.' Kitty tilted her head to rest on Gwen's. 'Running out of spring tension because of the extra weight on the other hand...'

Gwen snorted. 'Thank you, that makes me feel so much better.'

Kitty kissed the top of Gwen's head. 'You know I'm joking; to me you're perfect. And anyway, I have a feeling we're all going to lose some weight on Malta.'

'Yes... The situation doesn't sound very pleasant, does it? I can't imagine going through what we did last summer and not be able to stuff my face afterwards, or have a few bitters.'

'And apparently they ran out of tea two whole months ago! How can they even consider themselves British anymore?'

Gwen slapped her on the arm. 'That's not funny.'

'I know, sorry.' Kitty grinned, completely unrepentant, despite her apology. 'Seriously, though, I really don't know how they're coping.'

'I guess we'll find out soon enough.'

'I don't know; the amount of supplies we're taking with us, it's not as if we're going to be short of anything for a while.'

'I'm not sure the drink will last very long.'

Kitty laughed. 'No! At least not if we allow Mac anywhere near it.'

The two fell silent at the mention of the Scottish member of the Misfits. He hadn't been the same since they'd left Muscovy; the death of his lover at the hands of a traitor had sent him into a self-destructive depression which not even his long-time friend, Lady Penelope Bagshot, had been able to bring him out of. To make matters worse, since the Arturo had sailed he had spent half his nights in the brig after trying to pick fights with equally drunk naval officers.

'Abby's never going to let him continue drinking so heavily in Malta.'

'And she shouldn't.'

'Don't you feel sorry for him?'

'Of course I do, but grieving is one thing, drinking and flying is another, especially in combat; he's going to get someone killed and it won't be the Prussians.'

Neither of them knew what else to say and Gwen took the opportunity of the brief pause to change the subject, not wanting the mood to sour completely. 'How did the poker go last night? Are there any officers on the ship with any money left?'

Kitty smirked, Mac temporarily forgotten. 'Not many.'

Gwen sighed. 'Be careful, please; I don't want you being ambushed in a corridor late at night and thrown overboard by irate sailors.'

'I'll try to make sure to leave them with the shirts on their back. But don't get angry with me - I'm doing it for us.'

Gwen leaned back to frown up at her girlfriend. 'How is you fleecing unsuspecting naval officers possibly for us?'

'Well, I thought that we could use my winnings to repair your Zeppelin.'

Gwen craned her head to give Kitty a kiss, which the American returned with soft lips. When she eventually pulled back, she reached up to cup the blonde's cheek. 'That's very thoughtful, thank you, but you know neither of us need the money.'

Kitty grinned lopsidedly. 'I know and I haven't actually taken any money yet, just IOUs. I wasn't really planning on cashing them either; I just want to make the Biscuit Bangers sweat a bit.'

Gwen laughed and gave her another quick peck, then snuggled deeper into her side and turned back to the view.

The Rock had almost disappeared below the waves now, only its summit was still in sight, with the radar towers and the sinister silhouettes of the two huge guns, which were capable of firing far into Spain or at targets across the channel in Africa.

A hush fell over the flight deck as everybody stopped what they were doing to watch, as if it were some momentous occasion that couldn't be missed. Then, when it was finally gone there was a collective exhalation, almost like a sigh, and the naval personnel began to make their way below in dribs and drabs. As passengers on the ship, the two Misfit pilots had no duties to perform and there was no reason for them to go down into the metal corridors of the ship just yet, but the others had to get ready to go on duty - it was almost noon and time for the change of watch - and the Misfits were soon on their own, apart from the group of mechanics performing routine maintenance on the Sea Harridan fighters at the stern.

To the delight of the Arturo's pilots, the newer, more powerful and better-armed fighters had been brought on board while they were in Scotland to replace the American Hammond Martinets that the ship had carried previously. There were also four, doubling the carrier's previous compliment of two, but it was still a pitiful amount when compared to the more modern carriers in the British fleet, which could carry fifty or more aircraft and didn't have the problems launching that the Arturo had, with only one aircraft lift. One of those carriers, the *HMS Heart of Oak*, was escorting the force and would provide the main air defence when the convoy came under attack, which it inevitably would. The Arturo, meanwhile, had been relegated to a more cargo-carrying capacity. It would have been an unsupportable indignity for the venerable old ship, which had an illustrious history dating back to the First Great War, if it weren't for the fact that among the cargo was Misfit Squadron - the Arturo's association with the squadron gave her a prestige that placed her among the most famous of the Navy's ships, despite her rapid decline into obsolescence.

There was no land in sight anywhere now and for security and secrecy there wouldn't be for the ships of the convoy until it reached Malta, so the eyes of the two women natural turned towards the other behemoth sharing the sea with the Arturo, The Heart of Oak. It was only half a mile away and they had a clear view of the eight Sea Harridans in neat lines on the flight deck, about to go on patrol.

They watched them take off one by one, their powerful, but short-ranged springs and the new hydromatic airscrews invented by the boffins at Hawking giving them more than enough acceleration to get them to flying speed before the deck ran out. It was a far quicker operation than it was on the Arturo and in minutes they were all up.

The two women watched them until they were out of sight, but then Gwen gave a sigh and sat up. 'I suppose we'd better go down soon; we've got that briefing, remember?'

'How could I forget?' Kitty continued to stare out to sea, her blue eyes bright in the stark sun. 'I've enjoyed these last weeks too much...'

'Even the bit where we were almost killed by Prussian spies?'

'Yes, I even quite enjoyed that, in between the bouts of extreme terror,' the American's lips twitched up at the ends, but only briefly. 'But always in the back of my mind I knew that we were going to have to get back into the thick of things at some point. I thought it would be the same as before, that I would just be able to jump in Hawk and take to the sky as I always have, but now the time has finally come I find I'm... I'm...' She blinked, as if surprised by what she was going to say. 'I'm scared. I have something to live for now, a reason to survive and I'm afraid of losing it.'

'Join the club,' Gwen nodded earnestly, 'but we both know that if we run away from this, from our friends and our duty, then we will no longer be the people who fell in love with each other.'

'Yeah, I know.'

Gwen reached up and turned Kitty's face towards hers. 'Besides, we're Misfits and the Prussians wouldn't dare to shoot us down.'

Kitty laughed and allowed Gwen to pull her into a kiss.

Since the briefing was only for the Misfits, Abby decided to have it in the lounge of the quarters they'd been assigned rather than moving to one of the far less comfortable briefing rooms. The pilots were joined by the first officer of the Arturo, Commander Twining, as the representative of the Navy, and Sky Commodore Dorothy Campbell, who had been given overall command of the air defence of Malta by the king, due to her familiarity with the Misfits.

The sofas and armchairs had been rearranged in a semicircle around a couple of corkboards and Abby sat in an armchair next to the boards, watching her pilots getting tea, coffee and snacks from the table in the corner. They were laughing and joking as always, but she knew them well enough to read their tension and nerves in the slight tremble of a hand, or the stiffness in a gesture. She didn't blame them; the task ahead was gargantuan and fraught with more danger than even their mission to Muscovy. She didn't even blame Mac when he topped up his coffee with something from a hipflask, although she resolved to have a word with him about it before the night was over; what happened on the ground was his business, but she couldn't have him drunk in the air, where people depended on him.

She waited until everybody had settled down and had enough time to eat at least a couple of biscuits before she stood up.

'Alright then, people, I know you already know why we're going to Malta, but I'm going to bore you with it once more, just in case anybody slept through the previous eight or nine times.'

There were groans from just about everyone and Abby grinned. 'Don't worry, it's the short version this time - I'm not going to make you sit through another hour-long lecture.'

'Good, because we have food and we're not afraid to use it.' Owen picked up a sticky bun and cocked his arm back.

There was laughter and not a few of the pilots called out for him to throw, but he just stuck his tongue out at Abby, then stuffed the entire fist-sized pastry into his mouth, making his cheeks bulge horrendously.

Abby laughed and shook her head at his antics, but then took a deep breath and waved for the pilots to calm down. They did so quickly and she took a deep breath before launching into the short speech she'd prepared at Dorothy Campbell's insistence. 'Malta is the largest of the three major islands which make up the Maltese archipelago, the other two are Gozo and Comino. While there are army garrisons and coastal defence guns on the two smaller islands, it is on Malta itself where most of our forces are concentrated and where the three airbases, Hal Far, Luqa, and Ta'Kali are situated. The island is seventeen miles by nine miles and it would be insignificant in the grand scheme of things if it weren't for its location - slap bang in the middle of the Mediterranean and astride the main shipping routes. Consequently, it has been hotly contested by just about every sea-faring race through the ages, from the Phoenicians, to the Carthaginians, to the Romans and now us, and we'd quite like to hold onto it because from there we can pretty much stop the Coalition from supplying their forces in North Africa while making sure that we can at the same time. It also serves as a base for our undersea boat fleet in the Med as well as having a pretty decent harbour for our friends in the Navy, or so I've been told.'

She nodded at Commander Twining, who returned the gesture.

'Now that's out of the way, here's the plan for tomorrow...'

'Tomorrow, Boss? Won't we still be about a thousand miles away from Malta?' Bruce, the squadron's resident Australian, turned to squint suspiciously at Commander Twining. 'Unless this rust bucket is able to go a mite faster than you've been letting on this whole time.'

Abby rolled her eyes. 'Ignore him, Commander; he tends to speak first then let his brain catch up later.' She gave the Australian a withering look. 'Yes, Bruce, we'll be a little less than nine hundred miles from Malta when we take off and that is precisely why I had you all doing those long range efficiency tests - we are going to launch as soon as we can, at extreme range, with dual springs.'

Commander Twining spoke for the first time. 'We've lost a lot of shipping in the Mediterranean recently and with the fine weather there is no way we'll be able to make it to Malta without being spotted. The captain thinks, and Sky Commodore Campbell and Group Captain Lennox agree, that we can't risk the ship being sunk while you're still aboard.'

Abby nodded. 'This is a risk we're going to have to take.'

'But... Nine hundred miles, Abby?' said Owen. 'That's easy enough for me, Wendy and Chalky, but A and B flights will barely get to the island at that kind of range, even *with* dual springs. If you get lost...'

'We're not going to get lost, Owen, everybody here has more than enough navigation experience - or did you think I sent you off on those tests individually because I didn't want you bumping into each other?' Abby turned to the large scale map on the first of the corkboards and ran a finger along the thick red line marked on it. 'Malta is almost due east from our starting point, but most of the territory we'd go over in North Africa if we flew a direct route is enemy-controlled, so we'll be staying away from the coastline until we reach the northernmost point of Tunisia. From there it's a two hundred and fifty mile straight run and we have the island of Pantelleria one hundred and thirty miles out to give us another reference point. I'm confident that we'll make it easily enough.'

She paused and looked around, gauging the mood of her pilots. There was apprehension and doubt on many faces at the daunting prospect of such a long flight, which, despite her positive words, really was pushing their luck somewhat; there was no room for error and a strong headwind would mean a couple of the less tension efficient aircraft, namely Hummingbird and Swift, might not make it. She wasn't done, though, there was more bad news to come.

'Now, the reason why I wanted this briefing as late as possible before takeoff is because I was hoping that the situation would change, but it hasn't, so I'm afraid that C flight, with the exception of Hummingbird, will not be coming with us.'

'What? Why?'

Wendy's voice rose over the rest of the protests from the C flight pilots who had suddenly found themselves excluded from the mission.

Abby waved her hands to calm them. 'Don't worry, this is only temporary! The latest hydrogen shipment didn't make it, which means there is barely enough on the island for basic necessities and there is nothing to refuel your aircraft with.' She let that information sink in before continuing. 'All I'm saying is that you won't be coming with us tomorrow - there are two tankers with this convoy, but that doesn't mean we have fuel to waste, so your aircraft will remain in their crates here on the Arturo and be delivered with the Spitsteams four or five days from now.'

The three pilots grumbled, but nonetheless slumped back into their seats in acceptance.

'Right, back to tomorrow. Because we have no spring tension to waste we won't be forming up over the carrier like we would normally, instead we're going to stagger takeoffs a bit, with the slower aircraft of A flight going first and B flight following. Somewhere east of here we'll form into two flights and should arrive over the island at more or less the same time. Prussian raids have been more or less constant, so it goes without saying that we need to get down to rewind as soon as we can so that we're ready to go up again as quickly as possible.' Abby pointed to a sheet of paper on the board next to the route map. 'This is the order of take off. As you'll see, the aircraft are already in the correct order in the hangar so this should be a straightforward exercise. Having said that, though, if anything does go wrong and somebody gets into trouble, of *any* kind, you are to leave them and that is an order; we do not have the spring tension for any monkey business.'

There was more muttering and grumbling at that, but it quietened quickly; they could all see the logic behind her command, even if they didn't like it.

Abby turned to the map of Malta which almost completely covered the second board. She tapped the southern end of the island with a finger. 'This is our destination - RAC Hal Far. As I said before, it is one of three airfields on Malta, the others are Ta'Kali *here* and Luqa *here*. Now, if you get into trouble and have to put down, those are about the only places to do so on the whole island so make sure you memorise their locations. Forget about landing in a field like we used to in England, the fields on Malta aren't big enough and they're surrounded by stone walls - you try putting down in one of those and you'll have a nasty surprise. If you can't get to an airfield then bail out or ditch in the sea, *do not* try to land anywhere else.'

She looked at the pilots one by one, making sure they understood, then waved at the photographs of their new home, pinned next to the map.

'The Italians bomb Hal Far just about every day, but the people there have a very efficient repair team and it's never closed. At the south end of the runway, uh...' she searched the photos briefly until she found the one she was looking for. '...*here*, there is an underground hangar. A steel ramp goes down into it and during air raids it is closed to protect the aircraft and repair facilities within.'

'We're not going to have to bloody live underground as well, are we, Boss? I was looking forward to a bit of sunshine after Muscovy! I'm so pasty white someone asked me if I was a Pom the other day...'

There was laughter at Bruce's comment and some commotion from where Gwen, Kitty and Scarlet were sitting - it looked like tea was coming from Scarlet's nose.

Abby shook her head, trying desperately not to laugh herself at the much-needed levity. 'No, Bruce, we don't, although if you interrupt one more time I'll damn well pitch you a tent down there.'

'Alright, Boss, I'll keep it shut from now on.'

'Thank you. To answer your question, we'll be billeted in a requisitioned house in a nearby town called, uh,' she consulted the map, leaning in to peer at it,' Birzebbuga.' She struggled to pronounce the name and ended up making it into something that sounded quite rude. She realised what she'd done and smiled at Bruce, who had opened his mouth to comment, but stopped himself just in time. 'Nothing to say, Bruce? You wouldn't like to comment on the name of the town?'

The Australian shook his head vigorously.

'No? Doesn't *Birzebbuga* sound a bit, I don't know, *funny* to you?'

Bruce clamped his lips firmly together, fighting a snigger and shook his head again, while tears streamed down the faces of the rest of the people in the room.

Abby just continued to stand with her hands on her hips, staring at Bruce. She was tempted to repeat the word again, but decided to have pity on him. Besides, the sooner the briefing was over the better - there were too many preparations to be done for the morning to waste too much time on teasing the Australian. She nodded. 'That's what I thought.'

She turned back to the corkboard and returned to the briefing, ignoring Bruce's loud exhalation behind her. 'Luqa and Ta'Kali are home to four squadrons of medium bombers, Pickford Nelsons, which have been grounded since the Italian attacks began, but Hal Far is reserved for the fighter squadron. They have just been given the official designation *261 Squadron*, but everyone still calls them the "Hal Far Fighter Force" which is what they were known as before. They received a dozen Harridans the last time Arturo paid them a visit, but after six months of hard fighting they are down to three...'

'Two.'

Abby looked at Commander Twining. 'Two? I thought it was three?'

Twining nodded. 'It was. Gibraltar received a report last night from an undersea boat that one of the Harridans had gone down and the pilot killed.'

'Who?'

Twining turned to Gwen, who hadn't been able to contain herself. 'Sorry?'

'Who was the pilot? Was it Drake?'

'Uh, no. I think the man's name was Lloyd. I'm sorry I don't know his first name.'

While Gwen sagged in relief, Abby grimaced. 'Lloyd Hughes?'

Twining nodded. 'Yes, that's him. Apparently it was mechanical failure. His Harridan was badly damaged in a scrap. It fell out of the sky while he was on approach and hit a stone wall.'

Abby looked to Dorothy Campbell, who was sitting silently next to the corkboards. She had known Hughes for more than twenty years, the two of them having been posted to the same squadron briefly in the twenties.

Campbell met her eyes and shook her head minutely - there was no need to say anything; there would be time to mourn later. In private.

Abby gave her an equally small nod, then went on quickly. 'The Hal Far Fighter Force has been doing what they can, but as you can imagine that's not much against up to seven raids a day with more than a hundred bombers and the Prussians have been bombing almost with impunity. However, since there's not much of strategic importance on the island, beyond the airfields, and Malta is only really important for its location, the Prussians and Italians haven't seemed to care too much where they drop their bombs and the civilians have been taking the brunt of the attack. Especially in the capital, Valletta.'

'Bastards.'

Abby didn't respond to Mac's muttered comment and went on as if he hadn't said anything. 'The War Ministry, in their infinite wisdom, have decided that we, and a single Spitsteam squadron who will join 261 Squadron, are all that can be spared from the defence of Britain. They did at least supply them with fifty Spitsteams and plenty of spares, though, so replacements shouldn't become an issue for a while at least.'

'Will they be joining us for tomorrow's navigation exercise?'

Abby smiled at Derek's refined voice and well-phrased question which managed to convey his misgivings about the mission in a quintessentially British manner.

'I'm afraid not; there was no room on the Arturo or the Heart of Oak for their Spits to be carried assembled, so they will be delivered along with C flight.'

'Bloody typical. As always we're the poor fools who get to stick our necks oot.'

Again, Abby ignored Mac and just kept her gaze firmly on Derek. 'Don't envy them, though; while we're here being wined and dined, they are stuck on a troop ship with a couple of thousand soldiers... *Welsh* soldiers at that, so I think you can imagine what it smells like.'

'Hey!'

Abby winked at Owen, who crossed his eyes and stuck his tongue out. She chuckled at her friend's antics, then moved back to the first corkboard and tapped a map that showed Malta, Sicily and some of Southern Italy. 'Considering what we faced in Britain and Muscovy we should be used to these kind of odds by now, but this is a whole different prospect.'

She ran her finger from Malta to the neighbouring island of Sicily. 'The enemy are based here in Sicily, between sixty and seventy miles away. That means they can be over our heads in less than twenty minutes.'

Gwen grimaced. 'So, even if it only takes us a few minutes to spot them and take off, their fighters are always going to have a height advantage.'

Abby nodded. 'Quite right. Which is why we're going to divide our forces in two and have half our fighters in the air at all times. I've already spoken to the officer commanding the Spits, Squadron Leader Tiffin, and he has agreed not only to put his squadron under my command, but also to split it in two. So, Derek, you'll lead one flight with Kitty, Bruce, Monty and six Spitsteams and I'll be taking the rest. Any questions?'

When there were none, she returned to the larger scale map. 'The Ministry is confident that we can regain air superiority in a matter of weeks, at which time the bombers will come out of hibernation and we will begin to make our own attacks, not only on their airfields, but their ports as well.'

There were a few chuckles and scathing remarks at the Ministry's optimism and she waved her hands to quieten them. 'Yes, I know it's a tall order, but I *cannot* stress enough, just how important Malta is to the war. If we lose the island then the Prussians have a clear path to supply their forces in North Africa. That will likely result in us being pushed out of the only theatre where we actually have a chance to fight back and it will also render the Muscovites extremely vulnerable from the south.'

'Then why hasn't the Ministry sent more people?' Owen asked simply.

'Don't forget Britain still has to be defended. Aircraft are being produced as quickly as possible, but until enough pilots are trained up to fly them then Britain is going to be vulnerable. This is all that could be spared.' She grinned. 'Besides, we're Misfit Squadron - this is a piece of cake for us.'

Bruce and Monty simultaneously blew raspberries and, because the briefing was coming to a close, Abby let them get away with it. 'There is one vaguely positive piece of news, though, and that is that there has as yet been no sign of the Crimson Barons, although we know from the intelligence provided by Squadron Leader Drake that they will be joining the assault on Malta at some point, so don't let down your guard.' Abby rubbed her hands. 'Well, that's all people - after you've packed your bags and made sure everything is ready for tomorrow, then you're free until first light. And try to get some rest for once, please!'

Gwen and Kitty went directly to the hangar deck after the briefing to check on their aircraft. Despite the fact that all of the aircraft were in tiptop condition, completely repaired after the damage they had sustained in Muscovy as well as repainted and polished to a high shine, the fitters were there, fussing over them. They had been informed of the morning's flight at the same time as the pilots and, being the elite group of men and women they were, couldn't help but give their machines another look.

Excalibur's wings were designed to fold up on a carrier to save space, but with the cavernous hangar given over entirely to the Misfits there had been no need to do so and Gwen found her fitters, along with a couple of Navy mechanics who often helped out, standing on them, clustered around the cockpit, her chief fitter, Sergeant Jenkins, sitting inside.

They hadn't noticed her arrival and she didn't bother them, but instead just stood back to appreciate the sight of the aircraft she had been gifted with for Midwinter. Seeing one of her designs come to life was always a very special experience, but the fact that her entire squadron and the King himself had wanted to construct the aircraft for her as a present made it unique and every time she saw Excalibur her insides warmed with a glow that she'd thought only Kitty could ignite.

Having said that, the aircraft hadn't turned out to be quite as perfect as she'd been in her mind. Very early on in testing it had become very clear that, while she was just as fast and agile as she'd known she would be, she also had a few foibles. Most of them were easy enough to compensate for and she quickly discovered she could live with them, especially because they were a direct result of the aircraft's high-performance, but one - the tendency the aircraft had for one wing to stall before the other - was potentially fatal and needed to be put right.

The only trouble was that Gwen was too used to her designs being as good as flawless and she'd had no idea how to do so.

She had spent days in the design shed at Bagshot Hall, trying to find a solution, but no matter what she came up with it never seemed to work in her head. She had almost become resigned to the fact that she might have to completely change the wing shape, or do something else equally drastic, but when she mentioned the problem over dinner it had taken Lady Penelope Bagshot less than a heartbeat to suggest simply installing a stall strip. That strip, a simple, six-inch, triangular cross-sectioned piece of metal on the front edge of Excalibur's right wing, had not only made the stall much more predictable but had taught Gwen a valuable lesson - that even though she might be arguably one of the best designers in the world there were others who had far more experience than her and it was foolish to insist on working on her own out of pride and not ask for help when she needed it.

'Ma'am?'

While she'd been lost in her thoughts, the fitters had finished what they were doing and Sergeant Jenkins had come over to see what she wanted.

'Morning, Sergeant. Is something wrong in the cockpit?'

The grey-haired veteran grinned and shook his head. 'No, ma'am, nothing wrong, but I think you should come and have a look anyway.'

Gwen frowned, not sure why she would need to look if nothing was wrong, but nonetheless did as he asked.

She jumped up onto the back of the wing then made her way along to the cockpit and climbed in.

'What am I looking...? Oh!' Gwen's eyes widened when she noticed a new addition - a dark wooden slat, about two feet long and four inches wide, with *Excalibur* deeply carved on it in an ornate script, had been fitted above the main instruments on the panel.

A shadow looked over her and she looked up expecting to find Jenkins, but met the eyes of the captain of the Arturo instead. He was out of breath, but grinning even so.

'Captain Hewer!'

'Lieutenant Stone. I hope you don't mind.' He nodded at the piece of wood.

'No, of course not, it's beautiful!' She gazed at the slat, taking in the dozens of shallower, nautically-themed carvings woven in and around the name. She couldn't resist reaching out to run her hand over it, feeling its warmth, so different from the cold metal of the rest of the aircraft.

'It's one of the spokes from the Arturo's wheel.' Hewer said. 'I had it trimmed to shape, then carved by our best scrimshaw artist. The last few days it's been passed from hand to hand around the ship so that everyone could get a look at it, which is why it hasn't been installed until now.'

Jenkins had appeared on the other side of the cockpit and he smiled sheepishly. 'I hope you don't mind, ma'am, but I gave them a Duralumin strut from the fuselage to replace it. I was going to ask you for permission, but the captain wanted it to be a surprise and I was ordered to silence. Sorry.'

Gwen gave him a mock serious look. 'That's alright, I'll forgive you, Sergeant, as long as you put another one in its place.'

'Of course, ma'am.' Jenkins said, looking hurt. 'I wouldn't let you fly with a sub-standard aircraft, you know that!'

Gwen chuckled; Jenkins was very serious about his work, sometimes overly so and she should have expected him to take her literally. 'I do, Sergeant. It was just a joke.'

Jenkins blinked, puzzled. 'Oh. Alright. Sorry, ma'am.'

'Never mind, it wasn't a very good one.' She smiled at him, then turned back to the captain. 'So, Excalibur has a piece of the Arturo in her and the Arturo has a piece of Excalibur.'

'Indeed! The entire crew wanted to do something to honour your new aircraft and this was the best suggestion they came up with.' Hewer winked and leaned in to whisper to her. 'And it also did a marvellous job of raising morale after we were told we were becoming a bloody merchant vessel.'

'I'm truly sorry about that.'

Hewer shrugged. 'No need; it was going to happen sooner or later. This old lady has had her day and Britain needs more modern weapons if she's going to get survive the storm. At least we've been given a chance to be useful; they could have put us in mothballs or scrapped us for metal - Neptune knows we need as much of that as we can get these days.'

He gave the wooden slat a last look, then patted Excalibur fondly. 'Anyway, I have to get back to the bridge. Good luck tomorrow, Lieutenant, happy hunting and we'll see you on Malta in a few days.'

'Thank you, Captain.'

Hewer jumped heavily down from the wing and stomped away towards the bow, greeting those of his men who called out to him as he passed, leaving Gwen to wonder at the high regard in which she and her fellow Misfits were held and the effect they had on the British people's lives, far beyond their accomplishments in the war.

The bar in the officer's mess on the Arturo began serving drinks as soon as the sun was above the yardarm and Mac made sure he was there every day.

It wasn't that he didn't have plenty of alcohol stashed among his personal effects, because he did, but rather he knew that he was going to need that on Malta, which by all accounts had become a bit dry for his liking due to the blockade.

The briefing had delayed his trip down to the fifth deck a bit, but he'd made up for the lost time by putting a little something in his coffee. However, it wasn't nearly enough and as soon as it was finished he rushed out of the Misfits' quarters, going through the bulkhead door and into the stairwell. He had to pause there, though, and clutch at the railing as the world spun around him and he became suddenly unsure as to exactly where the top step was - he didn't want to come a cropper the day before he could finally start killing some Prussians. Or Italians. Whoever the enemy damn well were in the Mediterranean. He didn't care, all he wanted to do was kill them and start taking his revenge for...

'Mac, a word please.'

Mac suppressed a groan as Abby's voice came from behind him and managed to force a smile as he turned. 'Abby. What c'n I do fer yer?' He used the railing to help him stand as straight as he could and tried to focus on his friend's eyes, but they kept slipping off to one side and he was having trouble not leaning to one side in an attempt to follow them.

'We haven't had much of a chance to talk since the New Year's party and I just wanted to know how you were.'

'Oh, grand, grand. Thank ye fer asking.'

He turned to go, preferring to brave the shifting stairs than to face the inquisition, but was pulled to a stop when she put a hand on his arm. She stepped in and looked up at him, staring into his eyes, scrutinising him with a frown. 'You don't look "grand", in fact you look like something one of my cats dragged in.'

Mac scowled. 'How I look doesnae matter, now, does it? It's how I fly that makes me a Misfit.'

'You're right,' Abby nodded, 'and that's exactly what I want to talk to you about. I've turned a blind eye to your drinking up until now, but that ends now.'

'What I do on my own time is my own damn business.' Mac growled through clenched teeth.

Abby held his gaze, not backing off an inch in the face of his sudden belligerence or his breath. 'But it is if it effects your flying. If you're too drunk to do your job then it won't just be yourself you kill but the people who depend on you to cover their arses as well. So, right here, right now, I'm letting you know that if I ever get even just a whiff of alcohol on you before a mission I will make sure you never fly again.'

Mac opened his mouth to reply, but words failed him and Abby just continued.

'This is your only warning.' Her expression finally softened and she stepped back. 'Please, Mac, do the right thing. We need you.' She held his gaze for a few second, then turned and went back through the bulkhead, leaving him alone in the stairwell.

Mac spun on his heels and stomped down the stairs, even more desperate for a drink than before. However, before he'd even descended a single flight, he stopped and leaned heavily on the safety rail.

'Dammit...'

CHAPTER 2

Shortly after dawn, the pilots dressed in their flightsuits and gathered in the lounge area for breakfast.

Most of them looked and felt extremely tired, having become unused to the early mornings that were part and parcel of their lives over the holidays, but Mac's hands were shaking, making his teacup chink against its saucer and he had to rush out of the room after only a few sips.

When he came back, he caught sight of Abby staring at him and he growled at her, glaring at her defiantly. 'Dinna fash yersel.'

When her expression didn't soften in the slightest he eventually deflated and muttered 'I'm dry, alright?' before turning away, grabbing a bacon sarnie and slinking over to an armchair.

Gwen sat with Kitty and Scarlet, nibbling a slice of toast and sipping at a mug of tea. She didn't like to have too much to eat or drink before flying, not wanting the distraction of a heavy stomach or a sudden urge to pee. Her two companions didn't concern themselves with such things, though, and both the American and the Irishwoman were stuffing their faces and gulping down their coffee and tea thirstily.

It wasn't just the prospect of being uncomfortable during the flight that was preventing her from enjoying her breakfast, though; she was worried about the journey, not so much for herself, but for her two friends. Nine hundred miles really was pushing it for many of the Misfits' aircraft, including theirs, and, even though the forecast for the morning was generally good, there was no telling what kind of winds there would be off the coast of Africa.

Kitty saw her frown and grinned, showing teeth encrusted with breadcrumbs and brown sauce. 'Worry about yourself for once, darling.'

Gwen shrugged. 'I don't have to; Excalibur will make it with a couple of hundred miles to spare. You guys, though...' She tutted and shook her head regretfully.

Scarlet laughed, but there was a note of nervousness in her eyes that wasn't usually there and Gwen immediately regretted being flippant. There was no time to rectify the situation, though.

'Alright, everybody, time to go!' Abby called out from the door. 'There are packets of sandwiches and a thermos in everybody's cockpit for the journey in case you're still peckish, no need to stuff yourselves now.'

Gwen brushed her hands off over her plate and took one last sip of tea before standing up. She took Kitty's hand when she offered it and together they followed the rest of the pilots out.

Despite the early hour, all the Misfit Squadron fitters were in the hangar, even the ones whose aircraft weren't flying, as was a bleary-eyed Dorothy Campbell, who'd apparently had a few too many drinks in the mess the night before, trying to drown her sorrows over the death of another of her friends. There were also quite a few Navy mechanics hanging around, although none of them really seemed to have much to do, and even Captain Hewer popped in briefly to wish everyone good luck, before hurrying back to his post at the bridge.

The pilots ran through final checks with their fitters and then, while a few last turns were put on the springs, they gathered around Hummingbird, which would be the first to take off.

Everything that needed to be said already had been, so Scarlet merely gave Abby an ironic salute, hugged Gwen and Kitty, then flashed everyone else a cheeky smile, before clambering into her aircraft. The gyrodyne's overhead rotor was at full speed in seconds, creating a gale within the hangar which rocked the nearest people back on their heels and then the Irishwoman was gone through the hole in the side bulkhead.

The pilots watched as Hummingbird slowly built up forward speed, gradually pulling ahead of the Arturo, but then Scarlet switched to horizontal flight and the machine accelerated, quickly disappearing from sight and the pilots dispersed to their own aircraft.

Launching the other eight aircraft was a much longer and torturous process than it was for Hummingbird. It involved taking one of them up to the flight deck with the single lift, waiting for it to taxi to the stern, turn, and take off, before the process could be repeated with the next in line. It was necessary, though; the carrier harked from a time when the aircraft it carried flew a lot slower and therefore needed far less of a takeoff run, which meant that multiple aircraft could just stay on the deck. The Misfits needed every inch of the flight deck with the extra weight of dual springs, though, and it was only due to the new hydromatic airscrews that B flight could take off at all.

Eventually, after almost an hour, all the aircraft were in the air, strung out in a long line at ten thousand feet that stretched over more than a hundred miles, but as time passed the line slowly contracted until somewhere off the north coast of Algeria, the four aircraft of each flight joined up.

Scarlet had a head start of almost a hundred miles on the rest of the aircraft, but she was caught and passed after just over an hour, by first A flight, then B flight. It took three hours for B flight to catch up with A flight, though, and by that time Malta was in sight. Or rather the mayhem that was the airspace over the island was in sight.

A crackle in the ears of the pilots announced that they were in range of the fighter controller based at Hal Far and then a soft but authoritative woman's voice filled their ears. 'Badger flight, this is Haven control, we have you in sight. Welcome. Please be advised that there is an air raid in progress, repeat, air raid in progress. Advise holding off your approach for one hour. Over.'

'Haven control, this is Badger Leader. Thank you and acknowledged. Standby, please.'

Abby immediately switched over to the squadron channel. 'All Badgers, report.'

'Badger Two, I've got one quarter tension.'

'Badger Three, I've been on reserve for a while, Leader.'

'Badger Four, same here.'

'Badger Five is going on reserve now, Leader.'

'Badger Six here, I'm on my last ticks, Leader, situation critical.'

'Badger Seven. Um, I've got a wee bit left on my main springs. Mebbe a tenth.'

'Badger Eight. I've got one half tension on my reserve springs.'

Abby took a few seconds to assimilate the information. All the while, the island was coming ever closer and the black cloud over it was resolving into wave after wave of bombers, the grey and green

Prussian FU88's and HO111's which had been seen so often over England accompanied by much less familiar dark red and gold Italian machines.

'Alright, we have no choice, we have to take our chances landing. Badger Six will be first down, followed by Eight, Three, Four, then Five, in that order. Badger Five, you coordinate things. Take channel three, we'll take four. Two, Seven, we're going to stay up as long as we can to cover them, but as soon as we get low on tension we land. Everyone understand?'

As soon as the acknowledgements had finished coming in, Abby switched back to the Maltese frequency. 'Haven control, this is Badger Leader. Be advised, we are landing. Repeat, we are landing. Over.'

'Negative, Badger Leader...'

Abby cut the woman off. 'Haven, we land or bloody ditch. Which would you prefer? Over.'

There were a good few seconds of silence, before finally a different, harsher woman's voice come over the radio. 'Badger Leader, we cannot guarantee the safety of your aircraft. Land if you must, but do so at your own risk.'

'We have no choice, Haven. Be ready for us. Badger Leader out.'

'Leader, Five here. The Prussians have never been very good at bombing, I'm willing to take my chances on the ground. We can rewind for five minutes and then get back into the air with at least some tension and help out.'

'Roger, Five. Get everyone down, but don't take any risks. Get into that underground hangar of theirs and wait it out. We'll be there when we can.'

'Roger, Leader.'

'Good luck, Five.'

'Thank you, Leader. You too. Landing aircraft, form on me. Switch to channel four.'

There were a series of clicks as the five aircraft which were running low on tension switched radio frequency, then silence as the three pilots who were left, Abby, Gwen and Mac, watched them drop slowly away. None of them said what was on their mind: that they weren't sure who had the most dangerous task - the ones who were landing through the heavy bombardment or the ones who were left to take on the combined Italian and Prussian forces.

'Right, then,' said Abby, 'let's go and get the attention of a few Fleas.'

Gwen tore her eyes away from Kitty's red, white and blue aircraft with difficulty and followed Abby as she climbed towards the enemy.

Dozens of bombers were already heading back to Sicily, their payloads dropped, but there were enough still on their way to make life difficult for the landing aircraft if they decided to target Hal Far and any that the three Misfits could destroy or ward off would increase their chances of survival.

'Badger Leader, this is Falcon Leader. Two aircraft joining on your three o'clock high.'

Gwen all but leapt in her seat at the familiar voice and she turned her head to look up so quickly that she felt her neck crack.

She immediately spotted the two Harridan fighters above and to her right, but had to slot magnifying lenses in place over her goggles and look twice before she believed what her eyes were telling her.

The Harridans were a mismatched mess; there was barely any sign of their original paintwork, but instead they were a patchwork of colours, as if they had been repaired with whatever had been at hand, including - by the looks of several panels in strange shades of green, grey and dark red - enemy aircraft. Gwen also noticed that the lead fighter had a single long cannon barrel poking out of the front of its right wing with an improvised bubble allowing it to fit, that the fuselage of the second fighter had been crudely modified to hold the canopy of an MU9, and the spring of the leader had a squared-off, Prussian look about it.

One thing both fighters did have in common, though, were an inordinate number of victory markings on their flanks, with Italian eagles mixed with Prussian crosses and, curiously, they both had names painted on their noses, just behind the airscrews - *Hope* and *Faith*.

However, while the aircraft were battered and shabby, the pilots were in worse shape and Gwen couldn't help but gasp when the Misfit aircraft reached the same altitude as the Harridans and she caught sight of her old friend, Rudy Drake. He was almost unrecognisable, emaciated, with sunken cheeks and prominent cheekbones, his eyes a dull, almost lifeless blue in black pits. The only way she knew for sure that it was him was the cheeky half smile he flashed in her direction and the voice when it came over the radio again.

'Nice aircraft, Goosy. Who'd you steal it from?'

Gwen laughed, but she couldn't think of a witty rejoinder in the face of his skeletal appearance.

Thankfully, she was saved from the necessity by Abby. 'Let's leave the happy reunion until the job's done, please, people.'

'Roger, Badger Leader. Falcon flight is yours to command.'

'Welcome, Falcon and thank you. I take it you heard our comms?'

'Affirmative, Badger Leader.'

'Then you know we have to protect Hal Far as long as we can. I plan to attack the group of eighty-eights at one o'clock; they seem to be heading for the south end of the island, but you know the situation better than I do, so if you have another suggestion let's have it.'

'Negative, Badger Leader, that's as good as any other plan.'

'That's what we'll do - we'll ignore the fighters as much as we can and try to give those bombers a bit of a scare. Pick your targets and engage. Happy hunting, everyone.'

Gwen smiled grimly at Abby's words - there was no shortage of targets to be had and she was looking forward to seeing what Excalibur could do.

She'd had plenty of chance to test the aircraft's limits during the exercises Abby had insisted on running over England during the week or so after New Year's. She'd even had a chance to have a few mock dogfights with the other members of the squadron and had found that Excalibur was every bit as agile as Wasp had been, if not more so. Mock dogfights just weren't the same as being in actual combat, though, and she was also quite interested to see what effect the four cannons and six machine guns she'd been able to equip her machine with would have on the Prussian bombers.

She lined up on one of the large enemy machines, an Italian heavy bomber, leaving the leader to Abby, and flicked the safety off her guns.

'Bandits, nine o'clock high. Coming down.'

Gwen didn't recognise the woman's voice, but figured that it was Rudy's wingmate. She spared a quick glance upwards to find the enemy fighters, instantly concluded that they were too far away to make any difference to her first pass, then returned her attention fully to the targets that mattered.

She opened fire slightly earlier than she would normally have done, knowing that the enemy machine would be within optimum range by the time the slow-moving cannon rounds closed the gap. Almost as soon as she had squeezed the trigger she had to let it go again, though, as the bomber filled her windscreen, but she had just enough time to see cockpit glass shattering and gaping holes appearing, as if by magic, in the machine's nose before Excalibur rose up and over it, missing the vertical stabiliser, with its ostentatious golden roundel of *SPQR* surrounded by a laurel wreath, by inches.

She smiled, deeply satisfied, as she pushed her stick forward again and found her next target already lined up; for the first time in many years she had an aircraft that felt like an extension of her, like it was reacting to her thoughts even before she moved her hands and feet.

The enemy formation was so big that she could have kept going in a straight line and used her entire load of ammunition on bomber after bomber, but even as she'd been attacking her targets, half her mind had been on the fighters diving on them from above and, after she had poured fire into her third target, she had to turn to face them.

Excalibur was on her wing in an instant and the G forces piled on as the stick came easily back into Gwen's lap. She yelled to keep the blood in her head as her flightsuit, designed to help with just such stresses, proved completely inadequate to the task. The turn was so tight, though, that it was done in an instant and she was rolling out of it before she had even expelled a quarter of her breath.

She snatched a shot at a pair of MU9's as they flashed past her, but then rolled Excalibur onto her back and nudged the rudder to rake another bomber with cannon fire.

'Leader, this is Seven. Switching to reserve spring.'

'Copy, Seven. Disengage when you can.'

'Roger.'

'Two, what's your status?'

'Still got a good few minutes on my main, Leader.'

'Bloody hell, that aircraft is something else, Two.' Abby's voice cut off momentarily and out of the corner of her eye Gwen saw Dragon firing on a bomber. The big aircraft's port side engine flared and it began dropping out of the formation. However, despite her success, there was a note of frustration in Abby's voice when she came back on the air. 'I've been running on reserve for a couple of minutes. I'm going to have to leave you, sorry.'

'No problem, Leader, I've got this.'

Abby laughed as she destroyed one last bomber, but then Dragon inverted and pulled into a vertical dive towards the island, now almost directly below.

Gwen banished her wingmate from her mind and turned back to the job at hand. A quick glance at her instrument panel told her that she had less than half of her cannon rounds left, but with how little tension she had left in her main spring she didn't need to worry about conserving it and immediately set about finding some lucky Prussians to give it to.

She put Excalibur into a shallow dive which took her under the bomber formation and brought her airspeed racing up. In the mirror above her head she caught glimpses of several Prussian fighters following her down, but she pulled up well before they could get in range, sending cannon fire into the belly of one bomber and putting several of the large aircraft between her and her pursuers.

She led the fighters on a wild goose chase in and out of their companions for a minute or so, never giving them a chance to get a clear shot at her, but then bomb bay doors opened all around her, releasing black death on the island below and the bombers dipped their wings and turned for home, leaving her exposed.

With her spring tension now critical and no point in attacking the bombers any further, Gwen turned Excalibur in her sharpest turn yet, sprayed her attackers with her remaining ammunition, scattering them, then dove for the southern end of the island, pushing her throttle to the stop and giving Excalibur her head.

The airspeed indicator was just reaching five hundred miles per hour when there was a heavy clunk. At first she thought it was some kind of structural failure due to the high speed and was about to start pulling out of the dive, but then realised it was just her main spring announcing that it was done powering her. She pulled the throttle back to minimum, switched to the reserve, then pushed the throttle forwards again, but not quite as far as before, wanting to keep at least a little tension back in case she had to divert to a different airfield.

She glanced back at the airspeed indicator and was shocked to find the needle had gone past its maximum of five hundred and fifty miles per hour and was firmly against the stop. Most aircraft began to creak and squeal in a dive as the forces acting on their wings built up, but Excalibur hadn't so much as groaned in protest and there had been nothing to let her know she'd been going so fast.

She laughed, exhilarated; she hadn't had a chance to test Excalibur in a full dive before, there had just been too much else to do - it looked like she was going to have to challenge Kitty to a race; the American was so proud of the performance of Hawk, especially in a dive, but she was in for a bit of a surprise.

The altimeter was racing towards five thousand feet and she gently began to pull out of the dive, all the time looking for any Prussians who might have followed her down. She found none, but didn't stop her search, just in case. What she did find were two Harridan fighters on a similar course to hers, a few thousand feet above her. She throttled back and levelled off, steering towards them, letting them sink down towards her.

'Falcon Leader, this is Badger Two. I have you in sight. Nice to see that bucket of bolts is holding together.'

'What can I say, Badger Two? The Hawkings know how to make something that lasts. Even if it does fly like a brick.'

'You're just jealous of my lovely new aircraft.'

'Are you sure it's yours? I mean, it's not very *pink* is it?'

Gwen laughed. 'I've missed you, Digger. I'm rather glad you're not dead.'

'Funnily enough, me too.'

Gwen pulled up onto Drake's wing, on the other side from his wingmate and glanced across. He was already turned towards her, smiling, and, now that she was closer, she found that he didn't look quite as bad as she'd thought. He was still terribly thin and his eyes had black rings under them, but he wasn't nearly as skeletal and unhealthy as he'd seemed at first glance before the fight.

They were close to the southern end of the island now and Gwen searched the ground for the airfield.

It was easy enough to find, not because there wasn't much island to search, or that she knew exactly where to look, but because it was wreathed in black smoke.

She slotted lenses in place to take a better look, wanting to see if there were any obstacles she needed to avoid on landing, but instead was confronted with a terrible sight that made her heart skip a beat. 'Oh, no...'

The all clear had been sounded only minutes before, but teams were already out repairing the airfield. They could do nothing about the aircraft of Misfit Squadron, though, which for some reason had been out in the open during the raid and not safely tucked away in the underground hangar.

The aircraft that Derek had led in to land because they were low on tension had each received at least one hit from explosive ordnance and in most cases two or three, smashing cockpits, tearing off wings and twisting fuselages. That would probably have been enough to put them out of action permanently, but, to add insult to injury, the pieces had been liberally sprayed with cannon rounds and it more than likely wouldn't be possible to salvage anything from them, not even any Duralumin panels. Several of the nigh-on indestructible spring casings had also been cracked open by direct hits and there was razor-sharp brass ribbon everywhere, tangled with the twisted metal that was all that was left of the beautiful machines. Needless to say, none of them would ever fly again.

Gwen jumped out of Excalibur as soon as she had shut down and ran towards where a group of dejected pilots were contemplating the wreckage of their aircraft.

'How did this happen?'

They all looked up as she approached, but it was Kitty who answered. Her eyes were red, but it wasn't just with sorrow for Hawk, there was a hefty amount of anger as well.

'The bastards wouldn't let us down into the hangar and we were stuck out here when a bunch of MU10's and FU87's attacked.'

Gwen went to the American and wrapped her arms around her girlfriend's stiff body, wanting to comfort her, but knowing that there was nothing she could do or say which could lessen the loss of the machine which had been with her for years and carried her through innumerable battles. She didn't give up, though, and just held on as she looked around the pilots, needing answers for why the woman she loved had been hurt. 'Why, though? Why didn't they let you go down?'

'Because the hangar door will never be opened during an air raid. No matter who wants to get in.'

The Misfits turned to find Rudy Drake hobbling towards them. He was half-accompanied, half-supported, by the pilot of the second Harridan, a good-looking, if a bit thin, blonde woman in an RAC flightsuit, with small fading scars on her cheeks and a gap in her smile.

'Everything and everyone is down in that hangar during an air raid and I think you can imagine what kind of damage even one bomb falling on the ramp might do.' Drake looked around the group, meeting their eyes one by one, making sure that they understood. 'As you must have found out, there is a smaller, reinforced entrance for personnel to get down below without putting the rest as risk, but it's just not possible to do the same for the aircraft. I'm truly sorry, but that's the way it is.'

There was hostile muttering at his words, but Abby had arrived in time to hear and put paid to it quickly. 'That makes perfect sense and we were warned when we came in.' She looked around the group, just as Drake had before her. 'We just got here at the wrong time. It was bad luck is all.'

Drake nodded. '*Very* bad luck; they never attack the airfield like this because we don't usually have anything sitting out in the open for their dive bombers and heavy fighters to target. They must have spotted you coming in and diverted from somewhere else.'

'I suppose.' Abby gave the destroyed aircraft a sad look, then sighed. 'Well, even though there's not much left for me to command, I'm going to be taking charge in the air, but you should continue to run things on the ground until Dot Campbell gets here and relieves you. Any objection?'

'No, ma'am.'

'Good, thank you. And by the way - while you're flying with us, you two will be considered honorary Misfits.' She grinned at Drake and Tanya, then turned to the other pilots. 'Alright, there's no use crying over spilt milk and we've still got a job to do, even though it just got a hell of a lot harder. Those of us with aircraft are going to be very busy for a few days, so right now we're going get some rest and food so that we're ready to fly again as soon as possible. The rest of you... Squadron Leader Drake, can you organise some people to help them sort through the wreckage, see if there's anything at all we can salvage, please?'

'Yes, ma'am.'

Abby nodded. 'Right, then, let's get to it Misfits. Mourn later when we have time.'

The mess, like everything else on the base, was below ground, and Mac, Abby and Gwen accompanied Drake and his wingmate down the ramp and across the vast hangar.

The three Misfit aircraft and the two Harridans were already there and she was surprised to see that they were being rewound by hand, but then realised that, with the shortage of hydrogen, much of what could be done manually, would be. Despite the logical explanation, though, it was still quite shocking to see a pair of donkeys and what looked like a gang of locals helping the RAC servicemen push the long wooden poles, which could be attached to the winding machines in emergencies.

Gwen fell in beside Drake, who was still being helped along by the blonde woman and he flashed her a smile. 'Wotcha, Goosy.'

'Digger.' She looked down at the leg he was favouring. There was no sign of recent blood on his worn flightsuit. 'Are you injured?'

'I took a bit of shrapnel to the leg last week. I'll be fine, I just need to rest.'

'I'm sure a couple of the others would be glad to fly your Harridans for a few days.'

The blonde woman at Drake's side snorted and a sneer curled her lip. 'As if they would be able to handle them.'

Gwen frowned at the woman's words and especially the tone of her voice; it sounded far too much like the arrogance she'd encountered in Muscovy from Sergei Baryshnikov, the leader of Wolfpack Squadron.

Drake just laughed, though. 'Gwen Stone, meet Tatiana Guseva. Tanya is one of the Wolfpack pilots who were shot down the same day I was and it's thanks to her I'm not dead in the woods or being worked to death in a Prussian airship.'

There was a warmth in Drake's voice as he spoke about the Muscovite that went way beyond gratitude or comradeship and she turned her head to look at him. There was something different in him, a maturity that he hadn't had. For a moment she wondered if it was the situation and the responsibility that had been heaped on him, being in command of the losing side of a battle, but she realised why when she noticed the ring on his left hand and the matching one on the Muscovite's.

With a start, she lifted her eyes to the face of the woman who had captured her childhood friend's heart, wanting to see if she remembered her from Muscovy, but recoiled when she found icy blue eyes already staring coldly at her. The hand on Drake's arm tightened possessively and Gwen had no trouble reading the challenge in the Muscovite's expression.

Drake chuckled as he couldn't help but feel the sudden tension between the two women. 'So, Goosy! You and Kitty, then?'

Gwen groaned at Drake's typical lack of tact - at least there nothing had changed. 'Yes, Rudy, me and Kitty.'

'You were already with her in Muscovy, weren't you?'

'You knew?'

Drake shrugged sheepishly. 'Not at the time, but I managed to figure it out. That was what you were going to say to me that evening, right?'

Gwen grinned. 'Yes. I was actually quite relieved when I didn't have to have that conversation.'

'You were relieved that I was dead?'

'Exactly.'

'Lovely.' Drake laughed.

'Of course, when I found out you were still alive I got nervous all over again, but now I see I didn't have to be.' She peered around Drake again. 'Pleased to meet you, Miss Guseva.'

A little of the coolness had left the woman's demeanour as the conversation had progressed, but she still only gave the slightest of nods in reply as she looked Gwen up and down appraisingly. 'Tatiana. And you are the famous Gwen.'

'Famous?' Gwen wasn't sure how to react to the Muscovite's comment and her frown returned as she remembered the woman's scornful remark from before. 'I am, uh, well, Gwen, at least. And I'm sure any of the Misfits would be more than capable of handling your Harridans no problem.'

The Muscovite smirked, but before she could say anything more to antagonise Gwen, Drake interjected again. 'Tanya wasn't commenting on your quality as pilots, Gwen. It's just that our Harridans have been flying well beyond when they should have been scrapped and have developed quite a few foibles because of all the damage the fitters haven't had the resources to repair. The two of us have had a chance to adjust to each one as they cropped up, but anyone else wouldn't know how to handle them until they'd put in quite a few hours and we just don't have time for that.'

'Quite right; you will of course continue to fly your own machines. *After* you've had today and tomorrow off to rest and recover.'

The three pilots glanced over their shoulders at Abby, who had apparently been listening to the entire conversation.

'But...'

'No buts, Squadron Leader Drake. Two days' rest. That's an order.' She grinned. 'And if you complain, I'll make it three.'

Drake shared a glance with his wingmate and Gwen could see the conflicting emotions in their expressions. She knew exactly what they were thinking - like any pilot, they were keen to stay in the air and take the fight to the enemy, but they also knew exactly how strung out they were and that they needed rest. In the end, common sense, along with the fact that Abby wouldn't let them fly anyway, won out.

'Yes, ma'am. Thank you.'

Their slow progress, at the pace of the limping Drake, had finally brought them to an unpainted metal door at the very back of the hangar, with "MESS" stencilled on it in big black letters.

Gwen was fully expecting the mess to be a stark and dank concrete hole like the rest of the hangar, but behind the six-inch, blast-proof door was like something out of a dream she'd had as a girl and certainly didn't look like it was underground.

Hundreds of large plants, many of them as tall as trees, had been strategically placed around the room to create what she could only describe as a thick forest, completely hiding the walls. Not a single scrap of concrete could be seen, in fact, because the floor was covered with a soft moss, like a thick and very expensive carpet. A short path through the bushes flanking the doorway led to a huge central clearing where dozens of wooden tables were set out in groups beneath wooden gazebos, which protected them from the occasional drip of water or sap. The illusion was completed by the warm light, which filtered through the plants from overhead, like sunshine through branches, and when Gwen gazed up to try to find its source she was surprised to find that there were even small birds flitting freely around the room.

Whoever had built the underground complex had known that the men and women stationed on the base would be spending hours of their lives there and had made every effort to make it as pleasant as possible. They had succeeded admirably and there were even men and women scattered around the clearing, sitting on blankets, socialising or reading quietly, preferring to spend their off-duty time there rather than above ground.

The clearing was flanked by a decidedly under-stocked bar on one side and by a buffet table on the other, where a man wearing a white apron was doling out small portions of food, and it was there that Drake led them.

The table was almost as long as the space, but it held only a few things in clockwork warmers. There wasn't even the obligatory tea urn and Drake shrugged apologetically. 'I'm sorry, there's not much to choose from. There's fish stew, a few eggs, goat's cheese, goat's milk and goat meat. There's no bread to go with it, I'm afraid, but we've got plenty of seaweed.' He pointed out the dishes as he named them. 'All donations from the locals. They give us what they can, but it's difficult enough for them as it is, so we only accept what we need. It's going to be a tough few days with the eight of you here too, though.' He grinned. 'Almost makes me wish we were back in Muscovy. Even with all the bloody beetroot.'

The three Misfits stared at the meagre rations, then shared a glance. As one, they reached for the small bags, which had been all they could bring with them in the tiny luggage compartments behind their seats. Along with their spare underwear and toiletries, they had each chosen and brought a few luxuries with them from England.

The cook's eyes lit up at the sight of the bags of spices that Abby had brought and murmurs began when Mac brought out some flour, a late substitution for the whisky he had originally intended to bring. However, it was Gwen's addition of three large packets of tea from Selfridges that had everyone in the room on their feet.

Abby looked around the RAC personnel. There was only a single mess, so all ranks were represented, and she was, if not exactly pleased, then relieved to see that all of them were equally malnourished and the officers hadn't been receiving more rations than the others.

'This was supposed to be for our billet, but we had no idea that the situation was as bad - I think it's only fair that we share.'

'That's very decent of you, thank you.' Drake gave the cook a serious look and raised his voice slightly so that the whole room could hear. '*One* mug of tea per person per day until Lieutenant Stone's tea runs out. The rest of the supplies you can use as you see fit, although bear in mind that we're not getting anything else until the convoy gets here.'

'Yes, sir.'

'Blimey! This place is a bit special isn't it? And are those bloody birds?' The Misfits turned to find Scarlet in the doorway, gaping at the surroundings, a huge, bulging kitbag on the floor next to her. When she finally noticed that everybody was staring at her she grinned, completely unselfconsciously. 'Any chance of a cuppa? I'm gasping!'

CHAPTER 3

The Misfits couldn't wait around for the cooks to prepare anything from the supplies they had brought, so, after a thoroughly unappetising, but blessedly brief snack, they made their way back above ground.

They had only been down in the bunker for half an hour, but the airfield had been completely repaired and the wreckage of their squadron's aircraft was well on their way to being cleared away. What little could be salvaged - three panels of gaily-coloured Duralumin, a dozen support struts, a few springs, a dozen or so belts of ammunition and a couple of weapons - had been placed to one side, but everything else had gone on the pile of scrap to be melted down and reused when there was a chance.

Drake's fitter, Gertrude Forrester, approached the pilots as they climbed up the ramp. She saluted Abby, but then addressed her pilot. 'Sir. We've swapped out the springs in the Harridans with ones salvaged from the destroyed aircraft - they're much better than the Prussian rubbish we've been using - and all aircraft have been rearmed and rewound and are ready to go.'

'Thank you, Sergeant, but please stand down Hope and Faith; we've been ordered to take a couple of days' leave.' He grinned. 'So, if there are any repairs you think you might like to make...'

Forrester came as close to smiling as he'd ever seen as she replied. 'I think I might be able to find a few things to do, sir.'

Drake nodded. 'Carry on then, Sergeant.'

'Yes, sir.' Forrester drew herself up and saluted Abby again, before marching off and barking orders that had the crews of the two Harridans wheeling them back down into the darkness of the hangar.

Drake smiled at her back, then turned to Abby, Gwen and Mac. 'Sounds like you're ready to go. One thing you should know, though,' he pointed at the ammunition that had been recovered from the wrecks. 'That pile right there effectively doubles how much ammunition we have on the island. Tanya and I have had to be very frugal this last week or so and I recommend that you do the same; the Prussians have been coming five or six times a day and...'

The wail of the air raid siren drowned out the rest of his sentence and he just grinned and saluted as the three pilots raced for their aircraft.

Gwen found a young man, who didn't look much older than Jimmy, Abby's son, standing by Excalibur.

He followed her up onto the wing and leaned into the cockpit to help her with her straps. 'I'm Giuseppe, ma'am, I've been assigned to your aircraft until your fitters get here.'

Gwen spared the man a glance. If the name hadn't given her a clue, his olive skin would have told her beyond a doubt that he was a Maltese native. 'Pleased to meet you, Giuseppe, I'm Gwen.' She gave him a smile before she went back to her checks.

'I know, ma'am. Everybody knows who you are.' He flashed her a blindingly white smile. 'You're all ready. Happy hunting, ma'am.' He jumped down from the wing, then went to stand in front of the aircraft and watched Gwen start up.

When Excalibur was ready, Gwen gave Giuseppe a thumbs up and he raised his hand.

It didn't take long for the other two aircraft to be ready and then Abby gave the signal for them to release their brakes and begin taxiing into position for takeoff.

Gwen made sure she was in her place on Abby's wing, then looked towards Kitty. The American hadn't once glanced in her direction since she'd come back out into the sunshine, but she was watching her now and Gwen waved. She got only a briefly lifted hand in reply, though, without even a hint of an accompanying smile.

Gwen, Abby and Mac flew four more sorties that day. Conscious of Drake's warning about ammunition stocks, they only shot when they were certain of a hit, which reduced their overall effectiveness considerably. They still managed to destroy ten bombers and four fighters during the day, but that was not nearly enough to make an appreciable dent in the enemy numbers.

Once night had fallen and it was clear that the Prussians wouldn't be coming again, Abby sent her evening report to Dorothy Campbell aboard the Arturo, which was now well into the Mediterranean and in range of the radio, detailing the situation and their losses. The Sky Commodore in turn reported that the convoy had been attacked almost as soon as the Misfits had taken off. The Arturo had taken minor damage and one of the supply ships had been forced to turn back to Gibraltar, damaged below the waterline and taking on water.

The Misfits remained at the base to have a small, but sumptuous, evening meal in the wondrous mess, prepared mostly from the copious supplies that Scarlet had brought, and afterwards they were driven to their billet in the nearby town of Birzebbuga, less than a mile away.

Despite the town's proximity to Hal Far it was relatively untouched; along with the airfields, it was the Maltese capital of Valletta, with its port and the two warships under repair in it, which bore the brunt of the daily Prussian and Italian attacks. The only time Birzebbuga suffered any damage at all was when there were clouds and the bombers dropped their payloads indiscriminately in the area where they thought Hal Far was.

The house that the Misfits had been allocated was a four-storey building made of yellowish limestone, built in the Baroque style sometime in the nineteenth century, on the northern outskirts of the town, near the two anti-aircraft batteries that were manned by locals. A man in a black cassock was waiting for them on a bench outside the door, in the pool of light from the single candle set out to guide the pilots. They had seen him around the base accompanied by a group of locals who had brought food and other supplies, but he hadn't approached them, dealing instead with Drake as always.

'Father! Good evening.' Drake shook the man's hand warmly. 'Let me introduce you.'

'No need, Lord Drake; we all know who the Misfits are.' The priest gave the pilots a small bow. 'In the name of all the Maltese people, welcome, and thank you for coming to our aid. I am Father Bugelli and I am the liaison between the local councils and the RAC at Hal Far. If there is anything you need, then all you need to do is speak to any of my parishioners on the base or at my church in the town, St. Peter's, and they will know how to find me.'

Abby gave the man a smile and a nod. 'Thank you, Father. We will.'

The priest returned her smile warmly. 'I will leave you in Maria's capable hands,' he gestured at the now open door, where a young woman, the housekeeper, was waiting, 'but first,' he held out the small cloth bag, which had been slung over his shoulder. 'A gift, to ease your sleep. A couple of bottles of the wine we make on the island.' He winked. 'It's not French, but it's drinkable.'

The Misfits chorused their thanks as the man gave them another small bow, then, whistling to himself, wandered down the road in the direction of the church they had passed a couple of minutes before on their way through the town.

Derek snatched the bag from Abby and pulled out the bottles of wine. He held them up to the light of the lantern, inspecting them with a hungry glint in his eyes. 'I've heard of Maltese wines, but never had the chance to taste them.'

Abby reached out and took them back. 'Well, *we* have a chance now. But first, let's see where we're staying.' She looked in the direction of the housekeeper who smiled widely and beckoned them in.

The house was far more than they needed, boasting traditional Maltese balconies overlooking the sea, its own tiny private beach down some steps carved into the rock cliff on which it stood, a well, and a wine cellar, unfortunately empty, where it was possible to take cover during air raids. The ground floor was entirely taken up by two large rooms, a dining room and a sitting room, one on either side of the entrance, both with impressive views over the sea. The other three floors of the house comprised mostly of living quarters, making it seem almost like a hotel, and even with the temporary addition of Drake and Tanya to the ranks of the Misfits there were more than enough rooms for the pilots to have one each and still be a few left over for when the rest of C flight arrived. When they questioned Maria about it she told them it belonged to a wealthy and numerous family who had been on holiday in England when the war broke out and hadn't been able to return. They had, however, after hearing of the aerial defence of their island, sent a message volunteering its use as a home for the pilots.

The bedrooms all had adjoining bathrooms, something that most of the pilots took immediate advantage of. The water came from a well under the house and was pumped up to a cistern on the roof by a clockwork device which worked on the principles of an Archimedes' screw. There was plenty of it for baths and showers, but unfortunately it wasn't hot; the water heater used oil and there wasn't any to spare.

The Misfits didn't mind too much, though; compared to what they had encountered in Vaenga, the lukewarm water was almost a luxury.

The bedrooms had been cleared somewhat for the pilots, but there were still signs of the occupants and, judging by the decorations and the large bed with lace mosquito nets, the one that Gwen chose on the third floor for her and an indifferent Kitty had belonged to a young married couple.

Gwen dropped her bag just inside, then turned to the American and folded her arms around her, not giving her a chance to avoid her.

Kitty's anger towards the people that had left Hawk out in the open had been perfectly understandable, but she hadn't been so blinded by rage that she couldn't see they had no choice in the matter, that to save the aircraft would have put everybody underground in danger. She had thrown herself into the work that Abby had assigned her and the other pilots, keeping herself too busy to think or feel, but the anger had still been there, simmering away.

Gwen just held her, without saying anything, until she felt the stiffness start to melt away and the woman's arms lift and hug her back.

Eventually, she broke the silence. 'I'm so sorry, Kitty.'

'I know.'

It would take a long time, and maybe a new aircraft, for Kitty to get over the loss of something which had been almost as much a part of her as a limb, but in the meantime Gwen resolved to have a word with Giuseppe and get him to find something for her.

Half an hour later, after the pilots had had time to settle in, they met back downstairs in the dining room, where Maria had laid out a few snacks, mostly fish-based, as well as enough glasses for everyone to sample the wine.

Derek had decanted the wines before going to find a room and he declared them ready to drink, but before he could pour, Scarlet pulled a large bottle of whisky out of a bag and plunked it on the table. 'For those who need a *proper* drink.' She grinned at Mac. '*Irish* whisky. The best in the world.'

Mac snorted, not impressed, and when she leaned across the table to pour some for him he put his hand over his glass.

Scarlet frowned at him. 'Aw, c'mon, now, Mac! I was only joking!'

Mac smiled to show he hadn't taken offence and shook his head. 'Thank yer, Scarlet, but I'm not touching a dram while we're here. I made a promise.'

'Bloody hell! Who made you do such a thing?'

Scarlet turned to glare at Abby, who held up her hands. 'Don't look at me. I just told him not to be drunk in the air.'

'I promised meself, lass.' Mac said, quietly. 'I needed to mek a change and that's all I've got ter say about it fer now.'

Scarlet blinked at him, surprised, but then shrugged. 'Good. At least this way there'll be enough for the rest of us for once.' She held up the bottle. 'Who wants some?'

In the end only Derek, Gwen and Abby had wine, the rest, with the exception of Mac, who poured water from the carafe on the sideboard, chose the whisky.

Once everybody had a full glass, they paused, though, and looked to Abby.

Abby stared into the glass of deep red liquid in her hand for a moment before lifting her head and gazing around the group, a determined look in her eyes. 'We put a lot of ourselves into our aircraft, but they are *not* what makes us Misfits - it's the people around this table, the ones we left on the Arturo, and the ones in England waiting for us to come back who do that. Yes, we've been hurt and our ability to take the war to the Prussians has been hurt too, but we're still alive and we'll bounce back from this. I've already checked and there are construction facilities at Luqa, so when the supplies arrive we can start building new aircraft.'

She shook her head when faces lit up at this news. 'Don't get excited yet; the facilities are very basic so it will be very slow going - it might be months before we've all got our own aircraft. Meanwhile, though, I'm sure we'll be able to play around with the spare Spits; there's plenty to go around.' She lifted her glass. 'So, let us drink to the aircraft we lost today. To Sable, Raptor, Swift, Hawk and Dove. They did what was asked of them and more. But let us also drink to the aircraft to come; may they bring even more fire and destruction to our enemies than their predecessors.'

She drank and each of the pilots took a moment to reflect on her words before doing the same.

'What are we going to build, though, Boss?' Bruce asked, his voice slightly hoarse from the whiskey. 'Are we going to make them all like Excalibur? I mean, she's a wonderful machine and it would certainly be effective, but if we all had the same aircraft we'd be like a regular squadron.'

'I assume you five would like machines that suit your style of flying rather than Gwen's?' She met the eyes of the pilots whose aircraft had been destroyed one by one, receiving nods from each. 'Well, you're not going to have much to do until the convoy gets here, so I suggest you grab some paper and start drawing.' She gave Gwen a wink. 'But if they don't come up with anything decent we'll just make them keep flying Spitsteams.'

Monty spluttered, appalled at the idea that he wouldn't be able to design a "decent" aircraft. He coughed as his whisky going down the wrong way and doubled over, wheezing and gasping for breath. Scarlet laughed as she began banging him on the back and he tried to wave her away, but she avoided his feeble efforts and continued until he got enough breath back to round on her. 'Bloody hell, woman! I don't know what's worse - you or your whisky! Where did it come from anyway? And how did you manage to bring so much with you?'

Scarlet shrugged and looked around the table. 'I just left the ammunition for one of my guns behind; I thought we could do with a few things and it's not as if I ever get to shoot at anything anyway.'

Abby gave her a wry smile. 'I'm very glad you did, but we could probably have done with that ammunition...'

CHAPTER 4

The second day of fighting was much the same as the first and the three Misfits flew six sorties, with much the same results.

At the end of the day they were exhausted, but none of them for a moment considered handing their aircraft over to anyone else. Mac was especially tired, but for the first time since Muscovy he looked almost like his old self.

The grounded pilots hadn't been sitting idle while their fellows were in the air. Not only had they made a start on ideas for their new aircraft, but they had also gone out to the "Graveyard", as it was known. The Graveyard was a fallow field, not too far from the airbase, where the wreckage of all the Prussian and Italian aircraft that had crashed on the island had been brought, at the request of Sky Commodore Hughes, and it was from those aircraft that much of the material the Harridans had been repaired with had come. The Misfits had gone out with Gertrude Forrester, who knew where the best preserved aircraft were, and had begun salvaging what they could, in case the parts on the Arturo proved insufficient to construct their new machines.

On the third day, Drake and Tanya rejoined the defence.

Since they were flying with new pilots and so few aircraft, Abby decided to dispense with the Badger callsigns for the time being, apart from her own as Badger Leader, for clarity when contacting the ground and other squadrons and instead use the pilots' nicknames. That meant that Drake was Digger, Gwen, to her chagrin, was Goosy. However, they weren't exactly going to call Mac "Mad Mac", so he remained simply Mac, and Tanya had stated unequivocally that she did not have, or want, a nickname and insisted on being called "Tanya".

The fitters had used the two days to full advantage and repaired as much of the damage to the Harridans as they could. They had even used some of the small reserves of paint available to make them look a little more respectable. However, the British aircraft were put to the test in the very first sortie of the day, when they were swarmed by three whole squadrons of MU9's and Tanya's Harridan proved lacking. It was still not quite as manoeuvrable as it should have been, due to a fault the fitters hadn't been able to trace, and she wasn't able to fight her way clear. She did her damnedest and bagged two, but was forced to bail out when her tail was all but shot off. She was picked up off the coast by a fishing boat, wet and extremely annoyed, but unharmed.

The others fared better, each of them sustaining only minor damage, but for the first time they were beaten back before they could get close to the bombers harassing the island. They were unable to strike at the bombers during the rest of the day either and it seemed that the Misfits were doomed to fail in their defence of the island right from the start, but on the fourth day everything changed - with the convoy less than two hundred miles away it was now in easy range of the bombers and fighters on Sicily and the enemy diverted their efforts from Malta to attack it.

The British ships had known that they would face an attack from the air eventually, but they were completely unprepared for its ferocity - the Italians had known of the approach of the convoy for days, plenty of time to divert more than a hundred bombers to the Mediterranean, along with several squadrons of fighters, and it was these aircraft which made up the majority of the first raid.

The Sea Harridans from the Heart of Oak and the Arturo had been scrambled at the first sign that the raid was heading their way and intercepted it some miles from the convoy.

They were completely outmatched.

Despite having new aircraft which were much better than the Italian fighters and ideally suited to the role of convoy protection, the naval pilots lacked experience. They managed to bring down quite a few of the attacking aircraft but suffered heavy losses in return and were unable to prevent the bombers from reaching the ships.

Thankfully, conventional bombers are notoriously inaccurate in naval engagements, especially when flying at the heights that the Italians insisted on. Only three bombs of the hundreds dropped hit their marks, the rest dropped harmlessly in the sea. Of those three, the damage from two was relatively minor and didn't do anything to prevent the ships from continuing. The third, however, hit one of the smaller transports which, like most, was a civilian vessel roped into the war effort and was unable to withstand the hit. It sank quickly, taking with it an invaluable cargo of food and half of its crew.

The Italian bombers weren't the only threat, though. While the main force of Prussian undersea boats was engaged elsewhere - in the Atlantic attacking convoys bringing supplies from America, or harassing shipping around the British Isles - two were in the Mediterranean and they coordinated their assault with the bombers. They were forced off by destroyers, but only after they had launched a salvo which destroyed one of the hydrogen tankers in an explosion which rocked even the largest ships and dealt the Arturo a glancing blow below the waterline.

A trio of Italian undersea boats joined the attack as well, but they were so inept that the British didn't even realise that they were there and they slunk away, back to harbour, their entire load of torpedoes expended to no effect.

It was the single flight of obsolete torpedo bombers, only six of them, that did the most damage in that first raid, though. Two were destroyed by anti-aircraft guns while they were lining up the attack, but the rest put their torpedoes in the water only a few hundred yards from the Heart of Oak, the largest and most valuable target in the British fleet.

The bombers were destroyed as they tried to pull up, two by Sea Harridans and two more by anti-aircraft guns, but there was nothing that could be done about the torpedoes in the water.

Three scored solid hits and water began pouring in.

It was immediately apparent that the carrier was mortally stricken and the captain gave the order to abandon ship. As lifeboats began plunging from the decks into the sea the huge ship began to list heavily to one side, hampering the efforts to launch.

Explosions rocked the ship as cold sea water reached still-hot boilers, ripping her open, accelerating the process and less than two hours after the first torpedo had hit, the huge ship, pride of the British fleet, slipped beneath the waves and disappeared forever.

The Misfits could see the smoke from dozens of miles away and knew they were too late.

The Italians had been quite sneaky and had stayed too low to be seen from Malta until they were well on their way to the convoy. The

Misfits had been ready and waiting and were in the air almost as soon as they were spotted, but even so, the raid was already finished by the time they caught up and all that was left for them to do was try to take a modicum of revenge for the destruction that had been caused.

The four remaining aircraft had been reorganised into two pairs after Tanya had been shot down. Of the three single-spring fighters, Excalibur's performance best approximated that of Mac's twin-springed Jaguar so she was moved onto his wing, while Drake flew with Abby.

At first, Gwen had found the change extremely disconcerting. Her instincts had screamed at her that it was a mistake to separate her and Abby; they had flown together in combat so many times that they could read each other's intentions before even a single control was touched, complementing each other so well that it multiplied their effectiveness, as well as allowing them to survive through situations that would have killed anyone else. Mac had surprised her, though, and over the course of the previous day she had come to appreciate the opportunity to learn from someone new. The Scotsman was an extremely experienced pilot and just as cunning a warrior as the leader of the Misfits, but his tactics were vastly different, suited as they were to his faster, less manoeuvrable machine. Gwen had found that they suited Excalibur almost as well, though, and had adapted quickly, but she still didn't quite have the same connection with him as she did with Abby. The day before, that had proven to be a bit of a problem with the Prussians, who were good enough to exploit a weakness and make life even harder for the already beleaguered Misfits, but they weren't facing the Fleas that morning.

The Misfits approached the returning Italians from the east with the sun directly behind them. It was a trick that the Prussians had used against inexperienced British pilots in the early days of the war and their erstwhile victims now used it to the same effectiveness against their allies.

To the Italians it was as if the Misfits appeared from out of nowhere and they scattered in panic as the cannon of the British aircraft ripped through even the thickest Duralumin of the deep red aircraft. The carefully ordered formation disintegrated further as many of the bombers found themselves suddenly having to take evasive action as several of their colleagues lost control surfaces, engines, or in one case almost an entire wing and flew into their paths.

The Misfits thrived in the chaos that ensued. As they had done so many times before, the two most agile fighters ducked and weaved around the large machines, using them to confuse and frustrate the Italian fighters that tried to corner them. Mac and Gwen, in the meantime, kept their speed up, easily outpacing any pursuit, and used it to carry out repeated runs on any part of the bomber formation that showed signs of reorganising, keeping them disoriented and making them easy targets for Abby and Drake.

Unfortunately, though, the Misfits now found themselves at the same disadvantage that the Prussian fighter pilots had been over Britain; they had to fly so far to get to the battle that they didn't have much spring tension to spare to actually fight. They used what little they had to good advantage, though, taking a heavy toll among the enemy aircraft, but it was like the summer all over again; no matter how many they knocked out of the sky there never seemed to be any fewer.

The Sea Harridans had already retreated by the time the Misfits arrived. Their special springs, which sacrificed range for higher-power and in theory provided them with an advantage over a conventional fighter, now proved to be their downfall. With the Heart of Oak sinking and the Arturo unable to land them quickly enough, many of the remaining aircraft ran out of spring tension and the pilots were forced to bail out.

Only eight managed to land safely.

It took almost an hour, but finally the fires were out, the survivors from the Heart of Oak and the destroyed transport had been rescued, and the Sea Harridans were safely on board the Arturo being rearmed and rewound.

Just in time for the warning to come of another impending raid.

By the time the Misfits had landed back at Hal Far, the next enemy raid was already in the air. The pilots had enough time to stretch their legs and grab some food while the fitters worked, but then they were back in the cockpits and once again chasing after the enemy.

There were just as many aircraft in this raid as there had been in the first, but when the Misfits caught up they found it was made up mostly of green and grey aircraft - it appeared that it wasn't just the Italians who had finally realised that they should be dedicating far more resources to dealing with a target of such strategic importance. The three MU9 squadrons which had surprised the Misfits the day before were only a very small part of the additional forces the Prussians had brought in - there were more than double the number of HO111's and FU88's that had been seen over the island before, as well as four or five dozen heavy fighters to provide close escort, and even a couple of squadrons of FU87 dive bombers.

This time the Misfits were much closer when the raid arrived over the convoy, but that only meant they had front row seats to witness the far more effective Prussian bombing.

The bombers went in much lower than the Italians had, at five thousand feet, instead of twenty, exposing themselves to concentrated fire from the anti-aircraft guns of the convoy, but they were more than compensated for the few losses they sustained. Dozens of bombs found their targets, exploding mostly on the slower transports that were unable to effectively keep up an evasive pattern of course changes. Two took on more water than damage control teams could handle and began their last, slow voyage to the bottom of the sea, fires broke out on several more, but one blew apart with an enormous detonation when a bomb found its hydrogen tanks.

The transports weren't the only casualties. Two destroyers were struck, one taking a direct hit to its bridge, instantly killing the captain and several senior staff members. Both continued to pour fire into the sky from their anti-aircraft batteries, though; even without a bridge or a leader, the naval personnel knew their duty and would continue to do it until told to stop, even if their ship were sinking beneath them.

However, it was the Arturo that took the brunt of the attack on the military vessels. The Prussians, like the Italians before them, recognised the worth of the carriers, even an old obsolete one like the Arturo, and had chosen it as the target for the two dive bomber squadrons.

The FU87's came screaming out of the sky almost vertically. Far more accurate than their more stately cousins, more than half of their bombs hit the Arturo. The thick flight deck protected the ship from the worst of the onslaught, but unfortunately the carrier had been in the process of launching the recovered Sea Harridans and one of the aircraft had been on the lift, ready to be hoisted on deck. Two bombs found the hole and detonated within the hangar, killing the unfortunate pilot instantly and filling the rest of the confined space with shrapnel and fire.

When the Arturo suddenly found itself with double its usual compliment of aircraft, there just hadn't been enough naval mechanics to go around. Eager to contribute to the fight, Wendy, Owen and all the Misfit fitters immediately volunteered to help with the Harridans, rewinding and rearming them as quickly as they could, trying to get them back into the air to meet the raid that the tannoy system had announced was already on its way.

Standard procedure on the carrier was for the mechanics of an aircraft to clear the hangar once their aircraft had been taken to the flight deck. By the time the Prussian raid reached the convoy five had already gone up and there were only three left, so thankfully most of the ground crews were already gone.

Owen and Wendy were standing together by the starboard wing of the last Harridan in line, waiting to push the aircraft onto the lift, when the bombs exploded and a hot wind blasted them.

Gwen tore her eyes from the destruction taking place on the placid sea and looked back at the dark swarm on the horizon, awaiting them.

With barely any Sea Harridans coming from the carriers, the Prussians had placed most of their fighters as a screen between the Misfits and the bombers. It was impossible to accurately count them, but she estimated that there were at least five squadrons of MU9's and HH190's, possibly six, and two of MU10's. Even at the height of the summer, they hadn't faced such extreme odds. Her mouth went dry and her eyes flicked involuntarily to Dragon, a hundred yards off her left wing.

Before she could say anything, though, Mac asked the question that was on all their minds. 'Are we really going into that, Badger Leader?'

It was several seconds before Abby responded. 'Affirmative, Mac.'

Gwen heard the doubt in her voice and looked across to Dragon again, this time slotting lenses in place to see Abby better. Her old wingmate had her lips pressed tightly together and was sitting stiller than she ever did whilst in a combat zone, not even scanning the sky. Even as she watched, though, the woman seemed to shake herself out of whatever had been going through her mind and resumed her restless watch of the sky.

'We can't let these bastards know we're afraid of them, otherwise they'll keep doing things like this, but we're not going to press our luck, not today anyway, and we're only going to do a single pass through them. We'll wait until we're a bit closer, then pretend to lose our nerve and start to turn away, but at the last moment we're going to turn back into them and try to surprise them. I only want to have to do this once, so expend as much ordnance as you can on any target you can get in your sights, then, when you're through, dive and skedaddle back to Malta.'

Drake laughed. 'Sounds like a plan, Leader. First one back to Hal Far is a wet blanket!'

'*First* one, Digger? You're only saying it like that because you know you're in the slowest aircraft here.' Gwen chuckled, but even she could hear the note almost of hysteria in her voice. Of *fear*.

'Radio silence, Misfits.' Abby snapped, her voice tense, betraying her own nervousness. 'Turning left on my mark. Mark.'

Together, the Misfits stood their aircraft on their left wings and gently pulled back on their sticks, beginning a turn across the front of the enemy formation as if they were going to flee. They lost sight of the enemy fighters in the process, so they were unable to see if their ploy was having any effect, but it didn't matter; they would make their run whether the Prussians fell for it or not.

They held the turn for a couple seconds, presenting their bellies, but then, at Abby's command, they snapped back onto their other wings and pulled hard towards the enemy. In an instant they were facing the enemy once again, but thanks to their feint they were no longer facing the centre of the enemy formation but rather the flank and the Prussians were scrambling to adjust. The neat pattern of aircraft shifted and all but disintegrated as each of the flight leaders tried to manoeuvre their machines to get a clear shot at the approaching Misfits. Gaps appeared, as did overlaps, and suddenly more than half of the enemy were unable to fire for fear of hitting a friend.

The Misfits plunged into the disorder, cutting swathes through it as if they were the Dark Scythesman personified.

Gwen gritted her teeth as she pulled her trigger over and over, her eyes darting everywhere, her hands and feet unceasing on the controls as she slewed Excalibur back and forth, like a dog worrying a bone. There were so many aircraft around her that she barely had to do anything to find a target in her sights, but, as the British sliced through them, the Prussians were reacting in ever more unpredictable manners, crossing her path and closing gaps she had been aiming for, moments before she reached them, and she was being forced her to push her aircraft to the limit just to avoid a collision.

Fire reached out towards her as the highly-experienced Prussian pilots recovered from their initial surprise. It was far too hastily snatched, though, and most of it came closer to hitting their own machines than it did hers. At least two impacts made the stick shudder and jump in her hand, but she couldn't afford to take her eyes off the view through her canopy to see where she had been hit, so she ignored them and just kept going.

Suddenly, she was through and she instantly inverted Excalibur, pulling the stick as far back as it would go at the same time and feeling they familiar exhausting increase of weight as the G forces piled on. Her heart was already beating so fast that her vision barely greyed, though.

A flash of colour in the corner of her eye caught her attention and she found Mac's golden Jaguar keeping pace with her. She grinned and tried to lift her hand to wave, but it was so heavy she couldn't move it from the throttle where it was resting. She saw him grin back, even as threw his head back and shouted to keep the blood in his head, but then he was falling behind her as Excalibur's superior performance showed.

Gwen let up on the stick as the nose of her aircraft approached the horizon and, when she could, she looked around for pursuit.

She found Mac immediately, but it wasn't him she was worried about; Abby and Drake were in aircraft that were too similar in performance to the MU9's of the Prussians for them to easily outrun them like Excalibur and Jaguar could. She soon spotted them, several hundred yards behind and above her, a cloud of enemy fighters on their tails, closing rapidly.

She didn't think twice.

She slammed her throttle to full emergency unwind even as she pulled back on her stick as hard as she could. The G forces piled on, far stronger than they had before and this time Excalibur did creak in complaint as her wings were subjected to strains that would have folded up any another aircraft. Gwen kept the stick in her lap, though, and screamed, fighting hard to stay conscious. Blackness crept in on her vision as Excalibur's nose came above the horizon, but it receded again as the aircraft climbed, beginning to slow. By the time she was passing the vertical her vision was normal again and she was able to seek out her fellow Misfits and their pursuers.

The aircraft were a few hundred yards below, but still half a mile in front of her, so Gwen throttled back to half and when Excalibur's nose reached the horizon she kept her there. She waited patiently, judging her moment, and when Abby and Drake were just passing below her, she pounced, completing her loop and swooping down behind the Prussian fighters.

The Fleas had been so focussed on their prey that they hadn't even noticed she was above them and by the time any of them saw her it was too late; she was already on them.

It was like basic training all over again, shooting towed targets, except that there were living breathing men in these aircraft. Gwen put round after round into fighter after fighter and saw huge chunks spinning off them as her cannon ripped through them. She was able to attack seven of them before the rest scattered in panic.

Her intention had only ever been to get them off her friends so she let them go and formed up on Abby's wing, opposite Drake.

Abby glanced across at her and nodded her gratitude, but Drake pulled up slightly so that he could grin at her. 'Really, Goosy, you *have* to tell me who you got that bird from so I can thank them.'

'Um... Digger here, Leader. I've got a bit of a problem.'

The Misfits were on approach to Hal Far and Drake, in the most inefficient aircraft, was supposed to land first, but he had pulled out of his descent just before landing and turned out of the circuit.

'Report, Digger.'

'I'm pretty sure there's something wrong with my landing gear.'

'Wait one, I'll check. Goosy, Mac, go ahead and land.'

While Gwen and Mac continued towards the airfield, Abby banked away and formed up on Drake's wing.

'Put them down, Digger.' Only one of Drake's wheels came out and Abby grimaced. 'You've only got one leg. Give the manual pump a go.'

There was silence and Drake's Harridan bobbed gently up and down a few times as he pumped the lever of the hydraulic system that was supposed to put his gear down if the electrical system failed.

'This feels a bit loose, Leader.'

'It's not doing anything. Hang on, I'm going to take a look.'

Abby carefully manoeuvred Dragon until she was directly below the Harridan and sighed; there was a ragged hole in the wing where the right wheel was and the strut which connected it to the aircraft didn't anymore.

Drake heard her and chuckled. 'Sounds like you've got good news for me, Leader.'

'Not exactly, Digger. You're going to have to bail out. Point her out to sea and jump.'

Drake fell silent for a moment. 'I'm think I'm going to do a belly-flop, Leader.'

'Negative, Digger, it's not worth the risk.'

'I know what I'm doing, Leader, and we need this aircraft - if I can get her down without too much damage it *will* be worth it.'

'Alright, then, but don't blame me when you do yourself a mischief.'

Drake laughed. 'I won't!'

Gwen smiled at the waiting Kitty and stepped down from the wing of Excalibur. Her legs gave way beneath her and she staggered, but Kitty caught her before she fell. She closed her eyes and leaned against her, taking a moment to luxuriate in the feel of the American's strong arms around her, but then forced herself to pull back. She went on tiptoes to kiss her, then turned away and shaded her eyes against the sun to peer into the sky.

Kitty correctly guessed what she was searching for. 'What's happening with Rudy? We saw him on approach, but then he broke off.'

Gwen spoke without stopping her search. 'He has a problem with his gear. Abby was going to take a look for him.'

Kitty joined her and after only a few seconds pointed towards the end of the runway where Dragon had just come into sight, on final approach. 'There's Abby, but I don't see Rudy.'

It wasn't until Dragon was touching down that Gwen finally saw the Harridan. 'There he is.'

Relieved, she watched Drake's battered aircraft descend from the sky as elegantly as her pilot. Since he was coming in to land, she assumed that whatever problem he'd had was resolved, but when he was less than half a mile away she realised that his wheels were still up. 'What's he doing?' She knew exactly what he was doing as soon as the question was out of her mouth - for some reason he had decided to put the aircraft down with the wheels up instead of just taking to his glidewings.

It was typical Drake bravado, but there was one thing in his favour - the Harridan itself. She herself had designed the "Hawking Cage", which protected the pilot in the event of a crash landing. Drake had even been saved by it once before, when he'd been shot down by Hans Gruber, the leader of the Crimson Barons, in Muscovy. She just had to trust that it would again.

Dragon pulled over onto the apron next to Excalibur and Abby stood up on her seat to peer back along the runway towards the landing aircraft. Gwen briefly tore her eyes from the Harridan to glance at her, taking in her worried frown, but quickly turned away again and bit her lip as she watched the aircraft's final approach.

Faith crossed the fence surrounding the airfield with only yards to spare and Drake slowly throttled back and let her sink slowly towards the parched grass. When he was only feet from touching, he levelled the Harridan off, then shut off his spring.

He held the aircraft perfectly level as his airspeed dropped. It was an incredible piece of piloting, even if he did say so himself, and for a second it seemed like the Harridan would just settle gently to the ground like a butterfly, but then disaster struck.

The damage to the wing that had put his undercarriage out of action had also changed the characteristics of the wing itself, giving it a slightly higher stall speed than the other.

Drake felt it happen, but before he could send the message to his hands to compensate for it, the wing had stalled, dipped and lightly brushed the ground.

The machine, which looked so beautiful in flight and was so calm and relaxing to fly, instantly became a hell of tearing metal and shattering glass as it cartwheeled over and over. His straps bit painfully into his shoulders as he was thrown every which way, his head whipping from side to side, but there was nothing he could do except squeeze his eyes shut and wait for it to be over.

He must have passed out for a moment, because the next thing he knew Tanya was leaning over him, struggling with the quick release wheel for his straps.

He reached up and brushed away the hair that was tickling his nose, then cupped her cheek. 'I'm fine, dear; I've had some practice at this and I think I did it much better this time.'

She froze and lifted her eyes to stare at him. The corners of her mouth twitched, as if she were about to smile, but then her expression turned hard and she slapped his cheek and started shouting at him in Russian. The outburst only lasted a couple of seconds before she broke down in tears and began kissing him frantically, holding his head firmly between his hands.

When he was finally able to come up for air, Drake smiled at her. 'While I am quite enjoying this, do you mind if we do it somewhere a tad more comfortable?'

He finished the job of detaching himself from the aircraft and his glidewings, then let her help him stand on his seat. He shakily lifted a foot to swing it out of the cockpit, but then stopped.

'Golly.'

While he was in one piece, his aircraft certainly wasn't - one entire wing, half the tail and the forward part of the fuselage were still attached to the Hawking Cage which had once again protected him, but the rest of the aircraft formed a trail of broken and twisted metal leading back to where he had first hit the ground. About a hundred men, women and children, both RAC personnel and local volunteers, were already on the airfield, carefully picking up pieces of debris and filling in the huge divots he'd made in the airfield every time he'd bounced.

'Up to your old tricks again I see, Digger.'

Drake turned away from the cleanup efforts and found the Misfits standing in a loose group behind Tanya, watching him. Gwen was smirking up at him, her arms crossed across her chest. He wasn't sure if it was the bump he could almost feel growing steadily larger on the back of his head or the exhaustion, but in that moment she reminded him so much of the little girl who'd given him so many similar looks while they'd been learning to fly together that he couldn't help but cringe.

'Hey, this one wasn't my fault.' He glanced at the wreckage strewn across the airfield and grimaced. 'Well, not entirely, anyway.'

Gwen shook her head, but before she could say anything, Abby spoke up. 'Leave the bickering until later, please; we need to clear the airfield and you need to get to the infirmary, Squadron Leader Drake.' She beckoned to the crew of the wagon that was waiting to drag what was left of the aircraft out of the way.

Drake stepped out of the cockpit and hobbled over to the group of Misfits on Tanya's arm. He found his fitter, Gertrude Forrester, with them.

'Well, Sergeant, when can you have her back in the air?'

Drake winked at her, but she just gave him a sad look, then walked away.

Abby had been watching the mechanics hitch the wreck up to the wagon and even though she knew perfectly well he had been joking she still gave him a serious answer. 'I don't see much we can even salvage from her, actually. The spring, obviously, and most of the cockpit, but the frame is twisted to heck and the panels are worse. It was a valiant effort to save a valuable machine, but I'm afraid she'll just have to go in the Graveyard with the rest.'

'Excuse me, Group Captain.'

The Misfits turned to find Father Bugelli had been hovering discreetly behind them, just within earshot, with a group of strong-looking men.

'Yes, Father?'

'If you are going to discard her, then we would like to take her off of your hands.'

Abby blinked, puzzled. 'She'll never fly again, Father.'

'But she will still serve; Faith and her two companions became symbols for the people of this island and she will continue to be one, even exiled from the sky.'

Abby smiled her understanding. 'In that case, please, feel free to take what you want.'

The priest gave her a bow and made to turn to his parishioners, but something occurred to Abby and she called out to stop him. 'Father!'

He turned back and gave her a quizzical look. 'Yes, Group Captain?'

'Please leave the guns and ammunition with us, though. For your own safety.'

The priest chuckled and gave her another short bow. 'As you wish.'

CHAPTER 5

As the day progressed, the convoy crept ever closer to the island. Every mile it sailed meant a mile less that the Misfits had to fly, which in turn meant that they had more time to engage the Prussians.

The Fleas had learnt their lesson and no longer tried to block the Misfits en masse like they had before, but instead tried to swamp them from all sides. It was a much more effective tactic and they managed to force the Misfits away during their third sortie, but the British adapted and in the following two sorties used their greater speed and extra spring tension to draw them away and string them out, before sweeping past them and attacking the bombers.

It was a game of cat and mouse, but it was a game which the mouse couldn't possibly win; there were just far too many cats, and all the while the convoy was slowly being whittled down.

By the time the sun was going down, the remaining ships were only a handful of miles away from Malta, less than an hour from relative safety. With them so close, the Misfits now had a clear positional advantage and they were able to get back into the air far quicker than the enemy. They were already at thirty thousand feet when the enemy raid took off and they circled at a point midway between Sicily and Malta, ready to intercept it before it could attack the convoy.

The pilots couldn't help using the moment of calm to silently contemplate the extremely sorry state of the convoy. Of the twenty-two that had set out from England, only a couple of weeks before, less than half remained and most of those were trailing thick black smoke.

They were too high up to make out exactly what was going on aboard the vessels, but they could imagine the pandemonium as brave men and women fought the fires or encroaching seas, trying to save their badly-needed cargoes. They could imagine their fear as the incoming enemy aircraft came back time and again, promising a renewal of the nightmare after all too brief a respite. Worst of all, they could imagine all too well the pain of those unfortunates who'd been injured in the attacks and were in desperate need of better medical attention than they could receive on board their ships.

They were, however, able to see quite clearly that the Arturo was in trouble. She was low in the water and listing badly, the flight deck canted at something like a twenty degree angle, her belly exposed and vulnerable. Several tugs had rushed out from the island as soon as the ships had come within range, to help the worst damaged ones, and four had lashed themselves to the sides of the carrier in an attempt to stabilise her. Lagging behind the rest of the ships, she would be the last of them to enter the harbour. If she didn't sink first.

'Eyes up, Misfits, bandits approaching.'

Gwen tore her eyes from the disturbing scene below to look north and her mouth went dry at the sight of the black cloud that had gathered while she'd been distracted.

Seeing their chance to completely obliterate the convoy slipping away from them, the Coalition had marshalled their combined forces for one last attack and put more than three hundred machines in the air, rivalling the size of the raid which had been sent over the English Channel on September 15th of the previous year.

Two hundred British fighters had been sent up to face the Prussians on that fateful day, though.

The plan for this last, crucial engagement of the day was simple - the three British aircraft had a height advantage over the bombers and would use it to carry out as many sweeping attacks as they could. It was a tactic that B flight used often and to great effect, but they usually had the turn fighters of A flight to keep the Fleas off their backs during their runs. The three Misfits didn't have that luxury, though, and would be extremely exposed when they were clawing their way back up.

It was a risky tactic, but it was the only one that would allow them to punch their way through the fighters and actually engage the bombers, preventing them from having a clear run at the ships.

They began their attack ten miles out to sea, diving at the Prussian's at a thirty degree angle - any sharper and they would be going too quickly to get a shot at more than one bomber each run, any shallower and they would be going too slowly and would fall easy prey to the MU's.

The Misfits performed attack after attack, destroying or damaging two, three or even four bombers with each run. They knew it would never be enough, but they were hoping that the others would lose heart and flee or at least be scared enough for their aim to be off. It was a vain hope, though; a few, mostly red and gold Italian machines, did balk in the face of the continuous attacks, but most of the Prussian pilots were very experienced and weren't to be put off by only three enemies, not even if those three were Misfits.

Abby pulled up from her latest dive, her fifth, and swore when she glanced at her instruments; she was getting dangerously low on tension. Dragon wasn't nearly as fast as Excalibur or Jaguar and she'd had her throttle at maximum emergency unwind for the entire battle in order to stay out of the reach of the enemy fighters. She was going to have to break off and sprint for home soon, but she had enough for at least one more run.

She waggled her tail to look behind her for the Prussians. The nearest one was well out of range of even the most optimistic shot, so she dropped her left wing a touch and began a gentle bank while still climbing, hoping to skirt the swarm of fighters still chasing her.

She slotted lenses in place to take in the general disposition of the bombers, but instead spotted something that made her stomach sink as if she were pulling negative G's - a flight of FU87 dive bombers had somehow snuck in undetected behind the main bomber force and had just peeled off and dived away almost vertically, heading directly for the stricken Arturo.

She swore again, far more vehemently this time; the Arturo wouldn't be able to withstand a concentrated assault from the deadly accurate aircraft and she was far too far away to do anything except watch.

Suddenly, there was a flash of gold from within the bomber fleet and Jaguar broke free of the large machines to drop after the FU87's.

Mac was already going flat out from diving on the bombers and he caught them within seconds. Fire flashed from his wings and one of the bombers disintegrated, ripped apart by the cannons of the large fighter. He was in danger of overshooting the entire pack, though, and Abby winced as he began a dizzying spiral, bleeding off speed; she could only imagine the kinds of G forces he was subjecting himself to in an effort not to overshoot the bombers, which all had dive breaks that he didn't. However, in spite of the stress on his body and the confusion of the manoeuvre, Mac still managed to find his targets and he blew apart another Flea, then another, and another.

Abby spared a glance behind her, checking to make sure that the Prussian fighters on her six hadn't somehow caught up with her, but then looked back, needing to witness the Scotsman's heroic attempt to save the Arturo.

In the couple of seconds she had turned away Mac had scored another victory - he had cut the Prussian squadron in half, leaving only six. He was going to have to give up the chase, though; in her estimation they were at about two thousand feet and the FU87's were capable of pulling out of such a steep dive far later than Mac could.

'Pull up, Seven! Let them go!'

'Negative, Leader. These bastards will sink the Arturo.'

'I...' Abby started to respond, but then remembered a similar dive towards the placid waters of Loch Etive, what seemed like a lifetime before. She bit the words off, deciding to trust the Scotsman; he knew the capabilities of his machine far better than she did.

More fire sprouted from Jaguar's wings and two more FU87's disintegrated, leaving only four.

She tasted salt in her mouth and realised she had bitten her lip hard enough to draw blood.

The aircraft kept dropping and she kept watching.

Two more aircraft spun away, then a third.

There was only one left.

Mac blew it apart, moments after the bomb it was carrying detached from its belly.

Instantly, Jaguar stopped its tumbling and levelled off. Her nose came up towards the horizon as she began pulling out of the dive.

Abby's headphones crackled and Mac's voice sounded softly in her ears. 'It's been a laugh, Abby. Thank...'

The Scotsman was cut off as Jaguar struck the waves, sending up a huge plume of water and wreckage.

CHAPTER 6

The underground mess was just as spectacular at night as it was during the day. The overhead lighting gradually dimmed as the sun went down as the mirrored shaft that provided natural light gradually closed (if it wasn't already for an air raid) while at the same time lanterns on the tables were slowly brought up in intensity. Once the process had been completed, different lights came on behind the green canopy. Less bright, but a stark white instead of the warm yellow of the day, they sent shafts of moonlight to illuminate the tables and paths through the forest below. The birds, so active during the daytime, slept, and fireflies now took to the air, flitting through the trees.

It was beautiful, but the Misfits barely noticed, they just sat in silence, staring morosely into their dinners. The death of Mac would have been bad enough under normal circumstances, but the fact that most of them had been grounded and unable to do anything to prevent the tragedy just made it worse.

Bruce startled them all by swearing and shoving away his glass of water, knocking it over. 'We don't even have a decent bloody bottle of whisky to send him off with.'

There were murmurs of agreement from around the table, but it was Abby who reached out and picked up his glass and placed it back in front of him. 'It wouldn't be right to do it without the others, anyway, so we'll do it when they get here tomorrow. But we're not going to mope around with long faces until then because he wouldn't want that. Right?' She met his eyes and gave him a hard look.

Bruce held her gaze without flinching and for a moment it looked like he was going to continue his rant, even in the face of her unspoken command, but then the tension flowed out of him, his fists unclenched and he gave her his trademark grin. 'Yeah. Just cos *he* was such a miserable sod, doesn't mean *we* have to be.'

The Misfits laughed, the mood broken, and began eating in earnest. However, unnoticed by anyone except Abby, Bruce's grin quickly faded to nothing and he resumed toying with his food.

Drake had approached in the semi-darkness, unseen by the Misfits, who'd been too absorbed with their own thoughts and Bruce's outburst. He cleared his throat gently, drawing their attention.

Abby looked up at him. 'Yes, Squadron Leader?'

'I'm sorry about Mac. He was a good man.'

'Thank you.' Abby nodded. 'Was there anything else?'

Drake grimaced. 'Actually, yes. I've just had a long conversation with Commander Twining aboard the Arturo and he gave me a provisional list of casualties...'

He hesitated, reluctant to go on and Abby sighed. 'Just get it over with, please.'

'When the Heart of Oak went down her surviving aircraft landed on the Arturo and the Misfit Squadron fitters volunteered to help out with them. I'm afraid several of them were in the hangar when a bomb came down the aircraft lift. Um... as were the Llewellyns.' He looked down at the note he had hastily scribbled whilst speaking on the radio, unwilling to look at the pilots he'd come to know so well, not wanting to see their expressions when he gave them the bad news. 'Three fitters are reported as dead and four more are in critical condition. The Llewellyns...' He wet his lips before he continued. 'Owen and Wendy were together when the explosion went off. Owen was badly burned and hit in the back by shrapnel. He's also in critical condition.'

'And Wendy?'

'Apparently Owen tried to cover her with his body. She sustained only minor burns and the rest of her wounds are superficial. They are being evacuated with the rest of the injured to Valletta hospital and I've asked for regular updates to be sent.'

Abby nodded. 'Thank you.' She took a deep breath before continuing. 'Do you have the names of the dead?'

'Yes. Um.' He looked down at the paper again. 'Sergeant Jenkins, Airwoman Pierce and Airman Williams. Apparently they were assigned to the aircraft that was going to be next up the lift and were killed instantly in the explosion.'

All eyes turned to Gwen as she put her face in her hands; the men and women he had named were her fitters, people who had been with her since the day she'd joined the squadron, who had taken care not only of her and her aircraft.

Kitty put her arm around Gwen's shoulders and pulled her close.

'What about the rest of my people?' Abby looked back to Drake, wanting to get the bad news over and done with as quickly as possible.

'Most are still on board, helping clear the damage. Until it's cleared we won't be able to get at the supplies or C flight aircraft in the hold.'

'Are they still intact?'

Drake shrugged. 'Twining didn't know - there's extensive flooding in the lower levels of the ship and much of it is blocked by debris.'

He looked around the group, taking in the downcast expressions. 'If it's any consolation, Commander Twining told me that the damage from that single bomb from the 87 was nearly enough to sink the ship. They only just got her to the dock in time and they're still fighting to keep her afloat. He says that if any others had hit, the carrier would likely have gone down with all hands. Mac saved a lot of lives today.'

He nodded to them, then hobbled away - he was still station commander, even if Abby had taken control of the squadron itself, and he had more people to take care of than just the Misfits.

Abby glanced around her pilots and found them all looking back at her, even Gwen, whose eyes were red-rimmed, but clear. 'I'm going to the hospital. Who's coming?'

The pilots piled into two of the base's open-topped spring-powered autocars and raced off into the night at top speed for the short drive along the narrow Maltese roads to the capital.

They couldn't get anywhere near the hospital, though, because the roads were blocked by a wide variety of vehicles bringing a steady stream of moaning and screaming casualties from the ships. It seemed that everything that could possibly carry the injured had been mobilised and, as the Misfits made their way along the narrow pavement towards the hospital, they passed horse-drawn carts, delivery wagons, a couple of luxury autocars and even a few of the pedal-powered vehicles the postal workers used.

The situation when they finally got to the hospital was chaotic, but it was an organised chaos. A large part of the local population had mobilised and were pulling stretchers from the vehicles as they arrived, carrying them to the small square in front of the hospital where white-coated doctors and blue uniformed nurses were triaging the wounded as they arrived, pinning tags on them before they were taken inside.

The Misfits made their way through the crowd and into the building, but then came to a halt. They stood to one side of the entrance hall, trying to stay out of the way while they gazed around at the multitude of people, almost all of them in dark blue naval uniforms, that were laid out on the floor in neat lines, not knowing where to start to find their friends, or whether they were even there yet.

Thankfully, before they'd been there even a minute, a middle aged woman in a soiled black dress, carrying an empty stretcher, caught sight of them and pointed towards the back of the hall. 'Downstairs. Pilots in basement. Bottom floor.'

She hurried away before they could thank her and they moved across the room to a gaping door, through which a steady stream of the worst patients were being carried.

Beyond the door was a staircase, hewn into the rock, easily wide enough to accommodate six or eight people walking abreast. It spiralled down into the hill on which the hospital was built, winding its way around a pneumatic lift, which was being used to carry the worst patients up and down.

The hospital had been hit several times during the early weeks of the Italian bombardment and, while it hadn't sustained much in the way of damage, it was deemed unsafe for the patients. Luckily there was a ready-made solution - an extensive system of passages beneath it, dating back hundreds of years, which had originally been a barracks for the warrior monks who had used the island as a waypoint to the Holy Land. It had been a matter of only a few weeks' work to adapt the complex and now all of the patients were safely tucked away underground and the main building above was deserted.

They joined the long queue of locals carrying stretchers carefully downwards, around the outside of the staircase, leaving the middle for those who were coming up the stairs. At each floor, some of the wounded were taken into the adjoining corridors and by the time they reached the bottom, four floors down, they were alone.

It was immediately obvious that this lowest level was for the walking wounded, the non-urgent cases who could move about on their own, but nonetheless needed care. Two huge, open-plan rooms - sleeping quarters for the lowest-ranked monks - had been carved out of the rock on either side of the staircase and the pilots peered into them, wondering which way to go to find their friends.

A group of women were sitting just inside one of the wards, each of them with at least one part of their bodies bandaged or immobilised, and one of them, an older woman in her fifties with greying hair and her leg in plaster, waved them over.

'There's some Wreckers down at the back of this ward, luv. On the left. Can't miss'em,' she whispered. 'Keep your voices down, though; people are tryin' ter sleep.'

'Thank you. We will.' Abby smiled at her and nodded at the other women, then led the Misfits into the dimly lit room.

It was quiet in the ward, despite the pandemonium above, and most of the men and women were sleeping, exhausted after the events of the last few days. There were a fair few whimpers and half-cries of nightmares mixed in with the sounds of snoring echoing dully from the bare stone walls, though.

At the back, right where they'd been told, were the RAC personnel, including their fitters. Wendy Llewellyn and Dorothy Campbell were also there, but, unlike the others, they weren't sleeping - they were actually arguing, Wendy sitting on her bed while the Sky Commodore stood over her with her hands on her hips.

'He's still going to be here tomorrow! Just get some sleep and when you're feeling better I'll take you to see him.'

'I don't want to wait until tomorrow. I'm going now!' Wendy pushed herself up to her feet and stood unsteadily. She was taller than Campbell and far more corpulent, but the older woman didn't back down.

'Oh, just sit down before you fall down.'

Wendy glared at her as she continued to sway, but then her eyes crossed almost comically and she groaned as her legs gave way beneath her. Campbell was ready, though, and grabbed her under her arms and let her down gently.

The women had been too caught up in their disagreement that they hadn't seen the Misfits coming, but when Campbell straightened up from laying Wendy down, they both realised they had company.

'Abby!' called Wendy, whispering loud enough to wake the dead. 'Tell this old harridan to let me go up and see my husband, will you?'

Campbell shook her head. 'He's up on the top floor and the lift is off limits to patients. She'd never make it up there.'

Abby looked Wendy up and down. The whole of her upper body was swathed in bandages, as were her hands, there was a gauze taped to the side of her head and she had lost most of her hair, which she had thankfully been keeping short anyway. She looked dreadful and even if she hadn't seen her collapse she wouldn't have let her stand, let alone walk up a few flights of stairs. She smiled kindly at the big woman. 'I'm afraid she's right, Wendy. You're in no shape to go anywhere and it's a bit busy upstairs at the moment. You should wait until tomorrow, like the commodore says; things will have calmed down by then and you won't fall over and crack your head open trying to get up the stairs.'

'Bugger that, Abby! I want to see my husband!'

Wendy was getting more and more distressed as the conversation went on and her voice, not exactly soft at the best of times, was rising as well. They were in danger of disturbing patients who desperately needed their rest.

'Uh, Abby? Why don't we just carry her up the stairs? I'm sure between the lot of us we could manage even her.'

There were chuckles at Monty's comment, but rather than taking offence at it, Wendy's face lit up and she looked at Abby hopefully, beseechingly even.

Abby could see that Wendy wouldn't rest until she saw Owen and would probably sneak off on her own as soon as Dot Campbell's back was turned, hurting herself even more in the process, so she nodded in acquiescence. 'Alright,' she pointed a finger at Wendy, 'but only ten minutes and then you're down here to rest. Quietly. Agreed?'

Wendy nodded enthusiastically. 'Agreed.' She looked past Abby and scowled at the other pilots of the squadron. 'Well? What are you waiting for, you big namby-pambies? We're on the clock! Come and get me!'

There were only a few half-hearted chuckles at her taunting and she frowned. 'What's up with you lot?' She searched the group. 'And where's Mac?'

Abby took a deep breath, making sure that she had her emotions in check before replying. 'Mac died in the last sortie of the day, protecting the Arturo.'

'Oh.' All sign of Wendy's defiant attitude disappeared at the news and she deflated, what could be seen of her face going grey, as if finally realising exactly how hurt she was.

'We'll say goodbye to him properly when we have a chance.' Abby said softly, before waving the pilots forward. 'For now, let's just get you to your husband.'

Scarlet had slipped away as soon as the decision to take Wendy up to see Owen had been made and she had managed to scout out a stretcher. She laid it down beside the bed and the Misfits took positions around Wendy.

Bruce groaned theatrically as they lifted her down. 'Bloody hell! My back! What have they been feeding you?'

The big woman just gave him a scathing look, promising payback later and folded her arms, refusing to lie down.

Monty, Bruce, Derek and Chastity all lifted a corner of the stretcher and they started slowly down the narrow corridor between the beds.

Abby fell in behind her pilots, but Campbell took her arm and held her back.

Abby looked at her questioningly. 'What's up, Dot?'

Campbell just gave her a warning stare, then watched the rest of the pilots go. When she judged that they were out of earshot she started after them, keeping Abby pulled close against her so that she could speak as quietly as possible.

'It's bad, isn't it?' asked Abby, speaking out of the corner of her mouth while she smiled and nodded at a girl with her arm strapped to her chest, one of the few awake.

'Worse than bad.'

Abby found her smile faltering and she quickly turned away from the young naval officer so that she wouldn't be seen to be worried. 'In what way?'

Campbell took a deep breath as if steeling herself. 'Admiral Myerscough managed to get off the Heart of Oak before it sank and transferred his flag to the Arturo, but he lost so many of his staff that he asked me to help out. There wasn't much we could do, though, except let every captain try to survive as best he could and wait out the Prussian raids, so we spent most of our time compiling lists of the losses.'

Campbell paused as they passed the group of women chatting at the entrance of the ward. 'I thought you were going to sleep, girls?'

'We were just about to, Dot.' The same older woman who had directed the Misfits answered with a wide smile.

'Goodnight, then.'

''Night!'

Campbell waited until they were on the stairs, away from the women, who showed no signs of moving from where they were, or stopping their gossiping, before continuing.

'I won't bore you with what we lost - suffice it to say it's a long list, far longer than it should be.' She shook her head sadly. 'The War Ministry thought that between you and the Harridans on the Heart of

Oak the convoy would be relatively safe. They'd expected losses, obviously, but not on this scale. Your being knocked to shreds on landing threw a bit of a spanner in the works.'

Abby nodded. 'We should have been better prepared. There should have been something in place... I don't know, something, *anything*, to prevent such a disaster.'

Campbell shrugged as the two of them paused briefly, flattening themselves against the column of the lift to allow two men carrying an unconscious sailor on a stretcher to go past and down one of the corridors on the third floor. 'Believe me, I've been losing a lot of sleep, thinking what we could have done differently, but I just don't know, beyond taking off later, but that had its own inherent risks and might well have had the same end result or worse.'

Abby nodded. 'We heard about the attack on the Arturo and I think you're right.'

'Anyway. That's all water under the bridge, what's important is what we do from here.'

'Did you see my request to borrow a few Spitsteams?'

'That's what I wanted to talk to you about.'

Abby frowned. 'What? Tiffin doesn't want us to have any? That berk! As if his squadron...'

'It's not that,' said Campbell, interrupting. 'The Spits are yours. All of them. The transport carrying the pilots went down in the first attack of the morning. Squadron Leader Tiffin is dead, along with his entire squadron and nine tenths of the Welsh regiment they were travelling with.'

Abby sighed, regretting her hasty words. 'Poor sods, but at least we'll put their aircraft to good use.'

'Funny you should say that. Here. This came by undersea boat a couple of hours ago.' Campbell handed over a rumpled slip of paper. 'Read for yourself.'

Abby peered at the tiny writing on the telegraphic message.

BADGERS TO EQUIP ELLIPSES STOP REQUEST TO REBUILD DENIED STOP WARM

The signal was short, to the point and left no room for argument. However, Abby had to read it twice before she could quite believe it and even then she didn't really understand it, not even of the War Ministry.

'They know that we have the facilities we need, right? And plenty of materials to work with?'

'I did tell them, yes, but as you can see, they have other ideas.'

Abby growled and screwed up the message angrily. 'This is Cummerbund. He's finally managed to get what he wanted.'

'It looks that way. Sorry.'

Abby fell silent as they continued to plod up the stairs after the slow-moving Misfits. It was almost a full minute before she spoke again. 'My people aren't going to like this.'

'No. But they'll accept it. They have to.'

They found Charles "Chalky" Isaacs muttering to himself while he paced up and down the long corridor on the top floor of the underground facility, where the surgeries and intensive care wards were. The blonde man was looking even paler than he usually did, clutching his arm to his side and wincing with every step he took, but he still laughed when he saw his fellow pilots carrying Wendy like an Egyptian queen.

Wendy was in no mood to laugh, though. 'Chalky, why are you out here? Where's Owen?'

'He's in there.' Chalky pointed to one of the doors further down the corridor and grinned. 'They got sick of me hanging around and kicked me out.'

Abby pushed her way to the front of the group. 'Let me go and find out what's happening, you lot stay here for now.'

As she moved off, the pilots put Wendy on the floor to one side of the corridor, then sat down either side of her to wait, out of the way of the men and women who were still bringing in a never-ending stream of horribly-wounded sailors.

Gwen sat down next to Kitty and leaned her head against the American's shoulder. The floor was hard, but her flightsuit was padded and her Muscovite greatcoat was warm and no matter how much she tried to keep her eyes open, she was finding it extremely difficult to do so.

Gwen woke to warm sunlight and smiled, turning her face towards it. She snuggled into the soft bedding, pulling it close around her and reached out towards Kitty. She didn't find her, but that wasn't unusual; the American was an early riser, even when there wasn't a dawn patrol to be flown.

She gasped and bolted upright, throwing the covers off, and looked around with bleary eyes. She was in the room in the house in Birzebbuga and by the quality of the light shining on the mosquito netting it was mid-morning - not only was it well past the time when she should have been up in the air.

She swung her legs out of the bed, taking note of the fact that she was wearing the silk pyjamas they'd found in a closet, and staggered across the room to the door on unsteady legs. Before she got there it opened slowly and Kitty poked her head in.

The American smiled when she saw her. 'Oh, hi there, Sleeping Beauty! How are you feeling?'

'What's going on? Why didn't anyone wake me! I have to get in the air! The Prussians will be here any moment!'

Gwen started clawing at the buttons on her pyjamas while she scanned the room for her flightsuit. She was relieved to find it hanging on the wardrobe, where it always was.

She turn to go to it, but as she did the room spun around her.

She would have fallen if it hadn't been for Kitty's strong arms wrapping around her and holding her until the dizziness passed.

'No playing with the Prussians for you today, darling,' Kitty said, her voice soft in Gwen's ear, her breath warm on her cheek.

'What? Why? No! I have to!'

'Shhh.'

Kitty started to push her across the room and she tried to resist, but her legs were like jelly and her arms wouldn't obey her commands. In the end, she just had to give in and let her have her way.

She flopped onto the bed and looked up at Kitty. 'I don't remember coming home after the hospital, what happened?'

'I thought you'd just gone to sleep when we sat down in the corridor, but when we all got up to leave I couldn't wake you.'

'Leave? What about Owen?'

'That's my girl, always worrying about others before herself...'

Kitty smiled and stroked Gwen's cheek. She bent down to kiss her and Gwen's head swam momentarily, but for quite another reason. All too soon the American was pulling back again, though.

'The doctors wouldn't let us in to see him because the burns make him too susceptible to infection or something. They let Wendy in for a few minutes with a mask and a gown on, but that was it. We were going to take her back down afterwards and come home, but then we realised you were out cold.'

'What's wrong with me?'

'Oh, nothing much - just exhaustion, overwork and weakness from not eating enough.'

Gwen groaned. 'I'm such a wimp! Abby's done just as much as me, but I bet she's up in the air, isn't she?'

Kitty nodded. 'Of course, but she's a hell of a lot more experienced than you and she's better at pacing herself. You don't, darling, you give everything you have and more every time you go up.'

Gwen groaned again. 'So she's gone up on her own against all those Fleas?'

Kitty shrugged. 'I'm sorry to have to tell you this, but she's not on her own; Bruce took Excalibur up with her.'

'You let Bruce fly my aircraft?!?' The protest was out of her mouth before Gwen even realised, but she stopped herself before she said anything else; every aircraft was needed in the air and if she couldn't fly it was only natural that she give way to somebody else. She settled for crossing her arms grumpily. 'Hmph. Well, I hope he doesn't adjust the seat; it took me ages to get it right.'

Kitty laughed. 'I'm sure Excalibur will be just how you left her.' She eyed the pyjama top that Gwen had managed to almost completely unbutton before becoming dizzy and sighed in regret, then reached out to do the buttons back up. 'Come on, let's get you back in bed. You've got the day off and I'm going to make sure you actually use it to rest.'

Gwen allowed Kitty to help her under the covers and smiled up at her when she smoothed down her hair. 'Thank you.'

'My pleasure. Oh, by the way, the first of the supplies have come off the boats and we've got some actual food, if you want any? It's only canned stuff, but it's better than that damn fish stew we've been eating. I could do you some soup and I think I saw some fresh bread...'

'That would be lovely, thank you.' Gwen smiled, but she could already feel her mind shutting down as the warmth of the bed lulled her back into the oblivion of sleep.

CHAPTER 7

Abby had the pilots assemble on the airfield a good two hours before dawn the next day and they stood near where the ramp led down into the hangar, hugging their greatcoats around themselves against the morning chill.

Gwen was feeling rested and alert and was one of the more awake pilots - a single day in bed with decent food had done wonders for her and she was more than ready to get back into the air. At that moment, though, she was content to have her arm around Kitty and gaze up at the stars with her and she smiled when she saw that Tanya and Drake were only yards away from them, doing exactly the same thing.

'What the blazes are we doing here so bloody early, Abby? I was having a bonzer dream about this Sheila back in Brisbane. She was just about to...'

Abby cut Bruce off before he could go into details. 'Just wait and see, will you?'

Even as she spoke, a horn sounded, the ground cracked open behind them. Once the huge metal slab thudded into position, Abby led them down into the hangar, but then brought them to a halt once more.

The horn sounded once more and the ramp hummed and squealed as the clockwork mechanisms lifted it back into position.

The ramp closed with a loud clang, plunging them into absolute darkness as it blocked the faint glow from the moon and stars.

Silence fell once again and this time it was only ten seconds before Bruce felt the need to break it. 'If this is a surprise birthday party for someone I'm going to be a bit miffed, because *I* didn't bloody get one...'

The pilots grinned, waiting for Abby to tell the Australian to shut up or something, but in the end she didn't need to because, when the overhead lights came on with a crack as the electrical circuit was closed, every single one of them was rendered instantly speechless.

Half a dozen wagons had arrived during the night, after the Misfits had gone, bringing the first shipment of crated-up fighters. The squadron's fitters had come with them, as had most of the Arturo's mechanics, who had volunteered almost to a man and woman, to transfer temporarily to Hal Far. They had worked the night through and managed to assemble seven Spitsteam Mark IIb fighters, one for each of the pilots who didn't have aircraft. The brand-new machines were sitting wingtip to wingtip next to Excalibur and Dragon, extending in a long line across the massive space, their immaculate paintwork buffed and shining in the harsh white lights. The teams of RAC and Naval personnel were standing proudly next to them, grinning, waiting for their pilots to come and claim their aircraft.

Abby took a few steps forwards then turned to face her pilots. 'I could say something trite like "Today we start to take back the air"...'

'Uh, you just did, Boss,' interrupted Bruce with a grin.

Abby glared at him. '...but I *won't*. Instead I will merely say that today we will finally be able to begin the task that we were set by the King on New Year's Eve.'

'Mac would have hated this.' Scarlet muttered. 'Look at them all sitting there, identical, nothing individual about them, nothing to tell you who the pilot is and nothing of the pilot in them.'

'No,' said Gwen firmly, shaking her head, 'he wouldn't; it was Harridans he hated, he actually quite liked Spits. He told me once "at least they have character."'

Scarlet snorted and turned on Gwen, but Abby saw the argument brewing and acted quickly to forestall it. 'This mission was always going to be a difficult one, but now, with the Prussians firmly entrenched in Sicily, it is going to be a bit of an uphill struggle. We are *Misfit Squadron*, though, no matter *what* aircraft we are flying, and I am confident that we will get the job done.'

The pilots nodded and she smiled grimly in satisfaction. 'I had your flightsuits brought over from the house - they're in the ready room. Go claim your aircraft, make sure you thank your fitters in the name of the squadron, then have some breakfast and get changed. Briefing in fifty minutes. Takeoff in one hour.'

Gwen squeezed Kitty's hand and smiled at her. 'I'll see you in the mess, I just want to check Excalibur.'

'OK, don't be long.' Kitty gave her a quick peck, then trotted off towards her fitters, obviously more excited about the aircraft than the prospect of a good breakfast.

Gwen watched her go, then chuckled and wandered towards her own machine.

Bruce had apparently seen where she was going and hurried over to fall in by her side. She looked up at him suspiciously. 'I heard you flew Excalibur yesterday. I hope you took care of her.'

'Of course!' He said with a wide smile. 'She's a real beaut, is your machine, Gwen. Swap you a Spit for her?'

'Not on your nelly!' Gwen laughed, but then gave him a hard look when she detected a certain hint of nervousness behind his smile. 'What did you do to her?'

'Nothing!'

His answer was just a bit too quick for her liking and she scowled at him.

He grimaced. 'Well... I might have had a bit of a near miss, chasing an FU88 through the ack-ack barrage over Valletta.'

Gwen frowned and hurried her steps, wanting to see what damage he'd caused by doing such a stupid thing, however, when she got to her aircraft all she could see were a few scrapes in the paintwork of the nose. She reached out to run her finger over them. The paint had been taken back to the metal and the Duralumin was scored behind the airscrew, but only lightly. It was a fairly easy repair and she was relieved. 'I thought it would be much worse than that,' she said, to herself.

'Um...'

Bruce tilted his head towards the back of the aircraft sheepishly.

Gwen looked at him, alarmed, then ducked under the wing. She stopped short at the sight of the tail, hidden from her until then by the fact that she had approached the aircraft from the front.

Almost the entire rear of Excalibur, from the rudder to the roundel, was peppered with small holes and there was barely any of the black paint left on her underside.

Bruce saw her horrified expression and shrugged. 'It's not that bad!'

'Bruce, how is this not that bad? I've barely got a tail left!'

'Oh, come on, don't exaggerate! The control wires aren't damaged and she still flies perfectly well. She's just a bit scarred at the moment and that'll be easily fixed when we get the stores from the Arturo's hold.'

Gwen glared at him for a second, then smiled and reached out to pull the startled man into a hug. 'You're right, it's not too bad. I'm just glad you didn't get hurt. You'll have to give me a full report this evening when we're done for the day.' She released him, then began to turn away, but stopped when something occurred to her. 'Oh, and you know that any kills you got yesterday belong to me, right?'

She grinned, then ducked back under the wing, putting it between them so that he couldn't answer back, and went to tell Giuseppe that, after Sergeant Jenkins' death, he was now officially in charge of keeping a Misfit fighter in the air.

Drake smiled contentedly as he ran his hand over the gleaming paintwork of the sleek fighter. The Spitsteam was nothing new to him, but it had been a while since he had flown one and he couldn't wait to see what she could do with the new mark of spring and a hydromatic airscrew.

'Does she meet your approval, Squadron Leader?'

Drake gave the wonderful machine a last stroke then turned to face Forrester and her team, their ranks now swelled by naval mechanics. He nodded his thanks to them, before looking at his chief fitter. 'Very much so, Sergeant. Does she meet yours?'

Forrester shrugged, as dour as ever. 'She's not a Harridan, but I suppose she'll do.'

Drake nodded. 'Yes she will.' He smiled at her and, while she didn't smile back, he thought he detected a gleam in her eye that hadn't been there before.

Abby smiled contentedly as she watched her pilots rush off eagerly to their new aircraft, but then realised that two of them were still with her.

Predictably, Scarlet and Chalky weren't quite as pleased as the others, especially the small Irishwoman, who stomped up to her and stood with her hands on her hips, staring up at her, as confrontational as ever.

'Yes, Ophelia?'

'When are we getting one of those, eh? Or are we not good enough to kill Prussians with the rest of you?'

Chalky put his hand up. 'Actually, I'm fine without one, thank you; I'm not really a fighter pilot.'

'Quiet, Chalky.' Scarlet shot over her shoulder without taking her eyes off Abby. 'Well? *We* can do our bit too, you know.'

Abby glanced at Chalky and he shrugged helplessly, but kept silent, not wanting to antagonise Scarlet any more than she already was.

Abby nodded. 'Actually, I have something special in mind for you two, something far more in keeping with your particular talents and far more important than just shooting down a few enemies. I'll tell you about it at the briefing if we have time, if not, tonight over dinner.'

Scarlet stared at her for a moment, then nodded. 'It'll better be good.'

'It will be.'

With one last squinting stare, Scarlet turned and walked off towards Hummingbird, sitting lonely at the side of the hangar out of the way.

Chalky just gave Abby another shrug, then wandered off in the direction of the intelligence office, where he'd been immersing himself in the current situation since he'd arrived.

Abby had told Dorothy Campbell what she had planned and the Sky Commodore had been watching from the shadows at the side of the ramp. She now moved over to stand with her friend and together they watched the happy pilots clambering over their new machines.

'You haven't told them about the orders from the Ministry yet?'

'No, I didn't want them rejecting the Spitsteams before they'd even given them a chance. I'll give them a few days to fall in love, then break it to them.'

Campbell's doubtful expression spoke volumes, but she said nothing and just nodded, then wandered away to make sure everything was set up for the briefing.

The news of the successful destruction of one of the Misfit aircraft and the probable death of the pilot had spread like wildfire through the Coalition ranks, giving new confidence to Prussian and Italian pilots alike, and their morale had been at an all-time high the day before, as they had begun their campaign to destroy the few surviving British ships in Valletta Grand Harbour.

That confidence hadn't dampened in the face of the minimal losses they sustained at the hands of the two remaining Misfits and the fierce ack-ack barrage over the docks and they were certain that, with their overwhelming numbers, they would prevail eventually.

When the raid came over that morning and found themselves faced by the same two aircraft as they had the day before, they fully expected to once more brush them aside, drop their bombs on the ships with relative impunity, then go back to their bases for a slap-up breakfast.

The Misfits had other ideas.

Gwen squinted up into the sky through her canopy, her most powerful lenses in place over her goggles, but even knowing they were there, she couldn't find the seven Spitsteam fighters that were above her at thirty-five thousand feet. And if she couldn't see them, the Prussians had no chance.

The Misfits had barely been able to contain their glee when Dorothy Campbell had told them what she and Abby had cooked up to take advantage of the initial shock and surprise that the appearance of new aircraft would cause.

The plan was simple and very much like the one with which they had surprised the Barons over Lincolnshire. This time, though, it would be two Misfits acting as bait, not outmatched RAC pilots, and it would be the bombers who would be pounced on as soon as the enemy fighters had been drawn away.

It worked like a charm.

The Prussian and Italian fighters raced ahead of the bombers, eager to drive off the impertinent British and the two Misfits retreated, drawing them further away from their charges.

That was when the Spitsteams pounced and started knocking the aircraft the Coalition fighters were supposed to be protecting out of the sky.

The enemy fighters realised they'd been duped and seemed to hesitate for a moment, unsure whether to continue with their pursuit of their original targets or turn to protect the bombers from the new threat, and Abby and Gwen capitalised on it. They performed the sharpest turn they could, reversing course in seconds, and charged the fighters head on, cannons and machine guns blazing.

The Misfits poured all of their anger, sorrow and frustration into the engagement that morning and the bombers never made it anywhere near the island. However, they had used up the element of surprise and the enemy were ready for them after that. The following engagements were much less one-sided than they had been for weeks; even though they were still very much outnumbered, the fight for air superiority over Malta had taken a definite turn in favour of the British.

That afternoon, Wendy was told in no uncertain terms that she couldn't hang around the hospital waiting for Owen to recover and was discharged from the hospital. The Welshman had finally regained consciousness, but he was in an incredible amount of pain and was being kept so sedated that he had no idea of what was happening around him. It had been touch and go for a while, the doctors almost despairing of him living at one point, so extensive were his burns, but he had surprised them and pulled through. He was still in real danger, though, especially of infection, and contact with him was being kept to a minimum.

The big woman was understandably eager to get into the fight, but with Dreadnought still trapped in the Arturo's hold there looked like there would be no way of her doing so, unless she got into a Spitsteam, like Scarlet had wanted to. However, Abby told her the same thing as she had told Scarlet, that she had a few ideas for what the grounded pilots of C flight could do, and that evening, after the sun had gone down, she and Dorothy Campbell sat down with the pilots in the mess over dinner, to let them know exactly how they were going to conduct their little corner of the war.

After they all had food, Abby started things off. 'Today was encouraging, but we're not going to get very far taking the enemy apart piecemeal; the Prussians can get reinforcements here much quicker than we can and we can't afford to lose anyone else.'

There was some muttering at what she knew must sound like defeatism, but she just smiled and held up her hands for quiet. 'Which is why we're not just going to be knocking down their bombers, we're going to be going after their airfields as well. Then, when we've done that, we'll see about cutting their supply lines to North Africa, which is what we were really sent here to do.'

'Is that all?' asked Bruce with a snort. 'And what are going to do next week?'

'This is going to take a bit longer than that,' said Campbell, 'but I can always send you to Sicily to tell the Prussians jokes. I'm *sure* that would shorten the war *considerably*.'

'How's your German, Bruce?' Abby asked with a grin.

'Well, Boss, I had a bit of a fling with a Prussian Sheila in thirty-five. She taught me some German. And quite a few other things as well, I can tell you!'

'But you *won't*.' Abby cut him off.

The banter drew genuine laughter, but it didn't last long and Abby moved on quickly. 'Look, I know that the odds are still heavily against us, I don't need Bruce to tell me that.' She glared at the Australian, who smirked back. 'And if we're going to have a hope in hell of winning this fight, or even just surviving, we're going to need intelligence. Which is where you two come in.' She looked at Scarlet and Chalky Isaacs. 'We're blind at the moment and we haven't got the hydrogen to spare to send Vulture up, so you two are going to have to come up with another way of getting photographs of the airfields on Sicily.'

Chalky nodded, doubtfully, but Scarlet had a grin on her face which worried Abby. 'This is top priority. I want those photographs and you can have all the resources you need,' she grimaced, 'well, all the resources we *have* to get them. Having said that, though, while I don't care how you do it, I do want you alive and in one piece at the end of it.'

Scarlet pouted. 'Spoilsport.'

Abby just shook her head and turned to Wendy. The big woman was looking dejected and lonely and would need to be kept busy for her own good. 'Wendy. In the meantime you're going to be working with the undersea boat boys based at Manoel Island. That's in Marsamxett Harbour, which is only a *very* short walk from the hospital...' She gave Wendy a pointed look and the woman brightened considerably. 'Your contact there is a Lieutenant Commander Strangeways. I want you to work with her on a way for us to sink ships - the Italian torpedo bombers were pretty effective apparently and I want you to find out what the Navy have got that would mount on our fighters.'

Wendy nodded happily. 'Don't worry, I've already been working on a few ideas.'

Abby chuckled. 'I had no doubt that you would've been.' She looked around the group. 'That's it, unless anybody has anything else to say?' Bruce opened his mouth and she rounded on him. 'Anything *sensible* to say.'

Bruce shut his mouth with a pop to more laughter.

'Actually, I have something.' Drake spoke up, raising his hand like the good public school boy that he was.

Abby hid her smile with difficulty. 'Yes, Squadron Leader.'

'Even though I've handed command of the base over to Sky Commodore Campbell, the locals are still coming to me. I don't mind, as long as it's alright with you two?'

He looked from Abby to Campbell, both of whom gave him a nod.

'They're looking for permission to hold a service for Mac. I told them I would have to run it past you first because I wasn't sure if you would want something religious for him.'

Drake spoke carefully, not quite sure how the Misfits would react and wasn't surprised to see some scepticism.

'Does this come from Father Bugelli?'

'He was the messenger, but the request actually comes from Archbishop Caruana himself.

'And did he say why they want to have it for him and not the other men and women who have died for the island so far?'

Drake nodded. 'The service will honour them all, but it will hold Mac up as an example of the type of sacrifice which is being made for the people of the island.'

Abby nodded her understanding; quite apart from how Mac had given his life, the Misfits had long been used as role models in the British press. It had proven to be an effective way of keeping up morale back home and there was no reason why they couldn't do the same in Malta. She glanced around anyway, just to make sure that everybody felt the same way she did. Finding no objections she turned back to Drake. 'Permission granted.'

'Thank you. The service will take place this Sunday night in the Cathedral of St Paul. Oh, and they're asking for photographs of all the personnel who have lost their lives, along with any personal items that can be spared, which might represent who they were as people. They'll be put on display around the church for the service and left there for the duration of the war as a kind of memorial.'

Abby nodded. 'That sounds wonderful. We'll dig out something from his room at the house and I'll get a copy of his official RAC portrait from the files - he doesn't look too much like a belligerent Scotsman in it, so it should do.'

There were some chuckles, but they were extremely subdued; the squadron wouldn't feel completely comfortable making jokes about the mad Scot until they'd laid him to rest by sitting down to tell stories about him and drink to his memory.

Gwen spoke up quietly. 'Don't forget to get photographs of Jenkins, Pierce and Williams, please.'

'I won't forget, don't worry.' Abby gave Gwen a sad smile, then looked around the table at her pilots. 'Well, I suggest...' She stopped mid-sentence when she saw a junior officer from signals come into the forest clearing and head directly for them. She was holding one of the small pieces of cut up newspaper they'd been using as message slips since the paper supplies had run out. The woman halted in front of Drake and held out the paper, but he just smiled at her and tilted his head towards Campbell.

There were chuckles when the young aerial officer coloured with embarrassment, but they weren't unkind. She hurried over to Campbell and handed her the message instead, then gave Chalky a shy smile before hurrying away.

'You sly dog!' Bruce clapped the blonde man on the shoulder, knocking his fork out of his hand. 'Only just got here and you're already cracking on to the Sheilas!'

Chalky rescued his cutlery and fiddled with it while he peered around shamefacedly. He found himself the centre of attention, the message the woman had brought temporarily forgotten in the face of a new piece of gossip. 'It's not like that, Roberta's...' He sighed. 'Yes, it is like that.'

'Good on ya, mate!' Bruce slapped him again, a lot harder, and this time the fork went flying. It could easily have done someone a mischief, but Scarlet just casually reached out to snatch it from mid-air. She spun it between her fingers a few times before sliding it back across the table.

She shrugged at the impressed looks. 'Pitiless Pixie, remember?'

Campbell cleared her throat loudly, calling their attention back to the message. 'It's from the Admiral's office. Apparently three of the Sea Harridan pilots survived and they've volunteered to join us if we'll have them?'

She looked questioningly at Abby, who immediately nodded. 'Of course we will!'

'Good. They'll be here later tonight. I'm going to stay to greet them and I'll ask the fitters to put together another three Spits. They should be ready to go up with you at dawn.'

'Send them to the house when you're done with them, please, Dot,' said Abby, 'there's plenty of room to billet there and I'd like to have a word with them, see what kind of experience they have.'

'Will do, but don't wait up too late for them; they might not get here for hours yet.'

Abby smiled. 'Yes, ma'am!'

The Misfits were in high spirits during the ride back to the house in Birzebbuga, but as soon as the RAC drivers dropped them off they fell silent, then trooped up the stairs together to Mac's bedroom.

They stood just inside the door looking around.

Nobody had been in the room since Mac's death so it was just as he'd left it and they'd been worried what they would find, but they needn't have; there was barely any sign that he had ever been there. It was not surprising really, after all, he'd been able to bring very little with him on the flight to the island in the tiny luggage compartment behind his seat and the bulk of his personal effects hadn't yet arrived from the Arturo.

By unspoken agreement, it was the two people who had known him the best, Abby and Bruce, who went around the room collecting the few things while the rest watched from where they were.

It took only a few seconds to gather his toiletries from the adjoining bathroom and his clothes from the chest of drawers, but there was nothing even remotely like a keepsake to be found anywhere and it looked like they were going to be frustrated in their search for anything to take to the cathedral. It wasn't until Bruce looked in the nightstand that they found anything that they could say was truly Mac's.

'This is perfect!' Bruce chuckled. 'Look.'

He walked over to the door and the Misfits gathered around to see what he had found.

Tucked in between the pages of a leather-bound volume of Oscar Wilde plays, which Mac had borrowed from the small library on the second floor, was a photograph, serving as a bookmark. It was like one of the portraits that families got taken at a local studio, dressed in their Sunday best and smiling soberly for the camera, except that neither Mac nor Katerina had been dressed in their best or sober. By the address of the photographer in St Petersburg and the date scrawled on the back it was obvious that it had been taken the morning after the two of them had met.

They were posing in front of a backdrop representing a wooden hut deep in a Muscovite forest, Katerina in her plain brown army uniform with Mac's top hat on her head and Mac in his elaborate dress uniform with Katerina's flat cap on backwards. They were extremely bleary-eyed and looking very much the worse for wear, but still laughing their heads off, happy and full of life in each other's arms.

CHAPTER 8

The Navy pilots arrived just over an hour later. As soon as they'd heard their request to join the squadron had been approved they had commandeered a navy wagon and driver and raced to Hal Far. They had gotten there only ten minutes after the Misfits had left, but had wandered around the airfield for a good half an hour, not sure where to go or even if they were in the right place and it wasn't until a passing local had shown them where one of the intercom system boxes was that they gained entry.

Dorothy Campbell herself had welcomed them and she gave them a brief tour, ending up at the Spitsteams, which were being unpacked and assembled for them, before sending them on their way up the road to Birzebbuga with a Military Guard as a guide, just in case.

The Misfits were in the sitting room when Maria showed the Navy pilots in. It was becoming a habit for them to spend at least half an hour there as a group at the end of the day to unwind and chat about things like the day's flying and how the designs for the new aircraft were coming.

The three pilots, two women and a man, dropped their kitbags from their shoulders and came to attention as Abby put down her book and stood to greet them.

The leader, a woman in her late twenties with Lieutenant's bars on her shoulders, who was taller even than Kitty, nodded at her respectfully. 'Lieutenant Smith, Sub-Lieutenant Drummond and Sub-Lieutenant Farrier reporting for duty, ma'am.'

'Welcome, all of you.' She returned Smith's nod, then did the same to Drummond, a young man in his mid-twenties, who was trying, somewhat unsuccessfully to grow what the navy called a "set" - a full beard and moustache - then Farrier, a young woman with ginger hair who looked all of eighteen or nineteen and was shifting from foot to foot nervously. 'There's no standing on ceremony in this squadron, so, as you were, please.' She waited for them to relax then smiled. 'I'm Abby Lennox and these berks behind me are the Misfits - I'm sure they'll introduce themselves later.'

Abby smiled as the three pilots curiously gazed around the room, taking in the sight of the pilots they'd no doubt heard and read a lot about, lounging around in an assortment of pyjamas. 'There are rooms prepared for you upstairs, Maria will show you where they are - why don't you dump your kit, freshen up, then come back down and have a drink with us.'

'Aye, aye, ma'am.' Smith nodded and the pilots picked up their bags and followed Maria up the stairs towards the bedrooms.

'So, who exactly are we now, Boss?'

Abby turned and looked at Bruce. 'What do you mean?'

'Well, we've already accepted two strays and now we've got three Biscuit Bangers as well. Are we still Misfits? Or have we become something else?'

'Accepted?' Abby raised her eyebrow and looked around questioningly.

Her pilots immediately realised what she was asking and one by one she received nods from all of them. Drake had already earned their respect in Muscovy and in a very short time Tanya had demonstrated exactly why she had survived the calvary of Malta by displaying her brilliant piloting skills. She had also become well-loved by them all during the period she had been without an aircraft, keeping herself busy by scouring the countryside for supplies, bartering whatever she could for food and anything that the pilots or mechanics needed in order to keep doing their jobs.

Abby nodded and smiled at Drake and Tanya. 'Congratulations, you two. Looks like you're officially Misfits now.'

Drake beamed. 'Thank you!'

Tanya smiled, bemused, then leaned in to whisper in Drake's ear. 'Rudy, what just happened?'

Drake smiled at her. 'We found a home, darling.'

Abby waited for the chuckles and congratulations to subside before continuing. 'To answer your question, Bruce, yes, we are still Misfit

Squadron, but we are also all that is standing between the Prussians and this island, so we will accept help from whoever offers it, whether it is in the form of Spitsteams or Biscuit Banging pilots. The sooner we get this job done, the sooner reinforcements will come and then we'll be able to regain our identity and individuality. Which reminds me - she won't tell me how, but Tanya managed to scare up some paint from somewhere. We don't have much, but I'd like some individual touches on your aircraft, please; we can't have the Prussians thinking we're just a regular RAC unit, now, can we?'

'And when are we going to start rebuilding?'

It was Derek who asked the question and Abby thought she detected a note of suspicion in his eyes, as if he somehow suspected she was hiding something. She realised that it might be a good time to tell them about the War Ministry's order; they'd had a chance to fly their new aircraft and appreciate their virtues, but not enough time had passed since the order not to rebuild had come for them to be able to accuse her of hiding it from them.

However, before she could say anything else, the naval pilots returned and the opportunity was lost.

With the sudden influx of so many trained mechanics it had been a simple matter to assemble three more Spitsteams overnight and the squadron was up to twelve fighters for the morning.

Abby had drawn up a new squadron formation, rearranging it into Red, Blue and Yellow flights and recovering the Badger callsigns. After finding out that the Navy pilots lacked combat experience she placed them into Red and Yellow flights, which would be responsible for attacking the bombers, and put her best pilots into Blue flight, which would attempt to keep the fighters busy.

Gwen remained with Abby as Badger Two to form the first element of Red flight. They were joined by Kitty, who had been promoted to element leader, with the young Sub-Lieutenant Farrier on her wing as Badgers Three and Four.

Derek, with the most experience after Abby as a flight leader, was given Yellow flight, his callsign coincidentally remaining Badger Five. Chastity was moved onto his wing as Badger Six and Lieutenant Smith was made leader of his second element with the third pilot, Sub-Lieutenant Drummond on her wing as Badgers Seven and Eight.

Bruce took Blue flight and kept Monty on his wing as Badgers Nine and Ten, while Drake and Tanya made up the second pair as Eleven and Twelve.

It was immediately effective, although it was a lot tougher on Bruce and Blue flight than it was on the others and they came back with holes in their machines more often than not, something of which the Spitsteam was not nearly as forgiving as the Harridan and made for some hairy landings, and Monty was forced to bail when his wing was shot off.

Coalition losses mounted and they tried to compensate by reducing the number of raids to only three each day instead of five or six. This allowed them to put their entire force into the air, like they had during the final raid before the convoy had made port, instead of alternating between the Italians and Prussians as they tended to do. The tactic worked to a certain extent - the larger concentration of fighters preventing the British from scoring quite as many victories as they had - but it also meant that the men and women facing them had more time to rest between sorties and they weren't nearly as worn down as Gwen, Abby and Mac had been.

Despite their initial misgivings, the Misfits slowly fell in love with their Spitsteams and once they were able to put a few personal touches to them, the pilots really began to make them their own. It was an extremely elegant machine, a delight to fly, but best of all it was more than a match for anything the enemy could put in the air to face them. They continued to work on the designs for their own machines, though, Tanya and Drake included, now that they were officially Misfits; a Spitsteam was good, but it wouldn't ever be as good as a purpose-built machine.

Two days later was Sunday and, after the sun had set and the Prussians had gone home for the night, the Misfits wandered back to the house in Birzebbuga to change for the remembrance service.

Their luggage hadn't been in the main hold of the Arturo, but rather in one of the smaller storage compartments near their quarters, and it had been delivered to them the day before, which meant that they had their dress uniforms just in time.

Gwen stood in front of the mirror in the bedroom. She had fought to get into her corseted tunic, struggled with the awful and far too plentiful petticoats, given up on her hair and reluctantly applied makeup, but she had to admit that she presented a stirring figure, especially with the shiny new medal on her chest and Lieutenant's stripes on her cuffs.

Kitty appeared beside her in the reflection. 'You look beautiful, darling.'

'Keep telling me that and one of these days I might start to believe you.' Gwen looked the American up and down in the mirror. She had barely made an effort, but still looked stunning, her uniform doing things to her figure that had Gwen feeling decidedly weak at the knees. 'You don't look half bad yourself.'

Kitty laughed. 'Why thank you, ma'am.'

Gwen grimaced. 'Don't remind me. I still can't believe I outrank you now, it's so unfair.'

'You know I don't care about that kind of thing, besides,' Kitty grinned, 'I quite like it when you're bossy.'

'Is that right?' Gwen raised an eyebrow. 'Then I guess I order you to give me a kiss.'

'Yes, ma'am! Right away, ma'am!'

Kitty bent down to kiss her, but it was barely more than a peck; neither of them wanting to smear lipstick or rumple clothing that had taken more than an hour the previous night to restore to some semblance of respectability after its rough treatment on the Arturo.

Kitty pulled back with a sigh and Gwen frowned at her. 'Is everything alright?'

'Of course.' Kitty answered immediately with a smile, but then she took a deep breath and sighed again. 'No, it's really not; it was bad enough losing Hawk, but now we've lost Mac as well and we're flying Spitsteams with strangers on our wings... I don't know... It's almost as if we're not really Misfit Squadron anymore.'

'I know how you feel.' Gwen nodded. 'But we *are* still Misfits and nothing can change that. You heard how many people went to see the exhibition over Midwinter and you saw those children in the hospital when we went to visit Penny - "Misfit Squadron" has become more than just its machines or pilots, it's now a *symbol* which represents hope and the idea of a world free from the tyranny of the Prussians and it will live on long after *we* are dead and buried.'

Kitty shrugged. 'I supposed.'

'And as for Mac, well, this is war and we've been at the very forefront of it for months. We've been extremely lucky so far, but we always knew that our luck would run out eventually. Mac knew exactly what he was doing, though, and he chose when, where and how he was going to die - I just hope I'm as lucky when the time comes.'

It wasn't until the words were out that Gwen realised how much she truly believed them and when she gazed into Kitty's eyes she was sure she found the same belief, the same *certainty* in them.

As soon as they were ready, the Misfits piled into three autocars for the short ride to the town of Mdina, in the centre of the island. Father Bugelli had asked the Misfits to be at the cathedral two hours after sunset, but when they arrived there was hardly anyone there, just the priest and a few members of his congregation. The cathedral itself was completely dark apart from a couple of lanterns hung on the façade and there was no sign of the archbishop. There weren't even any people in the surrounding streets.

The father hurried out of the cathedral as they pulled up and came down the steps to greet them. 'Welcome, welcome! Thank you for coming.'

'Evening, Father.' Abby smiled, but then looked past him at the silent church. 'Are we too late?'

The priest glanced up at the clock on the right hand tower of the façade. 'No, you are right on time!'

'Then where is everybody?'

'They will be here soon.' The Father smiled enigmatically and motioned for them to follow him. 'This way, please.'

He led them up the steps to the cathedral, but instead of taking them through the large main doors and into the dark hole that was the nave, he led them to the tower with the clock and began to climb the stone stairs.

The pilots gave each other puzzled glances, but followed him without questioning.

There were small candles on the stone steps within, giving them just enough light to see, which was just as well, because the tightly winding steps were worn and uneven. It wasn't a long climb by any means, but the pilots were huffing and puffing by the time they were only half-way up, exhaustion and tight dress uniforms taking their toll, especially on the women with their corsets. Eventually, though, they reached the belfry at the top.

Four women, little more than shadows in the light from the final candle at the top of the stairs, were waiting for them, speaking in hushed tones, but when they saw the priest they gave him a small bow, then each went to an archway.

The peeling of the four large brass bells was loud, but not unbearable so, and they were joined by the four bells in the other tower, sounding out a call that must have reached even the furthest corner of the island.

After several minutes of surprisingly beautiful music, the bells stilled and the women gave the priest another small bow, then disappeared down the stairs, leaving them alone.

As the silence swelled around them, Father Bugelli ushered them forwards and the pilots moved to the arches and peered out past the bells into the night, searching the countryside beyond the thick stone.

St Paul's was on a slight hill and from their vantage point the entire island was laid out at their feet. They could see the sea all around, glittering in the moonlight, but Malta itself was dark, with not a single light to be seen.

Abby turned to the priest with a smile. 'That was lovely, Father, but now what?'

There was no need for Father Bugelli to answer, because just then Kitty's sharp eyes picked something out of the darkness.

'Look! There!'

The other pilots didn't have as good eyesight as she did and couldn't see what she was pointing at, but in a few seconds it didn't matter, because the single light she had spotted was joined by dozens, then hundreds, then thousands of others, from all over the island, as the Maltese people heeded the call of the bells. At the same time the sounds of movement in the town below carried up to them and the pilots leaned out to see the first of the townspeople appearing in the streets. Every single adult and most of the children were carrying candles and, as they began gathering in the plaza in front of the cathedral, bathing the church and surrounding buildings in a warm glow they began singing - a hymn of sorrow, but also of hope, uplifting, yet at the same time reminding them of all that had been lost.

The pinpoints of light in the surrounding countryside had begun to coalesce into larger groups as more and more people came from their villages or farms and joined the throngs on the roads. The biggest concentration of light by far was coming from the north-east, from the city, and the priest pointed it out.

'Archbishop Caruana is leading the procession from Valletta himself. It is six miles away and, even though he is riding on a cart, it will take a while for him to get here and the service will of course not start until then. Those of you who wish to stay and watch the processions may of course do so, but those of you who do not, if you'd like to accompany me there is tea and biscuits below.'

'Tea? Actual tea?' asked Bruce, his eyes shining eagerly in the candlelight.

'Yes, a donation from the British ships in the harbour.' The priest gave him a nod, then turned to begin the long climb down.

The tea Gwen had brought had run out in two days and what little the convoy had been bringing had gone down with one of the supply ships, so the Misfits were understandably eager to have some, and the promise of biscuits was just the icing on the cake. They hurried after the priest, piling down the stairs after him.

Soon only four pilots were left in the belfry - two couples who had both thought to remain behind to have some time alone with only the night and the beautiful view for company.

There was an awkward moment as Gwen, Kitty, Drake and Tanya looked at each other in silence, but it didn't last long before Tanya spoke up. 'Gwen. Can I ask you a very important question? It's about you and Rudy.'

'Uh, I suppose.' Slightly worried, she glanced at Drake, wondering what part of her childhood relationship with Rudy the woman might want to know about. He said nothing, though, and just gave her one of his half smiles.

'I just wanted to know...' The Muscovite chewed her lip as she paused, staring at Gwen. 'Was it you who gave him the nickname Digger?'

Gwen laughed, relieved. 'Yes, it was.'

'But why? What does it mean? He won't tell me.'

'Um.' Gwen grinned and again looked to Drake, but his expression was just as unreadable as before and she decided that was as good as giving her permission. 'Well, it's not that interesting actually - Rudy and I had flying lessons together for a couple of years when we were young and it took him quite a while to work out how to land properly. He used to slam the aircraft into the ground over and over, carving out great chunks of mud and grass every time. Hence the nickname.'

Drake chuckled and spoke for the first time. 'Just as well the undercarriage of the old Red Admiral was so durable.'

Gwen snorted at him, then grinned at Tanya. 'Rudy never noticed that our teacher, Manfred, had the undercarriage reinforced specially.'

'He what?' Drake stared at her, mouth open.

'Even then he had to repair it more than half a dozen times after Rudy bent it.'

Tanya frowned. 'But I've only ever seen him make perfect three-point landings. How did he get over it?'

Drake smiled wryly. 'Because Manfred came up with the idea of making me replace the divots in the airfield, as if I was on a golf course

- I learnt pretty quickly after that. It's one thing replacing a few ounces of grass after your three iron has carved a chunk in the ground, it's quite another for an eight or nine year-old to lug ten pounds of dirt around, more if it's been raining and the ground is soft.'

'Ah.' Tanya nodded in understanding, but then bit her lip as something occurred to her. 'But where do the nuns come into that?'

Gwen laughed and began to answer, but Drake cut her off quickly. 'I think that's enough gossip for tonight. Why don't we enjoy the view a little while longer, then go down; it's cold and I want some of that tea before Bruce and Scarlet drink it all.' He very deliberately wrapped his arms around Tanya, taking care not to wrinkle her uniform, then equally deliberately turned her away from Gwen and Kitty to face the view through the nearest arch.

Gwen watched Rudy lean forwards to put his chin on the Muscovite's shoulder, displaying an intimacy and comfort that was surprising considering how recently they had met. She marvelled at the twists and turns that fate had taken and found that she wasn't remotely jealous of Tanya or sad for losing what she could have had with Rudy. On the contrary, she was happy for them, especially because of how things had worked out for her.

She turned and met Kitty's eyes, ghostly grey in the moonlight - the American had been watching her watch the other couple. She reached up to cup the beautiful woman's cheek. 'I love you.'

Kitty put her hand over Gwen's and brought it to her lips for a kiss then tilted her chin at Drake. 'No regrets?'

Gwen glanced over her shoulder at them. They made a disgustingly good-looking couple, despite their dress uniforms having come from the quartermaster's stores at Luqa and not a tailor in London - although Gwen wouldn't put it past Rudy to have visited a local tailor to have them adjusted.

Gwen turned back to Kitty and shook her head. 'None whatsoever.'

The Misfits had their tea and biscuits in the sacristy, but didn't linger; they felt that they should be with the people who had come to pay their respects.

Father Bugelli took them back to the front of the cathedral and he positioned them at the top of the steps, to one side of the main entrance, where they stood, letting the music wash over them.

The crowd had grown immensely and the large plaza was almost full already, but not just with locals - there was a group of RAC personnel, probably from the nearby Ta'Kali, standing to one side, also cradling candles, and a few sailors scattered around. A few people were still drifting in, but it appeared that most of those who were coming were already there, ready for the main procession from the capital to arrive.

They didn't have long to wait.

A ripple of movement began at the back, where the main road fed the plaza, and passed through the crowd. Soon after, the music reached a crescendo and the hymn ended on a triumphant note, held by several thousand voices, which grew and swelled until it seemed that the whole world was filled by it, until suddenly it cut out.

Into the silence came a heavenly sound.

Where before the hymns had been rough songs of the common people, belted out at the top of, at times toneless, voices, this was the song of the angels.

Every candle in the plaza was extinguished as the crowd split down the middle, creating a passage from the steps of the cathedral to the main road, and into the void came a glittering vision - the archbishop in all his finery, riding in his ceremonial carriage, pulled by two pure white horses. Behind and on either side of him were hundreds of men, women and children, the candles in their hands making them seem to glow in their white robes.

The carriage pulled up in front of the cathedral and the archbishop got out, helped by two choirboys, who made sure his robes didn't catch on anything and cause any indignity. He climbed to the top of the steps, gave Father Bugelli a nod and winked at the Misfits, then turned to gaze solemnly down at his congregation.

The choir followed and spread out along the step below him, spacing themselves evenly to fill it from one end to the other. They continued singing while the rest of the people from Valletta filled the gap left for them in the plaza.

The procession had included not only the majority of the civilian population of the capital, but also representatives of the three branches of the British armed forces. The biggest group by far was from the Navy, the officers resplendent in their Napoleonic War-era dress uniforms. It was led by Admiral Myerscough, who was looking a lot older than he had when the Misfits had dined with him during the voyage. He was limping, leaning heavily on Captain Hewer, whose beard was a bit singed around the edges, and many of the men and women with them also showed obvious signs of injuries. The delegation from the RAC wasn't quite as big, but it was still sizeable and included Dorothy Campbell and the senior officers and staff from the three RAC bases. Only a few Army officers, led by a painfully-thin general in his sixties in a red regimental jacket, were present, though, because there weren't many soldiers on the island and most were stuck on guard duty in the various forts around both Malta and the neighbouring Gozo.

Once the last of the procession had come into the plaza and the people were still, the choirmaster brought the song to a close and absolute silence finally fell.

The archbishop raised his hand and drew a cross in front of himself, over his congregation. 'In nomine Patris et Filii et Spiritus Sancti.'

'Amen.'

The response was automatic, from every believer and there was a rustle of clothing as every one of them drew a corresponding cross on their own bodies before lifting their faces once more to the archbishop.

The man smiled down at them benevolently. 'Welcome friends. Please, join me in bringing light to this humble church on this solemn occasion.'

He gestured to the open doors, then turned and went inside.

As the choir began to sing again, Father Bugelli beckoned to the Misfits and they filed into the completely dark cathedral and went to stand with the archbishop a few yards down the central nave, between the rows of benches.

The glow through the doors grew steadily as the people made their way up the steps, relighting their candles from those carried by the choir as they passed through their line, and when the first ones passed through the door it was like the dawn had arrived.

Once inside, the congregation spilt up, most going left and right along the walls, while a few came past the archbishop and, as the wave of light slowly advanced down the long space, the Misfits were able to see what Father Bugelli and his helpers had been doing within when they had arrived.

The walls of the building were covered with hundreds of photographs of the men and women of the Royal Navy, Royal Aviator Corps and British Army who had given their lives in the defence of Malta, many accompanied by some personal item or other - a piece of scrimshaw, a medal, a uniform cap, a book, a toy.

It was to the front of the cathedral which Father Bugelli drew their attention, though, and as the wave of light progressed, the altar was finally revealed.

The photograph of Mac had been blown up to a few times its usual size and sat in the centre of a large display which included the images of the other pilots who had been part of the Hal Far Fighter Force. Sitting in front of them were a few personal items, including the photograph of Mac and Katerina, which Scarlet had made a copy of in the lab at the base. The finishing touch was provided by the side panel of Drake's aircraft, which had been placed at the base of the altar, leaning against it, with the stencilled letter "H", although pock-marked and scratched, clearly visible.

The pilots stayed where they were until the last of the people had come in, then, when the choir began to make their entrance in a double file, Father Bugelli ushered them into place and they joined onto the front of the procession with the senior officers, behind the archbishop.

Most of the pilots had been born during or soon after the Enlightenment and Gwen wasn't the only one to feel awkward and out of place as she marched down the nave of a catholic cathedral then went to her seat in the very front row for the service. However, one of the main principles of the Enlightenment was that everyone's beliefs were to be honoured, no matter what your own were, so, while they wouldn't actively take part in the prayers, they would witness the service respectfully, representing the squadron and by extension the Kingdom of Britain itself.

That didn't mean that Bruce couldn't comment quietly in his own inimitable way, though. 'Bloody hell, I hope I get this kind of send-off when I kick the bucket.'

'Are you religious, then, Bruce?' asked Abby.

'Nah,' he shook his head and grinned at her. 'I just like the idea of all the Sheilas I've known getting together in a place like this to shed a tear for old Brucey.'

'Just the Shei...' The leader of the Misfits sighed and corrected herself. 'Just the women, Bruce?'

'Of course, Boss! All the men'll be off down the pub for the real party.'

CHAPTER 9

The service had been extremely emotionally charged and had left many of the pilots in tears or on the point of them. However, Gwen hadn't cried until afterwards, when she had sought out the photographs of her fitters and found that Abby had included the one of her with the three of them in front of Excalibur from the Midwinter party at Bagshot Hall.

All thoughts of their lost friends and colleagues had to be put behind them for the next day, though, because they couldn't afford the distraction.

The Misfits enjoyed moderate success against the Coalition forces, bringing down several bombers and a few fighters, but it was impossible to stop them reaching their targets and the Grand Harbour took beating after beating. The accuracy of the bombers had become much greater since the Prussians had joined the fight, but quite a few stray bombs still fell on homes and public buildings and there was a near miss on the hospital, which didn't penetrate to the basement areas, but did destroy a few of the vehicles which had been acting as ambulances, killing their drivers.

However, it seemed that the civilian population, which had been so near the breaking point for so long, were rallying after the service of the previous night. Mac's sacrifice in particular had inspired them to renewed effort and the numbers of volunteers taking the supplies, which were ever so slowly being unloaded from the damaged ships, to the needy around the island were greater than ever.

There was also a measure of hope in the mess at Hal Far that night as well when Scarlet and Chalky announced that they had a solution to their reconnaissance and intelligence problems.

When Abby saw the grin on Scarlet's face she feared the worst. 'Please tell me the plan you've come up with is a bit more complicated than Charles sitting in a chair bolted to the side of Hummingbird and taking pictures while you dodge bullets.'

'A little bit. Although I'll jot that down in case our idea doesn't work.'

'The plan is to convert one of the spare Spitsteams to a reconnaissance aircraft.' Chalky began, ignoring the laughter that Scarlet's comments had provoked. He leaned over the mess table, pushing a few cups out of the way, and spread out a large piece of paper, fresh from the Arturo's stores. The paper had several detailed drawings on it, showing cutaways of a section of the fuselage of a fighter.

'The Spit will be lightened as much as possible by removing the guns and ammunition and as much of the armour as we can without weakening the structure. That will give it increased range to cover most of Sicily and increased speed to outrun any pursuit. We will then place a couple of the smallest cameras from Vulture in the middle of the fuselage, as close to the balance point as we can, and point them downwards through holes cut in the Duralumin.'

'Pointing downwards?' asked Abby with a frown. 'That means the pilot is going to have to fly directly over the airfields one by one.'

Chalky nodded. 'They will, yes.'

'Can't you mount them at an angle, like they are in Vulture?'

He shook his head. 'No, the platform isn't steady enough, this is the only way to get a decent picture.'

Abby grimaced. 'Alright, then I suppose this will have to do. When can you have it ready?'

'It already is.'

Abby blinked, then smiled. 'And what if I'd said no?'

'Then I seem to remember something about a chair bolted to the side of Hummingbird...' Scarlet answered before Chalky could.

Abby pointed a finger at her. 'I'll bloody bolt a chair to Dragon for *you* if you ever try anything so silly. You got lucky in Muscovy, don't push it, please.'

'I'll try not to.'

Scarlet's answer didn't convince Abby, but she had other, more pressing, matters to think about. 'How low does this have to be to get decent pictures?'

'Well, obviously the lower the better, but to just get an idea of the general situation and see what aircraft are on the ground I'd say thirty thousand feet will be alright.'

Abby nodded. 'Good, that'll take away some of the risk at least; by the time they can get anyone up that high it'll be on its way home.'

Scarlet gave her a look. 'That *was* kind of the general idea, Abby.'

Abby smiled. 'Right then. We'll do it tomorrow morning when we go up to meet the dawn raid; the reconnaissance aircraft can go up at the same time as us and just keep climbing, that way the Prussians won't realise anything special is happening until it's too late.'

Charles shook his head. 'We'll get better pictures as close to noon as possible, that way the shadows won't be as long.'

'Alright then. And as for who to fly it.' She looked around the table and was pleased to see universally eager faces, especially from the Navy pilots, who were always looking for an opportunity to impress. 'Well, it can't be me or Gwen, because the Prussians will expect to see Dragon and Excalibur. Unless you want to let Bruce fly Excalibur again, Gwen?'

Gwen's eyes widened in alarm and she shook her head vigorously. 'Not a chance! I've only just got her patched up after the last time!'

'That's what I thought.' Abby said with a grin. She looked to Scarlet and Chalky, both of whom met her eyes expectantly. 'Sorry, but it's not going to be either of you; I want someone with experience in a Spit, in case things go sideways.'

Neither pilot was particularly happy, but they nonetheless nodded in understanding.

Abby looked at the rest of the pilots. 'Which leaves *you* sorry lot...' She weighed up the options. 'Sub-Lieutenant Farrier, do you fancy becoming our high-speed reconnaissance expert?'

The fresh-faced nineteen-year-old girl's face lit up. 'Do I ever, ma'am!'

Bruce sighed exaggeratedly. 'Oh, to be that young and innocent again...'

'You were never that innocent, Bruce,' said Abby.

Bruce grinned. 'Too right!' He winked at Farrier, who went a bright red to match her hair and freckles.

The next day the Misfits, and Sub-Lieutenant Farrier especially, were keen to carry out the reconnaissance mission and make the first move towards striking back against the Coalition.

The weather had other ideas, though.

A storm moved in from the north overnight and with it came high winds, driving rain and low cloud that reduced visibility to as good as zero. There was no hope of carrying out the mission, but equally there was no way the Prussians were going to bomb the island, shrouded as it was from them.

It was the first bad weather since they had arrived, just over a week ago, but, instead of resting like they probably should have, the Misfits took advantage of the day off from flying, Abby's first, to go visiting. Father Bugelli had arranged for the pilots who'd lost their aircraft and been grounded to show their faces around Malta a few times to raise morale, but they had been relatively unknown at that time - just names and faces in newspapers. Now, though, after the service and weeks of flying, everybody knew who they were. So, Drake contacted the priest and told him they were going to the hospital first, but after that their day was his.

Wendy had been spending as much time with her husband as the doctors would allow her, but they hadn't let anyone else go to see him. However, he had come off the critical list a couple of days ago and no longer needed to be kept in sterile condition, so the Misfits could finally pay him a visit.

Wendy had been giving them regular reports on how he was, but it wasn't the same as finding out for themselves and, even though she had told them how badly hurt he was, they weren't at all prepared for the reality.

RAC work coveralls were fire retardant and had protected his body quite well, apart from where shrapnel had ripped through them, but his head and hands had been uncovered and had been completely ravaged. His hands had been reduced to blackened claws and the doctors were worried that he might have lost the nerve endings and wouldn't be able to feel anything ever again. The side of his face which had been turned towards the explosion was red and inflamed and his eye had been damaged, but the doctors expected him to recover at least some of his sight in it. His scalp was the worst, though, and had been the biggest worry; his hair had caught fire and the product he used to keep it in place had only fed the flames, making them burn far hotter. He had needed skin grafts and, when the Misfits caught a glimpse of the top of his head while the nurses changed the oiled silk dressings, it had looked like a crudely-sewn patchwork quilt.

According to Wendy he was rather down in the dumps because of the extent of his injuries and the Misfits had been hoping to cheer him up, but in the end he was barely even aware they were there; the medications he was on for the pain keeping him groggily drifting in and out of consciousness.

They did manage to cheer up just about everyone else in the hospital, though; they were spotted immediately on arrival and all but paraded from ward to ward by a succession of sailors, none of whom wanted their injured friends to miss out on meeting such important visitors.

Understandably, the Misfits weren't exactly in the mood to put on a brave face for the islanders afterwards, but that was what they did.

Father Bugelli had arranged transport for them and they were dispatched in pairs to the far corners of Malta.

Gwen and Kitty were sent to a pleasant seaside town on the north coast called Saint Paul's Bay and, for the second time in three days, found themselves in a religious building, this time the four hundred-year-old Church of St Paul's Shipwreck.

They thought that they were going to be asked to make a speech or something and were dreading it, not because they weren't used to speaking in public - both of them were, having presented papers in front of their peers - but rather because it would have to be something inspiring or uplifting and after the hospital they didn't think they would be able to. Thankfully, though, the father had just arranged an informal gathering, with food and plenty of local wines and spirits.

It wasn't only locals that were there to meet them, but also many injured sailors who had been sent to the town to rest and recover in its picturesque villas, which dated back to the 19th century. The two Misfits tried to dedicate as much of their attention as possible to the locals, but most of them only spoke the native Maltese language, which was a mixture of Italian and Sicilian, and Kitty's limited Spanish prove entirely inadequate so they couldn't help but keep gravitating back towards the British sailors.

Gwen and Kitty were plied with alcohol on all sides and, since they weren't flying and despite neither of them being really big drinkers, they decided to take the opportunity to sample some of the local vintages. They found that the limoncello was especially tasty, like a sweet lemonade, and seemed innocuous, certainly not alcoholic. For some reason, though, they didn't protest when the music began and they were pulled into the space which had been cleared in the centre of the nave to learn a local dance. Nor did they really notice when the energetic folkloric music gave way to something slower and more romantic, they just gave in to the sensations and, for just a short while, the only things that existed were the music, the dance and each other.

More limoncello found its way into their hands when the musicians took a break and they guzzled it down greedily to quench their thirst while sitting with a group of old men and women. It didn't seem to matter that they couldn't understand a word that was being said to them; the languages of laughter and happiness was universal. Even more limoncello was consumed during incomprehensible toasts, where the only words they recognised were "Malta" and a mispronounced version of "Misfit Squadron" and when the music resumed they found they were unable to stand up again by themselves.

That was when the woman, who had driven them there and been assigned to take care of them, discreetly pulled them into the sacristy and they all but collapsed onto the sofa within and started giggling like schoolgirls. She tutted, but smiled at them fondly, then brought them bread and goat's cheese and made them drink plenty of water before sneaking them out of the side into the night.

They fell asleep on the journey home, despite it being only a half an hour drive, and only half-woke when they arrived at the house and were carried gently up to their room by the female half of the small army of locals, which had been organised by Father Bugelli to take care of the returning Misfits.

Knowing all too well that the pilots desperately needed to let their hair down and relax, he had organised the visits as much for them as for the beleaguered Maltese people.

The bad weather lasted two more, blissfully quiet, days, during which the only sign of enemy activity was the drone of a few engines going over the east coast one time and the dull thud of bombs detonating out to sea as whoever it was dismally failed with their dead reckoning.

Aside from a couple more visits to the hospital, the Misfits used the time to rest and polish off the designs for their new aircraft. Abby had never gotten around to telling her pilots about the message from the War Ministry and, after discussing it once more with Dorothy Campbell, she finally decided not to, at least not yet, and continue with the plan to rebuild. Not only would obeying the order destroy the morale of her pilots, but in both her and Campbell's view it was completely irresponsible of the Ministry not to allow them to use all the resources at their disposal in such an important arena of the war.

With that weight off her mind, she was less hesitant about the amount of time that was being dedicated to the designs and she sat the Misfits down to have a serious discussion about which direction the squadron should go in.

The pilots had quickly come to the conclusion, some more reluctantly than others, that, with heavier weapons like Wendy's cannons, which were now being mass produced, and recent advances in spring power, a single-spring aircraft was more than capable of taking down even the heaviest of bombers and there was no real need to have more expensive and less manoeuvrable twin-springed aircraft in a squadron with their remit.

Most of the pilots were fine with the decision, having already been in single-springed aircraft, and Derek and Chastity readily agreed to switch over, but Kitty protested vehemently. She had wanted to redesign and rebuild Hawk and she pleaded with Abby to allow her to do so, but the group captain stayed firm. It was only when Gwen took the American to one side and promised that they would rebuild her aircraft together when they were on leave that she reluctantly agreed.

Bruce and Monty had decided to have identical aircraft once more, based on Excalibur, which Bruce had fallen in love with during his day flying her, and their design was ready by the end of the second day. It was sent to Luqa so that construction could begin using the Duralumin and other materials which had already been recovered or recycled from the Graveyard at Hal Far and stockpiled there. The others had to be put on the back burner again, though, when, on the third day, the weather cleared and the Prussians renewed their attacks. However, that also meant that the reconnaissance mission could go ahead and, at noon, Sub-Lieutenant Farrier took off with the rest of the squadron in the modified Spitsteam.

Abby had taken the aircraft up for a brief test flight between raids that morning, wanting to make sure it flew alright with all the modifications before letting one of her people in it. She had taken a few photographs of the island from thirty thousand feet to test the camera before putting the machine through a few evasive manoeuvres. The images turned out surprisingly well and Abby had been impressed with the handling of the Spit, so she had immediately given the go ahead for the mission.

As planned, the squadron climbed up to twenty thousand feet and circled around the island as they usually did, before turning to the north to intercept the impending raid leaving Farrier to continued circling and climbing. She was under orders to take the Spitsteam up almost to its service ceiling before heading directly towards the point of the boot of Italy, following the raid, which would be on their way home again by then. She would then descend to thirty thousand and fly a zigzag route over Sicily, which would hopefully allow her to spot all of the major airbases. It would be an extremely long flight of more than five hundred miles and she would be over enemy territory almost the entire time, but it was unlikely that the Prussians would even spot her. Just in case, though, she was under orders to break off and head for home at the first sign of pursuit, mission be damned.

The mission was timed so well that the last of the Coalition aircraft were back on the ground by the time she took her first photographs, which made it extremely easy to spot the airfields and pinpoint which were being used by the bombers and which the fighters. However, when the photographs were developed and blown up, there was something in the images which nobody had been expecting.

When the squadron returned from the final sortie of the day, Scarlet and Chalky were in the hangar waiting for them and Abby's feet had barely touched the ground before the Irishwoman shoved a large photograph in her face.

Abby grabbed it with both hands and peered at it through tired, bleary eyes. 'This is, what? The eastern coastline? This is Syracuse, right?' She pointed at a town on the coast.

'That's right.'

'I don't see any air bases, though. What am I supposed to be looking at?'

'Um...' Chalky pushed his glasses up his nose as he peered over the top of the photograph. When he found what he was looking for, a fair distance south-west of the town and almost on the edge of the image, he tapped it with his finger. 'That.'

Abby squinted at the object. It was an off-white rectangular shape and, if anything, it looked like nothing more than a blemish.

'Maybe this will help.' Scarlet grinned and handed her another photograph.

This one showed the object from much closer up and it became clear that it wasn't a flaw in the film or the developing process, but rather a man-made object and, instead of an indistinct rectangle, she could now make out that it was actually five long sausage-shapes placed side by side.

Abby looked up and searched the hangar. 'Drake! Get over here!'

Drake heard her tone and hurried over. Predictably, the rest of the squadron came with him, curious as to what all the fuss was about.

Abby shoved the photograph at him. 'Tell me if this is what I think it is.'

Drake needed only a single glance to confirm what she already knew. '*Bertha!*'

'Bertha?' asked Lieutenant Smith.

Abby looked at her in surprise, but then realised that the three Navy pilots had of course never heard of the airship, or heard the tale of how Drake and Tanya had escaped from it - the War Ministry, in their infinite wisdom, had decided to keep its existence a secret from the British armed forces "so as not to engender panic or defeatist ideas". She reclaimed the photograph and studied it while she came to a decision. 'Alright, go get changed and grab some food. Drake, can you grab your sketches from the file room and give us a quick briefing?'

Drake nodded. 'Of course.'

'Thank you. Briefing room in half an hour everyone.'

As the pilots moved away Abby held the photograph out to Scarlet and Chalky. 'Is there anything you can do to this to get any more detail?'

Chalky shook his head. 'No, sorry, this is blown up as much as it can be. If you want more detail you need to get closer.'

Abby grimaced. 'Alright. We'll cross that bridge if and when we come to it.' She looked around the hangar. 'Can you find Sky Commodore Campbell, please, and ask her to meet us in the briefing room?'

Scarlet grinned. 'I can smell a mission coming on!'

Chalky gave Abby a tired look as the tiny Irishwoman skipped away towards the administration offices. 'She's like that all day. *Every* day. Can you *please* find something that'll use up some of her energy?'

Abby smiled. 'I think I might be able to do just that. Remember what I said about bolting a chair to the side of Hummingbird...?'

She laughed at the blonde man's horrified expression, then walked off towards the ready room to get changed.

'The Bertha Berg or simply "Bertha" for short, is a five-hulled Zeppelin which acts primarily as the Crimson Barons' mobile base.'

The briefing hall was a rectangular concrete room with light green-painted walls, a thin maroon carpet, more than a hundred extremely uncomfortable wooden chairs and the obligatory corkboards. Unlike the ready rooms and the mess it was unadorned and deliberately functional, with nothing to draw the attention away from whatever briefing was taking place.

Drake stood at the front of the room, the diagrams he'd drawn of the huge airship pinned to the boards along with a large-scale map of eastern Sicily with the location of the Bertha marked in red. As he spoke he referred to the diagrams.

'The airship is moved by four fans placed at the bottom corners of the gondola. They are spring-powered, rather than hydrogen. This has brought down weight enough that its carrying capacity is much higher than a normal Zeppelin.'

'How are they wound?' asked Smith with a frown. 'If they have steam-powered winding machines, then wouldn't it be more weight-efficient to just power them with hydrogen?'

'It would, but they don't use winding machines. They are wound by hand.'

Smith laughed, but immediately stopped when he didn't smile. 'Surely not. You're joking, right?'

'I'm afraid not. You see, Bertha is also a flying prison camp and the prisoners of war are forced to wind the springs using devices something like a capstan on a ship.'

'That's... that's...'

'Inhuman? Barbaric? Believe me it's far worse than it sounds.' Drake gave her a half-smile. 'And that's before you know that they are all pilots, at Hans Gruber's personal request.'

'Why just pilots?'

Drake shrugged. 'Who knows? Although I will tell you that during our long conversations I did get the feeling that Gruber wasn't exactly the most rational of people.' He turned back to the diagram. 'Anyway, to facilitate maintenance and repair, the springs can be removed, just like the ones on normal aircraft, and that's how we escaped - the prisoners mounted a revolt in one of the four winding rooms and managed to jettison the spring. Tanya and I jumped through the hole left in the gondola wearing powered glidewings and made it here by the skin of our teeth. We left behind more than a hundred freed prisoners of war, at least a few of whom were armed with stolen weapons. They intended to jettison the rest of the springs, then do their best to destroy the airship.' He smiled wryly, then looked at the blown-up photograph. 'Gruber boasted to me that Bertha never needed to land, that it was supplied with everything it needed by aircraft. The fact that it is on the ground suggests that they were at least partially successful. Although I don't see much in the way of damage, so they were probably only able to jettison enough springs to force it to land.'

Drake shared a sad look with Tanya; they both knew what the presence of an intact Bertha on Sicily likely meant for their friends.

'What defences does it have?' asked Abby.

'It's fairly liberally covered with anti-aircraft guns, but what calibre or type I don't know. I did get the impression from Gruber that it relies more on stealth and inaccessibility than sheer firepower for defence; it's painted a light blue which renders it all but invisible and it flies so high that there aren't many of our aircraft that would be able to attack it.'

Abby exchanged a glance with Dorothy Campbell. 'Which means our best chance of destroying it is while it's on the ground.'

Campbell held Abby's gaze for a moment, then looked at the diagrams. She'd seen them, or at least copies of them, twice before - once when she'd been briefed about the new threat in Whitehall with a group of senior RAC officers and once more when she'd accepted the posting to Malta. She knew exactly what kind of threat the airship represented and what it would mean for British morale, and more especially for Prussian morale, if it were to be destroyed.

She turned back to Abby. 'What do you need?'

Abby smiled. 'Thank you.'

Campbell shook her head. 'Don't thank me yet; I'm not going to sign off on your plan unless I think it has a very good chance of working. We can't afford to waste pilots or resources on this, no matter how high-priority the target.'

'Understood, but in order to come up with a plan I need better information. I want Vulture to overfly the site.'

Campbell nodded. 'I can authorise the hydrogen for a single flight, no more.'

'Chalky?'

Abby looked to the blonde pilot, who adjusted his glasses and smiled happily.

'One flight is all I'll need.'

CHAPTER 10

It took a while to assemble Vulture and get together the hydrogen that was needed to fly her, but eventually everything was ready and Chalky took her up at noon, just three days after Bertha had been discovered.

There was no need for Vulture to overfly the site in order to get much better images than the ones obtained by Sub-Lieutenant Farrier in the Spitsteam; the large cameras that Chalky had designed himself, then built into his aircraft, could tilt and rotate however he wanted them to and, weather permitting, take excellent photographs from dozens of miles away with their Swiss-manufactured lenses. He could, therefore, have merely gone straight up into the sky over the island, hovered for a few seconds using the balloon system he'd incorporated into Vulture for extra stability, then come straight back down again. However, Abby wanted images from more than one angle, so he had taken the photographs from over Malta first, then flown an indirect route that took him to the east of the site to get others.

It took another half a day to develop and sort the photographs, but by the time the sun went down Chalky had pinned the best images on the boards in the briefing room.

Dorothy Campbell and the pilots gathered around to stare at the machine that carried the Crimson Barons into battle and for a long while nobody said anything.

Chalky's photographs were remarkable, giving them crystal clear images that almost entirely filled the large pieces of paper on which they were printed. Every detail was there for them to examine, from the anti-aircraft emplacements, to the open hangar door, to the scaffolding holding the airship upright. They could see the iron crosses, picked out in white against the off-white that was the sky-blue in the monochrome images and it was even possible to make out the silhouettes of a few people standing at the huge, floor to ceiling windows of one of the messes.

Most importantly, they were able to make out the damage Bertha had sustained.

The top of the gondola, on the hangar level, was black, as if there had been a fire within, two of the fans were twisted and had been detached - they were lying on the ground nearby with figures swarming over them, and the prow was buckled and split where it had apparently nosed into the ground, digging an enormous furrow in the fields in which it had come to rest.

Even though the five hulls were intact and untouched, it was clear that it wouldn't be flying anytime soon.

'Well, now we know why the Barons haven't showed up yet.' Abby pointed at the smoke-blackened paint around the hangar. 'I'm assuming the prisoners made it all the way up there and destroyed at least a few of the aircraft. You said that the workshops were there too, right?' She looked at Drake who nodded. 'Then they probably wouldn't have been able to replace them yet. Again.' She grinned at Scarlet; the Irishwoman had destroyed the entire squadron of aircraft, including Hans Gruber's personal machine, Hölle, in a daring nighttime raid on their base in Muscovy.

'I suppose it's too much to hope that bastard Gruber was killed.' Bruce grumbled.

Abby grinned at him. 'You mean you don't want the chance to shoot him down yourself?'

'Nah, I wouldn't want to get in Gwen's way; we all know what she's like when someone gets between her and something she wants... like a pint of bitter.'

The Misfits chuckled and all turned to look at Gwen, wondering what she was thinking. Bruce's comment was amusing, but he was only half joking; over a very short time, things had somehow become very personal between her and the leader of the Barons. Gruber had deliberately targeted her in Muscovy, to the exclusion of anybody else, including Abby, and he had then tried to kill her after he'd shot her down, when she'd been hanging from her glidewings. Not only that, but, according to Drake, the Prussian also had a rather disturbing exhibition in a secret room of his personal quarters on Bertha which included items from her childhood and personal life.

Gwen shook her head. 'Much as I would enjoy defeating him, I won't shed a tear if he was killed in the revolt.'

'Well, setting aside the question of the Barons for now, what are we going to do about this thing, Abby?' asked Campbell. 'I don't think a few strafing runs are going to do much.'

'There are the Nelsons at Luqa and Ta'Kali.'

'There's not enough hydrogen for them.'

'Not even for one mission?' Abby batted her eyelashes at her, making the pilots chuckle.

Campbell rolled her eyes. 'I'll ask around, but I doubt it.'

'Thank you.' Abby gave her a wild smile and a wink, then turned to the rest of her pilots. 'In the meantime we need to come up with another plan. We're never going to be able to put big enough bombs on the Spits to put a dent in that, but we had some success with rockets in Muscovy. Is there any chance you sneaked any onto the island, Wendy?'

The pilots smiled, remembering how the big woman had packed Dreadnought full of ordnance and tools for the voyage to Muscovy without anybody realising until they were well on their way.

Wendy shook her head, though. 'Sorry, not this time,' she thought for a second then shrugged. 'I might be able to put something together, but it'll take a while and I can't promise that they will be anything like as powerful; I don't know if they have any of the chemicals I need on the island.'

Abby looked to Campbell, who nodded. She turned back to Wendy. 'Make this your priority for now, please, put the torpedoes on a back burner.'

'Right oh.'

'Anyone else have any ideas?' Abby asked, then sighed when Scarlet grinned eagerly. 'Anyone *apart* from the Pesky Pixie?'

Scarlet pouted. 'It's Pitiless! The *Pitiless* Pixie!'

'Not any more it isn't!' crowed Bruce, before crying out in pain and doubling over after receiving a sharp blow from a tiny fist that was almost too quick to see.

Scarlet hadn't needed to look away from Abby to find her target and she ignored the strained noises the Australian was making and pleaded with Abby. 'Aw come on, let me give it a shot!'

Abby shook her head. 'Not a chance; this time they'll be expecting you.'

The Irishwoman crossed her arms, sulking, and muttered moodily. 'Doesn't matter. I would still get the job done.'

Abby ignored her and looked around. 'Anyone else?'

Nobody had any more suggestions, so they went back to staring at the photographs, but it wasn't long before the pilots started drifting away, going to the mess to eat, and soon Abby and Dot were left alone with their responsibilities.

The bombing raids continued unhindered and for the Misfits it was starting to feel very much like the summer all over again.

The Coalition continued to concentrate their efforts on the ships in the Grand Harbour and began to see results. They sank the last remaining transport, inflicted heavy damage on one of the three surviving destroyers and scored several direct hits on the Arturo. Thankfully, the transport was empty of crew, having already been unloaded and the Arturo's flight deck protected it to a large extent, but twenty-two men and women lost their lives on the destroyer, mostly because they were on deck manning the anti-aircraft guns.

After a few days the Prussians seemed to realise that raids on the shipping alone weren't going to win them the island, no matter whether they sank the ships in the harbour or not, and they resumed their attacks on civilian targets, trying once more to destroy the population's morale.

The people had evacuated to the countryside when the bombing had originally started, but returned when the focus of the attacks changed to the first the airfields, then the shipping. Now they fled once more, leaving Valletta and the surrounding towns deserted, apart from the volunteers manning the guns and the British forces. The hospital was hit by four bombs during one of the raids, demolishing part of the building, but the basement remained relatively safe, although access was blocked for several hours. Signals were sent to the enemy after that, informing them that there were shot-down Prussian and Italian pilots being treated there, and it was eventually agreed that a red Maltese cross would be painted on the remains of the roof and that the bombers would do their best to avoid hitting it.

The Misfits were becoming increasingly frustrated. Not only were their best efforts doing nothing to stop the bombing, but the Crimson Barons' home base was vulnerable to attack, well within striking distance, and they were unable to do anything about it.

That frustration boiled over into their flying and some of them began to make mistakes.

Bruce and Monty, normally so much in tune with each other, collided in mid-air when Monty banked in the wrong direction after an attack on a bomber formation. His airscrew clipped Bruce's tail, effectively destroying both Spitsteams and sending them spinning out of control. They managed to get out and take to their glidewings, but Bruce banged his head quite badly and Monty's left cheek was sliced open by glass when his canopy all but exploded with the impact. They were picked up almost immediately by a high speed Navy launch and spent the night in the hospital recovering. Bruce was bruised and had a concussion, but was otherwise untouched, however Monty would likely have a scar for the rest of his life to remind him of his error.

Chastity misheard one of Derek's commands and caused him to miss an MU9 kill. He thought she had disobeyed him deliberately and they spent the rest of the mission bickering on their private channel. Their argument continued on the ground and would have escalated if Abby hadn't sat them down and sorted out the misunderstanding.

Another time it was Abby who lost her cool, when she bawled a frustrated Gwen out for wasting almost all of her ammunition, stubbornly making run after run on one of the Italian Grand Eagle heavy bombers, trying, and ultimately failing, to take it down.

Even Kitty, who had more combat experience than anyone, else apart from Bruce, was out of sorts. She tried to land with her gear retracted and only just reacted to the abort flare in time to avoid disaster - unlike the Harridan, the Spitsteam was notoriously unforgiving of such slip-ups and many a pilot had died from inattention.

It was just as well that good news arrived when it did, otherwise somebody might have gotten killed, or killed someone.

Dorothy Campbell turned up to the house in Birzebbuga at nine one night, just after the Misfits had gone to bed and an impromptu meeting was convened in the sitting room. Most pilots pulled robes over their nightclothes, but a few hadn't found any and put on their greatcoats. Scarlet didn't bother covering up, though. She just came down in her negligee, a moderately revealing black silk number, and sat in an armchair by the fire, seemingly unconcerned by the looks most of the men, and a few of the women, gave her.

However, as soon as Campbell started talking, all thoughts of Scarlet's body were put out of even Bruce's mind.

'I found you some hydrogen for the bombers.'

'Where? I thought there wasn't any spare?' Abby asked.

'There isn't, not on the island anyway, but I had a word with Admiral Myerscough and he graciously allowed the ships in harbour to siphon off some of their reserves. Most of what we're getting is coming from the Arturo; she's so banged up that even if she does ever manage to sail again, it'll only be to a port in Britain for a complete overhaul and she's got more than enough for that.'

'That's great! How many raids can we carry out?'

'One.'

Abby's face fell, her contented smile disappearing instantly. 'One? There's no way that's going to be enough to destroy Bertha!'

Campbell shook her head. 'No, it's not. But it's all you're getting.' She grimaced. 'I've had a word with Whitehall and they agree that Bertha has to be a priority, but they refuse to strand the shipping in the attempt - if we take all of the hydrogen from the fleet there would only be enough for four or five raids and even just two would mean that what remains of the convoy will struggle to make it to a safe port.'

'But what good is one raid going to do?'

'Their thinking is that one raid should be enough to damage the airship and keep it on the ground until more resources can be brought to bear. Another convoy is under preparation for sometime in March. It will have at least another couple of tankers and will bring more aircraft and pilots. If it gets through we will be able to mount a proper assault with more of a chance of success.'

Abby sighed and shook her head. 'I have no idea what Whitehall is thinking. Everything they seem to be doing recently smacks of penny-pinching and half-measures.'

'That's because it is - penny-pinching that is.' Campbell said with a resigned shrug. 'The Kingdom of Britain isn't made of money and things are getting a bit tight. Trade with the rest of Europe is almost non-existent, many of our exports to America aren't arriving because our shipping is being destroyed and we're also supplying Muscovy with American weapons that we're having to buy on credit, putting us even further in debt. Cummerbund worked for the treasury as a young man, he's an accountant and he knows his checks and balances. He knows that if we keep fighting the way we are we'll run out of money before the year is out.'

'Can't he see that spending too little will lose us the war just as quickly, if not quicker, than spending too much?'

'I have no idea.' Campbell shrugged again. 'I will say this much, though, if his methods do not meet with results he will be out on his ear sooner rather than later.'

'What good will that do us if the drongo's already lost us the war?' Bruce broke in before Abby could say anything else, once again expressing in his own special way what they were all thinking.

'I'm sure the King will step in before things can go that far,' Derek said. He didn't seem too convinced by his own words, though, and there was silence as each of the Misfits contemplated what would happen if the War Ministry continued to act as it had been.

As always the Navy pilots were a bit lost, not having experienced Cummerbund's manipulations or apparent malice towards the King and the squadron first hand, and it was Lieutenant Smith who brought the conversation back to its original purpose.

'When are we going to carry out the raid, ma'am?'

'In three days - the bomber squadrons need some time to get their machines out of mothballs and ready to fly. Their commander and I both agree that, while it would be safest to carry out the mission at night, if we're restricted to one raid then we have to go during the day to be sure of hitting the target as hard as possible. We've tentatively agreed to go after the last Coalition raid of the day lands, when there's an hour or so of daylight left. That way they won't have had time to rewind their fighters and their pilots will already be thinking of bratwurst and beer.'

With a mission to look forward to, the Misfits regained their focus and effectiveness against the Prussian bombers. That didn't stop tragedy from striking the very next day, though, as Lieutenant Smith, badly injured after being hit by return fire from a Prussian bomber, crashed on landing and was killed instantly. Her remains were returned to the Navy so that she could be buried by her companions, her photo was added to the ones that graced the altar in the cathedral, and a memorial service was planned for her in Father Bugelli's church.

The two remaining Navy pilots were understandably upset about the loss of their leader; as the only surviving aviators from the Heart of Oak they had grown close, but it didn't affect their flying at all. If anything it made them more determined than ever to make a difference.

The day before the raid was planned, the weather worsened once more, grounding both sides.

Gwen stood on the deserted airfield, her head tilted up to the sky, feeling the drizzle on her face, not caring how wet she got. The water had soaked into the wool of her scarf and it was beginning to smell, but she didn't mind; the smell was familiar, it reminded her of home, of her father's coat when he used to hide her in it, protecting her from the rain while they ran along the path through the woods from the hangars to the house after they'd been working on her latest project.

'Penny for your thoughts?'

Gwen shuddered, a chill, which had nothing to do with the weather, running through her at the familiar question in a familiar voice, and turned to find Drake standing behind her at the top of the steps of the personnel entrance to the underground base.

He frowned when he saw the troubled expression on her face. 'Did I say something wrong?'

She forced a smile. 'No, nothing. It's just... never mind.' He obviously didn't remember asking her that exact same question in Muscovy, not very long before he "died" and there was no need to tell him that it had brought back some very unpleasant memories. 'I was just enjoying the rain and thinking of home.'

Drake pulled his waterproof closer and hunched his shoulders. 'I can't say I miss the rain. Home, definitely, but the rain.' He smiled at her. 'I'll take Mediterranean weather any day.'

'Just not this day's, right?'

'Right. Or tomorrow's; the forecast says this is going to last a couple of days.'

'And when are they *ever* right?'

Drake chuckled, but there was also laughter from behind them and they turned to find Kitty and Tanya huddled together on the steps, beneath the protection afforded by the thick metal trapdoor which lowered to cover the opening during raids.

'Could you two be any more of a cliché?'

'Sorry?' Gwen blinked at Kitty, as much to clear the rain out of her eyes as because she didn't know what the American was getting at.

'Two Brits, standing in the rain, talking about the weather. It might as well be a strip in the funnies.'

'Ah.'

Gwen glanced at Drake, who shrugged. 'She has a point.'

Tanya poked her head out from under the cover of the trapdoor and frowned at the clouds, but quickly retracted it and swiped her hand across her face. 'What's so interesting about the weather? It's just clouds and rain and snow. We can either fly in it or we can't. Why would we want to say anything else?'

Kitty grinned at Gwen and Drake before answering. 'Beats me. I think it's a metaphor for something sexual. It usually is with the British; they're very repressed sexually.'

Tanya nodded earnestly. 'That would explain it - Rudy was certainly quite inhibited when we were first together, but I'm teaching him to be more adventurous.'

Neither Gwen nor Kitty quite knew how to respond to the bald statement from the Muscovite, but Drake's cheeks reddened and he coughed. 'Yes... Um... Was there something in particular you two wanted?'

Kitty grinned at him. 'Change the subject all you want, Rudy, you know Gwen and I are going to have a nice chat with Tanya over a few drinks at some point.' She laughed as the colour that had so recently blossomed in Drake's cheeks drained away, leaving him white as a sheet, but took pity on him and didn't comment any further. 'We came to get you; Abby's called a meeting in the hangar in ten minutes. She says she's got a surprise for us.'

'Is this about the wagon that arrived about twenty minutes ago?' Gwen asked. When she'd come up to enjoy the weather, a heavily-laden RAC wagon was just trundling down the ramp into the hangar.

'Probably.' Kitty said. 'She was certainly very excited when she saw it.'

'Ooh, I hope it's that tea making machine I ordered from Selfridges,' said Drake. 'Corporal Doyle's tea isn't bad, per se, it's alright for you plebeians, but I prefer not to have my Brunel's Best Blend boiled for half an hour, thank you very much!'

Gwen aimed a kick for Drake's behind, but he skipped out of the way and ran past Kitty and Tanya and down into the bunker.

Abby was waiting for the pilots by a stack of wooden crates, piled up at the side of the hangar. With her were her fitter, Sergeant Potter, and the chief fitters from both Bruce and Monty's crews. When the two men saw their fitters standing with her, their eyes lit up and they glanced at each other.

'Please tell me those crates contain what I think they contain!' Bruce cried out, unable to contain his excitement.

Abby nodded at the fitters. 'If you would?'

The three men plied three of the crates with crowbars and the sides flopped down to reveal the contents - shiny new Duralumin panels.

'The people at Luqa have finished your aircraft, Gentlemen. I told them not to send anything until it was all ready so that it would be a surprise for you.'

Bruce whooped and danced, clicking his heels in the air and flapping his elbows in a rather ungainly display.

Abby watched him for a couple of seconds, then sighed and looked at Monty. 'Do you have names for them? Colour schemes?'

Monty tore his eyes from the spectacle of his wingman making a bigger fool of himself than usual and shook his head. 'We haven't been able to agree on anything,' he glanced at Bruce. 'Maybe *Chicken* would be a good choice for his.'

Abby chuckled. 'Or *Duckling*. It doesn't matter, you won't have time to paint them anyway if you want to fly them during the mission.'

Bruce froze in mid cavort, his left leg in the air and his arms bent like wings and grinned at Abby. 'You think they'll be ready that quickly?'

'Well, the fitters have got some work to do patching up the squadron's aircraft, but they've all volunteered to spend some of their free time working on your machines.'

Bruce whooped again and resumed his dance.

'Bruce, stop that now, please.'

Abby's coldly serious voice halted Bruce in his tracks, his smiled vanishing in an instant. 'What's up, Boss?'

Abby pulled the piece of paper with the message from the War Ministry from her pocket and handed it over to him. 'Cummerbund ordered us not to rebuild.'

'Badgers to equip ellipses, stop.' Bruce read. 'Request to rebuild denied, stop. Warm.'

The pilots absorbed the content of the message with expressions ranging from disbelief to disgust and more than one swore under their breath.

'Why the hell are you telling us this now, just when we're just getting our aircraft, Boss?' Bruce asked, incredulously. 'And what are we supposed to do with those?' He gestured at the crates. 'Just leave them in their boxes, while we wait for those bloody idiot Ministers to change their minds?'

'Of course not, Bruce.'

Abby exchanged a glance with Campbell, who shrugged and gave her an "I told you so" look in return. The Sky Commodore had argued against telling the pilots about the message so late in the day, but Abby had insisted, wanting to be honest with her pilots and thinking that they needed to know about Regis Cummerbund's continuing campaign against them so that they could be prepared when the next attack came.

She looked around her pilots, meeting their eyes one by one. 'This squadron was founded by me, at the King's command, and I have a charter somewhere with his name on it that allows me, no, it *requires* me to find remarkable men and women with remarkable aircraft and ask them to fly in defence of the country.' She looked pointedly at Monty, then Bruce. 'If you have aircraft which you have designed yourself and which have been constructed by you or any other British armed forces personnel, in your own time, using resources that don't belong to the RAC,' she smiled broadly and patted the Duralumin panel in the nearest crate, created using recycled metals from the Graveyard, 'but which the Prussians and Italians have been kind enough to donate, then I am well within my rights to ask you to use them.' The Misfits laughed and she turned to the fitters. 'Sergeants, there will be no flying today, so you and your crews may take the day off. Dismissed.'

'Thank you, ma'am.' Potter and the other two men smartly drew themselves up to attention, did a quarter turn to the right and marched a couple of steps in unison, just as if they'd been dismissed from a parade. Potter then put his fingers in his mouth and blew a piercing whistle which reverberated around the cavernous hangar.

Almost a hundred fitters, both RAC and Royal Navy, appeared, as if by magic, and swarmed the crates, breaking them open in a frenzy of efficiency, then carrying the contents away to were more men and women were waiting with two support frames, ready to receive them. In less than a minute, the crates were empty and half a dozen airmen and women were clearing up the packaging, placing it aside for later reuse.

Bruce whistled. 'Like ants on a drop of syrup!' He looked at Abby. 'If that's everything, I'd like to go and help them, please, Boss.'

'Me too,' Monty chimed in.

Abby nodded. 'Alright, but tonight we're having the sendoff for Mac and Lieutenant Smith.'

The two pilots froze in the middle of running off.

Bruce slowly nodded. 'It's about bloody time.' He gestured to Monty and they jogged away to join the fitters.

Saying goodbye to lost Misfits was usually a very private matter, but with Smith being only temporarily one of them they invited a few select guests to join them for a meal in the house at Birzebbuga.

Abby had tasked Farrier and Drummond with finding out if there were any of Smith's friends that would like to come and four Royal Navy officers showed up, along with Admiral Myerscough. As well as being the ranking Navy officer currently on the island, the admiral had been Smith's commanding officer on the Heart of Oak and had known her personally, so it was only natural that he come.

Owen, despite his pain, had been up and moving around the hospital under his own steam for a couple of days. His burns still needed treatment several times a day, but Dorothy Campbell had been able to obtain permission for Wendy to take him into her care for the night, arranging for the dressings and creams that were needed.

The meal passed pleasantly enough, with a couple of the chefs from a local restaurant being paid to provide the food, but it wasn't nearly as boisterous or lively as Misfit meals usually were.

Once the deserts were out of the way, Abby, as the person who had known Mac the longest, led the silent toast for the Scotsman, before the admiral, who had been briefed on what to do, performed the honours for Smith.

Afterwards, they retired to the sitting room to tell stories about the two pilots, the Misfits listening attentively as they learned more about the woman who had been one of them for far too short a time, and the Naval officers lapping up tales of the Scotsman who had earned his nickname of "Mad Mac" many times over.

CHAPTER 11

By the time the skies cleared and returned to their usual blue, the British bombers were fuelled and armed.

Since the Spitsteams had arrived, the Prussians had settled into a not-quite rhythm of three raids each day, each within a two or three-hour window - one in the morning, either before or after the Coalition pilots had their breakfasts, one sometime before lunch, then one in the late afternoon, which the British suspected was timed deliberately to spoil their tea. The crews at Luqa and Ta'Kali were ready and waiting, therefore, when the final raid of the day came over and, when the enemy aircraft had flown back out to sea, the ramps to the hangars gaped open and the British bombers streamed out of their underground hangars. Like Smith, Farrier and Drummond, each and every one of the bomber pilots had stepped forward when Sky Commodore Hughes had put out the call for volunteers to join the Hal Far Fighter Force. He had refused to accept them, though, knowing that they would be needed when the time came to strike back, so they were understandably more than eager to finally do their part.

The fitters at Hal Far rearmed and rewound the returning Misfit aircraft as quickly as they could on the airfield then, when everything was ready, Dorothy Campbell gave the signal for the raid to go.

The sound of sixty-four Pickford *Nelson* medium bombers powering up one hundred and twenty-eight hydrogen-powered engines reverberated around the island, reaching even the furthest corners. It greeted the Maltese people as they emerged from whatever shelter they took during enemy raids and caused a great many of them to look to the sky nervously, wondering if the all clear had come too soon. However, when the upturned eyes found no sign of Prussian or Italian aircraft, the word started to spread, until the entire island was alight with excitement - the British were striking back!

Hans Gruber was in his quarters, ensconced in his armchair, reading through the latest newspaper clippings from the British press while enjoying a glass of schnapps.

Pickings had been slim for a while after Christmas, as the Misfits had almost disappeared from sight. For almost a whole month there had only been the occasional unsubstantiated rumour of sightings and rehashed stories of past missions to keep the hungry British public satisfied. But then they had shown up in Malta and suddenly the newspapers were once again alive with the name *Misfit Squadron*.

By that time he had known as much as the press, more, actually, so he hadn't needed the reports, but he'd still enjoyed reading and rereading about how the Misfits had lost almost all of their aircraft on arrival at the island, the press once again reporting things that should have been kept secret. It was rather unfortunate that Mr F Featherstonehaugh hadn't been allowed to accompany the Misfits to the island; the reports from the pilot, Chastity Arrowsmith, were rather inferior, but he added them to his collection anyway, mentally filing away the few tidbits of a personal nature they contained.

When the alarm klaxon sounded, he was rereading the profiles of the three Royal Navy pilots who had joined the squadron, trying to glean some information that would help him kill them when he got back into the air. He tutted in annoyance and turned up the volume on his gramophone, trying to drown it out with Wagner. He would have to have a serious word with the signal lieutenant; he was becoming far too trigger-happy with the alarm. Only last week the man had sounded it as soon as the fire sensor in the officer's mess had lit up, instead of doing a little investigation first and finding out that the chef was merely serving Crêpes Suzette.

He turned the music back down, though, when Friedrich, his personal steward burst in.

'Sir, a raid!'

'Don't be absurd.' Gruber scoffed 'Have the Maltese landed in their colourful little boats, armed with nets and fishing rods?'

He waved the steward away and turned his attention back to his papers, but the man didn't move, so he sighed and set them aside. 'Oh, go on, then, tell me what's happening.'

'Italian spotters on the south coast report fifty or so bombers are in the air and heading this way, sir.'

Gruber considered the man's words for a second, then burst from his seat. 'Helmet, jacket and goggles, now!'

He didn't wait for the man to fetch the items, but just ran from the room and down the short corridor beyond. His pilots were in their rooms, changing into their dress uniforms for dinner and he growled at them in passing, making them scramble to catch up with him. He raced through the mess, brushing aside the steward laying the table, sending him flying, and making another fall as he stumbled backwards trying to get out of his way. He snarled in frustration at the bulkhead door, cursing the time it took to open it, then raced through and up the stairs and through the even more frustratingly slow airlock.

While he waited for the room to cycle he ignored the four pilots who'd made it in before he'd slammed the door in the face of the rest and tried to work out where the British could possibly have rustled up fifty aircraft to attack them. They were bombers, so they couldn't have come from a carrier and he would have heard about another carrier entering the Mediterranean anyway. Alexandria was a thousand five hundred kilometres away, Gibraltar one thousand eight hundred, so they couldn't have come from their either. There was nowhere else - they had to have come from Malta, but how? The British ships that had survived couldn't possibly have brought that many in their holds. Not even the Arturo could carry that amount of cargo.

The green light on the wall went on and Gruber let one of his pilots spin the wheel on the door and push it open, but then shoved him aside and ran towards Hölle.

'Is it ready?' His voice training allowed his shout to carry to his mechanics, even though he was still thirty metres away in a hangar that was loud with working repair crews, but his crew chief's reply was lost. The man's nod was enough, though and Gruber leapt up onto Hölle's wing and clambered into the cockpit.

His hands flew over the controls and his eyes darted from one instrument to the next as he ran through his pre-flight checks.

Friedrich arrived with his things and he shrugged into his flight jacket - he wasn't going to bothering with a flightsuit just for a few bombers and besides, there was no time to put it on - before donning his helmet and goggles and plugging himself into the radio.

The headset built into his helmet came alive with chatter, but he immediately broke into it, not caring who or what he was interrupting.

'This is Star Leader, get the damn hangar door open *now*! I'm ready to take off.'

He didn't bother listening to whatever response came, he just opened his throttle a crack and moved Hölle forwards onto the runway. He wanted to have as much airspeed as possible, so he turned towards the bow of the airship and accelerated away from the hangar door, not caring that he was breaking every rule by doing so on the runway and not using the taxiway. He turned at the very end, his rudder only centimetres from the far bulkhead, and came to a halt facing back the way he came.

The horn, announcing the opening of the hangar door, blared three times, loud even in his covered ears, and the red warning lights flashed. There was a thunk, a vibration which he knew could be felt through the entire airship, as the huge flap, several tons of reinforced Duralumin, started to move, but then there was a squeal of tortured metal and it ground to a halt with a deafening clang, sending another, larger shockwave through the metal beneath Hölle, rocking the aircraft.

'Get that damn door open!' Gruber shouted, silencing the chatter on the radio momentarily.

After a few seconds a new voice came over the airwaves which Gruber recognised as the admiral. 'Stand down, Generalleutnant. The hangar door mechanism is fused. You will not be able to take off.'

Gruber swore and slapped his hand against the instrument panel, smashing the airspeed indicator, before leaning over the stick and curling his fingers around the triggers of his cannon. He barely stopped himself from firing at the distant hangar door in time and released the stick with a growl. He threw his canopy back on its slides and stared up at the ceiling, high overhead, as he took several deep breaths. Eventually he calmed enough to click on his microphone and speak in a normal tone. 'Acknowledged, Admiral. Star Leader standing down.'

As the first huge impacts hit, sounding deceptively innocuous through the thick metal, but powerful enough to send tremors through the enormous airship, Gruber climbed out of his aircraft. He left it to be collected by someone else and stalked past the long line of Blutsaugers with their pilots, ready to take off, heading back towards his quarters.

Someone was going to pay. If anyone was left alive after the British had finished with them.

The enemy had been taken completely unawares and only when the first bombs were falling did the first fighters get off the ground. There was no way they would be able to catch the raid, though, because the Nelsons were already turning for home.

The Misfits watched from twenty thousand feet, ten thousand feet above the bombers, as flowers of flame bloomed in the half-light of the Sicilian dusk. A huge explosion flared brightly, making the pilots recoil involuntarily and there were cheers over the radio as an immense cloud of black smoke obscured the view.

'So long, Bertha!' crowed Bruce. 'Nice knowin' yer!'

The Australian's simple rhyme drew a few laughs, despite not being particularly funny, but Derek's voice immediately silenced them. 'Badger Leader, Nine here. Requesting permission to engage the incoming fighters.'

Abby looked down, searching for the enemy airfields west of them, assessing the situation. There were three bases on Sicily dedicated to fighters and each of them were undoubtedly putting their aircraft back into the air to face the threat. Two were on the south coast, one more than fifty miles away, the other almost a hundred, but the third was only ten miles from the Prussian airship and she could see a couple of squadrons of MU9's on their way up, climbing hard towards the retreating bombers, with a third squadron of MU10's only just taking off.

'Why the hell not, Badger Nine.' Abby said, more than eager for a fairer fight than usual. 'All Badgers, attack by pairs. Tally ho!'

Eleven aircraft dipped their left wings and fell from the sky, closing the ten miles to the enemy MU9's in just over a minute and blasting through them with cannons blazing. The Prussian pilots had been so fixed on the bombers that they hadn't even realised the Misfits were there until it was far too late and half a dozen of the small and far too fragile single-spring fighters were ripped apart and sent tumbling to the ground in just that pass with not a single shot fired in reply.

The Misfits, in a tried and tested manoeuvre, pulled up from their dive and went streaking back skywards, their momentum sufficient to take them several thousand feet above the enemy and putting them in an ideal position to strike again. However, when they banked around to do so, they found that the Prussians had already turned tail and were diving away for their base.

Not wanting to brave whatever anti-aircraft defences there were around the airfield, Abby called off the attack and ordered them home.

The RAC didn't lose a single pilot or machine in the raid, something that was almost unprecedented in the history of aerial warfare; even if there weren't enemy fighters defending the target there were usually anti-aircraft batteries in their droves around anything strategically important, yet there had been nothing protecting Bertha.

Farrier, in the reconnaissance Spitsteam, was going to go up to take a look at noon the following day, but everybody already knew that, by the amount of hits and the secondary explosion everybody had witnessed, the damage on the airship had to be substantial.

It was a satisfying conclusion to the first British attack on the forces massed against them and definitely something to celebrate. Which was exactly what the RAC did.

Luqa was the largest of the three RAC air bases on the island and as such had the biggest mess, kitchens and storage facilities, so it was only natural that the party was held there.

Every single member of the armed forces on the island, RAC, Royal Navy and Army - pilots, fitters, sailors and soldiers alike - was invited, as were many of the locals who had supported the British. In the end, more than two thousand people packed into the underground base, which was far more than it was designed to cope with, and the ventilation system struggled to cope, the fans whirring at an alarming speed, until someone had the bright idea to open the hangar ramp to let the air in, but cover it with a blackout curtain to keep the light from leaking out into the night.

Dorothy Campbell had insisted on a full debriefing after the mission, so the Misfits were the last to arrive and the party was in full swing by the time they were deposited on the airfield at Luqa, at the top of the ramp into the hangar.

A military guard had been posted to receive the guests and she saluted them. 'They're all in the mess. Go straight ahead between the Nelsons, then follow the noise to the left. Right old racket they're making already, you can't miss 'em!'

Abby thanked him then the Misfits tramped down the ramp, the metal echoing hollowly beneath their feet, then through the blackout curtain, held open for them by another pair of MG's.

The hangar was silent and lit only by the red lights used before nighttime sorties. It was completely deserted, all work on the aircraft apparently done for the evening and all personnel dismissed to join the festivities, aside from the few people on guard.

Bruce grumbled and tugged at the sleeve of his day uniform tunic. 'I know they said this was going to be informal, but we're Misfit Squadron, dammit! There should be someone here to welcome us!'

Abby grinned at him. 'I can go back to the guard and order her to salute you a few more times if you want?'

'She was only a corporal, find me at least a group captain and then I'll be happy.'

They walked across the hangar towards the sound of music, past the shadowy forms of the bombers, seeming much larger than they actually were in the ominous red light.

There were a couple more MG's posted outside the mess and they broke off their conversation as the pilots approached and stood to attention.

'Evening, ma'am.'

The leader of the two saluted, then, as soon as Abby had returned it, spun on her heel and thumped on the door.

For a second it seemed that nobody had heard and the Misfits glanced at each other, wondering why the guard wasn't just opening the door, but then it swung open, blinding them with white light that was all the brighter because of the contrast with the red.

The pilots walked in, squinting and shading their eyes with their hands, but then came stumbling to a halt when the upbeat jazz music stopped abruptly. It was only for a heartbeat, though, because the band immediately launched into a very different piece of music, one which the Misfits immediately recognised as *September Skies*.

It was a modern, yet martial piece by Benjamin Britten, a young and upcoming British composer, who had created it to honour the bravery and sacrifice of the RAC over Britain the previous summer, although he had later admitted that the Misfits had been the real inspiration behind it. The Misfits, along with a dozen other pilots who'd taken part in the battle, had been invited by the King, as guests of honour, to the premier performance in St James's Park. A huge, seven-tiered stage had been constructed for the occasion and the Royal Family and guests had sat in a special box to one side, in full view of the thousands of people who had filled both the park and The Mall. The event had been arranged not only to boost the morale of the British people, who travelled from all over the country to see it, but also as an exercise in disinformation, coming as it did two days before the squadron embarked for Malta, making it look like they were firmly settled in England and enjoying some well-earned time off.

The full piece, which had been played that day, called for a one hundred and twenty piece orchestra, a dozen Duralumin panels to be struck by metal hammers, machine-gun fire, and a fly-past by twenty-four bombers, although, if the performance is indoors, the fly-past can be substituted by twenty airscrews powered by hydrogen engines.

The full piece was over an hour long, but thankfully the band played only a few dozen bars of the reduced version for marching band before reaching a crescendo and coming to a crashing conclusion, which reverberated triumphantly around the mess hall.

In the ensuing silence, Bruce's whisper carried to all the pilots. 'That'll do, I suppose, but I'd prefer the Sheilas...' The rest of his words were cut off by thunderous applause which filled the room.

After a short speech by the Luqa base commander and another by Abby, the party resumed.

Gwen tried to hold on to Kitty as they were swamped by bomber crews and sailors, but it was impossible, and they were swept away from each other on a wave of congratulations and shouted questions. Her only compensation was the pint of bitter that was thrust into her hand - thanks to Freddy Featherstonehaugh's articles the whole world knew that was her preferred drink.

Eventually the furore died down, but instead of immediately seeking out her companions or joining the dancing, she found that her attention was drawn by her surroundings.

The mess was huge, easily as big as the hangar at Hal Far, and within it had been recreated the main exhibition hall from the Crystal Palace, complete with the rounded metal and glass roof, through which could be seen a star-studded night sky. The creators of the space had even faithfully reproduced the exhibits from the Great Exhibition of 1851, for which the Palace had been constructed, and they stood in their places around the room, along with the statuary, the fountains and the fully grown trees which had famously been planted inside.

Like most British children, Gwen had studied the Great Exhibition at school, and she had no need to actually approach any of the exhibits to know what they were, but she was actually looking forward to doing so later. However, at that moment she was more interested in finding out if something else that the exhibition had been famous for had been reproduced - the first ever pay toilets, which had given birth to the phrase "spend a penny". She was just about to go in search of them, when she felt a tap on her shoulder and turned to find a grinning Kitty with her arm around Polly Ames, the medical orderly from the Arturo that the two of them had befriended during the journey back from Muscovy.

'Look who I found.'

The words were barely out of the American's mouth before the young naval officer squealed and jumped at Gwen, knocking her back a couple of steps in her enthusiasm.

Kitty shrugged, her grin widening. 'She may have had a little to drink already.'

'You're not kidding.' Gwen gasped as Polly all but squeezed the life out of her.

The young woman pulled back slightly and smiled at Gwen from very close range. 'Gwen! I've missed you soooo much!'

Gwen struggled to breathe in the face of the rum fumes coming from the girl's mouth, but nonetheless smiled warmly at her. 'Polly! I'm so glad you're alright! Where have you been hiding yourself?'

'I've been working in the hospital.'

'Really? We've been by a couple of times, but I didn't see you.'

'I know you have; it's all some of the patients can talk about! And no, you wouldn't have seen me; I've been put on the night shift.'

'Oh, that must be hard.'

The girl grinned. 'Boring more like; now that everybody is safely under cover we barely have any new patients coming in and my job consists mostly of watching people sleep and helping people to the bathroom every so often.' She laughed, but then pouted and shook her head. 'Let's not talk shop right now, though; it's my first night off since the Arturo got in and I need to have some fun.' She grabbed Gwen's hand and started dragging her towards the middle of the room. 'Come on! Let's dance!'

Since they were flying the next day, Abby had ordered her pilots to be back at the bottom of the ramp by midnight, ready to take the autocars back to Hal Far, and the party was showing no sign of slowing down by the time they slipped out unobtrusively.

Polly had kept Gwen and Kitty on the dance floor most of the night, with only brief pauses for refreshments or when the band rested. They didn't mind one bit; it had been too long since they'd properly let their hair down and they hadn't been planning to drink much anyway, but it did prevent Gwen from finding the toilet or inspecting the exhibitions. When the time came to leave, Polly bid then a very noisy goodbye, kissed them both very enthusiastically on the lips and promising to use some of her time off to visit them at Hal Far.

Bruce followed the two women out. He had put his experience in Muscovy firmly behind him and had not one, but two girls on his arms - a petite naval officer and a pretty, but decidedly beefy-looking woman, in an army uniform. However, while Gwen and Kitty went straight towards the group of pilots already waiting, he stopped before he got to them and said a rather noisy goodbye to the women in the shadow of one of the bombers. He finally slunk over several minutes later, a wide grin on his face and his lips smeared with red.

He wasn't the last to show up, though; that honour went to Derek who, uncharacteristically, showed up almost ten minutes late, just as Abby was about to send someone to look for him. He was accompanied by a tall RAC officer with a thin moustache and was looking more relaxed and happy than he ever did, except when he had a bottle of expensive wine in his hands.

'Come on, Cinders!' called Bruce with a laugh. 'It's past midnight, you're going to turn into a pumpkin!'

Derek came to a sudden stop when he heard the Australian call out and even in the red lights they could see his face flush when he caught sight of the pilots watching him. He stared at them for a second, then seemed to draw into himself. He straightened and turned to the man with him, shook his hand brusquely, then moved towards the ramp. He came to a halt again after just a few steps, though, and seemed to speak to himself under his breath, then spun on his heels and jogged back, taking the man by surprise just as he was turning to return to the party. The man's eyes widened in shock as Derek planted a kiss on his lips, but then closed as their arms went around each other.

Derek knew what a spectacle he was presenting, though, so he pulled back after not long and gave the man a warm smile before leaving him again.

There was a spring in the usually restrained pilot's step and his fellow Misfits welcomed him with smiles, every single one of them thinking that it was about time he found someone. They said nothing, though, and just turned and went through the curtains into the night.

It was a different MG on guard outside and he saluted them, but said nothing and just kept up his watch.

The autocars hadn't arrived yet, so the pilots huddled together, speaking in hushed tones.

Mac's will, on file with the squadron, like every pilots', had been read out at the meal and, while his main possessions had gone to his relatives in Scotland, the few things he carried with him had gone to members of the squadron - his hip flask had been among them and he had left it to Chastity. The Misfits were fairly sure that he had meant it as a joke; his wingmate notoriously unable to hold her drink, but she had filled it with the best Scotch Whisky she had been able to find at the party and she passed it around now.

Abby took a small sip, then passed it on to Bruce. She waited for him to swig from it and pass it on to Monty before speaking. 'I've been meaning to ask you two - what have you decided about your aircraft?'

'Well, Boss,' said Bruce, 'we've decided we kinda like the grey and it goes with the names we've chosen.'

Monty grinned. '*Wraith* and *Ghoul.*'

Abby considered their answer for a moment, then nodded. 'Even though we're suddenly looking a lot less colourful as a squadron, I like it. I hope the Prussians don't.'

CHAPTER 12

The Misfits were on the flight line before dawn the following morning, waiting for the Prussians to take to the air for their morning raid. Mugs of tea and coffee steamed in the chill morning air and greatcoats were buttoned up against a cold front which had moved in overnight.

It was a beautiful morning, with the air crystal clear and a few fluffy clouds to catch the colours as the sun neared the horizon, but the pilots barely saw it; their minds were already on the day ahead and full of thoughts of what the Prussians might do as retribution for the raid of the day before.

'Really, what can they do?' asked Bruce. 'Drop a few extra bombs on us? Write more propaganda leaflets? Stick their arses out of their windows as they fly past?'

The pilots chuckled, but Dorothy Campbell's frown remained firmly in place. 'I'm not concerned about any immediate response, it's the long-term that worries me.'

'Why?' asked Abby.

Derek, always the strategist, saw the implications before just about anyone else and answered for Campbell. 'Because we're no longer just an undermanned fighter squadron, defending an island that has a few half-wrecked ships and an undersea boat base. The Prussians know we have bombers here now and we've become a greater threat that warrants greater attention.'

'Exactly.' Campbell nodded. 'We've been poking a sleeping dragon and it's just been batting at us half-heartedly, but now it might wake up and decide to squash us once and for all. It wouldn't be particularly hard, either; there's too few of us and they have aerial superiority, so if they sent a big enough invasion fleet we wouldn't be able to stop it. They could wipe us out without breaking a sweat.'

'That's a cheery thought!' Bruce said with a grin. 'I'm so glad I'm getting up this early in the morning every day to do my part in a lost cause.'

Campbell shook her head. 'I'm not saying this is a lost cause, Bruce. If last summer taught us *anything* it's that there is no such thing. I'm just saying that we have to be prepared for anything and make sure we are using what little we have to best advantage in an attempt to dissuade them.'

'Well, we've blown up their airship, that's a pretty good start in my book!'

'Yes,' Campbell nodded reluctantly, 'but I won't be sure we've done that until I see the photographs from the reconnaissance Spitsteam.'

'But we *know* it was destroyed; we saw the explosion. It was bloody huge!' Bruce protested.

'I want to see it with my own eyes.' Campbell said. 'Once I see that airship peeled apart like an orange I'll believe it, but until then...'

Unfortunately, the photographs taken by Sub-Lieutenant Farrier showed that Campbell had been right to wait until the destruction of the airship was confirmed before writing it off. She pinned them up in the briefing room and the Misfits gathered at the end of the day to gaze at them disconsolately.

The airship, or at least the top of it where the bombs had hit, was blackened and dented, but the thick metal covering the hulls had protected it, much as the flight deck had the Arturo, and the rest appeared intact.

'What the hell was that explosion, then?' asked Abby, her frustration showing in her tone of voice. 'Charles, do you see anything that would explain it?'

Chalky had far more experience than the rest of them in analysing reconnaissance photographs and, while everyone else had just been staring at the airship, he had been looking at the surroundings as well and he nodded. 'Look at this.'

He walked up to the boards and pointed at an image that showed the area of forest to the west of the airship. 'Most of the damage is concentrated around the airship, as you would expect from our bombers, but there is a line of fire damaged trees *here* leading away from it.' He followed the black line in the grey trees with his finger. 'Squadron Leader Drake's report stated that the electrical systems on the Bertha were powered by wind turbines. That kind of thing would be unreliable on the ground, so they would have to bring in something else to supply the system, a generator for example. I think this is what remains of the pipeline feeding whatever it was and the fireball would likely have been the generator going up.'

'So, the airship itself is probably completely undamaged.' Campbell sighed, then looked around the pilots. 'Well, we don't have enough hydrogen to mount another bombing raid and it would probably be useless anyway, so does anyone have any other suggestions as to how we can attack it? Rudy, did you notice any weaknesses we can exploit while you were there?'

Drake shook his head. 'Sorry, nothing.'

'I saw something.' Chalky flipped through the file of photographs from his own mission, a week before. He pulled one out and pinned it onto the board. 'The airship is surrounded by scaffolding, probably to hold it upright. If we took out a sizeable portion of that, maybe it'll topple over. We can use its own weight against it.'

Campbell shook her head. 'The thing already crash landed. If it didn't get wrecked then, flopping onto its side probably isn't going to do much.' She looked at Wendy. 'What about those rockets Abby was talking about? Did you get anywhere with them?'

'I've managed to construct a few. They're not as powerful as the ones I made before, but they'll punch holes in tanks and armoured vehicles no problem. However...' She looked at the images of the airship sceptically. 'If several dozen direct hits from five-hundred pound bombs didn't do anything, then I doubt a few rockets will; the gondola is probably almost as thickly armoured as the top of the hulls.'

'Then that idea's out of the window.' Campbell looked around the group. 'Does anybody have anything else?' When nobody spoke up, she sighed. 'Then I'm sorry, but we have to move on to targets that we do have a chance of destroying. I received word a few hours ago that a convoy is being assembled to supply Malta, Crete and Alexandria. They'll be here in a couple of weeks and we have to give them the best possible chance of getting through.' She turned back to Wendy. 'I want our fighters equipped with rockets to attack their bases, but go back to working on the torpedoes, please; I have a feeling we're going to need them soon enough.'

'Right you are, ma'am.' Wendy nodded, not at all upset by having her priorities continually changed; as long as she was working towards blowing things up she was happy.

Campbell saw the sour looks that were being directed her way and pursed her lips. 'Look, I know you all want to destroy that airship, and so do I, but we can't. Not until help gets here at least. So, in the meantime we have to focus on what we *can* do.' She met the eyes of the pilots one by one, making sure her point was getting across. When she was satisfied she nodded. 'Good, now get some food then go and rest, we're going to be a lot busier from now on.'

Most of the pilots drifted away, but Scarlet lingered, ostensibly to take a last look at the photographs as Dorothy Campbell packed them away. When the Sky Commodore's back was turned she took one and slipped it into her tunic, then hurried after her friends.

She closed the door of the briefing hall behind her and turned to go to the mess, but squealed in fright when she found herself face to face, or rather face to chest, with Tanya.

'Bloody hell! Don't sneak up on me like that!' Scarlet scolded her, but then paused, frowning and looked around. There was nowhere to hide and the door opened the wrong way for the Muscovite to have been behind it. 'Hang on, how *did* you sneak up on me like that?'

The tall woman just grinned.

Scarlet scowled up at her. 'What do you want? There's food waiting.'

'I was wondering what you were planning.'

Scarlet felt a moment of panic; if the Muscovite woman, who barely knew her, had realised she was up to something, there was no way her friends, or worse, that spoilsport Abby, wouldn't have noticed. She peered around the tall woman, worried, but found that the rest of the squadron were half-way across the hangar - it seemed that they either weren't as perceptive as she thought, or they were too wrapped up in their own worries. Still, she had no idea what the motives of the woman were in confronting her, so she decided to play it coy.

'I have no idea what you're talking about. I'm not planning anything.' She tossed her head as she brushed past Tanya and stalked towards the mess hall.

The Muscovite woman fell into step beside her. 'You know, I've seen your work first hand, experienced it, in fact. It was an excellent demolition.'

Scarlet was slightly mollified by the flattery and slowed down slightly. 'I know, I read Rudy's report and I'm sorry.'

Tanya shrugged. 'You had no way of knowing that we were there or that we were going to steal one of the aircraft you blew up. I'm just glad we weren't actually in the hangar when it exploded. It doesn't matter; things worked out for the best in the end.' She glanced down at the petite Irishwoman and grinned. 'So, *do* you have anything in mind for that airship?'

The Irishwoman shook her head vigorously and quickened her pace, wanting to get to the mess and have an excuse to change the subject. 'Of course not!'

Tanya sighed theatrically as she easily kept pace. 'That's a shame, because I happen to know how to get my hands on some high explosives and have nothing to do with them...'

Scarlet came to a sudden halt. The one problem she'd been unable to solve had been the matter of where to get the explosives to destroy the Bertha. In Muscovy all she'd had to do was find the right people, but that wouldn't work on Malta; everything was far too RAC and official, with quartermasters and far too many forms to fill in.

She turned to look up at the woman and smiled.

When they had first laid siege to Malta, the Italians had constructed three air bases on Sicily to handle the hundreds of fighters and bombers that they moved in. Then, when the Prussians joined the fight, they in turn built four more. Unlike the underground RAC bases on the island, they were conventional, with all facilities and hangars above ground so, despite being defended by numerous anti-aircraft guns, they were far more vulnerable to attack.

In Muscovy, the Misfits and their allies had targeted the enemy fighters, destroying their machines while they were on the ground and with them any hope that the Prussians could defend their bombers. It was only logical to do the same thing in Malta in order to gain air superiority, so that when the convoy arrived they would be better able to protect it. Accordingly, Dorothy Campbell chose the closer of the two MU9 bases and asked Abby if she would kindly attack it with her squadron.

Just three days after the raid on Bertha, the Misfits landed back at Hal Far after confronting the morning raid and, almost before the enemy bombers had reached their bases, took off again, rewound, reloaded and with a pair of rockets under every wing.

The squadron was going to approach Sicily as low as they could, giving the Prussians as little warning as possible and Gwen grinned as they screamed over Malta, barely higher than the rooftops. It was one thing to climb miles up into the sky every day to face bombers where there was freedom to carry out aerobatic manoeuvres to one's heart's content, but quite another to be going in excess of three hundred miles an hour at less than one hundred feet, seemingly close enough to reach out and touch the trees and houses as they blasted past.

They passed directly over the Grand Harbour. The damage from the most recent attack was still being tackled and the ships were wreathed in smoke, but many a face turned up to watch them go past and a few men and women paused in what they were doing to wave or roar in encouragement.

The harbour was left behind in a flash and then it was just the sea. The aircraft descended until they were only yards above the waves and the Misfits settled in and relaxed ever so slightly for the short flight.

It would take them only ten minutes to cover the sixty mile stretch of water between Malta and neighbouring Sicily and while quite a few pilots liked to spend the time before combat silently preparing themselves, others couldn't go without talking for that long.

Gwen preferred not to speak unless she had something to say and she listened idly to a few of the other pilots breaking down that morning's fighting while she studied, for the umpteenth time, the reference materials taped to her knees.

Chalky had examined the images they had of the Prussian base and identified the types of buildings and the best ones to attack. Abby had then assigned targets, hangars and storage sheds, to all of the pilots and Gwen's was marked in red on a hand-drawn diagram taped to her left knee. She compared it to the aerial photograph on her right, wanting to make sure that she would recognise her designated target when she saw it.

The plan of attack was very simple, as all the best plans were. They would go in at treetop level where the guns would have trouble targeting them, use their rockets on the flight line and their assigned buildings in the first pass, then make two strafing runs to finish off whatever aircraft had been left undamaged - three runs in total and then home before a response could be mounted.

It was simple, but it was going to be very dangerous even so, far more than attacking a massed bomber raid where many of the gunners were hesitant to target them for fear of hitting their own aircraft. It was well worth the risk, though; they could potentially halve the numbers of Prussian fighters in one fell swoop and leave the playing field much more even.

'Two minutes, Badgers. Arm rockets.'

Gwen had completely lost track of time and she started at Abby's command, cursing herself for her inattention. She looked up to find Sicily already a haze on the horizon and quickly checked her instruments, then gave her straps a quick tug to make sure they were snug, before turning her attention to the tiny brass panel bolted onto the left side of her cockpit. The panel had several electrical wires dangling from it and held two switches, one either side of a small light. She flicked the first switch and was relieved when the light turned on, burning steadily green, signifying that the electrical circuit running to the rockets was unbroken. She had tested the mechanism on the ground, they all had, but there was always the possibility that something could come loose during the flight because of turbulence or vibration.

'All Badgers, check in.'

'Badger Two, Roger.'

One by one the Misfits reported their readiness. Miraculously, everyone's rockets seemed to be armed and ready - Gwen had expected at least a couple of pilots to report failures, but Wendy's hurried work wasn't as slapdash as it seemed. It still remained to be seen whether all the missiles fired on command, though.

'Badger Eight, climb on my mark.'

The coastline was a thick muddy line only a few miles ahead and it was time for the Misfits to make sure that they were on the right heading. The only way to do that was to get visual confirmation of the location of the airfield, and the only way to do that was to send someone up to look for it. It would be silly for them to all go, so Abby had given the job to Sub-Lieutenant Drummond. After Smith's death, the young man had been moved into Kitty and Farrier's element and his temporary absence wouldn't mean someone would be on their own for the first run. He would rejoin them when they returned and use his rockets then on whatever target was left standing.

'Mark.'

Drummond's Spitsteam pulled up into a steep climb, going up to five hundred feet in a matter of seconds before levelling out. Abby had timed it superbly and he reported in just as the sea was replaced by trees and fields as the rest of the aircraft crossed the coastline.

'Adjust course ten degrees left, Leader. Target at three miles.'

'Roger, Eight, thank you. Now get your arse back down before they spot you.'

'Roger, Leader!'

The Misfits turned onto the new heading, each of them unconsciously beginning a countdown in their heads; three miles at three hundred and fifty miles an hour would take just over thirty seconds to cover.

Before they were even half done, Abby gave the word and they popped up to one hundred feet and got their first view of the airfield.

Gwen immediately found her target and knew by the tiny course correction Abby made that she had too.

'Look at that! Beeyootifull! Won't these bastards ever learn?'

It wasn't hard to work out what Bruce was talking about - the Prussian fighters were lined up in a perfectly straight line with customary Prussian efficiency. They were just begging to be strafed.

'Let's hope not, Nine!' Abby said with a laugh. 'Happy hunting, Badgers.'

There was no time for any more chit chat as light flared from under the wings of the ten aircraft and streaked towards the grey and green buildings. Fire bloomed everywhere, but Gwen didn't have time to see the resulting damage as she was already past and juking Excalibur back and forth. There was no anti-aircraft fire, though; the Prussians had been taken completely by surprise.

'Yes! Thank you, Wendy!' There was a loud whoop which made Gwen wince and automatically curse Bruce under her breath, but then she blinked in surprise when she realised it had been Derek's voice, not the Australian's - he really was coming out of his shell.

There was answering laughter from a few pilots, but then Kitty's panicked cry drowned them all out.

'Eight, what are you doing? Eight! Break off!'

Drummond was supposed to have orbited the airfield and joined with his element on the far side, but in his enthusiasm he had flown straight in to launch his rockets without even dropping to the deck first.

Gwen held her breath as she watched the lone Spitsteam dip towards the line of buildings, but before he could launch his rockets, the anti-aircraft batteries finally woke up and fired at the only aircraft left over the airfield.

The young Naval pilot didn't stood a chance and what was left of his Spitsteam dropped from the air like a rock to hit the grass of the airfield near the perimeter fence and disappeared in a huge ball of flame as his live rockets exploded.

Gwen stared at the fireball, mesmerised by the beauty and horror of it. She thought she heard gasps from the other pilots but couldn't be sure that it hadn't been her.

'Focus, Badgers! Come on! Round two! Let's get those fighters! Turning now.' Abby's calm voice brought the shocked pilots' attention back to the job at hand.

Gwen tore her eyes away from the spectacle and saw that her wingmate had begun to swing back towards the airfield. She flung Excalibur on her wing to follow and increased throttle to catch up.

'Still with me, Two?'

'Yes, Leader. Sorry.'

Metal streamed into the sky from the anti-aircraft guns as the Misfits came in from all directions for their second attack. Tracer rounds reached out for Gwen and she kicked her rudder, seeking to throw off the gunner. It was the oldest trick in the book and she grinned with satisfaction when the deadly fire slewed, seeking to follow her non-existent turn. By the time it started to track back she was past the gun and her own were chattering.

Fighters broke apart in her sights, pieces flying off them as if they were made of paper, as she walked her cannon fire from one to another, but then she was too close and it was time to worry about the Prussian weapons again.

'Leader, Three here. I'm hit.'

Gwen's body twitched violently as she heard Kitty's calm report and she barely caught Excalibur before she nosed into the trees. She kept half an eye on Abby, staying with her while they made random evasive manoeuvres, but dedicated most of her efforts to searching for Kitty's Spitsteam. The aircraft was easily identifiable due to the red, white and blue stripes the American had painted on it, diagonally from the tip to the tail, but she couldn't find it anywhere and panic began to set in.

'Report, Three.'

'I've lost rudder control and my elevators feel sluggish. I can barely turn, Leader.'

'Get home, then, Three.'

'Roger, Leader, breaking off now.'

'Good luck, Three. Four, escort her, please.'

'Aye aye, Leader.'

Gwen sighed in relief; if Kitty couldn't make it home she would have said so.

'One more run, please, Badgers,' said Abby. 'Let's make it a good one.'

Gwen followed Abby round in a hard turn, her wingtip almost brushing the tops of a row of cypress trees planted around a rather lovely villa. She got a glimpse of a Prussian officer in a green uniform standing on the lawn, shading his eyes to look up at her, and half a dozen near-naked men lounging around a pool, before they were once again hidden from view and she grinned as she levelled off behind Dragon.

For this run she and the other wingmen would fall back behind their leaders, then mop up anything they missed so Gwen moved her stick and pedals back and forth randomly, swinging wide to allow Abby's yellow aircraft to get half a mile or so ahead of her.

Anti-aircraft fire started up again just as the smoking wreckage of the Prussian base came into sight. The hangars were all but destroyed and a couple of the other support buildings had also taken damage, but there were a few aircraft left, seemingly relatively intact.

'Two, do you see the pair on the left?'

'Roger, Leader, I see them.'

'Good. They're mine, go find your own.'

Abby flew over the perimeter fence and dropped until Dragon's airscrew was throwing up dust and grass with the wind of its passage. Being so low meant she was forced to fly straight and level, because any roll at all would put her wingtip into the ground, but it didn't matter because it also made it absolutely impossible for the Prussian guns to target her.

Gwen chuckled. 'Showoff.'

She shook her head, then looked along the long line of fighters, trying to find the best use for her final run. It was hard to decide; most of the forty or so aircraft were so beaten about that it was hard to imagine them ever flying again, but she could always put a few holes in them, just to make sure.

She was just lining up on a trio of MU9's near the ones Abby was going for when she saw him.

Hans Gruber.

He was one of several officers who had just emerged from the back of one of the smaller buildings and were running towards a waiting autocar, but there was no mistaking him; not only had Gwen, to her shame, seen his movies far too many times, but he was also wearing a very distinctive black uniform, which, as far as she knew, was unique in the Prussian armed forces.

She had no memory of making a course change, but suddenly, Excalibur was pointing directly at the running figure and her world narrowed until it became just her and him. She usually hated firing at men, had nightmares of the effect that her guns had on their soft bodies in fact, but she found that she had no such qualms about Gruber. Her finger curled around the trigger of her guns and gradually began to put pressure on it as she approached firing range - she didn't want to jerk it and spoil her aim; a single man was a hard enough target to hit at the best of times.

Gruber reached the autocar and pushed another officer bodily out of the way so that he could get in, but then he paused as if sensing something and spun in place to look directly at her.

The look of sheer terror on his face as he recognised his doom approaching was delightful and Gwen savoured every moment as she closed to within five hundred yards and took up the rest of the slack in the trigger.

Excalibur shuddered as four powerful cannons and six machine-guns flared in the corner of her eyes, perceptibly slowing with the recoil. Lines of fire reached out from her wings and huge clods of earth flew as Gwen walked death towards the autocar and its intended passenger, just as Abby had shown her.

A huge impact threw Gwen sideways, putting off her aim, and she fought for control as Excalibur lurched, only just preventing the machine from nosing into the ground. The white face of a petrified, but very much alive Gruber flashed past, almost close enough to slap and she shouted out her rage as she put Excalibur into a maximum-rate turn, recklessly brushing the treetops with her wingtip. However, by the time she was able to look back at where Gruber had been the autocar was gone and so was the leader of the Crimson Barons.

She snarled and slammed Excalibur onto her other wing and headed directly away from the airfield, racing to catch up with Abby.

She pulled up on Dragon's wing and found a grinning Abby looking across at her.

'Find something interesting to fire at, Two?'

Gwen took a deep breath, calming herself and letting go of her frustration before answering. 'Only if you can call Hans Gruber interesting, Leader.'

There was a pause as Abby stared at her, her mouth working but no sound coming out. Eventually the older woman swallowed with some effort and coughed before speaking. 'Repeat that, please, Two; I don't think I heard you right.'

'I spotted Hans Gruber and decided to get a little payback, Leader. Any objections?'

'Please tell me you got him!'

Gwen was surprised when she heard Bruce's voice, but quickly realised that Abby must have switched them over to the squadron frequency so that everybody could hear.

'Unfortunately not, Nine, but not for lack of trying, believe me.'

'Bugger.'

'I think I might have made him wet himself, though, if that's any consolation.'

'That'll do me, Two. Good job!'

Gwen landed at Hal Far and taxied to the top of the ramp, lining up behind Dragon. She smiled at Giuseppe, who had come running to meet her with the rest of her fitters, men and women who she was only just getting to know. He smiled back, but then his gaze strayed to the fuselage behind her and his eyes widened in horror. 'What have they done to my beautiful bird?'

Gwen finished shutting down, then undid her straps and leaned out of the cockpit, curious as to what had him so upset.

She didn't have to look very far. There was a gigantic hole, fully two feet wide, in her fuselage, through which she could see the interior of her aircraft. It had impacted just behind the cockpit, missing her by all of eighteen inches, and had to have been what had knocked off her aim and saved Gruber.

The young Maltese man clambered up onto the wing and peered through the hole. 'What did this? This is too big for a single anti-aircraft round.'

Gwen climbed out of the cockpit and joined him. The hole was clean and perfectly round, as if the Duralumin were merely a piece of paper being prepared for filing, and she could see all the way through it to the blue sky.

'I think it's from an ack-ack gun. I'm fairly sure they have a minimum altitude they can be set to explode, but they must have been using them anyway.'

Giuseppe grumbled, looking unhappy. He stroked Excalibur soothingly. 'We'll fix you up, don't worry.'

Gwen nodded at him. 'Thank you.'

Dragon had now disappeared down into the hangar and the controller was waving Excalibur forward so Gwen clambered back into the cockpit to cover the brakes while the hangar entry team manhandled the aircraft down the ramp.

As soon as her eyes adjusted to the relative darkness she gazed around the hangar, searching for the two Spitsteams that had left the fight early, but could find no trace of them. She jumped down to the ground and headed towards the communications room, wanting to ask if they were in contact with the two pilots, but changed direction when she spotted Dot Campbell speaking to Abby in front of Dragon.

The two of them looked up as she approached and she stumbled to a halt when she saw the expressions on their faces - a worrying mixture of regret and sympathy.

'What is it? Where's Kitty?'

Gwen's breath caught in her throat as she looked back and forth between them and warm darkness suddenly began to envelope her. Her legs turned to jelly beneath her and she felt herself going down, but then strong hands gripped her under the arms and she was half-carried to a crate of parts and sat down. Something was thrust into her hand, accompanied by a voice telling her to drink and she did so automatically before realising that it wasn't water, but a hip flask filled with rum. She coughed, gasping for air, but the shock cleared her vision and she lifted her head to find Scarlet kneeling in front of her.

She nodded her thanks and handed back the flask then looked past her to Campbell.

'What happened?'

'She's alive.'

'But?'

Campbell grimaced. 'But she had to bail out over the sea. She deployed her glidewings and managed to get close to a fishing boat. Farrier loitered long enough to make sure she was safely aboard, but she reports that the boat was Sicilian, not Maltese.'

'So, she's a prisoner of war.'

'Probably.' Campbell nodded. 'Don't worry, though, I'll contact the Italians, see what we can do about a trade - we've shot down quite a few of their pilots and we'll get Kitty back, even if we have to hand them all over.'

Gwen nodded, a spark of hope igniting within her, but she couldn't help but wonder if Abby had told Campbell about Gruber being on the base yet; knowing him, Kitty was probably already on her way to Bertha.

The damage to Excalibur was more extensive than it had seemed at first glance. The aircraft had been twisted by the impact and some of the frames had bent, meaning that repairs wouldn't just be a matter of patching up the holes, but would require the aircraft to be partially dismantled which would take a lot longer.

Unsurprisingly, with her mind on Kitty, Gwen didn't really feel like flying, but when the noon raid came over she did her duty and jumped into a spare Spitsteam to take to the skies with the rest of the Misfits.

The loss of fully half of their escorts had affected the bomber crews and they were far more timid than they had ever been.

The nine Misfit aircraft intercepted the incoming raid half-way between Sicily and Malta. The red and gold Italian machines dumped their entire loads and turned tail as soon as they spotted them, diving away for their bases, but it took the loss of almost a dozen of their bombers to persuade the Prussians that it might be for the best if they didn't press their luck. They eventually dropped their bombs into the sea, less than ten miles from the Maltese coast and performed an orderly, if hasty, retreat.

They didn't bother coming back that afternoon.

As soon as she landed from the noon raid, Gwen went in search of Sky Commodore Campbell.

She found her in her office, staring at her radio receiver, a half-eaten bacon sandwich on her desk, along with a stone-cold and forgotten mug of tea. She didn't seem to have heard Gwen's knock and didn't look up, even when she was standing right in front of her.

Campbell was looking tired, far more than she ever had in Muscovy, even at the height of the fighting around Murmansk, even when the situation had been at its most desperate. Her hair, which had still been mostly black when she had been Gwen's station commander at Didchurch, was now almost entirely grey and the frown lines on her forehead were more deeply marked than ever.

'Ma'am?'

'Yes?' Campbell looked up and for a moment her eyes were empty and unseeing, but then they cleared and she smiled, albeit weakly. 'Oh, Gwen, sorry, I was miles away. I don't have much for you, I'm afraid; nobody seems to know where Kitty is.'

Gwen frowned. 'What does that mean?'

'Well, I've been in touch with the commander of the Italian forces on Sicily. He was very friendly, but after a long conversation in which he invited me to his villa in Tuscany and flirted with me several times he told me that he couldn't help and that he would put me through to the admiral in charge of the naval forces. The admiral made me wait for fifteen minutes while he had someone ring around the ports before finally telling me that they had no reports of any prisoners being handed over to the authorities. He told me he would contact the civil authorities who run the police and local prisons and would have the Governor of Sicily ring me back when they had any news. That was...' Campbell looked at the antique aviator's chronograph that she habitually wore on her wrist, 'bloody hell, almost an hour ago.'

'What does that mean?'

'Not very much, actually. Just that the Italians are doing what the Italians do best - a lot of talking and very little working. I'm sure Kitty will turn up sooner or later. Maybe the fishing boat is still out at sea, or maybe it's from a remote village and it'll take time for someone to collect her. There could be any number of reasons why nobody knows where she is.'

'Do you think Gruber's got her?'

Campbell shook her head. 'No. The Italians would know if that were the case. I don't think they're going to hand her over to him, either; I've told them we're willing to exchange some of their officers for her. They'll hold onto her.'

Gwen frowned, not particularly convinced; Gruber seemed to have a habit of getting whatever he wanted and he would *definitely* want Kitty if he found out about her. 'I hope so.'

'I'm sure they will. Anyway, right now there's nothing else you can do, so leave it with me, don't worry too much about her and try to keep your mind on your flying; you want to be alive when she comes home, right?'

Gwen grimaced; the woman must have been listening in to the radio chatter in the control room and had undoubtedly heard Abby scolding her more than a few times for stupid mistakes she'd made in the attack on the bombers. She'd been distracted, thinking about Kitty instead of paying full attention to what was going on around her and had been as much a danger to her wingmate as she had been to the Prussians.

'That would be nice, yes.' She did her best to give the woman a smile, but she just couldn't. Campbell did slightly better, but it was a politician's smile and not entirely convincing.

'Good. Then off you toddle. If I have any news I'll come and find you. I promise.'

'Thank you, ma'am.' Gwen nodded and left the woman to her thoughts.

There was no word on Kitty's whereabouts that day, though, and it wasn't until mid-morning of the next that Campbell got a call saying that the aviator had been found.

She was waiting on the airfield when the Misfits came back from the morning sortie and as soon as Gwen saw the broad smile on the woman's face she sighed in relief, letting go of the breath that she seemed to have been holding for twenty-four hours.

Before she'd even shut Excalibur down, Campbell was up on the wing and crouched down beside her. 'The Legione Aerea have Kitty and that's the best thing that could have happened to her; the Italian Army or Navy might not have been interested in an exchange, but they definitely will be and I'll do what I can to make it happen.'

'Thank you.' Gwen smiled at her. 'How long do you think it'll take?'

'Sorry, but I have no idea. These things take time even in the best of circumstances. You'll just have to be patient, I'm afraid.'

Campbell squeezed Gwen's shoulder, then made her way back off the wing.

Gwen looked down at her instrument panel, where she had taped a photograph of Kitty, one of the ones that the photographer from The Times, Mr Jones, had taken in Muscovy. She reached out to stroke it gently. 'Don't do anything stupid, darling.'

CHAPTER 13

Tanya crept down the hall and snuck into Scarlet's bedroom half an hour before midnight.

The Irishwoman came awake instantly when she put a hand over her mouth and her eyes flared open, but to Tanya's surprise, she didn't cry out or struggle, instead her eyes just flicked downwards to take in the dark clothing the Muscovite was wearing before she nodded in understanding.

Tanya removed her hand and stepped back, giving Scarlet enough room to slide out of bed. In just a few very efficient movements, the Irishwoman's negligee was on the floor and she was stepping into equally dark clothing - a male child's by the look of it. The black trousers and dark grey shirt fit her well, though; Scarlet had quite obviously altered them to fit and Tanya nodded in approval at the demonstration of foresight and preparation.

They slipped out of the room and moved towards the staircase at the end of the corridor, but froze when a noise, like a cry, came from Gwen's room. They stood stock still, listening for the sound of someone getting up to relieve themselves or investigate, but moved on when no other sound came, apart from a few low moans of a woman in the throes of a bad dream.

'Poor thing,' muttered Scarlet under her breath when they had reached the relative safety of the stairs. 'She's been having nightmares again ever since Kitty was shot down.'

Tanya said nothing, she just nodded and tried to put on a sympathetic expression, even as she was promising herself that she wouldn't ever become so weak as to be similarly affected if anything happened to Rudy.

The two of them had spent time finding out which stairs squeaked, which floorboards creaked and made sure that the hinges of every door they had to pass through were well-oiled. That, added to the fact that the house was never locked, meant that it was extremely easy for them to leave undetected and less than five minutes later they were out in the moonless night, padding softly up the road towards the village.

Once they were safely out of earshot of the house, Scarlet frowned up at the slightly deeper darkness that was the Muscovite. 'How did you sneak up on me? Again! Nobody can sneak up on me.'

'When you hunt in Siberia you learn to be very quiet so as not to be hunted yourself.'

'But I set traps!'

'They were quite childish.'

Scarlet huffed in annoyance; ever since she was a child, nobody had ever managed to get that close to her without her knowing, even when asleep. And it wasn't as if nobody had tried. Always before, though, she had come awake as soon as she had sensed someone approaching, had the chance to assess whether the intrusion was welcome or not, and been able to act accordingly. She smiled back at the woman, albeit grudgingly. 'You'll have to show me how you did it.'

Tanya frowned down at her. 'Why? Whose bedroom do you want to sneak into?'

Scarlet giggled. 'How long have we got?'

Tanya glanced at her chronograph. 'Five and a half minutes. Why?'

Scarlet thought that the Muscovite was playing with her and grinned, but then saw that she was genuinely puzzled and sighed. 'Never mind.'

They entered the town and passed between the stone buildings of the main street.

Scarlet kept her eyes moving, scanning for threats. 'Where are we meeting them?'

The whisper sounded far too loud in the dead silence and Tanya just gave her a warning look in reply and turned off into the square in front of the church. She led Scarlet to the side entrance and slipped into the deep shadows of the doorway, becoming instantly invisible.

Scarlet stood next to her, feeling ungainly and far too conspicuous for the first time since she'd gone on the course at the Infiltration and

Sabotage school and found she had a talent for the stealthier side of things.

After a few minutes of awkward silence she peered at her chronograph. It was nearing midnight and there was still no sign of any explosives. Or anyone at all.

'Are you sure they're coming? Who are they anyway? And why are we meeting here of all places?'

'You ask too many questions, Irish.' Tanya said. 'If you closed your mouth every so often, the rest of your senses might give you your answers.'

The Muscovite gave Scarlet a pointed look and the Irishwoman frowned at her, not understanding what it meant, but then heard the faint clip clop of a horse's hooves against the flagstones of an adjoining street. She peered around the stone frame of the doorway just in time to see a horse and cart emerge from the lane which led to the sea.

She glanced back at Tanya, wondering if she was going to meet it, but realised that the woman was no longer there. She spotted her a couple of seconds later, already most of the way across the square, and swore under her breath, using one of the saltier phrases her grandfather had taught her and which she used only on special occasions, then moved quickly after her.

The cart reeked of fish and had three occupants. To the Irishwoman's surprise, one of them was Father Bugelli.

'Father.' Scarlet heard Tanya whisper as the cart gently creaked the last few yards to the church. 'Any problems?'

'None, Tatiana, the enemy were as greedy as we knew they would be.'

The driver of the cart pulled the horse to a halt next to the same doorway the two women had taken shelter in and, while the other man jumped down and began undoing the tailgate, Tanya handed the priest down.

Scarlet watched, unsure why the Muscovite was helping Father Bugelli, a youngish man, down from the low cart, but when Tanya dropped to a knee and the priest made a sign over her she understood that it had simply been out of respect. She looked away, uncomfortable with the religious demonstration, and waited until Tanya was on her feet again before approaching the priest.

'Father.' She nodded at the man when he looked her way, peering into the darkness in an attempt to make her out.

'Miss Flynn, good evening.'

'And a very good evening to you too.'

As Bugelli went to open the door, Scarlet and Tanya helped his companions pull two heavy crates, stamped with the Italian Imperial crest, from beneath a filthy tarpaulin. They carried them into the sacristy, where the priest had lit a few candles.

The priest handed the two men a bottle of wine each and they left after exchanging a few words with him in the local dialect. Tanya waited for the door to close behind them before producing an iron crow from somewhere about her person and applying it to the lid of the first crate.

Scarlet crouched down beside her and examined the other wooden box while the Muscovite worked. During her *I and S* training she'd been made familiar with the various types of explosives used by the military of both sides and she recognised the names and numbers written on the crate immediately.

She grinned. 'These are exactly what I asked for! How did you get them?'

'That is a long story of bartering and exchanges that is far too convoluted for this late at night,' said the priest, 'which started with one high-ranking Prussian naval officer's love of a certain type of fish and ends with an Italian Army quartermaster and his taste for lederhosen.'

'Lederhosen?'

The priest grinned. 'You really don't want to know.'

Scarlet was fairly sure she did, but right then the lid came off the crate with a loud crack of splintering wood and, while Tanya placed it to one side, she peered into it. It was stuffed to the brim with wood wool and she dug her hands into it, immediately finding one of the hard metal cylinders, about eight inches tall by five wide, that she'd been expecting.

She fished around in the crate again, pushing aside a dozen or so more of the black demolition charges until she found what she was looking for - a small rectangular metal box.

'Have you used this kind of thing before?' she asked Tanya as she brushed a few wood chips off the box, then snapped open the catch and flipped up the lid.

The Muscovite shook her head. 'No. My basic training was limited to guns, knives and bayonets and we threw boules instead of grenades because we didn't have any.'

Scarlet snorted. 'The French should have thought of that; they would have scared the Prussians right away and saved us a lot of trouble.'

Inside the metal box was a detonator, packet in cotton wool to protect it, and Scarlet pulled it out and showed it to Tanya.

'This is the radio detonator.' She flicked a switch on the front of the rectangular gadget and one of the three small lights in a row under the switch, the red one, lit up. 'Red means that there is nothing in range. If the green one goes on...' She fiddled briefly with the base of the explosive, flicking a switch, and the red light went off at the same time as a green one ignited. 'Then it's ready to blow. Then we just have to press these two buttons at the same time.' She pointed to the red button underneath the lights, then showed them a second button on the side. The two were close enough together to be pressed simultaneously by one hand, but far enough apart not to be pressed together by accident.

'You mean it's live now?'

'It is.'

'Yes.' Scarlet nodded and the priest, who had been following along, jerked back involuntarily, but the Muscovite didn't even flinch.

A little disappointed, Scarlet made the bomb safe again and turned off the detonator.

Tanya took another of the cylinders from the crate and turned it over in her hands. She didn't look impressed. 'Are you sure these will get the job done? Don't we need something a bit bigger?'

Scarlet nodded enthusiastically. 'Oh yes, these will be more than enough, trust me. The Italians might be a bit lackadaisical and rather comical when it comes to most of warfare, but they know how to destroy stuff, and the reason I asked you to get these in particular is that they contain an acidic compound that is designed to eat through metal like a hot toddy through a constipated sheep.'

Scarlet stopped abruptly when she realised what she had said and put her hand over her mouth. She stared at the priest, wide-eyed. 'I'm so sorry, Father.'

The priest just waved away the apology. 'I grew up in a community that farms and fishes, Miss Flynn, I have heard, and seen, far worse.'

'What's the third light for?' asked Tanya as if she hadn't heard the Irishwoman's crude analogy, pointing to the light in between the red and green ones.

'That's the test circuit.' Scarlet turned the explosive back on, then pressed a yellow button on the top of the radio controller. An orange light went on, along with a corresponding one on the top of the explosive. 'It's how we'll make sure everything is working. We need to unpack both crates and turn all the explosives on one by one to make sure the circuits inside them haven't been damaged.'

'Do we have time to do that now, Father?' Tanya looked at the priest.

Bugelli glanced at the clock on the wall, linked to the same mechanism that ran the one in the tower with the bells. 'I have Lauds at six, but the congregation will arrive at five-thirty to start cleaning and preparing the church for the day. You have until then.'

Tanya looked at Scarlet, who nodded. 'This will only take me half an hour, unless there's something wrong. I suggest you go and get some sleep; you need to be alright to fly tomorrow, whereas I've just got more paperwork to look forward to.'

The Muscovite pursed her lips and glanced at the explosives, obviously wanting to stay and help, but then seemed to see the sense in Scarlet's suggestion. She stood up and brushed her hands off. 'Alright. Try not to blow yourself up.'

'Aw! You do care!'

Tanya shook her head. 'Only about the explosives.' Something occurred to her and she turned to the priest. 'Oh, and Father Bugelli and his church, of course.'

Bugelli laughed. 'I'm glad, thank you!'

Tanya bowed her head to him solemnly. 'Goodnight, Father.'

'Goodnight, my child.'

Tanya gave Scarlet a last look, then slipped out of the door.

When she was gone, the Irishwoman looked at the priest. 'You don't have to stay if you don't want.' She grinned. 'Unless you don't trust me not to steal your communion wine?'

'Actually, I think I'd like a glass myself, if you'd care to join me?'

'Bless you, Father!' Scarlet gave him one of her best smiles, then turned her attention to the explosives while he went to fetch a couple of glasses.

The two women sneaked out again the following night, just before eleven. This time they didn't stop in the town, but jogged through it towards Hal Far. They didn't go all the way to the airfield, though, but turned off just before they got to it and made their way through the trees to a clearing, a few hundred yards from the perimeter fence. A dirt track ran from the fence directly to the clearing and that was what Scarlet's fitters had used to move Hummingbird there.

'Any problems, Aviator Sergeant?'

Scarlet's chief fitter, Bob Skidmore, jumped and stifled a shriek when the Irishwoman spoke in his ear.

She grinned at him when he spun to face her and stamped his foot.

'I've told you before not to do that!'

'I know, but it's just too much fun.'

'For you.' The man pouted, but then smiled broadly. 'She's all ready, ma'am, and raring for something to do.'

'I know she is, Bob, I know.' Scarlet reached out to pat her machine. 'Don't worry, darling, we've got something special for you tonight.' She gave Hummingbird a last stroke then turned back to the fitter. 'Did the priest bring you the explosives?'

'Yes, ma'am!' The man grinned. 'They were in with the potatoes in the daily supplies, but I rescued them before somebody in the kitchen tried to peel them. They're with your bags on your seat.'

'Good, thank you.'

The man rubbed his hands eagerly. 'Are you going to be taking photographs again?'

'I have my camera all ready, don't worry.'

'Hurray!' Skidmore clapped his hands in delight, then skipped away happily and began removing the straps holding Hummingbird's overhead rotor in place.

'Interesting character.'

Scarlet had to work extremely hard not to jump out of her own skin as Tanya did exactly the same to her as she had done to the fitter.

'He's a brilliant mechanic and understands Hummingbird almost as well as I do. For that I will forgive any over-enthusiasm or familiarity.'

Tanya nodded. 'As it should be. Let's check the explosives, shall we?'

In the red light of a small emergency lantern, the two of them took the crates of explosives off the seat and placed them on the floor to do a quick final check of the radio control mechanisms, making sure they were wound fully and that they hadn't run down overnight for some reason. They then packed them into two of the knapsacks that Scarlet used for such missions.

When Tanya found that there were items already inside her knapsack she looked up at the Irishwoman.

Scarlet shrugged. 'Food and water for three days, a med kit, and a few other essentials, in case something happens and we need to walk home.'

The Muscovite brought a large knife out of the bag and smiled at it. She pulled it half out of its sheaf, examined the blade, then thrust it back and tossed it to Scarlet. 'I won't need this.'

'Why?'

Even before the question was out of the Irishwoman's mouth, two wicked-looking knives had appeared in Tanya's hands. 'Because I have my own, thank you.

Scarlet had been watching her the whole time, but even so she had no idea where the blades came from, they were just suddenly there. Nor did she see where they went back to, they were just gone again and the woman was standing and hefting the packed bag. She put it down to the poor light playing tricks on her and picked up her own knapsack and followed the Muscovite to Hummingbird.

While Scarlet was running through final checks, Tanya got dressed. She would be riding on the outside of the aircraft in one of the bolted-on stretchers that Scarlet had improvised in Muscovy to carry rescued pilots, so she needed warm clothing. She had found a winter coat and trousers, a hat, scarf, gloves, a balaclava and three thick jumpers in a cupboard at the house - one of the family was evidently a skier. She'd brought the lot with her and proceeded to put every single piece of it on.

She caught Scarlet watching her and shrugged as best as she could through so many jumpers. 'I don't like the cold.'

'But you're from one of the coldest places in the world!'

'And we have proper clothes to protect ourselves from it, not this... rubbish.' She turned her nose up as she fingered the trousers, feeling how thin they were.

'I'm sure you'll be fine, it's not as if it's very cold anyway.'

Tanya smiled wolfishly. 'Then you won't mind if I fly and you ride outside.'

Scarlet laughed. 'Not a hope in hell! Now, if you're quite finished complaining, it's time we were in the air.'

Hummingbird flew south, directly out over the sea, before turning to the east and skirting around Malta, a mile or so off the shore.

While the other Misfits were flying, Scarlet and Chalky had been in the intelligence office at Luqa, poring over copies of the surveillance photographs that the blonde man and Farrier had taken of Sicily and updating maps of the island with Prussian and Italian military assets.

There was no problem finding landing places for Hummingbird which were far enough away from population centres or troop concentrations that even the quiet aircraft wouldn't be heard, but they were all at least half a dozen miles away from the airship and would require a hike through pitch black forests and unfamiliar territory. There was no way they would be able to do that safely and make it back before dawn and finding a bolthole for the day was out of the question.

And then there was the question of where and how to actually set the charges.

Scarlet had sneaked a glance at a copy of the blueprints of Bertha that Drake had drawn up and gotten a good idea of where they needed to place the explosives to do the most damage. The trouble was it would require either infiltrating the airship itself, which would be nigh on impossible, or scaling it on the outside, which would leave them extremely exposed.

In the end, Scarlet decided that the best approach would be the boldest one.

She would approach from the sea as fast, but as stealthily, as she could, and go directly for the fans, which had been extremely conveniently left outside of the main scaffolding which held up the airship. Then, while Scarlet kept Hummingbird hovering above a fan, Tanya would hop off and plant a single charge on its centre, which should be more than enough to completely destroy it. They would repeat the exercise with as many of the other fans as possible until they met with resistance, at which point Scarlet would take them up on to the top of the airship, where they would plant their remaining explosives above the five envelopes.

After the two of them had gotten through with Bertha, the Prussians would be left with a completely intact gondola, the biggest and most expensive in the world, but no way to lift it into the sky.

Thirty-five minutes after takeoff, the grey surface of the sea gave way to the darkness of the land.

There were no landmarks to be had on such a dark night so Scarlet was flying by dead reckoning, but she wasn't concerned; not only was she used to such missions, having carried out many over France in the early months of the war, but Bertha was too big a target to miss, especially since her light blue paintwork, which rendered her almost invisible in the air, would stand out against the ground.

'Two minutes!' Scarlet called out of the window.

While remaining strapped in, Tanya carefully divested herself of the thick clothing, stripping down to the work coveralls she was wearing underneath and stuffed them deep into the cowl, which Scarlet had added to the front of the stretchers to protect anyone using them from the wind. She then took two of the cylinders from the bags which she'd shared the ride with, armed them, and put one into each of the voluminous thigh pockets of the coveralls.

'Thirty seconds!'

Tanya undid her straps and carefully pulled herself up to a crouch, grabbing hold of the curved cowl to keep herself from being blown off the back of the stretcher.

Scarlet had told her that Hummingbird was at her most quiet flying at one hundred and thirty miles per hour and that was the speed at which she would make her final approach before transferring power to the gyrodyne's overhead rotors to bring her to a hover. It felt like they were going far faster, though, and she was having trouble maintaining her grip on the smooth metal, which hadn't exactly been designed for the use she was putting it to.

'Ten!'

There was a note of uncertainty in Scarlet's voice, evident even over the noise of the air rushing past her and Tanya glanced at her. She found the Irishwoman peering over her aircraft's nose and frowning down at the ground, her features dimly lit by the faint red lights of her instrument panel.

Tanya crouched lower, back into the shelter of the cowl then stuck her head out the side, into the wind, and peered down over the edge of the stretcher.

It took her a few seconds to get her bearings, comparing the shape of the nearby coastline to the image she had in her mind, but she soon realised they were in exactly the right place - Scarlet had pulled off a very impressive piece of navigation.

The only problem was, Bertha wasn't there.

'Gone? What do you mean, gone?'

'Exactly that - Aviator Sergeant Guseva and I went on a little sightseeing jaunt last night and we found Bertha.... gone.' Scarlet grinned at Dorothy Campbell.

Campbell sighed. 'And what exactly was the purpose of this little unsanctioned trip?'

'Oh, we were just going to say hello to the Prussians and ask them if they wouldn't mind terribly if we blew up their airship from underneath them.'

'With what explosives?'

Scarlet waved in the direction of the two crates she had repacked the explosives in on their return. She had left them with Hummingbird, which an extremely disappointed Skidmore had brought back to the hangar in the early hours of the morning. The man had had a long night, rewinding and servicing Hummingbird in case she was needed again, and was snoozing, snoring loudly, propped up against the crates, using his greatcoat as a pillow. 'Tanya managed to get hold of some really nice Italian stuff which would have made short work of that airship. I brought them back, in case I find someone else to donate them to.'

While most of the Misfits could hardly hold back their laughter, Drake had been staring at Tanya the whole time and when she glanced at him he spoke to her accusingly. 'You crept out of our room last night and flew to Sicily with Scarlet?'

She smiled and patted him on the cheek. 'Oh, Rudy. I've been creeping out of our room most nights since we got here. Or did you think I was getting hold of all those supplies we needed by just making a few calls?'

Drake blinked. 'I... but... This is different! You weren't putting yourself in such danger before.'

Tanya just gave him a crooked smile.

'You... Were you?' Drake's voice had gotten higher and higher as the conversation had gone on and he was beginning to sound like a schoolboy. 'How? What did you do?'

The Muscovite shrugged. 'Better you don't know, darling.'

Gwen was only very vaguely aware of the conversations going on around her because, ever since Scarlet had told them that the airship had disappeared, all she could think about was whether it had taken Kitty with it.

Negotiations had stalled when the Italians had made unreasonable demands. They were fully aware of who Kitty was, her picture having been splashed all over newspapers around the world, and they knew that she was worth a lot to the British who had turned her into a symbol of American involvement in the war. However, nobody could reasonably expect Malta to surrender just to get her back, but that was what they were asking for, and as the days dragged on, Gwen was becoming more and more convinced that she would never see Kitty again.

The other Misfits had tried to cheer her up and, when that failed, plied her with alcohol, but the only thing that took her mind off of the American for even a second was being in the air and she had thrown herself into her flying, using it to escape her worries. It was something she had done since she was a child - whenever she felt unhappy, or needed to clear her mind, she would jump into one of her aircraft and use the sheer joy and freedom of flight to wash everything away. However, her time on the ground was a seemingly endless ordeal of sleepless nights and nervous days spent watching the door to Dorothy Campbell's office. It had gotten so that she barely recognised herself in the mirror in the mornings when she prepared for the day. Her hair, which Kitty so enjoyed running her fingers through, was lank and greasy, her nails had been bitten to the quick, something she hadn't done since she was five, and there were thick black blotches under her eyes.

The voices of her friends faded away completely as her fears surrounded and consumed her and she closed her eyes and drifted away into a nightmare vision of Kitty wasting away in the hellhole that Drake had described in the depths of the airship.

Which was why she didn't react when there were gasps from the Misfits and only did so slowly when strong arms went around her from behind and pulled her into a soft body.

She spun within the embrace and shoved whoever it was away to arm's length, but found herself caught and held by bright blue eyes.

She stared into them for long seconds, wondering if she had gone mad, but when the beautiful vision didn't disappear she flung herself back at the woman and broke down into tears.

'Shh...' Kitty cupped the back of Gwen's head, holding her against her chest while she kissed the top of it. 'It's alright, I'm here now.'

Gwen had no idea how long she stayed like that, but it was a catharsis and her fears and doubts flowed from her, evaporating in the fresh morning air. Eventually, she pulled back and wiped her eyes with the back of her hand, but then wrinkled her nose and sniffed her fingers. She looked down at the American's red flightsuit and sniffed again. 'You smell of fish. Why do you smell of fish?'

'I'll tell you everything later, for now we have an island to defend.' She looked at Abby. 'If you'll have me?'

'Are you up to it?'

'Oh yes.' Kitty nodded eagerly. 'I'm rested, well-fed and more than ready to get back into the fight.'

'Then of course we'll have you.'

The Misfits had held back from the two in silence, allowing them their private moment, but now they swarmed forward to surround them, welcoming Kitty and comforting Gwen, who felt tears coming again, despite the wide smile on her face.

It wasn't just the pilots who were happy to have Kitty back, the entire base had been on edge, while they waited for the situation to be resolved, and when she told her story at dinner that night, she had an audience of more than a hundred people.

While most of the support staff found places on the mossy forest floor, Kitty sat on one of the tables so that she could be seen better, directly in one of the pools of light, as if she were some old-world pagan priestess, imparting her wisdom to the people. She looked incredible, like something out of a baroque painting, her hair loose and shining gold, her skin a light bronze. The Italians had obviously been taking care of her and the time she'd had off from flying, almost a week, had done her a world of good.

She spoke between mouthfuls of food and the Misfits and the rest of the staff, starved of decent entertainment, lapped up her words hungrily.

CHAPTER 14

The week before.

Kitty swore as the Spitsteam slewed sideways and she fought for control, trying to stop the machine from nosing gently down into the trees and killing her. The trouble was, things didn't seem to be working quite as they should - the stick was spongy as she drew it gently back and as for the rudder pedals... She kicked them one after the other, but all they did was clunk uselessly against the forward bulkhead.

While she continued to try to coax the machine into obeying her commands, she glanced in the mirror over her head.

'Well, that kinda explains it.'

Usually, the vision in the small round mirror attached to the canopy framing was bisected by the tail of the Spit. It wasn't anymore, because the vertical stabiliser was no longer there.

'Leader, Three here. I'm hit.'

Kitty finally managed to bring the Spitsteams nose a safe distance above the horizon, but without a rudder and only very weak aileron control she couldn't risk making much of a turn and was heading almost directly eastwards towards the coast and the open sea and if she kept going that way she would end up in Tunisia.

'Report, Three.'

'I've lost rudder control and my elevators feel sluggish. I can barely turn, Leader.'

'Get home, then, Three.'

'Roger, Leader, breaking off now.' She stifled a laugh; she'd already "broken off" mainly because she'd had no choice.

'Good luck, Three. Four, escort her, please.'

'Aye aye, Leader.'

Kitty glanced to her right and found Farrier still faithfully on her wing, despite the fact that they'd been flying more or less straight and level for the last few minutes and had been sitting ducks for any Italian or Prussian with a gun who cared to point it at them. She switched to their private frequency. 'Report, Four.'

'All Bristol fashion, Three.'

'Um, good.' When Kitty had joined the squadron she hadn't been quite sure what many of the Misfits were saying half the time, especially Bruce and Mac, but she'd managed to work out what most of the quirky phrases they used meant over the years. However, the naval aviators had brought with them a whole new set of sayings and slang and she was once again struggling. Why they couldn't all just call a cog a cog was beyond her.

Below her, the land gave way to sea and she breathed a sigh of relief - she know it was a false sense of security, that the water was just as hard as the ground if you hit it fast enough, but it just felt a lot safer. Also it meant that there were no more anti-aircraft guns to fret about.

The Spitsteam had risen to three hundred feet and she decided it was as good a time as any to coax her around to the correct heading.

'Four, I'm going to try turning towards home. This might take a while, don't get bored.'

'Aye aye, Three.'

Kitty took a deep breath. 'OK, then. Here goes nothing.'

She gently pushed her stick to the side and lifted her right wing about ten degrees. Then, as the aircraft began to slide and the nose dip slightly, she pulled back slowly to compensate.

The nose lifted almost imperceptibly and the aircraft began to come around, turning south, but then there was a twanging noise, accompanied by a minute vibration that she felt through her seat, and the stick came backwards as all resistance went away.

The nose dipped again and she quickly levelled her wings, but it was too late - she had completely lost her elevators and the Spitsteam was in a shallow, but inevitable, dive towards the waves. She tried pushing the throttle forward, to see if the extra lift would help matters, but it had no effect.

'Dammit!' There was only one thing for it and she thumbed her radio switch. 'Four, it's no good, I'm going to have to hit the metal.'

'Understood, Three. Best of British.'

As death dives went, it was a fairly sedate one and Kitty had plenty of time to get out of the Spit. She unlatched and pulled back the canopy, locking it open, before undoing her straps and standing on the seat.

The Spitsteam was too low for her to risk a standard exit where she would deploy her glidewings after she was safely away from the aircraft, so she gripped the handle of the glidewings with one hand, the frame of the canopy with the other, then stepped onto the lip and leapt straight upwards while simultaneously deploying the wings to their first level.

Normally, what she was doing was tantamount to suicide, but the fact that she had no stabiliser meant that there was nothing to cut her in half as it went past and she was merely swept away by the wind as her aircraft kept flying. It was then an easy matter to open the Duralumin wings to their fullest extent and arrest her fall.

The Spitsteam continued its slow dive and she took a moment to thank it for its faithful service, before taking stock of her situation.

She was about a hundred feet up, perhaps ten miles out over the sea, with Farrier's aircraft circling her about half a mile out. She was confident in the naval pilot's ability to pinpoint her position and relay it to Malta when she got in range of the naval rescue services. However, it would take some time for them to get to her and, even though the small life jacket she was wearing would keep her afloat indefinitely, she would quite possibly have frozen to death or been moved somewhere else by the currents before then.

Luckily, there was another option - a fishing boat a few miles away. If she could get Farrier to call their attention to her, then they could pick her up. It would almost certainly be a Sicilian boat, but she would be alive and there was always the possibility that she could bribe them to go to Malta with the gold sovereigns in her survival kit.

She turned towards the boat and pointed at it to signal her intention to Farrier. The blue and white-tailed Spitsteam waggled its wings and turned towards the boat, abandoning her temporarily.

All that was left for Kitty to do was to prepare herself and she ran through the procedure for bailing out over water in her mind.

During basic training, she and the other Misfits had taken it in turns to jump off a scaffolding tower on the shore of a lake, just like every RAC pilot did. There they had had divers and a boat on hand to rescue them if they botched it up. Many pilots did, including Kitty, and ended up being dragged down under the water by the weight of their glidewings before the slack could be taken up on their safety harnesses and they could be pulled back to the surface. There was no such safety measure for her here, no drill sergeant to bawl at her and send her back to the top of the tower, sodden and shivering, and she would have to get it right first time.

She made sure that the lenses on her helmet were secured in their up position, then removed her goggles and tossed them away. Next to go were the maps and documents from her thigh pockets - the water-soluble ink would make them unreadable, but it was best not to tempt fate. Lastly she pulled the toggle that released the liquid from the pockets of her flightsuit; she couldn't afford her mobility to be restricted.

Thirty feet above the waves, she prepared the quick release on the harness of the glidewings.

Twenty feet.

She dived slightly to get her speed up then flared five feet above the water, as if she were a bird coming in for a landing, carrying out a manoeuvre that Gwen had made look so simple and elegant over the summer when Abby had insisted they needed to "test" their glidewings.

Too late she realised she had overcooked the dive, put on too much speed and was regaining far too much height. She had no choice but to continue, though; it was either dump the wings or be forever attached to them.

In theory it was a simple manoeuvre - at the apex of the climb, at that so brief moment of stillness before you began to drop, you released the catch, then, as you began to slip out of the harness you simply raised both arms and fell away from the wings while they still held the air.

Kitty had done it over and over, first on dry land over mattresses using the specially-constructed zip-line, or "death slide" as the Brits *so* encouragingly called it, then over the lake under glidewings, but had *never* quite gotten the knack of it, so she was understandably nervous.

She released the catch, then raised her arms up over her head.

She didn't quite get the coordination right and one of the straps snagged on her elbow.

She tumbled sideways, arms and legs flailing wildly as her mind told her to grab onto something, *anything*, despite knowing perfectly well that there was nothing.

'Oh, sh...'

Her expletive was cut off as she hit the water extremely hard and very awkwardly. Her breath was knocked out of her and water filled her mouth, making her cough and expend what little air she had left.

She sank, her flightsuit and survival pack dragging her down. Bubbles surrounded her and she twisted and turned, not sure which way was up, flailing mindlessly as the urge to breath became more and more powerful. Fear overwhelmed her as she realised she was going to die and the image of Gwen filled her mind, along with regret that their hopes and dreams wouldn't come to fruition.

Curiously, though, the British woman was looking at her with that expression she so often had on her face which meant that someone, usually Bruce, had said or done something idiotic.

Kitty would have groaned at her own stupidity if she'd had the breath to do so. With the last of her energy she groped for the toggle which inflated the life vest that she'd completely forgotten about in her worry at the landing. She seized it and jerked at it over and over, but she had left it far too late and her movements became more and more sluggish until finally she gave up, stopped struggling and filled her lungs.

It wasn't water that flooded in, though, it was deliciously cool air; in her frantic struggling she hadn't noticed that she'd broken the surface.

She coughed weakly and choked as she inhaled the water splashing into her face, trying to vomit it back out at the same time as she desperately gulped in huge mouthfuls of oxygen. Finally, she was able to breathe properly again and she closed her eyes and just lay there, bobbing up and down gently, luxuriating in the feel of the sun on her face and thanking whoever was listening for the fact that she was still alive.

She slowly became aware of a buzzing noise and lifted her head to squint into the sky. Almost immediately she found Farrier's Spitsteam. The woman was pulling a hard turn around her position, the white of her face showing under her dark blue helmet as she craned her head to peer down at her. Kitty raised an arm so that the young woman would know she was alright and waited until she saw a hand lift in reply before exhaustedly dropping her head back into the water, the effort of holding it up too much.

A new sound soon drowned out the Spitsteam, though - the chugging of a rather old steam engine - and she twisted around to find the fishing boat she had seen from the air, black smoke pouring from its chimney. There was a man standing in the front of the boat and when he caught sight of her he shouted something she couldn't hear over the noise of the labouring engine and pointed.

The boat veered to head directly at her and for a second she thought it was going to run her over, but the fishermen obviously knew what they were doing because it made a slight course correction at the last moment and she passed down its side, close enough to touch it if she'd had the energy to do so. Two men were waiting in the middle of the boat, where the gunwale was closest to the water and she smiled at them, but they were too intent on their job to see. As she drew level with them they reached down for her. Strong fingers grasped her life jacket and they pulled her bodily into the boat as if she weighed nothing and deposited her onto something soft.

One of the men, actually just a youth, left, but the other, a grizzled veteran of anywhere between sixty and eighty years of age, bent down to offer her a bottle. 'Drink?'

Kitty struggled to sit up, then looked at the bottle sceptically. It was a cloudy green, with a round bottom and no label and was wrapped in a decidedly greasy-looking netting. It was the kind of bottle that, in her experience in Mediterranean countries, was filled either with dregs or moonshine from illicit stills.

'Is good!' The man grinned at her with a mouth that was more gaps than teeth, then took a long swig. He smacked his lips and wiped his mouth with the back of his hand, then held it out again.

Kitty contemplated refusing, but she needed to get on the good side of the men on the boat if she was going to persuade them to take her to Malta and that same experience told her that the best way to make friends with Mediterranean people was to drink with them.

She smiled, took the bottle and saluted him with it, then tipped it up, trying not to think about how the man's cracked lips had been wrapped around it so recently.

The drink was surprisingly refreshing, but incredibly powerful and she found her eyes watering, even as a lovely warmth spread through her belly, contrasting nicely with the cold of the water and her clammy leathers.

She gave the bottle back with a smile and a nod and, as he went to hang it from a hook on the single mast, took a look around.

She was sitting on a pile of netting, which, unfortunately, had been recently used, was filled with silvery fish scales and smelled to high heaven. The boat itself was metal, with white sides, a red-painted deck, a small white wheelhouse and a black funnel with a red ring around its top. She was no expert on ships, but she knew engines fairly well and could tell by the sound of it that it was coal fired, which made it at least twenty years old, if not more. The boat was filthy, filled with crates of fish, and blood was smeared everywhere, but it had definitely been well looked-after and she couldn't see any signs of rust.

The sound of the engine grew and she looked up as black smoke billowed from the chimney. Something occurred to her and she searched the sky for Farrier, but the Spitsteam was gone - understandably the woman had only waited long enough to see her rescued before hightailing it out of enemy territory and heading home to report.

The boat heeled as it turned and she caught sight of the haze on the horizon that was Sicily, only ten miles or so away. If she was going to persuade the fishermen to go to Malta instead she was going to have to speak to them soon, before anyone watching for approaching vessels caught sight of them.

The old fisherman reappeared, but before she could say anything he beckoned to her and motioned to the back of the boat. 'Come. Wet, cold.'

He pantomimed rubbing his arms and shivering and Kitty nodded. She could feel her body temperature plummeting as the wind of their passage across the water cooled her flightsuit and her within it. It would be prudent to get warm and dry before speaking to the captain; there was no point in getting home if she died of pneumonia when she got there.

She pushed herself up, but toppled as her legs gave way beneath her. She flailed, trying to reach anything to stop herself from nosediving into the metal deck, but bony hands shot out to catch her, arresting her fall almost before it had begun. Despite taking almost her full weight, the old man barely shifted and when she grabbed his arms to steady herself she felt corded muscle through his filthy jumper.

She found her feet again, and when she felt secure she pulled back and gave him a smile. 'Sorry.'

'You're welcome.' He gave her another of his broken smiles and shook his head, then beckoned again, but this time he offered her his arm as if they were going to promenade together.

She laughed and took it gratefully, then stumbled with him past the wheelhouse to the rear of the boat, where there was a companionway.

The stairs led directly into a small single low-ceilinged room which acted as kitchen, dining room, living room and bedroom. There was a table and four chairs, all bolted to the deck, in the middle of the space, a tiny stove and a sink along one wall, and two sets of bunk beds along another. It was tidy and organised and far cleaner than she would have expected, as were the towel and spare clothes the man pulled from the wardrobe built into the wall between the bunks and gave to her.

She thanked him and took her life jacket, helmet and gloves off before starting work on her flightsuit. The man's eyes widened in panic when she began to pull down the zipper on the front and he coloured and spun to face away from her.

She grinned, amused, but was quite glad he'd turned away when she found that the tight leather was stuck to her - she wasn't very modest at the best of times, you couldn't be in a mixed military, but the way she had to wriggle her way out of it, sitting on one of the beds and sticking her legs in the air, was beyond indecent. The exercise was good for getting the circulation going in her limbs, though.

Soon enough, she was dressed in the clothes - a rough shirt, woollen jumper and canvas trousers - and on her way to being warm again.

'You can turn around now.'

She wasn't sure that the man understand the words, but he got their meaning and, after a cautious glance over his shoulder at her, he turned.

'Are you the captain?'

He gave her a puzzled look. 'Cosa?'

'Captain. Uh.' She drew herself up to attention and saluted. 'Aye aye, Captain!'

'Ah! Il capitano!' He shook his head. 'No.' He pointed up, towards the wheel house over their heads. 'Il capitano there.'

'Can I speak to him?' When she got another blank look she racked her brain for the words in Spanish, knowing that the two languages were similar. 'Parlar con el capitano?'

'Ah, yes, yes! Of course!'

As they came back on deck, Kitty glanced nervously in the direction of land and heaved a sigh of relief when she saw it was still only just above the horizon - the boat was even slower than she'd expected.

The captain, a weather-worn man in his forties with black hair, was at the wheel with the youth beside him and he smiled at her when she appeared in the doorway of the wheelhouse. He nodded at the boy to take over the wheel, then came towards her with his hand extended.

'Welcome on board the Cassandra. My name is Marco Marino. And you are one of the Misfit pilots, yes? Kitty Hawk is it?'

'Kitty Wright, Hawk was my aircraft.'

'Ah, I am sorry. My son, Orazio,' he tilted his head in the direction of the youth at the wheel. 'He has been talking about you non-stop since you came on board and I am afraid I was too busy to listen to him properly.'

Kitty looked over the man's shoulder and caught the youth staring in her direction. The man, Marco, glanced over his shoulder at him and grinned, shaking his head, then pointed forward. The boy looked away guiltily and made a show of concentrating on piloting the boat.

Marco turned back to Kitty. 'Did my father look after you?'

'He did, thank you.'

'Good. I'm sorry that I can't offer you any hot food or drink right now; the fire must remain off while we are moving, but we will be in port in an hour.'

'That's what I wanted to talk to you about, Captain.' Kitty said, putting on what was, she hoped, her most winning smile. 'I was wondering if I could persuade you to take me to Malta.'

'I'm sorry, I can't.'

'Not even for...' she fished around in the deep pockets of the trousers and pulled out the ten sovereigns she had rescued from the small survival kit that had been attached to her life jacket. 'This?'

The man's eyes widened at the sight of the gold, but it was only in surprise - Kitty couldn't detect a single trace of greed in his expression. 'I'm sorry, no.'

'Is this not enough? I'm sure that I can get you more when we get to Malta. How much do you want?'

The man looked at the money wistfully. 'That amount of money would keep my family fed and clothed for many years, but I can't take it.'

'Why? Please!' Kitty tried hard, but couldn't keep her desperation from showing in her voice; being delivered to Sicily would mean the end of her war and, with Bertha on the island, probably her death, working as the slave of Hans Gruber.

Marco shook his head. 'You don't understand - it is not because I don't want to, it is because it is impossible. The Navy keeps close watch on us fishermen, they have regular patrols out and if they catch us going in the wrong direction with a full catch there will be dire consequences for me and my family.'

'Oh.' Kitty said, her face falling as she realised that there was nothing she could do. 'I wouldn't want anything bad to happen to you, or your family.'

'Thank you.' Marco smiled kindly. 'That is not the only reason, though; we are down to our last lumps of coal and would not make it even half of the way to Malta - we were already on our way back to port and will barely have enough to get home after turning around and pick you up.'

'Thank you for doing that, by the way.'

'Don't mention it.' The man shrugged. 'I would have done the same, even for a Prussian.'

The man said the word with such vehemence, almost spitting it out, that Kitty couldn't help but be curious. 'You don't like Prussians?'

The man glanced nervously in the direction of his son, then took Kitty back out onto the deck where his words would be more easily lost in the wind. 'The Prussians are greedy. They are like children who take more cake than they can possibly eat, just because it is there.'

'But your emperor decided to side with them.'

'Because he is as greedy as they are, but worse, he is stupid. He can't see that he is being used by the Prussians and when they are done with everyone else they will merely take away what he has gained.'

'If they win.'

'If?' The man gave her a sad look. 'It is far too likely, I'm afraid.'

Kitty shook her head emphatically. 'The British will stop them.'

Marco chuckled. 'I can tell you are American; so optimistic.' He sighed, his smile evaporating. 'Ask your British friends if they think they will win this war. I think you will find less hope and more stubbornness - that upper lip of theirs.'

'They stopped the Prussians from conquering Britain and they've been held back from Muscovy.'

'But for how long? Muscovy will fall soon enough and then Britain will be alone. Unless your countrymen follow your example and do what is right. However, if I read the newspapers correctly, I don't think your President Taft is going to let that happen any time soon.'

Kitty looked impressed. 'For a fisherman you seem to know a lot about the world. And how come you speak such good English?'

'I studied physical oceanography and marine evolution at Tilbury University.'

'Ah, OK.' Kitty nodded in understanding. She didn't have much of an idea about or interest in most British institutions, but even she had heard of the marine university in the London estuary, one of the three great universities, famously founded by Darwin to study and teach about the three natural worlds of land, air and sea. People came from all over the world to study at them, one of her friends from Ohio had gone to Bury University, in the South Downs, to study Dendrology in fact, and Derek was a graduate of Merthyr Tydfil University, up in the Brecon Beacons, which was dedicated to the study of the creatures of the air. 'Do all Sicilian fishermen have your education?'

'The older generation are not; their education was the sea and their fathers, but men and women of my age were offered the chance to study in France or England after our participation in the Great War and most of us took it. So yes,' he grinned, 'I am far too qualified to be slinging a net, but I am happy.' The man glanced into the wheelhouse to make sure his son was still concentrating on his job before continuing. 'My son was awarded a scholarship to Tilbury, but the war broke out just as he was due to take up his place, the same month in fact. He is not happy as a fisherman, he wanted more for his life and to be honest, so did I.'

The man shrugged, then sighed. 'At least as a fisherman he is protected from being dragged into the war; the armies need food.'

He turned to stare out across the water towards the approaching land. After a few seconds of silence he seemed to come to a decision. 'We will be at the dock in just under half an hour. There are no authorities in my village so you will be my guest tonight, but then tomorrow I will have to take you to the police in Vittoria, sorry.'

'I quite understand.'

He gave her a nod of thanks. 'We will speak again later, but for now, I must prepare for our arrival. You should remain below; unloading is a dangerous enough job without a famous pilot distracting everyone, especially my son!'

Kitty grinned. 'OK, will do. Oh, and while I'm down there, can I have some fresh water to wash my flightsuit in? I should get the salt out before it dries.'

'Of course,' Marco nodded, 'we no longer need to conserve it, so use as much as you want. My father will give you what you need.'

'Thank you, Captain, for everything.'

'You are welcome and please, call me Marco.'

Marco's father, who turned out to be called Matteo, took Kitty back down into the living area and showed her how to work the water pump which fed the tap in the sink, as well as the tiny shower in a cubicle under the stairs. She wound it up by hand, refusing to let the old man do it when he offered, then put her flightsuit, gloves and helmet in the sink and ran fresh water on them. It wasn't an ideal solution to the leather having been soaked in sea water, but it was the best she could do until she got hold of some proper cleaning and conditioning materials.

After the third rinse, she realised that it was as good as it was going to get and she held up the dripping suit and looked at Matteo quizzically. He took her to the shower and pulled a drying rack out of the wall. Once the suit was draped over it he opened two grills in the walls, one high up, through which could be seen the sky, and the other at the base of the opposite wall.

Hot air with a whiff of engine oil immediately began to fill the minute space and he frowned and closed the bottom panel more than half way until the air was only slightly warm before grunting in satisfaction. He closed the door and smiled at her. 'Dry well.'

Kitty laughed. 'Thank you!'

There was a shout from on deck - the youth, Orazio, calling for his grandfather - and Matteo grinned apologetically, then climbed up the stairs to the deck.

There were small portholes on either side of the cabin and Kitty went to first one, then the other, trying to catch a glimpse of the fishing town they were heading for, but she couldn't see far enough forwards and could only make out an as yet distant coastline of trees through the cloudy glass.

She gave up and began pacing up and down the small room, considering her prospects for the future.

Prisoners of war usually made their way home either through exchange or escape. By far the most likely in her situation would be an exchange and she had no doubt that Dorothy Campbell would already be preparing to contact the Italians. However, her status as an American national complicated things somewhat. If things were kept unofficial, as she was sure Campbell would try to do, there would be no problem, but if things moved into official channels then difficulties would almost certainly arise because of her status as an American national. She wasn't sure if the British could even legally negotiate for her and if they weren't and it was left up to her own countrymen then her prospects became less than encouraging; the American government had made it perfectly clear that her involvement both in the Iberian conflict and with the RAC was unsanctioned and that she was on her own. Which meant they wouldn't lift a finger to liberate her, no matter who her grandfather was.

That left escape, and she had very few options there either. She couldn't steal a boat because, not only were the Italian Navy watching the seas, according to Marco, but she also had absolutely no idea how to sail - while her friends at school had been riding horses and learning to sail their father's yachts she had spent all her time in the air and she barely knew which end of a boat was which. Paying someone to take her was out as well, because she didn't want to risk someone getting caught for her, although if she could find a smuggler who routinely made the trip that would be alright. The last option would be to do what Drake and Tanya had tried in Muscovy and steal an aircraft, but she lacked Tanya's skills and willingness to kill someone with a knife and didn't think she could ever get up the nerve to go sneaking around an enemy air base in the middle of the night.

All in all, it didn't look like she was getting back to Malta anytime soon. If ever.

Her increasingly disheartening train of thoughts was interrupted when there was a change in engine note and the boat began a slow turn. She went to the porthole and peered out just in time to see the Marino's village come into view.

A long row of picturesque, single-storey stone houses fronted a small marina with a couple of boats, similar to the Cassandra, tied up to it, while a few smaller vessels were pulled up on the adjacent beach. People, mostly women, were coming out of the houses and making their way down to the sea front to meet the boat, many of them waving and calling out to the Marinos.

It looked like a charming and extremely friendly place. It was just a shame it was enemy territory.

The boat pulled up to the marina and Kitty watched as ropes were tied down and then crate after crate of fish were handed off the boat to the villagers, who carried them away to one of the nearby buildings, a nondescript stone block with few windows.

It took almost an hour, but finally it looked like the job was done and the villagers made their farewells and went back to their houses.

'Miss Wright! You can come up now!' Marco's voice called down the companionway.

Kitty was ready and immediately went to the stairs, but something occurred to her before she got there and she stopped and looked around. Spotting what she wanted, she loped over to the kitchen area, fished the coins out of her pocket and put them in the coffee tin next to the sink. She grinned - when she was taken to the police, the gold would have undoubtedly disappeared as if it had never existed, at least this way it could do some good and would pay the Marinos back for their kindness in a small way.

She made sure the lid was on tightly and the tin was back in exactly the right place before hurrying back to the stairs and climbing into the sunlight.

There were two women with the three Marino men and they regarded her curiously as she went to join them.

'Hi.' Kitty smiled at them, trying to hide her nervousness at how, as an enemy, she would be received. She needn't have worried, though, because the women, Marco's wife, Adolorata, and daughter, Giulia, greeted her warmly, kissing her cheeks, like they did in Spain.

'Welcome to Scoglitti! Come, I show you round!' Giulia, who was only a couple of years younger than her, grabbed her hand and dragged her through the gate in the side of the boat, down the short marina and onto the shore.

She took Kitty along the row of buildings, chatting continually in Italian, only some of which was close enough to Spanish for Kitty to understand, pointing out the sights as they went. That included the whitewashed building where they had taken the fish, from which could be heard the sound of an engine gently turning over and which she thought she understood was a refrigerated storage facility, where the fish was kept temporarily until it was loaded up on wagons and taken to the nearest military bases.

As they passed the houses, curious people appeared and the girl called out to each of them in turn, answering their inevitable questions. Kitty heard her name quite a few times, along with "Americana" and "aviatrice" - the feminine form of aviator. The girl was obviously very popular and Kitty was almost glad she was appearing in public for the first time in her company; between the girl's babbling and her obvious acceptance by the Marinos it made it easier for the rest of the community to accept her too.

The Marino residence was near the end of the line of buildings. Like all the others it appeared to be just a simple stone house, but when Kitty was taken inside she found that the façade hid a secret.

The original building had been expanded greatly, but instead of building upwards, like in most towns and cities where floor space was at a premium, the fisherfolk of Scoglitti had built backwards more than fifty metres, making room for growing families.

A doorway had been cut in the back of the old two-room house, which was now used only as a receiving area for visitors. It opened into a small open-air courtyard, with a covered walkway around the outside and a small fountain and wildflower garden, surrounded by benches, in the middle, which served as a buffer between the public front and the private family rooms at the back.

Beyond it was a sitting room which took up the entire width of the house and was filled with chairs of many different styles and ages, from deep leather sofas to an intricately-carved wooden rocking chair. The walls were covered with portraits, some of them so old and grimy that the faces were unrecognisable. The vast majority were of men and, as she glanced around, Kitty wondered why more of the women of the family hadn't had their portraits painted, whether it was some sign of a patriarchal society. Her question was answered immediately, though, when the three fishermen came in behind her. They went directly to the side of the room, where there was a crucifix hanging above a shelf which held a model of the Cassandra and pictures of the three men - a small oil painting for the father, and photographs each for Marco and his son. With no ceremony whatsoever they took their pictures off the shelf, hung them on the wall next to it, quickly crossed themselves, then continued across the room and disappeared through the door on the far side.

While they waited for the men to come back, the women sat Kitty down in one of the chairs in the centre of the room, within reach of a low table where an older woman placed coffee and snacks. Giulia finally fell silent as they bit into sweet cakes, but she still managed to mumble the name of them, *cannoli*, around a mouthful while rolling her eyes in a comical expression of how good they were. All the time, the older woman, Marco's mother, watched Kitty from the rocking chair, smiling benevolently.

When the men came back they also tucked in hungrily, knocking back several small cups of the strong black coffee each.

During the afternoon a steady stream of fishing boats, including three large vessels like the Cassandra and several smaller ones, came back in and the Marinos were called away to the marina to join the rest of the village in unloading. Kitty offered to help, but Marco refused, once again stating that it was dangerous for the uninitiated, so she was left at the house with the older woman, Matteo's wife, Arcangela. However, when the woman retired to take a nap, Kitty was left on her own so she went to sit on one of the benches in the courtyard and tilted her head back to catch the sun.

She had fully intended to think about her situation and how best to get back to Malta, but the sound of the babbling fountain must have lulled her to sleep, because the next thing she knew the shadows had lengthened and she was being gently shaken by Giulia.

The girl gave her clothes, something that was far too frilly and feminine for her liking, and then it was time for dinner.

When Marco had said that she was to be his guest, Kitty had expected a family meal, but apparently the village had insisted on having a party. Every single one of the families brought out their dining table and they were placed end to end in the road along the sea front and filled with food and drink. It then became a kind of free for all, with people moving from table to table and no set groups, apart from the two obligatory ones of old men and old women sitting in chairs at opposite ends of the festivities.

She was taken around by Giulia, who introduced her to all and sundry and kept her plate filled. The young woman hadn't batted an eyelid when Kitty had explained with hand signals and halting Spanish that she was vegetarian and made sure that she fended off any offers of meat herself so that Kitty didn't offend anyone.

The villagers were very welcoming and friendly, but she thought she caught more than a few pitying looks shot her way and the manner in which they plied her with drinks made her think that the night was less about hospitality than it was about trying to make sure she enjoyed her last night of freedom.

After most of the food was gone, some of the villagers brought out musical instruments and the beach became a dance floor. Kitty was dragged onto the sand over and over to dance dances that were simple and hadn't changed in generations. Kitty picked them up easily enough and found that she was enjoying herself far more than she had expected. The only thing missing was Gwen, but she tried not to dwell on that too much.

The evening passed in a blur of good food, good wine and good company, but all too soon it was over, the fishermen having to rise early to go back out onto the sea. A bed had been made up for Kitty in one of the spare rooms in the Marino house - apparently the family had been much larger at some point - and she collapsed onto it gratefully, falling asleep almost as soon as her gently spinning head hit the pillow.

She was woken before dawn by Giulia, who brought her coffee and bread, thickly spread with butter and marmalade. As soon as she was finished and dressed, the young woman took her down to the refrigeration building. A large wagon was being loaded up for delivery to Vittoria and she and Marco were going to hitch a ride.

The entire Marino clan was there to see her off, along with quite a few of the other villagers.

A grinning Matteo had brought her flightsuit, helmet and gloves, now dry, and she took them from him with a smile, but immediately turned to Marco.

'Would you hold on to these, please?'

When she'd put the gold coins in the coffee jar she'd realised that she couldn't take her gear with her when she was turned in to the

Italians; she wouldn't be allowed to keep it in a prisoner of war camp and it would just end up as someone's trophy, probably Gruber's. She had decided to leave it with the Marinos - it was worth a lot of money and they could probably sell it after the war to a collector.

The man immediately understood and nodded. 'Of course.'

He handed them to his wife, who cradled them carefully, then motioned for Kitty to get into the back seat of the wagon with him.

Once the two of them were in she turned to him urgently, knowing it was her last chance to save herself. 'Are you sure you or someone you know can't take me to Malta? Is there no way?'

'I'm sorry, no. I tried to arrange something with a, um, *friend* of mine, but the authorities radioed all the fishing villages last night - you were seen coming down and they are making enquiries as to whether any of us picked you up. They will check everybody who was known to be in the area if you do not show up in a couple of days.' He grimaced and looked away from her as if ashamed of what he was saying. 'Too many people have seen you and would say something if I were to try to hide you or get you to Malta, even in this village.'

The journey was extremely uncomfortable, not just because the roads were rough and the shock absorbers of the wagon were inadequate, but also because the noise of the engine prevented comfortable conversation and the two of them had lapsed into an awkward silence after Marco had crushed her last hope of escape.

Kitty spent the time staring out of the window, not really seeing the beautiful countryside that was going past. At one point she caught a glimpse of something in the sky and pressed her face to the window, trying to see what it was, but it had already disappeared amongst the broken clouds.

Less than half an hour after they had left Scoglitti, they arrived in Vittoria. The driver dropped them off in front of a small building with "Polizia" painted rather crudely over the door, but Marco didn't go straight in, instead he turned to Kitty.

'We might not have a chance to speak after we go in, so...' He stopped and shifted uncomfortably, not at all reconciled with what he had to do.

Kitty smiled warmly. She barely knew him, but felt sorry for him nonetheless; she wouldn't have liked to be in his shoes at that moment. 'Thank you for making me so welcome in your home and for pulling me out of the sea. You're a good man.' She leaned forwards and kissed him on the cheek.

'Thank you. I hope everything turns out alright for you.'

'Thank you.' She took a deep breath and looked towards the open door. 'Right. Let's get this over with, shall we?'

There was no need for Marco to say a single word to the two young grey-uniformed policemen inside the station. They took one look at Kitty and leapt out of their seats, spilling their coffee, then one of them ran towards the back, shouting wildly, while the other watched her wide-eyed, his shaking hand clutching the handle of the gun at his side.

Thankfully, a sergeant with a clearer head arrived in moments. He exchanged a few words with Marco, making sure that Kitty was who she seemed to be, then ordered the two young men to take her into custody. As they led her away, Kitty glanced over her shoulder at Marco, but he was already being shepherded into an office by the sergeant and didn't look back.

She was taken down to the basement and locked into a tiny cell with no windows and just a bare bulb for illumination. After ten minutes, one of the young men arrived with strong coffee and cannoli. Not taking his eyes off her for one moment, he put them on the floor just inside the door. It was as if he thought she were some kind of predator, which she supposed she was, in a way, but only in the air. She tried to give him a reassuring smile, but it only frightened him more and he hurried out again before she could say a word.

The cannoli weren't quite as good as the ones Adolorata had made, but were still delicious and she wolfed them down - she usually liked to have a large breakfast and the bread Giulia had brought her when she'd woken her up hadn't nearly satisfied her.

She had fully expected to be kept waiting while the police decided what to do with her, but not for nearly as long as she was and the hours dragged on and on and still nothing happened. Lunch, a simple pasta dish, was deposited on the floor for her, then a few hours later an afternoon snack of more cannoli and coffee was brought. She was beginning to think that she would be spending the night there when finally the door opened, but, instead of one of the young policemen, a dashingly handsome man with a thin moustache and elaborately-coiffed black hair in a sky blue uniform walked in.

Kitty barely had time to take in the wings on his chest and the gold stripes on his shoulders before he beckoned to her with a wide smile and spoke in a cheerful, singsong voice. 'Chao! Come, you are now a guest of the Legione Aerea!'

The man, who introduced himself as Colonnello Leonardo Vitelli, led her back through the police station to the reception area. As they went, Kitty looked through every open doorway that she could, but there was no sign of Marco anywhere and she hoped that they had just taken his report and let him go instead of detaining him for keeping her overnight or something. After the colonnelo had signed a piece of paper with a flourish, officially taking custody of her, he took her out to road in the front of the station where, instead of a guard wagon or some other such military vehicle, a sporty, red, open-topped two-seater autocar was waiting, surrounded by a crowd of admiring people.

The man opened the passenger side door for her and waited for her to get settled before closing it, then made his way around to the other side, all the while smiling to the crowd, receiving their adoration as if he were some kind of movie star and answering the questions that were called out to him. There was a gasp from the crowd when he announced that the woman in his autocar was one of "il famoso Misfit Squadron" and much of the attention transferred to Kitty, but she barely noticed; she was searching the crowd. TO her relief, she eventually found what she was looking for - Marco. Their eyes met and he gave her a half-smile and lifted his hand, but she immediately lost him again because, right at that moment, the autocar surged forwards. The crowd cheered wildly as the rear wheels slewed, fighting for grip on the old road, its stone worn thin by centuries of use, but they were left behind in seconds, along with the town itself as the man took them into the countryside.

They said nothing during the journey, not so much because there was nothing to say, but rather because the man sang the entire way. She wasn't sure, but she thought it was an aria from a Puccini opera and she cracked a small smile, her first in hours, when the thought that Gwen would undoubtedly recognise it popped into her head.

With no need to make any small talk, something that had never come easy to her, despite her mother's efforts, she sat back and enjoyed the countryside, the last of the sunset and the man's voice, which was actually extremely good.

It was only a short ride to the Italian air base, a dozen or so miles north of Vittoria and at the speed with which the colonnello drove it was over very quickly. They sped through the gate without slowing, the guards warned by a honk of the autocar's horn to open the barricade in the nick of time, and raced around the perimeter track, past a very short line of Grand Eagle bombers and enormous Zeppelin hangars, empty now after the Misfits had shot down all their occupants. They finally came screeching to a halt in front of one of a row of long, thin, brick buildings which just screamed "barracks" and the man sounded the horn again.

By the time he had hopped out and jogged around to open her door for her, there were three young women in sky blue uniforms standing on the steps of the building.

He led Kitty to them, then gave her a small bow.

'I leave you with them for now. See you for dinner. One hour! Chao!'

He gave the women a wide, movie star smile, then jogged back to the autocar, jumped in without bothering to open the door and went racing off.

Kitty caught the longing looks on the women's faces as they watched him go and she half expected at least a couple to swoon dramatically. One of them caught her watching and giggled, blushing. 'Is very handsome, no?'

Kitty shrugged. 'I suppose.'

The woman giggled again, then turned to go back into the building. 'Come! We dress for dinner.'

The women, all junior officers with very little English, who worked in the signals shed, took her to their quarters where she was stripped of the rough men's clothes she was wearing - all that could be found in her size that was suitable to travel in - and thrust into the shower. She was then rushed into their room, where there was a dress laid out ready for her. It was a ball gown in a lovely cornflower blue, which was probably the closest they could find at such short notice to the rather unfeminine colour of the RAC uniforms. She put it on and stood still while one of the women pinned it with the practised skills of a seamstress, then removed it again so that adjustments could be made on a sewing machine sitting in the corner. While that was being done, she was sat in front of a mirror and fussed over by the other two women. One brushed her matted hair, causing her to wince in pain every few seconds, while the other began pulling bottles and vials out of a large makeup bag. Kitty stepped in before they could start work, though, guessing their intentions and told them in broken Spanish and using quite a few gestures, that she would take care of herself.

The women pouted, disappointed, but agreed, and left her to her own devices while they worked on their own appearances.

A few subtle touches had Kitty looking less a shipwrecked mariner and more her usual self again and she sat and watched as the women hurried around the small four-person room, putting on far too much makeup for her liking and curling their hair into overly elaborate styles, making her feel very glad she had insisted on doing her own. They were impressively efficient, though, and in less than twenty minutes, something unheard of in Kitty's experience with her sisters, they were all dressed and ready and hurried out into the night.

A passenger wagon was waiting for them and they climbed in, joining a dozen other women already waiting inside. As the wagon trundled around the perimeter track, the women chatted animatedly, speaking far too quickly for Kitty to have any hope of understanding any of it, although she didn't care too much, she was enjoying just watching them; there was so much gesticulation going on that it was almost as if they were putting on a puppet show.

The wagon took them to another air base about half an hour away. This one had smaller hangars and Kitty thought she recognised it from the reconnaissance photographs as being home to a couple of Italian fighter squadrons. It was in more or less the right place, about fifteen miles north of the main airship base, near Caltagirone, one of the larger Sicilian towns.

She sat up and pressed her face to the window, wanting to get a closer look at the Italian operation and machines, but they didn't go onto the base itself. Instead they went past the main entrance and turned onto a track that went around the outside of the perimeter fence. Once past the hangars and other service buildings they came to a secondary, smaller entrance round the back of the barracks buildings and there they turned away from the airfield and onto a gravel driveway.

Kitty couldn't help but stare in awe as their destination came into sight. Much like Bagshot Hall, the airfield had been built in the grounds of a stately home. However, instead of the quintessentially English mansion, this one had a sprawling Roman villa as its centrepiece and it and its grounds had been dressed up to create a fantasy setting, like something out of *A Midsummer Night's Dream*.

The driveway was lined by cypress trees, each of which was hung with hundreds of tiny electric lights, creating a magical passageway at the end of which a spray fountain spread its wings, the high plumes of water creating shimmering rainbows as the tiny water droplets drifted inexorably earthwards, shrouding the faerie world behind it in mystery. Beyond, two immensely powerful anti-aircraft searchlights thrust two thick, seemingly solid columns into the sky, creating a gateway that visitors must brave if they would have their audience with the Queen, Titania. But, even if they plucked up the courage to pass through, there was no guarantee that entry would be granted, because rank upon rank of soldiers in burnished and shining bronze armour, holding aloft flaming torches, stood guard on either side of the entrance to the house itself.

The Italians had managed to create something wondrous in the middle of a world that had turned very ugly and Kitty found tears in her eyes as once again the realisation that she couldn't share it with Gwen sprang unwanted into her mind.

There were a dozen or more vehicles parked unobtrusively to one side in the shadows, including several wagons much like the one that had brought them, and quite a few private autocars, among them a familiar red sports autocar, but the wagon didn't join them. Instead it went around the fountain, passing through the spray, then stopped in the centre of the driveway, directly opposite the villa.

The women looked at each other, wondering what was happening, but then the door opened and the colonnello boarded. He stood at the front of the bus, searching the faces of the passengers until he found Kitty.

He gave her a smile that brought forth at least a couple of sighs from the women around her and held out his hand. 'The guest of honour is here at last. Please?'

Conscious of the envious glances being thrown her by most of the women, Kitty made her way down the aisle and allowed him to hand her down onto the driveway, where a long red carpet had been laid, as if at a royal banquet.

The villa sat on top of a low mound with a wide stone stairway leading up to it and waiting for her at the bottom of them was a delegation of four officers. A couple were in air force uniforms similar to Colonnello Vitelli's and another was in a dark blue uniform with white trim and a flat cap, but the last was in what could only be described as a Roman officer's uniform, complete with red plume on a shining gold helmet, red cape, leather kilt and an anatomically correct golden breastplate with exaggerated musculature and, of all things, nipples.

She'd thought the soldiers standing guard in front of the house were just wearing costumes, but apparently that was now the Italian army's dress uniform. Unless, of course, the elderly man with scrawny legs and hairy toes in his leather sandals had actually chosen to dress that way.

Vitelli brought her to a halt in front of the group and saluted the senior air force officer, who was a dignified white-haired man in his sixties, with so many medals on his chest and gold on his shoulders and cap that it was a wonder he could stand.

'Aerial Officer Wright, may I present our host for the evening, Generale De Luca, commander of the Legione Aerea forces here on Sicily. Generale, this is Aerial Officer Wright of Misfit Squadron. '

The man smiled and gave her a small bow. 'Welcome, Aerial Officer Wright.'

'Please, I'm not in uniform. Call me Kitty, or Miss Wright if you feel you have to.'

De Luca inclined his head in agreement. 'Very well, Kitty. And you must call me Giovanni.' He smiled widely, then turned to indicate the other men, who nodded in turn as he introduced them. 'My second in command, Generale Mancini. My counterpart in the navy, Ammiraglio Costa. And the overall commander of the Imperial Italian forces here on Sicily, Generale Jilani.'

He introduced the army officer in the Roman uniform last and the man stepped forwards to offer his arm to Kitty.

'Would you allow me to escort you, Miss Wright?'

Vitelli shifted at Kitty's side and she glanced at him. He had obviously hoped to enter the party in triumph with her on his arm as his trophy and was looking quite miffed to have rank pulled on him by the army general. Kitty flashed him one of her most winning smiles, which brightened his expression somewhat, then turned back to Generale Jilani. 'I'd be delighted, Generale.'

The fact that the elderly man had chosen to call her "Miss" made it quite obvious that he was used to the manners of the past and she adjusted her behaviour to match, taking his arm as if they were entering a ball.

Despite being in his seventies or possibly eighties, there was nothing infirm about Jilani and his arm was solid corded muscle beneath her hand as he escorted her through the searchlight gateway then slowly, but steadily, up the stairs towards the villa.

When their feet touched the top step, the ranks of legionaries thrust their torches aloft as a fanfare blared out on both sides from soldiers holding huge curled brass horns straight out of the history books.

Kitty jumped, startled and squeaked before she could stop herself; she was used to guns and explosions, but not sudden assaults by musical instruments.

The old general chortled in delight, but not unkindly, and leaned in close to speak in her ear. 'Sometimes there are distinct advantages to being half-deaf, Miss Wright; it would not be dignified for someone of my rank and position to have a heart attack every time a few trumpets play.'

Kitty chuckled, not at all offended, but then her breath caught in her throat as they passed through the wide doorway and into the atrium where the party was being held.

Jilani brought her to a halt just inside, both so that she could take in the spectacle and also so that she could be seen by the hundreds of people waiting for them. For her.

The generale had managed to let go of her without her noticing and he took a step back, leaving her completely alone in the limelight, as a brass band, stationed near the back of the room, broke out into the national anthem of the United Federation of American States. She cursed him under her breath, even as she kept her smile firmly in place and held herself to attention.

She would have thought the Italians would have hard feelings towards her, after all, the Misfits, and the Hal Far Fighter Force before them, had sent a lot of their pilots to meet the Dark Scythesman, but all she saw on the faces gathered in the room was respect for the anthem being played and anticipation of a good night ahead. There was nothing of hatred or resentment that an enemy should be treated so well and she relaxed ever so slightly, knowing she wouldn't have to suffer through the veiled insults and whispering behind her back that she'd had to in the formal occasions she'd been forced to attend back home.

Unlike her sisters, Kitty didn't enjoy being the centre of attention, but thankfully the band only played the short version of the Sousa march before Jilani reclaimed her arm and led her forwards, as the men and women applauded.

'Do you dance, Miss Wright?'

Kitty grimaced; she enjoyed dancing and had been told she had a talent for it by her teachers, but balls had also been more her sisters' style. 'I have been known to.'

'Just as well.'

When the two of them reached the centre of the floor, the band began to play again and Kitty sighed in relief when she heard a waltz, something even she couldn't mess up.

The generale moved her across the floor, competently and elegantly, but the climb up the stairs had taken its toll and he almost immediately began to tire. He was saved from making an embarrassing spectacle of himself, though, when they were joined by the other senior officers and their partners, the colonnello leading Luisa, the woman who had said he was handsome when he'd dropped Kitty off. That was the signal for the rest of the couples to swarm onto the floor and gave Jilani the opportunity to retire gracefully from the dance floor. He led Kitty to a long bar at the side of the room and got them both drinks, before turning with her to watch the dancing.

Kitty was more interested in their spectacular surroundings, though. The anachronistic nature of the two-thousand-year-old Roman army uniforms among the modern military ones was reflected perfectly in the setting, where the past had been juxtaposed with the present: the atrium had once been open to the sky, but at some point it had been covered over by an immense glass ceiling, the large panels supported by entwined wrought iron in the shape of an enormous cog wheel. A single massive golden chandelier hung from the centre of the wheel, illuminating the dancers with the soft light of hundreds of candles. Now that she had a chance to look properly, Kitty noticed that the floor they spun around was actually a giant mosaic, as she imagined it would have been when the villa had been built. The spiralling pattern of tiles was entirely modern, though, and, instead of ceramic tiles, it appeared to be made up of gold, brass, a shiny black stone like obsidian, and some kind of crystal which sparkled in the candlelight, an ode to Italian extravagance as it had been before the war. The rest of the atrium retained much of its original form, however; the smooth walls were painted in red and gold and the walkways around the outside of the slightly sunken mosaic still had their terracotta awnings, despite the glass and iron roof rendering them unnecessary.

Kitty tore her eyes from the sight and turned to Jilani. 'Do you always throw such extravagant parties?'

He shook his head. 'No. This is all to honour you - a gallant enemy.'

Kitty sipped at her drink, a superb Italian white wine which Derek would probably have had a fit over, then set it aside regretfully. 'Thank you, but I don't think I'll be able to enjoy myself very much; I am after all a prisoner.'

'On that matter, we have already been contacted by your superior, Commodore Campbell, and your exchange will be arranged soon. So, until then you must please consider yourself not a prisoner, but rather our honoured guest.'

She blinked at him in surprise, then slowly grinned. 'In that case.' She picked the wine up again. 'Cheers!' She saluted him with the glass then took a long drink.

He laughed and did the same, before turning back to the room with her.

The mosaic floor where the dancing was taking place was a foot below the walkways around the edge of the room - it had probably been a pool at some point - so Kitty had a good view of the people dancing and she wasn't surprised to find that, as well as women in civilian clothing, there were a good few in uniform. Unlike Prussia, Italy didn't forbid its women from joining the armed forces, they did however keep them firmly in support roles and away from any real fighting. They would never have a chance to show how well they could pilot an aircraft, for example, which was a shame; Tanya had apparently never flown an aircraft before the war but she had quickly become one of Misfit Squadron's best pilots, rivalling even Chastity and Abby. Would one of the vivacious women she'd shared the wagon ride with proven to be just as talented if she'd been given the chance?

She spotted Luisa and Vitelli in the crowd. The woman was enjoying herself immensely and it looked like the colonnello was too. She smiled; perhaps, because of her capture, there might be a few romances started that night and it looked like she would be able to resume her own in just a few days.

The thought of Gwen brought a warm feeling that had nothing to do with the alcohol, but it was banished almost immediately when she spotted a black uniform in amongst the shades of blue and shining breastplates. She remembered what Drake had said about Gruber's dress uniform and almost panicked at the thought of him being at the party, but then saw that there were a few other men in similar uniforms scattered about the room. She didn't know how she hadn't noticed them before; they were making a lot of noise and a few of them looked like they were already drunk. She frowned at one, a portly man who was laughing while he swayed unsteadily on his feet, pawing at an unfortunate woman in a dark blue uniform who he had trapped up against one of the columns. He caught her staring and shot her a look of such hatred that it made her reel back and bump into Jilani.

The generale looked at her in concern. 'Miss Wright?'

'Sorry,' she smiled at him. 'I was distracted. Who are the men in black?'

Jilani's nose turned up. 'They are *le Camicie Nere*, the black shirts, the Emperor's bully boys. They are the ones who make sure that everybody does what they can to realise his vision of a new Italian Empire and punish those who resist.'

Kitty shuddered at the thought of being forced to conform to a megalomaniac's whims; it went against every value of freedom that she had grown up with and fought against for years. She smiled sympathetically at the man. 'So, now I know why you wear that ridiculous uniform without complaint.'

The man laughed, but then stopped abruptly and looked around in concern. 'Please,' he hissed, 'don't say things like that too loudly; even as a foreigner and my guest you are not beyond their reach.'

'And you? Are you beyond their reach?' Even as she asked the question, Kitty knew the answer - the man wouldn't have looked so worried that they'd been overheard if he wasn't accountable to the black shirts himself.

The man brushed aside the question by putting his glass on the bar and holding his hand out to her. 'I am recovered now, would you dance with me a little more?'

Kitty knew when not to press her luck and gave him a small, but extremely elegant curtsy - one of the few things her teachers had been satisfied with. 'Of course.'

She took his hand and allowed him to lead her back onto the dance floor. However, Jilani only danced for a couple of minutes before pleading that he needed to rest. He thanked her for "humouring an old man" then led her to the side of the floor and handed her off to Giovanni De Luca, the generale in charge of the Legione Aerea, who bowed to her and immediately spun her back onto the floor for a quickstep.

De Luca proved to be an enthusiastic, if not particularly talented dancer, and Kitty was fearful for her toes, but thankfully, after only a few stumbling and awkward minutes, a gong rang announcing dinner and the dance came to an end.

As the host, De Luca could safely claim the privilege of escorting her in and she was sat at his right hand as the guest of honour, with Jilani opposite her, Ammiraglio Costa next to him and Colonnello Vitelli by her side. Curiously, an empty seat was left next to the admiral and she wondered if it was some tradition of theirs, perhaps to honour a pilot who had been shot down recently, but, when the soup course was almost over, a man in black sat down.

Remembering what Jilani had said about *le Camicie Nere*, she pointedly didn't look at the man, however, his fluent and American-accented English when he apologised for being late caught her attention and she couldn't help but glance in his direction.

Gruber!

She hadn't realised she'd shouted his name out loud until her end of the table fell silent and everyone around her turned to stare at her.

'Quite right, Miss Wright.' Gruber grinned, as if he'd said something amusing. 'It's a pleasure to finally meet you in the flesh and I'm looking forward to getting to know you *much* better after you join me on board my airship.'

'Aerial Officer Wright is the prisoner of the Legione Aerea, Herr Gruber,' said De Luca from his place at the head of the table. 'She will not be joining you anywhere.'

Gruber chuckled. 'As I was saying before I was interrupted - the reason for my tardiness was because I was speaking to the Kaiser precisely on this very matter. He has promised to speak to your Emperor about Miss Wright's status and remind him that the attack on Malta is under Prussian direction now, which means that any prisoners taken belong to *me*.' He grinned malevolently at Kitty.

'Nonsense. That is not how things work and you know it - a prisoner "belongs", as you say so erroneously, to whoever they surrender to. The Emperor will never agree to handing her over to you and that is the end of this conversation.'

De Luca stared at Gruber, daring him to say more; as the host he would be well within his rights to have the Prussian thrown out.

'Very well.' Gruber nodded, but his confident smirk never faltered, even as he picked up his spoon and rapidly began to shovel soup into his mouth.

Kitty had followed the exchange closely, well aware that her fate was being decided as much, if not more, at the table that night as it was in the palaces of Europe. Despite De Luca's words, she wasn't sure that the Italian generals would dare go against Gruber if the man outright demanded Kitty even if the Kaiser didn't back him up.

A rustle from her side alerted her and she turned to face De Luca as he leaned in to speak to her quietly.

'Don't worry, the Emperor will never let him take you; we have too much to gain by exchanging you and I would never forgive myself if you were to end up in that man's clutches.'

'Thank you, Giovanni.' Kitty smiled warmly, but wasn't particularly reassured and, as the dinner went on, she found she had no appetite for any of the wonderful food that was put in front of her, especially because every time she lifted her gaze from her plate she found Gruber staring in her direction, as if she were his property and he was deciding what to do with her.

The two hours that it took for the meal to conclude seemed like an eternity, but then it was back to the atrium for more dancing and, while she could ignore Gruber at the table by simply not looking at him, it was impossible to avoid him when he was free to approach her when he willed. There was nothing she or anyone else could do, therefore, to stop him when he cut in on Colonnello Vitelli and whirled her expertly away into the crowd.

Kitty was too stunned to do anything except continue dancing. For a moment she wondered at his temerity in doing such a thing; a Brit would never consider such a thing and even an American would at least warn the man first, but then again it was Gruber and Gruber was *all* temerity. She briefly considered causing a scene and putting him in his place, but the conversation at the table had shown her how low an opinion the man had of the Italians and it would mean very little to him to be shown up in front of them. It would also deprive her of an opportunity to get the measure of him as a man and not just a pilot. Unfortunately, that meant enduring his touch and trying to breathe through his halitosis.

'That was a very practised move. How many women have you stolen away from their partners like that?'

Gruber laughed. 'More than I care to remember.'

'And does it usually work or do you get what you deserve?'

'You'd be surprised how many women fantasise about being swept off their feet by me.'

'I'm not one of them, believe me.'

He leered at her. 'Oh I know perfectly well you have other... *leanings*.' As the music ended he took the opportunity to illustrate his words by dipping her, putting her off balance and leaning her more than sixty degrees. He held her there, seemingly effortlessly, and only brought her up again when the orchestra had launched into a new tune and it was too late for anyone to rescue her diplomatically.

To her horror, the next dance was a tango, one of the dances most associated with romance, and Gruber immediately pulled her into a very close embrace as he began to move her.

If anything he was even more adept at the tango than the foxtrot he'd cut into, which didn't surprise her one bit, considering it was one of his main seduction methods. However, while he was keeping his face carefully schooled, like the good actor he was, she could tell he was actually finding the energetic dance quite hard; not only was there a faint sheen of sweat on his brow and a slight labouring to his breath, but she could feel something ribbed around his waist as he pressed his body against hers, betraying the fact that he wasn't quite as fit as he wanted it to seem he was.

She smiled to herself as she remembered that one of her dance teachers, a woman, of course, had described the tango as a battle and that, while the man was nominally in charge, it was the woman who had the real power. So, by forcing her to keep dancing with him, he had provided her with a way to attack him where he was vulnerable - his ego.

A man led a dance by giving the woman subtle clues as to what he wanted her to do or where he wanted her to move, like shifting his weight or pressing with his hands. She didn't *disobey* those commands; that would have been disastrous, instead she simply *resisted.*

A truly great tango dancer, a proper one, would take her resistance and use it to create something remarkable, something which belonged to both of them, but Gruber was only *technically* proficient. He wasn't a true dancer, he didn't *feel* the dance as much as carry out the steps and he was obviously not used to a partner showing any reluctance whatsoever. He began to struggle and in a very short time his breathing became ragged. He began to sweat properly and his hair, so carefully slicked back, began to come loose, strands falling into his eyes as the product in it was diluted.

He barely lasted the dance and when the music ended there was no fancy flourish, just a simple pose, held for a few short seconds, before he released her and stepped back.

'That was amazing! Invigorating.' Gruber huffed breathlessly, very pleased with himself. He looked around as if expecting applause and pouted when none was forthcoming.

'Meh.' Kitty made a non-committal sound, raising her voice slightly so that the people around them could hear. 'It was... *adequate*, at best, much like your flying.' She slapped his stomach with the back of her hand. It made a hollow sound which more than proved her theory about his fitness. 'You might dance better if you loosen your girdle.' She started to go, but then turned back with a smile. 'Oh, and your bald spot is showing.'

Amid titters from the onlookers, Gruber's eyes widened in alarm and his hand shot up to his hair. He brushed the loose strands back into place frantically before coming to his senses and realising what he was doing. He looked around and found himself surrounded by dozens of people, all thoroughly enjoying the spectacle of his discomfort.

He scowled and snarled at Kitty. 'You'll pay for that.'

He stormed off in the direction of the exit, pushing his way through the crowd to more laughter and Kitty just couldn't resist a parting shot. 'Lord Drake sends his regards, by the way!'

Kitty was probably one of the few people on the planet who didn't like Gruber's movies and she had never had a particularly high opinion of him, having heard tales of his exploits from friends who had encountered socially. However, ever since she'd read Drake's report, she'd felt that he didn't even deserve the respect that pilots normally showed each other, or to even be considered one of them, and had been looking forward to putting him in his place in the sky when the Barons finally showed up. Doing so on the ground, face to face, had been almost as satisfying.

'That was well done, Kitty, but are you sure you want to antagonise him? All you're doing is giving him more of a reason to mistreat you if he ever gets you as his prisoner.'

Kitty turned to find Generale De Luca watching. 'Do you know what he does with the pilots he has as prisoners of war?'

De Luca nodded. 'I have been made aware. That is why we will be doing what we can to keep you out of his clutches.'

Kitty laughed. 'That was very melodramatic! You sound like you're an actor in one of his awful flyvies!'

'Really? How horrible!' De Luca shuddered exaggeratedly, then shrugged. 'I'm sorry, but I wouldn't know, I've never seen any of them.'

'Believe me, that's for the best.'

'So I've been told.' He grinned and nodded, but then turned serious. 'Anyway, I promise that we will do whatever we can to keep you from him until you can be exchanged. We all wanted the privilege of playing host to you, but in the end it was decided you would be safer and more comfortable with Generale Jilani and his staff at his headquarters. He will naturally want to wine and dine you while you are there, but I hope you will agree to accept the hospitality of the Legione Aerea at least once and Ammiraglio Costa has asked that you pay him and the Legione Marina a visit in Palermo.'

'Will negotiations take that long?'

De Luca shrugged. 'These things take as long as they take.'

The musicians, who had paused for a couple of minutes to allow the dancers to get their breath back after the Tango, started up again and De Luca smiled wryly and held out his hand. 'Would you allow me a chance to make up for my clumsiness of before?'

Kitty smiled. 'Of course, Giovanni, although you were not at all clumsy.'

'You are too kind.'

She relaxed into his hold for a sedate waltz, which wouldn't put her feet in as much danger as the quickstep had.

It didn't take long for the party to end; the pilots were flying at dawn and, as the hosts, it would have been rude to keep going without them.

Generale Jilani took Kitty to the villa that he had requisitioned for his headquarters in his luxurious autocar and his second in command was rousted from his suite to make room for her.

Over the next few days she was kept in the lap of luxury with the best of food, plenty of rest and some very interesting company. There was even a swimming pool and, after a bathing suit was found for her, that was where Kitty spent most of her days, either lounging around with a book from the villa's extensive library, swimming laps, or simply enjoying the early spring sunshine with the dozen or so other army officers that found themselves with too much time on their hands. The evening after the party at the villa she made her way to Palermo with Jilani for a formal dinner with the Italian Navy and the very next day it was the turn of Colonnello Vitelli, although his party was far less formal and much more fun, with a jazz band, plenty of alcohol and not a single black shirt, Italian or Prussian, in sight.

She tried to relax and have fun, but, even knowing that she would soon be reunited with Gwen and her friends, there was always the shadow of Gruber looming over her, preventing her from fully enjoying herself. She couldn't help think that he would manage to get his own way somehow; he always seemed to come out smelling of roses and it seemed that the Kaiser would do anything for him.

She was right to worry.

She was lounging in her bathing suit at lunch, an informal buffet set up on the patio overlooking the pool with no dress code or set time, when a messenger arrived on a motorcycle and hurried straight up to the generale, who was sitting next to Kitty at one of the small tables. The woman saluted, handed him a folded sheet of paper, saluted again then left, but only after a furtive look and shy smile at Kitty, which the American returned warmly, before going back to her delicious meal of pasta.

She paused, her fork half-way to her mouth, when the generale screwed the message up into a ball and started swearing, using many of the more colourful phrases that she'd asked the younger officers teach her over the last few days so that she could take them back for Scarlet to add to her collection.

Eventually Jilani ran out of steam and he turned to her, frustration evident on his face. 'Orders from the Emperor. We are to deliver you to Gruber before his airship takes off this evening.'

The fork dropped unnoticed from Kitty's hand, splattering tomato sauce on the red and white checked table cloth. 'But... the exchange! I thought...'

The generale deflated in his seat and looked at her for long seconds, his sympathy clear in his eyes, but then he suddenly sat up straight and started bellowing orders in Italian too fast for her to understand.

The change in the half-dozen men lounging around the patio was instant and they abandoned whatever they were doing and raced into the villa. When they were gone, the generale lounged back in his chair and picked up his drink. He sipped at it, then gazed out over the beautiful grounds of the villa as he spoke slowly and deliberately. 'Oh dear, it seems that we have already exchanged you and won't be able to comply with the Emperor's orders.'

Kitty blinked, puzzled, but then smiled as understanding dawned. She stood, her meal forgotten, and hurried towards the house, but then stopped and ran back to the old man. 'Thank you, generale.' She bent and kissed him on the cheek, then raced into the villa.

When she came out of the front of the villa, half an hour later, she was dressed in nondescript green Italian army coveralls belonging to a female mechanic, with the woman's uniform hat on her head, hiding her golden hair. Jilani was waiting for her, along with an army wagon, and she marched up to him and saluted with a grin.

He laughed and returned the gesture, thumping his hand against his chest. 'My men will take you to the village you came ashore in. I have already spoken to the Marinos to arrange passage for you and the Navy have been told to ignore their boat.'

'Thank you, but what about the exchange?'

'Sky Commodore Campbell strikes me as an honourable person, I trust her to give us what she thinks is right.'

'I'll make sure she does.'

'I know you will.' He stuck out his hand. 'I hope we meet again under better circumstances, Miss Wright.'

'So do I, Generale. So do I.'

The Marinos welcomed Kitty back with open joy, but this time there was no big party for her; her presence in the village needed to be kept as secret as possible to prevent the Prussians from finding out that she wasn't already back in Malta.

It was just after midnight when the Cassandra sailed with a single passenger for the six-hour journey to Malta.

Kitty slept most of the time, while the Marinos took it in turn to pilot the ship, but she had asked them to wake her when they were nearing Malta and Orazio did so when they were half an hour out.

The young man shyly handed her a bundle, wrapped up in brown paper and she opened it to find her flight suit. It still smelled faintly of fish, but it had been treated and was almost as good as it had been when she'd taken off in it days before. He also had her helmet and gloves in a hat box, the lenses wrapped in felt to protect them.

'Thank you!'

The boy grinned. 'You're welcome.'

He took a newspaper off the table behind him and she saw that it was an Italian one with a report on her capture. She scanned it quickly, getting the gist of it, and grinned when she saw that the Marinos were mentioned a couple of times and hailed as heroes. She went to hand it back, but the boy held out a pen.

'Please?'

He waved the pen, making his intentions perfectly clear, even if he didn't know the words and she grinned.

'To Orazio, thank you for saving my life. Lots of love and kisses. Kitty.' She signed it with a flourish and handed it back to him.

He beamed and surveyed it happily, but she hadn't finished. The Marinos had held on to her survival kit as well and she dug around in it for the penknife. After some quick work at the stitching she pulled the Misfit Squadron patch off her flightsuit and held it out.

He gasped and stared at it in shock. Then looked up at her. 'Davvero?'

Kitty smiled at him and nodded.

'Grazie!' He turned and sprinted for the companionway, almost tripping over the stairs in his haste to get up them, all the time calling for his father.

Kitty grinned and started getting putting on her flightsuit. It wasn't too long before dawn and she wanted to be ready to fly with the Misfits as soon as she got back to Hal Far.

It seemed that the British had been expecting them, because when they steamed into the Grand Harbour, just as light was seeping back into the world, there were four patrol craft, filled to the brim with cheering Royal Naval personnel, and a few dozen fishing boats waiting to escort them to their berth.

As they neared the shore, Kitty leaned against the rail of the Cassandra and peered into the gloom, searching the people on the shore, but was disappointed when she didn't see Gwen or anybody in an RAC uniform. It had been a forlorn hope; she had known that the pilots would be sleeping as long as they could to be as rested as possible for the day ahead, but she had thought that Sky Commodore Campbell would be there at least. Instead, the delegation on the pier was made up entirely of Royal Navy personnel and led by Rear Admiral Pritchard, the commander of the Navy base on the island. There were at least a dozen Italian airmen with them, under a very loose guard, and she briefly wondered if Jilani would be satisfied with that many men as an exchange for her, or whether he had been holding out for more.

Marco brought the boat in smoothly and, while Matteo and Orazio were throwing ropes to the men on the shore and tying up the boat, he approached Kitty.

'A happy ending.'

'For now at least. Thank you again, Marco.'

'It has been a pleasure; I am very happy to have been the one to bring you home.' He grinned. 'And thank *you* for the coffee. It will make things a lot easier in the village for a long while.'

He held out his hand for her to shake, but she slipped past it and threw her arms around him. 'Take care of your family, Marco.'

She held him tightly for a few seconds, then turned and went down the gangplank and back onto Malta.

CHAPTER 15

The Misfits flew with renewed vigour in the week after Kitty's return, but they were never able to turn the bombers away again, like they'd done that first raid after they had destroyed half the Prussian fighters. They did drop their payloads far more haphazardly, though, in a hurry to get home and out of range of the British fighters. Most bombs fell harmlessly in the water of the harbour or on the deserted city, but another freighter was destroyed and the Arturo was hit dozens more times, but her flight deck continued to absorb the worst of the attack and repairs below decks continued unhindered. In fact, on one of his few visits to Hal Far, Captain Hewer reported that they were making good headway, despite the difficulties of the situation and the lack of proper facilities.

The battle for the skies over Malta quickly turned into one of attrition. The Coalition had the same problem they'd had over England; British pilots who bailed out were being recovered by rescue boats or simply gliding to safety on the island, but the Italian and Prussian pilots were going straight into captivity and there were noticeably fewer bombers in each raid as they ran out of crews.

However, the supply of Spitsteams was beginning to run dangerously low. Of the fifty that had been delivered, there were only five left in their crates. The rest had either been destroyed or condemned as beyond repair and cannibalised for spares to repair the ones they were flying. The Misfit aircraft, with their better performance and much sturdier construction, hadn't fared nearly as bad, but every one of them had sustained damage which had forced them off the flight line for days at a time. Luqa reported that Drake and Tanya's machines were almost ready, though, and their arrival would hopefully take a bit of the strain off the Spitsteams.

If both sides continued to fight as they were and nobody was resupplied, it would be a close run thing as to who would run out of aircraft first.

Dorothy Campbell wasn't one to sit and wait for an outcome if she could do something to affect it, though, and she decided the time had come to tip the balance further in the favour of the British and hit the enemy while their morale was low.

Wendy had finally managed to get together enough rockets for the Misfits to carry out another attack and Campbell authorised a reconnaissance flight by Vulture in order to find the best fighter base to target.

Chalky's photographs were disappointing, though; the enemy had learnt from their mistake and moved their fighters back from the south coast of Sicily, spreading them around several airfields so that no more than a single squadron was based in any one place. Not only would the Prussians have far more warning and be able to intercept them on the way home, but the possible gains had been reduced so far as to render it almost pointless to attack them.

However, with the British convoy only a day or two from Gibraltar, something had to be done to secure air superiority.

Up till then, the Misfits hadn't been properly engaging the enemy fighters. With four squadrons of MU9's, two of MU10's and one more each of Italian T202's and older T200's, there were just too many of them and Bruce, Monty, Drake and Tanya's job as Blue flight had just been to keep them occupied and away from the Misfits attacking the bombers. They hadn't always been successful and occasionally the Coalition fighters had been able to force the British away, but, with such inferior numbers, it was a game the Misfits were forced to play if they were to have a chance at putting the bombers off from their targets.

Campbell wanted to scrap those tactics completely, ignore the bombers and target the fighters. Wendy's rockets could then be used to destroy the bombers on the ground instead. The larger machines couldn't operate from the small or hastily constructed airfields that the fighters could; they needed proper infrastructures like hydrogen supplies as well as a much larger takeoff run, so they were still clumped up on their four bases around the south coast of Sicily. They would be sitting ducks when the enemy fighters were no longer so much of a threat.

The plan was simple, but it had its risks, not least of which was that the bombers would have a clear run on their targets in the Grand Harbour, with only the anti-aircraft guns to dissuade them, so Campbell went to speak to Admiral Myerscough, to warn him about the change. He was understandably doubtful at first, but when she gave him her reasoning he finally agreed; even though his ships would take a pounding they were next to useless stuck in port, whereas the convoy was desperately needed.

None of the Misfits liked leaving the Navy high and dry, especially Farrier, who already had to suffer seeing her fellows in the Navy attacked every day, but they saw it as a necessary evil and, from the very first sortie, they couldn't deny how effective it was.

As with most times the Misfits did something new, the enemy were taken by surprise. They expected to be playing the same game of cat and mouse as usual and were thrown into chaos when instead the British engaged them head on with all their fighters and two of them even collided.

The Misfits took down a dozen enemy fighters in the first sortie, fully twice as many as they had been able to destroy in the weeks since the raid on the Prussian fighter base. They shot down a further twenty more during the next two raids, leaving the Coalition reeling, a third of their fighters gone.

The Navy paid the price for the Misfits' success. During the course of the day, the last two remaining freighters were sunk, along with one of the destroyers and the Arturo added more than a dozen new potholes to her already scarred flight deck.

Campbell had initially thought that it would be at least a couple of days before the Misfits could attack the bomber bases in relative safety, which would be cutting it fine; the convoy would be almost in range by then. However, after seeing their success and hearing reports of fighters breaking off and fleeing almost before the fight had begun, she decided to take a risk and had the fitters ready the first load of rockets.

Wendy's rockets had been produced by the mechanics in the workshops of the undersea boat squadron on Manoel Island and the men and women there had been fully aware of the use that they were going to be put to. They had taken the time to engrave the names of the friends they had lost on them, making the simple brass tubes into things that were as beautiful as they were deadly. The Misfits, by unspoken agreement, took the time that their aircraft were being rearmed and rewound to read as many of the names on the weapons as they could instead of resting. Nothing was said, but not a few of the Navy mechanics working on the aircraft did so through reddened and moist eyes.

Rockets were notoriously unreliable and difficult to aim, but for some reason every single one of them hit their targets that evening and the Misfits left two entire HO111 squadrons lying broken and burning in the smoking ruins of their base in the west, near Marsala.

They repeated the feat the next morning, directly after the first raid of the day, then once more after lunch.

In less than 24 hours, all three of the Prussian bomber bases and almost their entire fleet of bombers were destroyed, along with twenty more fighters. The Misfits left the fourth base intact, though; it was Colonnello Vitelli's base and they wanted to show their appreciation for how well the Italians had treated Kitty.

A few days later, the thirty-ship convoy made it to Malta almost completely unscathed, with the loss of a single destroyer, which had fallen foul of the torpedoes of Prussian undersea boats.

Only a quarter of the merchant vessels were stopping at Malta, the rest were destined for Alexandria and the island of Crete and continued straight on, deeper into the Mediterranean, taking with them most of the survivors of the convoy that had brought the Misfits, including Admiral Myerscough and his staff. However, those few ships brought with them desperately-needed food, materials and, vitally for the defence efforts, eighty more Spitsteams, sixteen pilots to fly them, and two tankers of hydrogen, enough for the bombers at Luqa and Ta'Kali to finally be let loose.

The tide had firmly turned in favour of the British.

With air superiority now firmly in their hands and the Coalition unable to bomb Malta, the Misfits were able to turn their attention towards the shipping supplying the enemy forces in North Africa.

Wendy had been tasked with finding a way to mount torpedoes on the Misfit fighters, but neither she, nor her contact in the undersea boat base at Manoel Island, Georgina Strangeways, a tiny woman in her early fifties, had been able to do so. They had quickly come to the conclusion that it would be impossible without making the torpedoes a lot smaller, and therefore ineffective, or completely redesigning the aircraft, defeating the object. It had been easy enough to design a system to mount them on the Nelsons, though, and the workshops at Luqa and

Ta'Kali had immediately started producing them and attaching mounts to the bombers, while the two turned their minds to new and interesting ways to blow up ships with fighters.

Nothing they came up with was practical or destructive enough to guarantee the destruction of a target with only a few hits, though, and they had more or less given up, with Strangeways returning to her vital work on the undersea boats, when Scarlet and Tanya had flown their stillborn mission against Bertha.

Curious about the Italian explosives, Wendy had stolen one and it hadn't taken long for her to realise that they would be ideal for her purposes. However, while redesigning them to be deployed from a fighter would be easy enough, they would be useless unless they could replicate the special metal-destroying acid they contained.

Thankfully, as well as being just as enthusiastic about destroying things as Wendy, Strangeways was a member of the Chemists' Guild, and she proved equal to the task. By the time the convoy arrived they had a prototype of the deployment apparatus ready for testing on the Spitsteam she'd been given for her experiments, but it wasn't until the munitions supplies were unloaded that Strangeways had the raw minerals needed to create the acid.

Without telling anybody what it was for, she had the carcass of a Grand Eagle bomber hauled from the Graveyard and placed in a field next to Hal Far. Then, first thing the next morning, she arranged for the Misfits and Dorothy Campbell to meet Strangeways by the perimeter fence overlooking it and took off in the Spitsteam from Ta'Kali.

The sight of the pilots wandering over to the perimeter fence with bacon sandwiches in one hand and mugs of tea in the other was already enough to draw a fair amount of attention, but after Strangeways was quietly quizzed by one of the fitters there was such an exodus from the underground bunker that it was left almost entirely deserted.

'Wrecker, this is Chemist. Ready when you are, over.' Strangeways had brought a portable radio transceiver and she used it to contact Wendy.

'Chemist, this is Wrecker. Coming in hot!'

The pilots and the group of more than two hundred men and women looked skywards as the buzzing of an airscrew became audible over the sounds of the countryside.

The Misfits had an advantage over everyone else in that they were wearing their helmets, ready for the morning's sortie, and they slotted lenses in place to better see the Spitsteam as it came into sight. The two long thin tubes under the wings, one on each side, immediately provoked excited comments and Bruce glanced at Strangeways.

'What the hell has she got under her wings? Are those bigger rockets or something?'

Strangeways said nothing, she just tilted her head in the direction of the bomber, gave him a wink, then turned to watch Wendy make her run. The Australian grinned and gave the woman a speculative look before doing the same.

The Spitsteam came in straight and level on a flightpath parallel to the perimeter fence, which gave them a perfect view, but also meant that there was no possibility of disaster if something went wrong. Everyone, except Strangeways of course, was expecting either the nose of the aircraft to dip and rockets to fire or the tubes to fall away like bombs, but they did neither. Instead, they split down the centreline on approach, opening up like bomb bay doors, and half a dozen small metal objects fell from each.

The Misfits flinched back, expecting one of the enormous explosions that was customary during any display related to Wendy's inventions, but there was only a clang, almost drowned out by a disappointing dull coughing sound, and a few small clouds of earth thrown up by the ones that had missed.

Many of the onlookers began muttering and a few even started to wander away, but Strangeways kept her eyes on the Grand Eagle, a stopwatch in her hand. 'Wait for it...'

There was a sudden squeal of tortured metal and then the Italian bomber just seemed to collapse under its own weight.

Strangeways clicked the button to stop the timer, then scribbled something in a small notebook. When she looked up she found every single one of the pilots looking at her.

'Uh. Yes. Wendy will explain. And don't let anyone touch that aircraft for a while, just in case.' The small woman turned and hurried away through the crowd, deliberately not meeting anybody's eye.

Abby chuckled, then looked back to the wreck. 'I don't care how much of a bang it makes; if it can do that to Duralumin that thick, then I'm looking forward to seeing what it can do to a ship.'

Wendy's Spitsteam buzzed overhead, on the downwind leg of a textbook circuit of the airfield, betraying her nervousness with the handling of the fighter, and the pilots started back to the hangar to meet her.

Wendy had landed and was crouched beneath the Spitsteam with Strangeways when the Misfits arrived, the two of them speaking animatedly and fiddling around with one of the tubes.

They waited patiently for the big woman to come out and she grinned at the pilots while she brushed the dust off her hands.

'Well?'

'You tell us,' said Campbell. 'What did we just see?'

Wendy pulled one of her bombs from a canvas bag on the floor and hefted it in one hand.

'This is based on those explosives that Scarlet and Tanya got from the Italians. Those things can melt through anything metal, but they have to be placed so that the explosive charge is pointing in the right direction, which would make throwing them out of the cockpit of a Spitsteam pretty ineffective and a bit silly. I'm fairly sure we've solved that problem.' She held up the bomb. It was black, roughly conical in shape and about eighteen inches long, with a couple of small fins at the fat end. 'The fins create resistance as it drops and orient it point downwards. The tip is lead, which is broken off on impact, up to here.' She pointed to a seam running around the cone, about six inches from the sharp end. 'That breaks the glass vial inside which contains the acid and then, when the weak explosive in the tail goes off, the liquid is sprayed through the tip, keeping it concentrated in a fairly small area. As you saw on the Grand Eagle, it takes a few seconds for the acid to have an effect, but once the process starts it is unstoppable and it will keep burning a hole through a ship until it reaches the sea. Even just one of these might be enough to sink a relatively large vessel. Oh, and they will set off anything explosive they come across, so if they find their way to a magazine or hydrogen tank they'll make one hell of a bang!' Wendy grinned, obviously looking forward to witnessing the explosions her weapons caused.

'What if someone gets hit by the acid?' asked Kitty in a quiet voice.

Everyone went silent as a horrific vision of men with their flesh melting off of them springing into their minds - not even the enemy deserved that.

Wendy shook her head, though. 'Nothing would happen to them. The acid only eats through metal.'

Quite a few of the pilots sighed in relief and a couple of green faces started going back to their normal colour.

'Um.' Gwen looked at the device thoughtfully. 'Do you think you could put a warhead like that on a rocket? For if we come up against Bertha?'

Wendy exchanged a glance with Strangeways, whose eyebrows raised, expressing her surprise.

The tiny woman shrugged and nodded. 'We'd have to make the glass receptacle a bit thicker to survive the initial acceleration, but I don't see why not.' She pulled her notebook out of her pocket and flipped to a clean page. 'Don't know why we didn't bloody think of that before. Perhaps we could...' She trailed off, mumbling to herself while she wrote furiously.

The Misfits watched her for a few seconds to see if she would speak to them again, but the woman just wandered off distractedly, so they turned back to Wendy, who shrugged. 'She does that a lot. When she comes back she'll have the solution and probably a better proposal.' She looked to Campbell. 'What do you think, Commodore? Are we going to be able to use these?'

Campbell nodded. 'Oh yes. When can you have them ready?'

'It depends how busy the undersea boat people are. A week? Two? Maybe three if a boat comes back in a bad shape.'

'Make sure they know that this is a priority please.' She waited for Wendy to acknowledge, then gazed around the group. 'In the meantime, the bomber squadrons are ready to start torpedo operations as soon as we have a target.' She looked at Chalky. 'You're authorised to fly tomorrow. I want the shipping lanes scoured every six hours.'

'Yes, ma'am!' The blonde man beamed happily at the prospect of getting back in the air.

'As for the rest of you, I'm pleased to announce that my request has been approved. The boys and girls who just arrived will take over the 261 Squadron designation and Misfit Squadron are now themselves once more and authorised for independent duty.'

She smiled and waited for the boisterous celebrations her announcement sparked to die down before continuing.

'So, I'm going to keep 261 here in reserve, in case the Prussians decide to try something silly, but you lot are going to be flying escort for the bombers - we'll see if we can't cut those supply lines completely.'

Bruce laughed. 'Yeah! And next week we'll conquer Italy!'

CHAPTER 16

Chalky flew regular reconnaissance missions, just as Dorothy Campbell had ordered, but it wasn't until the fourth day that he actually spotted something for the Nelson squadrons to do with their new weapons - twelve ships leaving Tripoli, eight supply ships and four escorts. It was unfortunate that they were sailing towards and not from Italy because they would probably be empty, but that was no reason to let them pass safely.

As Wendy's bombs wouldn't be ready for a while, the Misfits were relegated to a supporting role and were forced to circle and watch as the Nelsons carried out their first ever torpedo runs. Only the thirty-two Nelsons from Luqa had been sent on the mission, the commander of the bomber wing thinking that sixty-four torpedoes would be more than enough to sink all of the ships, but the destruction wasn't quite as comprehensive as he'd hoped.

The Nelson hadn't been designed as a torpedo bomber and the pilots had never trained for it either, so understandably they made quite a few errors, like making their runs too fast or dropping the torpedoes from too high so they couldn't deploy properly. Two of the bombers were also lost to anti-aircraft fire because their pilots had flown straight and level for far too long, trying to get the release exactly right.

Only seven of the ships, including one of the escort destroyers, received direct hits and of those, only five of the supply ships were sinking by the time the Nelsons were on their way home, but it was an encouraging start, despite the losses, and the pilots knew that they would only get better with practice.

That didn't mean the remaining Italian ships made it safely home, though. The bombers from Ta'Kali were given their chance and they sank almost all the remaining ships, for the loss of a single bomber, leaving only one of the faster-moving escort ships to report back to Italy.

With the prospect of very little flying to do over the following weeks until the Coalition could move further aircraft into the area, the Misfits were given a week of leave, with the only stipulation that they remain in contact and be able to get in the air within four hours of an enemy convoy being sighted.

Unfortunately, that meant that Chalky had to remain on duty. He didn't mind one bit, though, and even insisted that he stay in the air the entire day, arguing that it was more hydrogen-efficient to use his balloon to float around, rather than continually going up and down. He used the time to catch up on his reading and service his cameras, although a couple of mornings he was spotted sneaking a woman on board Vulture in the darkness of the hangar.

Several spring-powered RAC vehicles, autocars and motorcycles, were put at the disposal of the rest of the pilots, in case they wanted to go to other parts of the island, and a few of them did just that.

Derek borrowed an autocar so he could tour a few of the vineyards around the island, bringing quite a few samples back with him, which were more than appreciated by the rest of the Misfits. The first day he went with a friend, the RAC officer from Luqa he'd met at the party, but the man had only been able to get that single day off from duty. After that Derek was joined by Scarlet. She wasn't nearly as enthusiastic as he was about wine, but, in the absence of pubs to crawl around, leapt at the opportunity to consume alcohol.

Bruce had somehow managed to make the acquaintance of quite a few women in his brief moments off-duty and he used one of the motorcycles to race around the island, visiting a different one each day. His joking around and easy-going nature, as well as his status as a Misfit, had always made him popular with women, but he had never before been with more than one at a time. However, after he'd been hurt so badly in Muscovy, something had changed in him and on Malta he was flitting from one to another, avoiding any possible commitment by having several "on the hook", as he put it, at a time.

Monty missed his life with the flying circus and secured permission to take Ghoul on an aerial tour of the island, putting on impromptu stunt shows over any village he came across. After the first day every village and town was clamouring for him to visit them and he had to draw up a schedule and publish it in the newspaper, although many of the islanders, especially the children, followed him around to watch show after show.

Wendy had very little to do while Strangeways and the undersea boat squadron workshops created her munitions and spent most of her time with Owen, who was expected to be discharged within a week or two at most.

For some reason, Freddy Featherstonehaugh had not been granted permission to accompany the Misfits to Malta. The British press had almost revolted, threatening to turn the public against the War Minister, whose decision it had been, so he had reluctantly allowed them to appoint Chastity in his stead as an unofficial correspondent. She had made plenty of notes, since arriving on the island, but been kept too busy to do much more than send a weekly digest, so she spent most of her time off at the house or the private beach, writing up reports on the various attacks on the Prussian air bases, the destruction of the Italian convoy and the heroic circumstances of Mac's death. Once she was done, she took them to the undersea boat base to be carried to Gibraltar, where they would be transmitted to the Ministry for approval before being published.

Farrier went and stayed with her naval friends for the entire week in one of the houses they had been assigned on the west coast. It wasn't that she hadn't been fully accepted by the Misfits or made friends with them, it was just that she missed the men and women that she had gotten to know and love from her old ship, the Heart of Oak, and there were so few of the left alive that she felt even more compelled to spend as much time with them as she could.

Abby spent most of her leave with Dorothy Campbell, keeping her friend company while she remained on duty at Hal Far, sitting in her office and rereading the letters from Jimmy which had come with the convoy. He had protested as much as ever when he'd been left behind, but had been quickly won over when the King himself had found him a place with the Royal Guard Squadron at Hyde Airfield to continue working as a fitter.

With the help of Father Bugelli, Tanya and Rudy found a small house in a picturesque area just north of Birzebbuga. They moved in for a few days to have some time alone for a kind of anticipatory honeymoon, not knowing whether they would ever get the chance to do so again.

Neither Gwen nor Kitty much cared what they did, as long as they did it together. They went for walks in the town, along the beach and spent a lot of time in their room in the house, taking advantage of the fact that hardly anyone else was there. Gwen did ask to have a few hours to herself, though and Kitty was puzzled by her request, but agreed because she wanted to speak to Dorothy Campbell about contacting Generale Jilani and making sure that the Marinos had gotten home alright.

Gwen walked to Hal Far in her work coveralls first thing in the morning, while Kitty was still getting her uniform on, and went in search of Giuseppe. She'd already let him know that she would be coming and he had what she'd asked him to get from the Graveyard, so many weeks before, ready for her in the small workshop.

The Misfit aircraft had been so comprehensively destroyed on the ground when they'd arrived that there was very little left of Hawk for Gwen to play with. The wings and fuselage had been so filled with holes that Giuseppe had only been able to cut away four small pieces of Duralumin, but, rather surprisingly, two of the instruments had survived the ruin of the cockpit - the air speed indicator and the artificial horizon that sat next to it. It made a depressingly small pile on the workbench, but it was enough for what Gwen intended.

She had never been particularly artistic. Her drawings had always been true to life or strictly functional and her efforts at sculpting clay had been laughable at best, but she knew how metal went together and she could see how the instruments and metal panels could be joined to make something that would be pleasing to the eye. Especially for an aviator. The only really artistic choice she had to make was what part of the panels to use to best show off the colours of Hawk.

She held the picture of the finished piece in her mind and began to cut. For someone with her background in aircraft construction it was an easy matter to shape the panel into what she wanted and it took less than half an hour for her quick hands to finish with the Duralumin. It was then only a matter of fitting the instruments and attaching them to the small clockwork mechanism she'd asked Giuseppe to acquire for her so that they wouldn't just be dead things.

She took another ten minutes to smooth the edges of the metal and polish it to a high shine, but then it was done and she stood back to admire it, inspecting it from all sides. Satisfied, she wrapped it in a felt cloth and hefted it in her arms for the walk back to the house.

'I think you've thanked me enough now.' Gwen gasped, wiping the sweat from her brow.

The American smiled down at her from where she was propped up on her elbow, her free hand trailing idly over Gwen's belly. 'I don't know if I'll *ever* have thanked you enough...'

Gwen groaned. 'You're going to kill me...'

'I doubt it,' Kitty laughed. 'What a way to go, though.'

She bent down and stole Gwen's remaining breath away with a deep kiss.

When they came up for air, Gwen rolled onto her side and Kitty cuddled up behind her and together, they looked towards the nightstand, where what Gwen had created sat, shining brightly in a beam of sunshine from the open window.

It stood about two-foot tall and was made from a single piece of Duralumin, which was mostly blue, apart from thin red and white stripes at the very top. Gwen had bent the panel ninety degrees, about a third of the way from its bottom, then gently curled it back under itself, forming a base so that it would stand on its own. She had rippled the top of the horizontal surface and scored it gently so that it looked like the sea over which they flew every day. From that sea, the vertical plate rose like the sky and, at the very top, Gwen had engraved the metal, incorporating the red and white into the familiar silhouette of Hawk, forever climbing into the air.

To finish it off, she had embedded the instruments in the base, where it curled back on itself, so that they faced outwards and hidden the clockwork mechanism behind them. The wind up device kept them powered, their indicators live, and a tiny switch on the back of the base toggled their interior lights on and off.

Gwen had been afraid she would be reopening an old wound with the sculpture, but Kitty's expression when she had first seen it had told her that the wound had never healed and probably never would. She hoped that her gesture would provide a modicum of closure for the woman, though, at least until they could rebuild her aircraft.

She turned over to face Kitty and stroked her hair absently while gazing into her clear blue eyes.

Kitty must have seen something in her expression because a frown creased her smooth and lightly sun-browned brow. 'What's up, darling?'

'Nothing.'

Kitty raised an eyebrow and grinned at her sardonically and Gwen grimaced; Kitty knew her too well and was too American to let her get away with being so British.

'I'm, er, wondering if we'll ever get a chance to rebuild Hawk for you.'

Kitty chuckled. 'Right... and what else?'

'What do you mean?'

'I mean you've been very clingy since I got back. Don't get me wrong, I'm not complaining, and it's not as if I haven't been too, but I'm the one who was captured and threatened with being Gruberized, not you.'

'*Gruberized?*' Gwen laughed. 'That sounds like one of the processes people keep inventing names for, like vulcanized rubber, or teslarized batteries.'

'It does a bit, doesn't it?' Kitty grinned. 'It's pretty catchy, maybe I'll invent a new waste-management process that I can use the name for after the war.' She put on a voice like a radio announcer. '*Has your garbage been Gruberized? Never flush a toilet again, just Gruberize!*' She chuckled then turned serious again. 'Now, stop changing the subject and just bloody tell me what's on your mind!'

Gwen started at the commanding tone in Kitty's voice. She considered jokingly reminding her who had the highest rank, but decided against it; there was just something about the young woman's expression that told her she wouldn't put up with her beating around the bush any longer.

She sighed. 'Alright. Yes, I'm being "clingy" these days because I was sure I was never going to get you back, but that's only part of it, it's...' Gwen took a deep breath as she tried to sort out the thoughts and feelings she'd denied for so long but had been unable to keep under control since Kitty's capture. 'When we arrived and the aircraft were destroyed, things were damn hard for a while, then when Mac was killed I thought he was just going to be the first of us to die, that me or Abby would be next. But that didn't happen and we got the Spitsteams and now it looks like we're winning somehow. Yes, we've lost Drummond and Smith, and Owen is...' she stopped, unable to continue as her stomach heaved involuntarily when the vision of the horribly scarred man swam into her mind. She pushed the image away and forced herself to continue. 'Look, all I'm trying to say is that things are going *far* better than they should be. We're *so* vulnerable her it's laughable, and if the Prussians realise that, then things will start going very badly, very quickly, and we've got nowhere to go...' she trailed off, her thoughts too jumbled to express herself clearly. 'Do you know what I'm saying?'

'Of course!' Kitty smiled. 'And everybody's thinking that, darling, you can see it in their faces.'

'Can you? Because I can't.'

'That's because your daddy's not a psychiatrist. Mine is. Anyway, that stuff Rudy said to you in Muscovy is true just as much for the *possibility* of losing people as it is for *actually* losing them - all we can do is fight as hard as we can in the air and live our lives to the fullest on the ground. That way, when our time comes, and it will, there are no regrets.' She reached out to tuck a lock of Gwen's unruly hair behind her ear. 'And believe me, I *do* intend to live what time we have left to the fullest.'

A slow smile spread across the American's face. 'Speaking of which, I still don't think I've thanked you nearly enough for my present yet.'

Gwen looked at her in alarm. 'Don't you dare! I haven't...' Her voice trailed off in a moan as Kitty leaned forwards to kiss the soft skin of the side of her neck. 'That's not fair; you know I can't resist... oh!'

Gwen felt herself melting into the pillow and losing all sense of herself, but, before she let go completely, there was something she needed to say. 'By the way, I quite liked it when you went all bossy. Feel free to do it again sometime...'

CHAPTER 17

The week was over far too quickly and the Misfits returned to duty. There was still no sign of any movement by the Fliegertruppe, the Legione Aerea, or any ships, but, instead of extending leave, Abby let the Misfits know in uncertain terms that the fun was over and that they had work to do. So, the next morning, after a moderately lazy breakfast, they wandered down to the airfield together.

Normally, when they passed through the town at the crack of dawn it was deserted and quiet, apart from a few fishermen making their way down to the sea, but it was later than usual and it was alive with people.

Things were still hard for the islanders. The government was worried that the convoy might be the last to arrive for a while and had imposed rationing, just in case. The ships had been unloaded directly into storehouses scattered around the island and supplies were parcelled out from them. It was a lot of extra work, with each village having to collect and then distribute the food every day, but it was a hardship that the islanders faced willingly, knowing that the British were dealing with them as fairly as possible and suffering the same privations that they were.

The inhabitants of Birzebbuga turned out en masse to meet the wagons each morning and many of the men, women, and children paused in what they were doing to wave or shout a greeting as the Misfits went past and the pilots cheerfully responded.

Hal Far was a short distance from the town along a quiet country lane and as they crested a slight hill the pilots caught sight of the airfield. They were surprised to see their aircraft lined up on the apron, but they were even more surprised to see that there were two unfamiliar grey machines among them, in place of two of the Spitsteams and more than one pilot crammed their heads into the helmets they'd been carrying so as to get a better look with their lenses.

'Our fighters!' Tanya exchanged a glance and a grin with Drake and then the two of them broke out into a run, racing each other.

The other Misfits laughed and called out encouragement, but just kept to their leisurely pace; the pair were still wearing standard issue RAC flightsuits and they would never have been able to keep up with them in their custom suits with the pockets of liquid in their thighs stiffening their legs.

The two pilots had put on weight since the arrival of the Misfits and the lessening of their duties, but they still hadn't recovered fully and the Misfits jeered and catcalled good-naturedly when neither of them made it anywhere near all the way to the flight line. Drake and Tanya didn't pay them a blind bit of notice, though, they only had eyes for their aircraft.

While the Muscovite went straight to her aircraft and began clambering over it with her fitters, Drake slowed and stopped a few feet away from his, not because he didn't desperately want to do the same, but because there was something he had to take care of first.

Gertrude Forrester was standing in front of the aircraft, her hands on hips, gazing at the grey machine, *smiling*.

'Well, Sergeant? Will she do?'

Forrester started and blinked at him, surprised. Her smile immediately disappeared, replaced by her usual dour expression, but it was too late; he had seen it and she knew it. She sighed and shook her head, then gave him a wry smile. 'Yes, sir, she'll do.'

Drake grinned. 'Come on then, show me around.'

Forrester gave him another smile, which made her seem much younger and almost carefree, but then it was gone as she got down to the serious business of showing the pilot around *her* aircraft.

Drake and Tanya had listened to Bruce and Monty's reasoning for why they liked to have identical aircraft and had decided that they were going to do the same. They had begun designing a fighter around a Hawking cage, something that Drake insisted on, having had his life saved by it twice already, but, no matter how many drawings they had done, it had always come out looking quite like a Harridan. They wouldn't have minded too much because they both loved the aircraft, but they had known full well that it could be improved on and had enlisted Gwen's help to do so, knowing she had always wanted the chance. Their aircraft were the result of that collaboration and in the end bore only a passing resemblance to the Harridan, with an elongated and sharper nose, a fuselage that lacked the distinctive hump and wings that were more similar to those of a Spitsteam.

Campbell came to meet the Misfits as they sauntered up to the flight line. She grinned and jerked her thumb over her shoulder. 'Looks like the children are happy with their new toys.'

'Wouldn't you be?'

'Of course!'

'And we've got some toys to play with too.' Abby nodded towards the tubes hanging beneath the wings of fighters. She raised her voice. 'Drake! Guseva! When you are *quite* finished!'

Drake and Tanya quickly hopped down from their aircraft and rather sheepishly joined the rest of the squadron.

'What are you calling them and how are you painting them?' asked Abby.

Drake looked at Tanya who shrugged with one shoulder as a signal for him to speak for them both.

'They're called Lion and Wolf,' he said, 'to honour our pasts. And as for the colours - no pink, thank the fates.'

There were chuckles from the Misfits, who all looked at Gwen, who tutted and shook her head.

Drake waited for quiet before he continued. 'We're going to use the standard camouflage pattern, but in colours that mean something to us as well.' He gestured to the aircraft in turn. 'Wolf will have white and grey camouflage and I was going to use red and yellow on Lion, but with red being such a complicated colour right now I've decided on a lovely regal purple instead.'

'Ouch!' Bruce said, wincing. 'It hurts just thinking about that. It's not too late to go with the pink...'

'I think I'll pass, thank you,' Drake said, winking at Gwen.

'Any word on when everyone else's machines are coming, Abby?' asked Derek quietly.

Abby shook her head. 'Sorry, Derek, it doesn't look like they're going to be coming any time soon; Luqa only finished these for us because they were already pretty well advanced, but with the bombers operational now, they can't afford to devote their time to making our aircraft, although they have told me they wish they could. It looks like the rest of you are going to have to go without for the foreseeable future.'

With the arrival of Wolf and Lion, only Derek, Chastity, Kitty and Farrier were still flying Spitsteams. Farrier of course wouldn't have an aircraft constructed for her because she was only temporarily a Misfit. She had already been reassigned to the Arturo and would go with her when she sailed.

'Right then, I'm sure that Rudy and Tanya are dying to get in the air and frankly so am I, so let's get to work.' Abby changed the subject before people could start to feel too sorry for themselves. 'As some of the more eagle-eyed among you may have noticed, we've all got Wendy's thingamabobs on our wings.' She looked at the big woman. 'Have you come up with a good name for these things yet?'

'I'm thinking *Peas* in *Pods*.'

'Peas in...' Abby trailed off and stared at Wendy, who nodded sincerely.

There was an awkward silence as the pilots tried to reconcile Wendy's name with the bombs and the tubes they were carried in. Admittedly, they were very much like peas in a pod, but the name really didn't do their potential destructive power justice.

Wendy laughed. 'You should see your faces! I'm only joking! The tubes under the wings I *am* calling Pods, but the munitions I'm calling *meltbombs*.'

Abby shook her head. 'You do know I'm your commanding officer, right? And it's not a good idea to tease me?'

Wendy gave her a half smile and shrugged. 'What are you going to do? Make me stop developing weapons for you?'

'Actually I was thinking I might ground you.'

Wendy laughed again. 'Ground me? But I'm not flying...' She stopped speaking suddenly as she realised what Abby was implying and looked from her to Campbell and back again. 'Do you...? Is...? Can I...?'

Abby nodded. 'Dreadnought has been cleared for operations and so has Bloodhound, whenever Owen is ready to take her up.'

Wendy nodded gratefully. 'Thank you, I'll let him know. I'm sure he'll be over the moon.'

'As soon as you can put your machine back together and equip her with torpedoes and or meltbombs you'll be joining us for the raids on enemy shipping.'

Wendy rubbed her hands together gleefully. 'It's about bloody time I got to have some fun!'

Bruce rolled his eyes. 'Oh come off it, half the island has heard the "tests" you've been doing every day for the last month or so. You can't tell me you haven't been having fun.'

Wendy grinned at him. 'Ah, but some things are so much more fun in the air...' She paused deliberately and turned to look at Chalky. 'Isn't that right, Charles?'

While the Misfit fighter pilots trained with the new weapons and Scarlet aided Wendy with Dreadnought, Chalky continued to watch for enemy ships. After the destruction of the first convoy, it was more than likely that the Italians would start giving Malta a wide berth as they tried to reinforce and supply their forces in North Africa, so he was now flying a route of more than five hundred miles in order to cover all possible shipping lanes. First thing in the morning he went west to within sight of Tunisia, where he deployed his balloon and hovered to look up and down the coast with the powerful lenses on his cameras to make sure that no ships were sneaking along the coastline of Africa. After a few hours, when he was sure there was nothing in the offing, he flew east, back to the island, where he changed course slightly to the north, in order to inspect the shipping lanes off the coast of Greece, one of Britain's few remaining allies.

The Italian and Prussian forces in North Africa were under considerable pressure from the British and were in desperate need of supply, but, even so, it was a whole ten days since the last convoy before Chalky spotted the next one. The reason for the delay was immediately apparent, though; the Italians were putting all their eggs in one basket and sending a large convoy with as large an escort as they could. They weren't trying to sneak past either, but were taking the direct route to Libya, relying on force rather than stealth to get them past Malta - an understandable tactic given that the convoy was far too big to effectively conceal.

It had only been four days since the Misfits had come back from their time off and to Wendy's disgust, Dreadnought was not yet ready to fly, but the other pilots and aircraft were.

The Misfits had mastered the technique required to drop the meltbombs in the first few hours of practice, but Abby had insisted that they continue to train. However, after the first day of serious, focussed, and extremely tiring work, she allowed them to relax a bit and make a game out of it.

A target, less than five yards across, comprised of concentric rings like an archery butt, was painted on the airfield, and the Misfits took it in turns trying to hit the bullseye. To make things interesting, their scores were added up and the prize for the overall winner at the end of each day was to be served breakfast in bed the next morning by the lowest scorer.

Bruce was the clear loser the first two days. His scores weren't bad and he never missed the target by much, but he never quite managed the accuracy of the others; his talents definitely ran to other things than bombing. He ended up having to serve Chastity breakfast one day, which he didn't mind one bit, but Monty the second. His subordinate and wingman made the most of the opportunity to lord it over his leader, demanding that he call him sir, serve him with a tea towel over his arm and that he bow before he left the room.

Bruce took it in his stride with a smile, but after he had performed his duties he informed his wingman that he would be getting his own back that day.

It looked like the Australian would make good on his promise, as an inspired Bruce scored bullseye after bullseye and an increasingly nervous Monty lagged well behind the others. However, he was ultimately denied his chance for revenge when Chalky's alert came in at lunchtime and further training was cancelled indefinitely.

Abby, Campbell, Scarlet and Chalky were called to Luqa to analyse the photographs and prepare an assault plan after lunch and the rest of the Misfits drove to Luqa after dinner that evening for a briefing with the combined RAC forces.

It was a far less festive occasion than the last time they had visited the base as a squadron, but they were made no less welcome. This time they were met on the airfield by the base commander himself, who shook their hands before leading them down into the enormous hangar and through it to a briefing hall that was easily large enough to hold several thousand people. Like the one at Hal Far it was sparsely decorated, with bright lights overhead and the same green walls and maroon carpet. The Misfits immediately saw that the wooden chairs were identical as well and remained standing as long as they could, remembering exactly how uncomfortable they were. Abby, Scarlet and Chalky had done their jobs and they joined them now. Scarlet and Chalky had plates full of sandwiches, which they shared with anyone who was still peckish after dinner, but when Bruce asked for a swig of Scarlet's beer instead she told him to "bog off" and downed the rest of it in one go, to laughs from the bomber crews gathered around, discreetly watching them.

The Misfits were among the last to arrive, so they didn't have long to wait before the senior officers mounted the dais and the briefing was called to order.

When everybody sat down, the Misfits got their first clear view of the corkboards on the raised platform at the front of the room. They had been expecting to see blown-up photographs of the convoy, but were surprised when there were only the same maps as they had at Hal Far on the boards.

While the rest of the officers took their seats at the side of the stage, Dorothy Campbell remained standing, and, when everyone was settled, she used a microphone, set up at the front of the stage, to address the room.

'Evening, ladies and gentlemen. As you may have heard, we have some work for you to do - a new and much larger convoy has left Italy and is steaming southwards. We're obviously going to attack it, but before we get into details of the plan, I've asked Captain Hewer to give us an idea of what we're going up against.'

Campbell nodded to Hewer, who smiled back as he stood and moved over to take her place, ignoring the microphone and just raising his voice.

He nodded to a woman standing next to a projector in the central aisle of the hall and the woman bent and cranked a handle on the machine. A soft ticking noise began and a light started to flicker behind its glass lenses. The overhead lamps were then turned off one by one, until the room was in darkness, apart from the beam of light shining onto a white canvas screen on the wall at the back of the stage.

'Oh, goody! I hope this one's got that Gruber chap in it; I like him! Lovely hair!'

'Lieutenant Walker!' Campbell called out from her seat after the jeering at Bruce's comment had died down. 'Don't make me come down there and put you over my knee!'

'Yes, ma'am!'

There was more laughter, but it was quickly replaced by an expectant silence when the first images came on to the screen.

One of the improvements Chalky had made to Vulture over the Midwinter period was the addition of a movie camera. Unlike the gun cameras that were sometimes fitted to fighters, which resulted in very poor quality images because of the small size of the camera and the vibration of the fighters, Chalky had been able to requisition and install a Hollywoodland-quality one. He had fit it with lenses of his own design and the resulting images were almost as clear as if he'd been hovering just overhead in one of the camera Zeppelins they used for the bigger-budget flyvies.

It was an impressive bit of camerawork. First, the entire convoy was held perfectly framed, giving the audience a chance to take in its sheer size and see for the first time that the sleek grey shapes of the ships, with their wakes streaming out behind them, shining brightly in the sunshine, were accompanied by the white lozenges of airships. After a few seconds the image magnified smoothly, homing in on the lead vessel so that it filled the entire screen with enough detail not only to identify its type, but also read the identification number on the bow. The image held for a few seconds, then there was a slight break before the next vessel was shown; Chalky had evidently stopped recording while he swung the camera onto his next target, preventing the sickening swoop that was typical of less expertly shot surveillance movies.

After a few minutes the reel on the projector clattered as it ran out of film and the technician switched over to static display mode, bringing up a photograph of the convoy in its entirety as Hewer began to speak.

'The maritime convoy is made up of thirty-six cargo vessels of varying types and ten military vessels. The cargo vessels are lightly-armoured and most are unarmed, however a few have small-calibre anti-aircraft guns mounted on their fore and aft decks. There are two battleships and six destroyers, but they are there to tackle ships and undersea boats and have very little in the way of anti-aircraft weaponry, so they shouldn't be too much of a bother to you either. No, it's these blighters that you're going to have to worry about.'

The technician brought up a photograph of a wide ship, bristling with guns, all of which were pointed skywards.

'As far as we know there are only three of these in existence and two of them are with the convoy. They're called *Giavellotto*, or "Javelin" anti-aircraft ships and are relatively new, having been built only a few years ago. So, unlike the majority of the Italian fleet, they are not obsolete relics of the last war. They are dedicated to naval air defence and are typically armed with forty of the latest ack-ack guns and another forty thirty-seven millimetre cannon, both of which are capable of engaging targets at up to twenty-five or thirty thousand feet.'

Hewer looked over his shoulder at the photograph still being projected and held his hand up to cast a shadow on it. 'As you can see, the top deck is completely clear of any obstructions, apart from safety rails - there are no funnels, no masts and no bridge to get in the way of the guns, meaning that each of the eighty guns has almost a full hemisphere in which to target enemy aircraft, down almost to sea level.'

He let the information sink in for a few seconds before he continued. 'These aren't the only threat you'll be facing, though. Commodore?'

Hewer stepped back and Campbell took centre stage again. 'Next photograph, please?' Campbell waited for the next image, that of a large airship, to click into place before beginning. 'There are twelve of these with the ships. The Italians call them *Cittadelle Volanti* - "Flying Citadels" - although we used to call them "Bristly Pigs" back in the last war. They are far larger than the airships that dropped bombs on Malta at the start of the siege, but are still several orders of magnitude smaller than Bertha. They are single-hulled and have twenty-eight anti-aircraft cannon emplacements which are concentrated mostly on the top or sides, with only four mounted underneath. The guns are of a lesser calibre than those mounted on the Javelins and are much shorter ranged, having been designed to counter much slower and lower-flying aircraft. Unless they've been replaced, of course, which is a distinct possibility. The Pigs were phased out towards the middle of the Great War, as aircraft technology advanced and they were rendered completely useless in the offensive role for which they were intended, but Captain Hewer and I agree that they are an inspired choice for the job of convoy defence.'

The photograph changed back to one that displayed the whole convoy and Campbell used her hand like Hewer had to point to the airships ringing the ships. 'Unless the wind picks up, we expect the Pigs to maintain this formation - low, in a circle around the supply ships, but inside the screening ships, as a secondary line of defence after the Javelins. Lights please.'

Campbell waited for the light level to slowly come up, giving everyone a few seconds for their eyes to adjust before she went on.

'Now that you know what the enemy has, here is the mission plan. Aviator Lieutenant Isaacs will take off at oh four hundred hours tomorrow so that he will be in position to spot the convoy at first light. By that time the convoy should be somewhere between one hundred and one hundred and fifty miles east of Malta, but he will relay the exact coordinates to us so that when the rest of you take off at oh six hundred hours you'll have a precise heading. Arrival over the convoy will be staggered, with two minute intervals between the groups. Misfit Squadron, will go in first and use their new weapons on the Javelins. Once they've had their chance, 261 Squadron will go after the Pigs.

Then, when 261 are fully engaged, the Nelsons will go in with their torpedoes to attack the supply ships, ignoring the screening battleships and destroyers as much as possible. I leave it up to the individual squadron commanders to decide how best to carry out their tasks, but they will be given precise timings for when to start their runs. However, we all know that these things never work out quite as well in practice as they do on paper, so Group Captain Lennox will have command in the air and the authority to make changes as circumstances dictate.' She turned her eyes on Abby. 'There's no need for me to tell you how vital your role in the battle is, but I'm going to anyway - if those ships are left untouched they will annihilate the Nelsons. So, if you can't knock them out then that's it, mission's over and you pull everyone out. Understood, Group Captain?'

Abby nodded, but her reply was drowned out in a wave of protests from the bomber crews.

Campbell held up her hands for silence, but had to wait for a good twenty seconds before she got it. 'We all know how important it is to our people in Africa that convoys like this don't get through and I know you all want to have a go at it, but if the Misfits can't knock out the Javelins first, then there's nothing we can do. The boys and girls in the undersea boats are already poised to do their bit and we'll just have to let them get the glory this time. There will be more chances later, I assure you.'

Voices were raised in complaint once more and Campbell glared at the culprits. 'No!' Her magnified voice drowned out the protests, but the subsequent squeal of feedback stopped them completely, causing most people to wince. 'This is non-negotiable! I hope it doesn't come to it, but you *will* return to base if told to do so and I will personally make sure that anyone who disobeys *never* flies again. Squadron Leader Dunstable.'

'Yes, ma'am?' The man in charge of the Spitsteam squadron stood.

'If Group Captain Lennox falls in the assault on the Javelins, you will assume command and make sure that everyone else is brought home safely. Understood?'

'Yes, ma'am.'

As the squadron leader took his seat again there were a few discontented mutters, but no more arguments.

Looking around, Gwen could see from their faces that, while they didn't like the Sky Commodore's decision one bit, they at least understood it. She just hoped they would obey it, otherwise the defence of Malta might well be brought to an abrupt end.

'Good.' Campbell nodded in satisfaction, then looked around the room. 'Right then, does anybody have any questions?'

Abby put her hand up and the Sky Commodore pointed at her. 'Yes, Group Captain?'

'I have a question for Captain Hewer, ma'am. Captain, you said that the guns on the Javelins can target *almost* to sea level. What does that mean *exactly*?'

Hewer moved to the front of the stage before answering. 'According to the information we have on these ships, the barrels of the thirty guns in the lower, outer ring are thirty-six feet above the sea and cannot depress below the horizon.' Hewer smiled. 'Why? Are you thinking of flying under that?'

Abby nodded earnestly. 'Yes. Unless anyone has a better way of attacking them?'

Hewer blinked at her, then turned to look at the men and women sharing the stage with him. When none of them said anything he turned back to her and shrugged, giving her a wry smile. 'Looks like they haven't. Best of luck to you, Group Captain, and watch out for the wave tops!'

Abby grinned. 'Thank you, Captain.'

There was silence in the wagon on the way back to Birzebbuga, as the pilots contemplated the task ahead of them and it lasted until they gathered in the lounge of the house to hear Abby's plan of attack for the morning.

'Eighty anti-aircraft guns... That's a hell of a lot, Boss.'

Abby grinned. 'There could be a thousand of them and it still wouldn't matter if they can't target us.'

'You weren't serious when you said we would fly underneath their guns, were you?' Farrier scoffed and looked around, obviously expecting the other pilots to support her, but when they all just smiled knowingly her eyes widened and her voice rose about an octave. 'But we'd have to be on the deck as soon as we were within range! That's five or six miles! We can't possibly survive that low for that long; if there's a rogue wave or a gust of wind we'd just hit the water! Hell, if we sneeze we'll probably end up in Neptune's grasp!'

'I'd rather rely on my own skill and that of my pilots than face those guns.' Abby said calmly. 'The only other alternative is to fly to them maximum height then dive at top speed, but even then we'd be under fire for almost a minute and they'd have to be very unlucky not to hit any of us in that time.' Her expression turned hard and she looked around, meeting the gaze of her pilots one by one. 'Having said that, this is a volunteer mission only. Anyone who doesn't feel up to the challenge can join the Spitsteam squadron in the attack on the Pigs.'

Her eyes came to rest on Farrier and her eyebrows raised questioningly.

There was an awkward moment as the young woman blushed in shame and looked away, shaking her head, but then Bruce tutted, breaking the tension and rolled his eyes. 'Blimey, Abby, you're as melodramatic as Gruber. Of course we're all bloody in, so just hurry up and tell us what the plan is so that we can go to bed!'

CHAPTER 18

The Misfit aircraft, weighed down with Wendy's weapons, slowly climbed towards the rising sun, following Chalky's directions. It had been dark on the ground when they had taken off, but the higher they had gotten, the brighter the horizon had become until suddenly, at ten thousand feet, they had broken into sunlight. Darkened lenses were brought down on helmets, but they weren't nearly enough and the pilots had to squint against the glare every time they looked ahead, straining to catch their first glimpse of the convoy.

Gwen looked past Dragon to where Kitty's Spitsteam, which the American had found already painted for her on her return from Sicily, was on Abby's other wing as Badger Three. The group captain had changed the squadron formation and reassigned callsigns, then split it in two, allocating one of the Javelins as a target to each five-aircraft half. Gwen had been extremely relieved to hear that the American would be staying with them; in a fight that was going to be this tough she didn't want her out of sight for even a second.

'Badger Leader to all Badgers, we're ten miles out. Looks like the Javelins are still fore and aft of the convoy.'

Gwen cursed when she realised that she had gotten distracted. She dragged her eyes from the red, white and blue striped Spitsteam and peered over Excalibur's nose and down at the convoy. Even with her lenses in place the ships were still little more than grey rectangles with the thin white cones of their wakes stretching out behind them, but it was easy to distinguish the two Javelins, with their much wider beam, on either end of the untidy clump of merchant ships.

Any doubts the Misfits had over whether they had been spotted or not were dispelled when the first black clouds of ack-ack fire burst in the air at least a mile in front of them.

'Three here, Leader. Those came from the outlying destroyer. I saw the flashes of their guns.'

'Thank you, Three. Looks like we've made them nervous.'

'Just wait until they see what we do next.' Bruce chuckled.

'Indeed, Seven.' Abby said. 'All Badgers, prepare to dive on my mark.'

Abby drew the moment out for a few seconds, unnecessarily as far as Gwen was concerned, and she glanced across to find her wingmate grinning, her excitement evident, despite the calm of her voice.

'Mark!'

Gwen's stomach, or rather the bacon sandwich and mug of tea she had ingested an hour before, made its presence known as the Misfits nosed over sharply, going from level flight to a forty-five degree dive in an instant.

It was none too soon, either; Abby had judged the distance to the convoy very finely and, just as they manoeuvred, both of the Javelins were lit up brightly.

Seconds later, the air where the Misfits would have been erupted in black smoke, which was instantly ripped to shreds by the passage of heavy calibre cannon rounds.

'Cutting it a bit fine, weren't we, Leader?'

Derek's dry voice brought a smile to Gwen's lips, even as she concentrated on the rapidly plunging altimeter and the dark sea, seemingly so close below.

'Perfectly calculated, Six.'

'Uh, Boss, I think they've worked out what we're doing.'

Bruce's comment puzzled Gwen for a second, but then a bright flash and a puff of black, accompanied by the ping of metal striking Excalibur, startled her and she realised that the barrage from the Javelins had not only been following them down, but had caught up with them.

'Damn, Hewer said the guns wouldn't be able to traverse that quickly. All Badgers, follow me.'

Gwen fought to keep up as Abby pushed her stick forwards once more, steepening the dive almost to the vertical.

The airspeed indicator on Gwen's instrument panel surged upwards, even as the altimeter began to rotate alarmingly fast, counting down the feet to the unforgiving sea below.

If before it was going to be a risky proposition, pulling up from a moderate dive only a few feet above the waves, now it was going to be almost suicidal and Gwen spared a thought for Drake, Tanya and Farrier, who were stuck in standard issue flightsuits and would have no help resisting the extreme G forces they would have to pull. The move had taken the Italian gunners by surprise, though, and the deadly black clouds were once again bursting safely above them.

The altimeter passed five thousand feet, spinning dizzily, and Gwen had to fight the urge to jerk her stick back, her survival instincts, yelling at her that it was already too late, warring with her piloting ones, which calmly insisted there was still plenty of time.

'That should be enough. Whenever you feel like it, Badgers.'

Unlike a normal squadron, where everybody was flying the same type of aircraft with similar characteristics and capabilities, the performance of the Misfit aircraft varied widely, especially with the addition of the heavy weapons under their wings slowing them and changing their flight characteristics. That was why they had practised this manoeuvre so many times and that was why Abby had to let everybody judge for themselves when they needed to pull up.

The Spitsteams were first and from Gwen's perspective it was as if they had reached the end of an elastic and rebounded into the sky, even though they were still descending at a tremendous rate. She watched Kitty's aircraft for a second, but then forced herself to concentrate on her own flying.

She had tested Excalibur extensively in England before embarking and knew perfectly well how quickly she could pull out of a power dive, exactly like the one she was in. She had never done it under such extreme conditions, though, and also had no idea how the battle damage she had sustained since then, or the piece of shrapnel that had just hit her, had affected her aircraft's performance.

She decided to play it safe and gave herself an extra two hundred feet to carry out the manoeuvre, doing it rather more gently than she could have. Even so, she was the last of the Misfits to pull up and when she had levelled off above the sea she was well out in front of everyone else and she throttled back to give everyone else a chance to catch up.

Abby was first to come into her peripheral vision and as Gwen tucked Excalibur in on Dragon's wing she spared a split second to glance over at her.

'Mac would have enjoyed that, Leader.'

'Yes, he would, Two. Yes he would.'

There were murmurs of agreement from many in the squadron, but then silence fell as they each concentrated on just staying alive.

After a single glance at her altimeter Gwen pointedly ignored it and fixed her gaze on the horizon instead; the needle was wavering slightly with minute changes in air pressure, going from one side of the nought to the other in an extremely disconcerting manner.

Thankfully, the Mediterranean was normally quite placid and weather conditions in the last few days had been very good, so there were almost no waves to worry about, but even so, every so often a freak convergence in the currents or the wind, something that Gwen didn't really understand, would send spray reaching up for the aircraft.

However, while the sea below was calm, a storm raged less than a five yards above them.

The flak created a solid bank of black clouds which roiled and flashed as explosion after explosion rocked them, sending tiny shards of metal floating down to patter relatively harmlessly on the aircraft.

It was hard not to flinch away from the death above, but the death below was just as real and the Misfits were caught between the two, flying a narrow passage of safety where a single slip or moment of inattention would surely end everything in a heartbeat.

An aircraft routinely made random up and down and side to side motions during flight because of wind, air currents and such, and a pilot would usually pay no heed to them, but Gwen's hand was a death grip on the stick and her legs were in constant tension as she fought each and every deviation the instant she felt it, in an attempt to keep Excalibur exactly where she was in the very centre of the thin patch of clear air.

Making matters worse was a worrying creaking noise, easily audible over the thunder of the barrage. Every chance she could get, Gwen shot glances at her wings and instruments, trying to find the problem, wondering if something was coming loose and would plunge her nose first into the drink.

It took her a good thirty seconds to work out that it was her own teeth making the noise, that she was grinding them unconsciously, something she hadn't done since her first nervous presentations in front of the Société Aéronautique.

Realising she was being ridiculous, that she had a good ten feet to play with, both above and below her, she forced herself to relax her hands and legs and worked her jaw to get rid of the stiffness.

'Thirty seconds to target. Good luck everybody. Badger Six, B flight is yours.'

'Thank you, Leader.' Derek replied. 'See you on the other side.'

The Misfits had been heading for the centre of the enemy formation, so as not to give away their intentions, but now they split into their two groups and changed course abruptly towards their assigned Javelins. A Flight, led by Abby, with Gwen, Kitty, Farrier and Chastity as Badgers Two to Five turned for the one at the front, while B Flight, led by Derek as Badger Six, with Bruce, Monty, Drake and Tanya as Badgers Seven to Ten, aimed for the rear one.

'Ten seconds.'

'For what we are about to receive...'

The old blasphemy, muttered almost under his breath by Monty, drew no reactions - the pilots were far too engrossed in their own thoughts and fears to even hear him properly, as the seconds counted down to when they would have to pull up into the hell that waited for them in order to drop the meltbombs onto the decks of the Javelins.

The ack-ack had stopped as they had drawn too near for the shells to have time to arm, but the near-invisible cannon fire was still there, still providing a layer of metal above them in which nothing could survive. The Misfits had one last surprise for the gunners, though, and, right before they had to come up off the deck, the pilots kicked their rudders hard, splitting the flights and slewing their aircraft to either side of where the fire was concentrated.

Sticks came back into laps and the aircraft popped up, surging to a hundred feet in less than a second, taking them above the fire that was desperately trying to follow them. Again, the enemy tried to compensate, but a stomp on the opposite rudder swerved the aircraft back in the opposite direction, confounding them again, before sticks went forwards, bringing the noses of the aircraft back below the horizon at exactly the same moment as the ships came into their sights.

Levers were pulled and meltbombs were dropped, then the Javelins were past and the Misfits dived back down onto the safety of the wave tops, their aircraft suddenly so much more responsive after ridding themselves of their excess baggage.

All eyes went to the mirrors above their heads, looking for the results of the attack.

The one drawback with the meltbombs, at least as far as Wendy was concerned anyway, was the lack of a satisfyingly big explosion, which meant that there had originally been no way of knowing if the munitions had actually hit their target or not. Georgina Strangeways had solved that problem, though, by adding a small smoke packet to the bombs and, as the Misfits watched, red smoke billowed up from multiple points around the decks of the Javelins.

Almost instantly the flashes from the guns came to a halt as the gunners found they had other, more important things to do.

'How long until...' The words were barely out of Gwen's mouth before a huge explosion rocked the Javelin behind her, then another, and another. 'Oh, not long then.'

The laughter began slowly but picked up pace and volume as every single pilot joined in, some of the tension of the attack flowing from them. It took a while, but gradually it died down and then Abby's voice came over the radio. 'Is anybody hit?'

'Six here, I have a rather lovely new hole in my wing, but it's not giving me any gyp.'

There was silence for a couple of seconds as Abby waited for anyone else to report, but nobody did - it was just Derek who had been hit and he had only sustained minor damage.

'Bloody hell, we've been damn lucky.' Abby's voice was soft and full of emotion and Gwen realised with a start that the woman had most likely been expecting to lose some, if not most, of her pilots that day. She wondered if she would ever be capable of leading a group of men and women she loved into the face of almost certain death.

'How about we use a bit of that luck and give the Spits a hand with those airships, then, Boss? My guns are feeling a bit left out...'

'Good idea, Seven, let's...'

Before Abby could finish her sentence she was interrupted by a shout from Chalky, who was watching the attack from forty thousand feet, ten miles away. 'Badger Leader, I have incoming enemy fighters! Repeat, incoming enemy fighters! Fifty plus aircraft, fifty miles north-west of the convoy at angels twenty.'

'Acknowledged, Eleven.'

Even as Abby replied to Chalky, Gwen was running the numbers and she had no doubt that everyone else was as well: the enemy fighters were only a few dozen miles from the Nelsons, while the Misfits were on the far side of the convoy from them - they would never return in time to prevent them from attacking the bombers and even if the Nelsons turned for home immediately, the enemy would catch them easily.

There was a chance to save them, though, and, even as Gwen realised how, the radio crackled.

'Badger Leader, this is Gladiator Leader, we are turning to engage the enemy. Request you engage the Pigs, then escort the Nelsons, over.'

'Roger, Gladiator Leader. Go get them.' The strain in Abby's voice left it perfectly clear that she didn't like it, but had come to the same conclusion as Gwen that it was the only solution. 'Trafalgar Squadron, start your run now, we'll clear the field for you.'

'Roger, Badger Leader, we're on our way.'

'Right then, Badgers, let's make some bacon as quick as we can, then go help the Spits. Everyone pick a target and go after them individually. Stay low, remember they are lighter armed on the underneath, and use cannons only; save your machine guns for the incoming fighters. Happy hunting.'

The Misfits turned hard, back towards the convoy, their wingtips only feet above the water, and got their first good look at the results of their previous efforts.

Smoke was rising from both Javelins and both were looking decidedly low in the water, but more importantly lifeboats were streaming away from both - there would be no more fire from them. Without a word, ten very relieved pilots gently pulled back on their sticks and each gained at least a hundred feet.

Gwen chose her target, then searched for Kitty. She immediately found her; the American had sneaked up on her and was tucked in behind her wing, as close as she could get without actually climbing into the cockpit with her.

The American slid up her tinted lenses, revealing her eyes in their goggles, and gave Gwen a wide smile, then blew a kiss.

Gwen laughed. She wished they could exchange a few words in private, but she only had that luxury with Abby and she had to be satisfied with just returning the kiss.

They were approaching the convoy now so, with a last regretful smile, they pulled away from each other and concentrated on their target.

While the Misfits had been attacking the Javelins, the rest of the convoy, apart from a couple of the escort destroyers who had moved to pick up the survivors, had just kept steaming as they had been and the Pigs, the *Cittadelle Volanti*, were still floating above the slow-moving cargo ships.

Gwen slotted lenses in place to get a better look at the curious beasts.

It was easy to see why they had been named "Flying Citadels" by the Italians. Their grey hulls were made up of rectangular steel panels, which looked quite like the stones of a castle, and the protruding anti-aircraft guns were each protected by thick armour, shaped like battlements. To cap it all off, enormously long banners, the colours of the army divisions stationed on the airships during the First Great War, streamed gaily in the wind of the huge machine's slow progress through the air, flying from the gun emplacements they had serviced, and might still do for all she knew.

At the same time, it was clear why the British had called them "Bristly Pigs"; the hulls, instead of being the familiar, sleek, long tube of the common Zeppelin-type airships were short and fat, almost exactly the shape of the animal that could be seen on many farms in England, and, by the looks, they probably handled about the same.

It was hard to believe that these airships had ruled the skies above the battlefields of Belgium and France during the first eighteen months of the previous war, but they had, and Gwen remembered reading about them in Aviation History class at school. By all rights they should be in a museum and she hoped that the Italians had a few more lying around somewhere, because after she and her fellow Misfits had finished with them, they wouldn't be in such good condition any more.

The Pigs didn't open fire until the Misfits were a couple of miles away - it seemed that the Italians hadn't upgraded the weaponry since they had been mothballed, just like the grey hadn't been replaced by the red and gold livery of the Legione Aerea's fleet.

The fire from the Pigs was nothing like as intense as what the Javelins had been able to lay down, but it was comparable to what could be encountered over a Prussian airfield and it would have been a mistake to underestimate it. Scattered anti-aircraft fire had already been coming from the screening ships and Gwen had already been carrying out evasive manoeuvres, but she increased her zigzagging movements, throwing herself dizzily from side to side as she closed the gap at full throttle.

She dipped down to the sea, out of the arcs of most of the anti-aircraft batteries, just before she came into range, but then almost immediately pulled up again.

The Pig filled her vision, impossible to miss, but merely spraying it and hoping for the best wouldn't bring down such a large and heavily armoured aircraft. However, the experts at Luqa had found the designs for the airships buried in the archives at the airfield and discovered that the airship had all of its gas in only two bags, so if one of them could be deflated, it wouldn't be able to hold itself aloft.

Excalibur juddered and decelerated noticeably as Gwen opened fire with her cannons. She kept her sights fixed on a point just above the small gondola where the pilot sat and saw the steel disintegrate under the concentrated fire. She hoped that two seconds of fire would be enough to break through to the bag, because that was all she could give it, as she was forced to push the stick forwards again or risk a collision.

The gondola flashed past, only inches away, and she instantly put Excalibur onto her wing, banking away, looking for her next target.

Farrier's dark blue Spitsteam flashed past in the opposite direction and she lined up on the Pig that the woman had just come from.

There was a loud scream over the radio, quickly cut off, and Gwen immediately put Excalibur into a sharp turn and searched the sky for the source.

She was just in time to see a huge splash as an aircraft hit the water near to one of the cargo ships.

'Did she get out?'

'Did anyone see…?'

'What happened…?'

Too many Misfits started speaking at the same time to distinguish individual voices, but Gwen could only stare at the boiling water, trying to catch a glimpse of the wreckage, wanting to see what colour it was, dreading it being…

'Gwen? Gwen? Are you alright? Answer me!'

Kitty's panicked screams drowned out the other pilots and broke through to Gwen. She tore her eyes away from the sea and took a shuddering breath. 'I'm here, Kitty. Who was it? Who went in?'

'It was Chastity.' Derek's voice was colder than it usually was. 'She managed to get out, but only a second before she hit the water. I don't know if she survived, I can't see her.'

'Get your heads back in the game, Badgers!' Abby bawled at them with her best parade voice. 'We have a job to do! Worry about Chastity after we've taken down these things; the Nelsons are counting on us!'

Gwen clenched her teeth and pulled a maximum rate turn back towards the Pig to carry out the run she had aborted.

A few of the Italian airships needed numerous attacks to bring them down, but eventually the last one sank almost gracefully to the sea and quickly disappeared beneath the waves.

Only then could the Misfits spare a thought for Chastity.

'Leader to Six, take Four and search the area around where Five went down.'

'Roger, Leader.'

'Everybody else, regroup; we're going after those fighters.'

The squadron formed on Abby and climbed, passing over the incoming Nelsons, following Chalky's directions towards where 261 Squadron were going up against the enemy fighters.

To everybody's relief, Derek radioed in shortly after they left the convoy behind.

'Leader, this is Six.'

'Go ahead, Six.'

'Chastity's on board one of the motor launches picking up survivors from the Pigs. She doesn't seem too hurt.'

'That's a relief, thank you, Six. Come and join in the fun when you can, please.'

'Roger, Leader.'

The Spitsteams had engaged the fighters, which turned out to be Italian, some thirty miles from the convoy, heading them off before they got anywhere near the Nelsons. They were outnumbered quite badly, but the Misfits weren't too concerned; the Italian aircraft they'd been facing were nowhere near as good as the Spitsteams, nor were the pilots any great shakes, and 261 Squadron should be able to more than hold their own until reinforcements got to them.

It wasn't until they got closer and were able to listen in to the panicked shouting and occasional agonised scream that was 261's comms that they found out they couldn't have been more wrong.

'Five, you've got one on your six! Break, break!'

'I've.... aargh!'

'I'm hit! I'm hit!'

Gwen switched off the channel quickly, not wanting to hear any more, but she couldn't help but slot lenses into place and she watched the dogfight, trying hard to analyse it clinically, even as she felt for each and every one of the British pilots she was forced to witness being shot down.

She frowned; even though she couldn't see them very clearly, she could tell that the Italian machines were of a design that she didn't recognise. They were longer and thinner in profile than the stubby fighters they'd been up against previously and seemed to be at least comparable in performance to the Spitsteams, possibly even superior to them, and the pilots looked like they knew how to use them well.

'Gladiator Squadron, this is Badger Leader, we are thirty seconds out, break off and head for home.'

'Roger, Badger Leader. You heard her, Gladiators, disengage!'

Only five Spitsteams were left to dive away from the melee, but at least a dozen of the fighters followed them down.

The Spitsteam was extremely good in a dive, reaching speeds that were unheard of in any other production aircraft due to its aerodynamic design, and it was clear that the remaining British fighters were slowly outpacing the Italians. One of them took several hits before getting out of range, though, and spun away.

Of the sixteen aircraft which had taken off that morning, only four escaped west back towards Malta. However, there were at least half a dozen silver glidewings floating towards the distant sea, where a scattering of fishing boats were discreetly waiting to pick them up when the Italians had gone. Gwen was also very pleased to see that there were at least ten golden glidewings accompanying them down.

For a moment it looked like the remaining twenty or so Italian aircraft were going to turn to engage the Misfits, but suddenly they banked sharply and dived away to the north, towards the Italian mainland, fleeing in the face of the legendary British squadron.

'Looks like the bloody Eyeties don't want to dance, Leader.'

'Yes, thank you, Seven, I had noticed.' There was a brief pause, but then Abby made the only decision she could under the circumstances. 'Let them go, our job is to cover the Nelsons.'

The Misfits turned and headed back towards the convoy, where smoke was already pouring from half a dozen stricken ships.

CHAPTER 19

As the day went on, soggy and bedraggled pilots from 261 Squadron were brought to Hal Far in ones and twos, but finally, after the sun had gone down and no more were forthcoming, they were forced to face the fact that they had lost five of their sixteen pilots. There were plenty of spare aircraft to replace the ones that had been destroyed, but pilots were another matter and the squadron would be undermanned until another convoy could be sent.

The bomber squadrons had fared better, losing only two aircraft, but, because they had to make their torpedo runs so low, both entire crews, ten men and women, had been killed.

The Misfits, on the other hand, seemed to be leading very charmed lives and, to everybody's surprise and relief, Chastity was delivered to Hal Far that evening. She had gotten out of her aircraft almost unharmed and been rescued fairly quickly by a launch from a destroyer, suffering only a few fairly deep scratches on her cheeks and chin from when her canopy had exploded, hit by a cannon round from the Pig she'd been attacking. She had barely gotten dry and warm, though, before the destroyer was struck by torpedoes and sunk from under her, plunging her once again into the cold water. This time she didn't come through her adventure unscathed; when the ship lurched she had been sent crashing into a bulkhead and had broken her nose. It was a small price to pay for her freedom, though, because she had finally been rescued by a fishing boat which had been picking up survivors and, in the chaos, the fishermen had been able to hide her and, after they had delivered their catch of Italian sailors to one of the last remaining destroyers, they had carried her home to Malta.

The losses of the Spitsteam pilots was offset to a certain extent by the success of the raid. Chalky stayed up as long as he could, watching the evolution of the efforts of the *Legione Marina* to save its ships, and reported that, by the time it was too dark for him to see, both Javelins, one battleship, two destroyers and eighteen cargo vessels had been sunk, with fires raging on a further three cargo ships and one destroyer.

It was an impressive bag for a single raid and the only thing that had been stopping the British from carrying out another and completely destroying the convoy was the lack of torpedoes available for the Nelsons. The dearth of supplies meant that explosives were scare once more and there hadn't been sufficient to make enough for a second go at the Italians. Thankfully, the Royal Navy were there to cover the RAC's deficiencies and undersea boats intercepted the convoy that very night, sinking another six cargo ships, the last battleship and another destroyer, which left only half a dozen cargo ships to deliver their badly-needed supplies to the coalition forces in Libya.

Without any more torpedoes, the RAC would be able to do very little to prevent any other convoys from making their way across the Mediterranean, but the Coalition didn't know that and, as the weeks went by, there was no sign of any further convoys. The mysterious fighters weren't seen again either, and the Italians showed no intention of moving more forces onto Sicily or continuing the assault on Malta.

Things became exceedingly quiet all of a sudden, but Chalky kept flying his patrol; the British wanted no more nasty surprises.

Another British convoy made its way through a week later and, although again the majority of the supplies were destined for Alexandria and Crete, stocks of explosives, hydrogen and food were delivered, along with another fifty Spitsteams to replace 261 Squadron's losses and one hundred and fifty Harridan Mark IIC's with forty-five pilots to fly them. Not including the Misfits, the RAC presence on the island was now three full fighter squadrons - a reinforced 261 Squadron and 185 and 126 Squadrons equipped with the Harridans. There were now sufficient forces on Malta to defend it effectively and it seemed that Misfit Squadron's job was done, however, there was no word from the War Ministry on when they might expect to go home.

By all accounts, the war in Greece was going well, with the combined British and Greek forces pushing back the invading forces, but in mid-April, an undersea boat returning from Alexandria reported that the Crimson Barons had been spotted over Greece, supporting a large-scale invasion by the Prussians.

While the Misfits were relieved that they wouldn't have to face the Barons any time soon, they felt sorry for the men and women in Greece, who would find their lives a hell of a lot more difficult all of a sudden.

The Misfits took advantage of the quiet to relax and recover. They flew two training missions a day to keep their combat edge, but that left plenty of time in between to swim in the sea from the beach near the house in Birzebbuga, or play cricket on a pitch marked out on the airfield, watched by cheering locals, some of the new pilots having sneaked some equipment into their baggage.

They had good food, excellent wines, plenty of rest and as much tea as they could drink. It was idyllic and they could almost forget that there was a war on.

Then, a week into May, all hell broke loose.

The day started the same as so many others had previously.

Chalky got up in the darkness and hurried to the airfield. He stuffed a couple of bacon sandwiches in his mouth, washed them down with a mug of tea, then picked up the picnic basket that the cooks prepared for him every day. He hopped into Vulture and was in the sky just before dawn for his daily patrol.

Some hours later, the rest of the Misfits emerged from their rooms and drifted down the road to the airfield for a late breakfast and the first day of the inter-squadron cricket tournament that Campbell and the other base commanders had arranged. To make the tournament last as long as possible, each base was providing several teams and it was going to be a round robin, with all the teams playing each other in one day matches. It was promising to be an exciting first day, with the Hal Far Fitters XI taking on the Luqa Aircrew 2nd XI and then, time permitting, the Misfit XI would face the Arturo 3rd XI.

The Luqa team won the toss and elected to bat, so the Hal Far Fitters took the field. Right from the start it was clear that the fitters were superior, with some particularly good leg-break bowling from Sergeant Potter, who had taped the arms of his glasses to the side of his head so they wouldn't fall off.

At eleven, when the teams came in for a tea break, it wasn't looking good for the Luqa team, who had lost six wickets for only fifty-two runs, although their current pair were putting up a valiant defence and had scored more than twenty runs between them in the last five overs. However, after the restart, a revitalised Potter and some inspired medium pace from one of Kitty's fitters soon put paid to them and the lower order collapsed, adding only fifteen more runs until they were finally all out for sixty-eight.

It was Hal Far's turn to bat, but no sooner had the opening pair padded up and made their way out onto the field, than the air raid warning siren sounded.

The airfield went completely still, as everybody froze where they were in surprise, not quite knowing what to do, but then chaos ensued as people began running in every direction.

Gwen and Kitty had been sitting on a blanket on the grass at the edge of the improvised pitch and they were among the closest to the ramp down into the hangar, which someone had had the foresight to keep clear. They left the blanket and the remnants of their snacks where they were and sprinted down the ramp to the ready room, where their flightsuits were hanging. They were joined almost immediately by the rest of the Misfits.

Abby stripped quickly, then grabbed her flightsuit from where it had been hanging next to Gwen's and stepped into it. She grinned as she pulled the zip up the front. 'Saved by the bell, eh?'

'Indeed!' Gwen chuckled. One of the first things that the two of them had found they had in common was that they disliked cricket, despite it being the most popular sport in the world. They had both been roped into playing for the Misfit team, though, because, with Chalky flying, Owen not well enough to play and Kitty's unfortunate status as an non-cricket-playing American, they were needed to make up the numbers. 'Any idea what's happening?'

Abby shook her head. 'I'm hoping it's just a drill - Dot's idea of a joke or something. We'll find out soon enough.'

One by one, the Misfits finished dressing and ran or waddled, depending on the tightness of their flightsuits, to where their machines were ready and waiting for them.

Gwen clambered up onto Excalibur's wing and hopped into the cockpit. Usually she would strap herself in before doing anything else, but she wanted to know what was going on, so she plugged in her radio and switched to the base frequency before letting Giuseppe help her with her safety harness. She was just in time to catch the end of the conversation between Chalky and Campbell.

'...similar numbers coming from the north west of the island.'

'And only the single flight of fighters?'

'So far, Haven, yes.'

'Thank you, Seeker. If the situation changes please inform us.'

'Roger, Haven, I...' Chalky's clinically professional voice faltered and was filled with terror as he almost screamed his next words. 'Oh, god, Bertha! Abby! It's Bertha! The Barons...'

A squeal of feedback made Gwen wince, but then there was silence until Campbell's voice filled it. 'Seeker, repeat your last, please. Seeker, are you there? Chalky? Come in please!'

There was a note of despair in the woman's voice as she tried to raise Chalky, but after a few tries she stopped. There was a long pause, during which only the background static could be heard, but eventually Campbell came back on, her voice composed and professional once more, although Gwen though she could notice a catch in it, as if there was something in her throat.

'Badger Leader, this is Haven. Did you get that?'

'Roger, Haven.'

'We have one hundred plus bombers incoming, with an escort of two squadrons of Italian fighters, but don't worry about them; the Spits and Harrys can handle them. Chalky's last known position was fifty miles east at twenty-five thousand feet - go find the Barons and take the bastards down.'

'Roger that, Haven. With pleasure. All Badgers, you heard her - let's go.'

Gwen powered up the ramp, a tricky manoeuvre that was nonetheless second nature to her now, after so many sorties, and turned onto the airfield. She immediately threw her throttle wide open and followed Abby as she accelerated away.

Nothing needed to be said about Chalky's fate; it was easy enough to work out what must have happened to him. Bertha was nearly invisible in the air and he wouldn't have been looking out for her - she must have been waiting along his flight path and launched fighters when he approached. Vulture was a peacetime aircraft, built for stargazing, it had no armour whatsoever, no manoeuvrability to speak of and was very slow - there was no way it could have survived and it was extremely unlikely that her pilot had either.

Once the Misfits were in the air and climbing hard to the east, Abby called Campbell again. 'Haven, this is Badger Leader. Where did those bombers come from?'

'Seeker spotted them taking off from the airfields on Sicily.'

'I thought there weren't any aircraft left on Sicily?'

'They must have moved them there in secret and put them together in the hangars where we couldn't see them.'

'We should have been bombing those hangars, Haven...'

'We don't have the resources to waste on flattening a few buildings we thought were empty, and even if we did they would have just rebuilt them, or put them somewhere else. Now stop worrying about what we *should* have been done and concentrate on punishing them for what they *have* done.'

'Roger, Haven.' Abby sighed, but didn't argue any further.

Gwen kept a good watch as they flew up into the sky. A fighter could fly fifty miles in a very short time, especially if they were willing to sacrifice height for speed, and the Barons could well be over the island already, waiting to ambush any aircraft that took off. She thought that it was more likely that they would be back on Bertha, though, concealed by the camouflage and steaming away from the scene of the crime. She doubted that the Misfits would find the airship that day.

Unfortunately, she was right.

'Haven, this is Badger Leader. There's nobody here. We're going to broaden the search.'

'Negative, Badger Leader; incoming aircraft are now three hundred plus, return and engage, please.'

'Are the Barons with them, Haven?'

'Negative, Badger Leader.'

'Damn and blast!'

Bruce laughed at Abby's feeble swearing. 'Gruber's never going to do escort duty, Leader, you know that! Don't worry, we'll have a chance at him soon enough I reckon.'

'I know, Five.' Abby sighed. 'Come on then, Badgers, let's go take care of this little raid.'

The Misfits banked around to reverse their course and Gwen peered over her wing at the sea below as she did so, hoping to find some trace of Vulture. The Mediterranean was calm, though, with no sign of any wreckage and none of the fishing boats seemed to be moving to rescue anybody. Chalky was gone.

As her wings came level, her view of the sea was hidden and she resumed her search for the huge airship that had to be there somewhere.

As the massed formations of Italian and Prussian bombers, droned towards them, the islanders rushed for the nearest shelter, abandoning the homes they had dared to return to in the major population centres like Valletta, praying that the repairs that they had made during the recent weeks of peace wouldn't be destroyed.

The Misfits were rested and had in no way lost their fighting instincts. They tore through the ranks of bombers, furious at the loss of their friend and seeking vengeance.

Gwen tried to stay on Abby's wing as she usually did, but she was finding it hard to maintain her usual discipline and it showed in her flying.

After her wingmate had strayed from her wing for a third time in only a couple of minutes, Abby tutted. 'Oh, just go and blow off some steam, would you, Two?'

'If you insist, Leader.' Gwen couldn't help but grin as she pulled back on her stick, sending Excalibur rocketing into the sky, before spiralling down again, directly into the middle of the Italian bomber formation. Her wild actions surprised not only the group of bombers, who belatedly tried to scatter, but also the four MU9's who had been following her and Abby as they'd made their run. She blasted one of the fighters to bits, before giving two of the larger machines much longer bursts as they passed across her nose.

Her path took her under the bomber formation and she continued her dizzying loop, coming back up towards the bellies of the next flight of bombers. However, before she could get in range, a couple of Harridans shot through them, cannons spurting fire. Only one of the bombers was hit enough to drop out of the formation, but she ignored the rest and aborted her run when she saw the flight of Italian fighters on the tails of the British fighters.

She got her first good look at the new model of fighters just before she pulled her trigger and raked the first one with machine gun fire. They were streamlined and sleek, with long noses, tails which tapered to sharp points and wings that were very similar in design to the MU9. They were a lot tougher, too, as the hits she scored on the fighter failed to knock it out of the sky as they would have the older models.

She pulled in behind the fighters and gave the trailing one a quick burst of combined fire. She was very pleased to see that her cannon were just as effective on them as they were on any other aircraft and, as that fighter disintegrated and fell away she adjusted her aim to the next one, but the Italians had had enough and abandoned their chase, scattering and diving away from her. She let them go and banked hard, bringing Excalibur around directly underneath a flight of big Prussian HO111's. She sprayed two of them liberally as she climbed up at them, but was then forced to kick her rudder and turn away as the bombers began dropping their bombs.

As she rolled around she was briefly inverted and she snatched a glance at the ground, wondering what the target was, and found the familiar sight of Hal Far almost directly below her, smoke and dirt blossoming as it was pounded remorselessly. With so much going on around her she couldn't afford to watch for very long, so she put the airfield out of her mind, sure in the knowledge that the men and women working there were safely below ground, and got back into the fight.

From high above and twenty miles east of the island, Hans Gruber munched on a bowl of popcorn while he watched the bombs exploding on the airfields of Malta. He wasn't expecting the raid to do any lasting damage, with the facilities on the air bases underground, but it wasn't as if there was anything else worth bombing on the island anyway; the civilian population was already terrified and the ships in the harbour were more of a liability to the British than they were an asset - an ancient aircraft carrier that was worse than useless and a couple of damaged destroyers that were using up resources to repair that they wouldn't be able to replace.

'What is the purpose of this?'

Gruber frowned in annoyance as he retracted his lenses and turned from the spectacle to look at the man standing next to him at the window of the officers' mess. The admiral had brought a huge antique brass telescope to watch the attack, mounting it on an equally antiquated wooden tripod. It was a wonder he could see any of it.

'This attack will not do anything to inconvenience the British, save give their ordinary airmen practice at filling holes in their fields. All I can see is that it we are wasting pilots, aircraft and munitions.'

The admiral was nominally in command of Bertha, but after the success in Greece, the Kaiser had promoted Gruber and placed him in charge of the assault on Malta, which meant the elderly man now had to obey his orders rather than granting his requests as before.

Since the change in circumstances, the admiral had done nothing to conceal his distaste both for Gruber and the situation he had been placed in. However, instead of trying to make peace in the interest of cooperation, Gruber used any opportunity he could to rub the man's nose into the change of seniority by keeping him out of the loop and only telling him what he needed to know for the operation of Bertha.

He met the man's eyes and deliberately sipped his schnapps, then took the time to wipe the back of his hand across his lips before answering.

'You'll see, Admiral, you'll see. All in good time.'

The man frowned in annoyance at being put off once again and Gruber grinned, delighted, as he turned back to the window, the same window through which he had watched the Misfits earlier when they had come searching for their companion, Charles "Chalky" Isaacs, hoping to find him still alive.

It had been a vain hope, though, because the man had already disappeared beneath the waves, entombed forever in his machine.

CHAPTER 20

'Damn it, Dot, we should have been doing something to protect Chalky instead of playing bloody cricket!'

After chasing the raid back over the sea the Misfits had flown straight home. They'd had to orbit the field for twenty minutes while enough potholes were filled in before they were able to land, but as soon as she was down, Abby had left Dragon in the care of her fitters and stormed over to Dorothy Campbell, who had come to watch the fighters return.

'What the hell *could* we have done, Abby? We thought the Barons were in Greece and we were watching Sicily for threats. There was no way we could have prevented his death, unless we had him grounded, in which case we would have been blind, or escorted him the entire time, exhausting pilots with long shifts, in which case we probably would have lost them too.'

Abby opened her mouth to continue arguing, but then shut it again when she realised that Campbell was right - there was nothing they could have reasonably done differently that would have affected the outcome in a positive manner. At the end of the day, like it or not, they were at war and Charles had known what he was getting into and known the risks when he'd agreed to join Misfit Squadron. And just like Mac he hadn't died in vain, but with his dying breaths had warned the British that the Barons were there - it might not seem like much, but if the Barons launched unexpected into the middle of a fight from the nigh on invisible Bertha, even the Misfits would be hard-pressed to survive.

She sighed and dropped her head. 'You're right, of course. Doesn't mean it doesn't hurt, though.'

'Of course it hurts. I would be worried if you ever got to the point where you *weren't* affected by the loss of one of your people because it would mean you were no longer the woman I helped start this squadron.'

'I just hope that I have a squadron left after this nightmare ends.' Abby turned to walk away, but came to a sudden halt when she saw that the rest of the Misfits had been standing silently behind her. There were long faces, as she'd been expecting, but more than anything else there was determination and she nodded. 'We'll have a drink and take Charles' photograph to the cathedral tonight, but right now I want you ready to fly again; I'm pretty damn sure the Nelsons are getting ready to retaliate as we speak and I for one want to be with them. Be back on the flight line in fifteen minutes.'

Without another word she stalked off towards Dragon.

The Misfits watched her go, then drifted away, a few to their aircraft but most towards the ready room and the snacks that were always there between missions.

Gwen slipped her hand into Kitty's and together they clomped down the ramp, but she pulled her to a halt before they got half-way. 'Hang on a second, there's something we should do.'

She pulled Kitty back up into the bright sunshine and over to Campbell, who was watching the last of the Harridans land. She saw them approaching and smiled weakly.

'What can I do for you, ladies?'

'I was just thinking that someone should tell Roberta Leyland, Chalky's girlfriend, about him. She works in signals. We've gotten to know her pretty well, so we could do it if you want.'

Campbell grimaced and sighed, shaking her head sadly. 'I suppose there's no way you could have known; I've only just been informed myself.'

'Known what?' Gwen asked, a sinking feeling in her stomach.

'I'm sorry, but Aerial Officer Leyland was on Vulture when she went down. It was their anniversary or something and she sneaked on-board to surprise Charles.'

While the fighters at Hal Far could make do with a narrow strip of just a few hundred yards to take off and land on, the bombers at Luqa and Ta'Kali couldn't; they needed far more room, especially when they were taking off fully loaded, so repairs to their airfields took far longer than the fifteen minutes Abby had predicted and in the end it was more than forty-five minutes before Luqa and Ta'Kali were open for business again. Not only would the delay have given the Coalition fighters ample time to get home, rearm and rewind, and get back into the air, but there was also the matter of the Barons' ability to appear out of nowhere, thanks to Bertha. Campbell and the other station commanders came to the inescapable conclusion that, if they went ahead with the attack, loses would almost certainly be high, if not total.

The reprisal raid was cancelled, the fighters at Hal Far stood down and the pilots trudged, disappointed, back to the ready room.

'Are you really just expecting us to sit on our thumbs and do nothing?' Bruce asked, slamming his mug of tea down on the coffee table between the sofas with far more force than necessary, spilling some of it and startling a couple of the more inexperienced Harridan pilots sitting nearby. He glared at Campbell. 'Since when have the RAC been afraid of a fight?'

'We are not cowards, if that is what you're accusing us of, Mr Walker.' Any conversations that were still going on after Bruce's outburst came to a halt and all eyes went to her as she turned cold eyes on the Australian. 'It is not cowardice, it is prudence. If the Barons are here, it means that Greece has either fallen or is on its knees, and that means we're next. We're going to need those bombers; they will be vital in stopping the invasion fleet when it comes, and we're not going to put them at risk just to destroy a few bombers that can't do much to us anyway and which you can shoot down easily enough.'

'So, what?' asked Abby, who hadn't cooled down after her outburst on the airfield. 'We just wait for them to decide they're ready to send in their ships and scrape us off this godforsaken island?'

'Unfortunately, yes.' Campbell nodded, retaining her calm in the face of her long-time friend's confrontational attitude. 'We no longer have control of the skies, so all we can do is go back to weathering the storm as best we can, while taking advantage of any opportunities that present themselves. Which is what we've mostly been doing already anyway.' She looked around the room taking in the long faces. 'If Greece really has fallen, then the War Ministry *has* to support us and send proper reinforcements, otherwise we'll lose all the Eastern Mediterranean and probably North Africa as well. We have to bunker down and last until then. There's nothing else we can do.'

'Actually, there is; we could destroy Bertha.' Tanya's quiet statement silenced the mutterings that had begun at Campbell's rather disappointing statement. She looked around at the pilots who were now staring at her and shrugged. 'That way we win this game.'

'Game?' Drake grinned at her.

'Yes, it is like a chess game. First they move, then we move. Unless we take their most important piece we will go back and forth until the King must commit suicide.'

'Resign, darling, resign.'

Tanya shrugged again. 'Resign, die, suicide. It is much the same in war because the winners get to do what they want afterwards.'

There was a brief silence as the pilots contemplated Tanya's bleak outlook on things before Bruce spoke up.

'I'm all for knocking Bertha out of the sky and Gruber along with it, but how are we going to do that if we can't find the damn thing? I mean, even the Barons need special instruments to find it.'

Tanya smiled and craned her neck to peer over the top of the high-backed chairs. 'You can help with that bit, right?'

'I should be able to.'

The pilots swivelled in their seats to see who she was speaking to and were shocked to find Owen standing by the door - in all the fuss they had completely forgotten that he was being released from hospital that morning. He had come in unnoticed while all the attention, apart from Tanya's apparently, had been on the Muscovite, and was accompanied by Wendy, who watched him with some concern as he hobbled stiffly over to them. He was being as nonchalant as possible in the face of their surprise, but there were obvious signs of pain in his eyes as he moved. They faded somewhat when he was still again, but it was telling that he leaned on the back of a wooden chair rather than sitting down.

It was the first time the Misfits were seeing their friend since he'd been burnt, without him being swathed in bandages, and for a few seconds they were lost for words and could only stare. They had all seen what had happened to pilots who had been caught in a burning aircraft, it happened far too often to bomber crews for them not to have, but they had never expected one of their own to end up the same way, especially because, since the advent of springs, fighter aircraft no longer had anything combustible in them, which made the sight all the more upsetting.

When the bomb had exploded on the Arturo, Owen had wrapped his arms around Wendy and held her against his chest, lowering his head over hers to try to protect her further, leaving half of his face and the back of his head exposed to the intense heat and flames. His once thick and proudly cared-for hair had burnt away and most of his scalp had been seared and only a few untidy patches were growing back, but it was what had been done to the left half of his face, the side that had been turned towards the explosion, which had many of the Misfits fighting tears. It was almost as if the skin of his face had melted and run, pulling the corner of his eye and his mouth downwards and distorting his nose. The eyelid over his slightly milky left eye was thicker and didn't seem to open fully and he had no eyebrows or eyelashes on that side. Neither did he have an ear.

Owen saw the looks and smiled, although only half of his face moved. 'Well, I don't think it looks *that* bad and just think how much I'm going to save on haircuts!'

The silence lasted a second or two, but then Abby cleared her throat. 'Yes, but you're going to have to spend a fortune on hats.'

There was a shocked silence as everyone stared at Abby, wondering how she could be so callous, but then Owen started laughing.

It hadn't been a particularly funny joke and certainly didn't warrant Owen's reaction to it, but, as Gwen looked back and forth between the two friends, she realised what the woman was doing. Owen didn't want pity from his friends, he didn't want a big thing to be made of his injuries, he just wanted to go back to how things had been. Abby had picked up on that and, in following his joke, had made sure that everybody else knew that he didn't need treating with kid gloves and his laugh owed as much to relief as anything else.

She smiled and chuckled, earning a puzzled look from Kitty, then raised her mug of tea. 'Welcome back!'

'Yes, welcome back, Sheepish!' called Bruce. He drew a few uncertain laughs from the other pilots but one by one their frowns disappeared and they each called out a greeting to the Welshman in their own way.

Abby caught Gwen's eye and gave her a small nod of thanks before leaning forward and banging her mug on the low table. 'Alright, settle down, we'll do this properly later.'

Once the room was quiet again, Abby turned to Owen. 'I take it you want to get Bloodhound in the air to find Bertha. Are you sure you're up for that?'

'For sitting on my arse and looking at a few screens?' Owen leaned over the chair and slapped its back with a hand which was covered in scar tissue. 'I think I can handle that. I've already checked Bloodhound - my fitters have done a good job and she's ready to fly immediately.

Let me do this, let's destroy that monster for...' He swallowed, welling emotion cutting off what he'd been about to say.

Abby took a deep breath. 'Unfortunately, knowing where Bertha is won't be enough, though. There's no way we can destroy her; we bombed her once before and barely even scratched her paintwork.'

'And that's where I come in.' Wendy said, holding up her hand and grinning. 'A shipment of brand new meltrockets will arrive tonight after the sun goes does. Lieutenant Commander Strangeways has managed to get together enough for the entire squadron, including Dreadnought.'

'Meltrockets?' Bruce asked, raising an eyebrow and smirking.

Wendy glared at him. 'You think of a better name! It's not easy coming up with good names for all the interesting stuff in my head, especially because they all do more or less the same thing.'

Bruce pursed his lips thoughtfully, but said nothing and after a couple of seconds Wendy nodded triumphantly. 'See? So next time you start to criticise my name choosing...'

She never got to finish the sentence because Bruce's eyes lit up and he cut her off with a shout. 'Bertha Busters! Let's call them Bertha Busters!'

Wendy automatically rolled her eyes and opened her mouth to pooh-pooh his idea, but then stopped herself when she actually thought about it. 'Actually, that's not bad at all.' She sighed. 'Alright, let's call them that.'

Monty groaned. 'Can we at least call them "Bertha Breakers" or something? "Buster" sounds so... I don't know, *Antipodean*.'

He stuck his tongue out at Bruce, who crossed his eyes in return.

After the laughter had died down, Abby brought the room to order. 'We haven't got time for this people; the Prussians will probably be back soon, so let's have a serious conversation please.'

'With those two in the room?' Owen asked.

'Yes,' Abby gave the two men a stern look. 'And if I have to separate them, I will.'

'We'll behave, I promise,' Bruce said earnestly.

'Scout's honour!' said Monty, putting his fist to the side of his head and puffing out his chest.

Abby stared at him as he held the ridiculous salute, then shook her head in exasperation. 'Yes. Well.' She pointedly turned away from the two men and looked at Campbell. 'Dot?'

The Sky Commodore just shook her head as she finished her tea. She stood up and looked down at Abby. 'This is your show. You plan it. Use whatever resources you need, just run it by me when you have something, please.'

'Will do.' Abby nodded. She waited until Campbell was out of the room before addressing the pilots.

'Right then, we're only going to get one chance at this, because as soon as Gruber knows we can see Bertha he'll pull back beyond our reach, so we have to make it count. We'll do it tomorrow, while the Prussians still think they have us over a barrel, but if the weather is bad, Bertha is too far away, or any of us sees *any* other problem, then we call it off and try again another time.'

She looked around, making sure everybody understood before continuing. 'The fitters will install the rockets tonight. Owen will go up in the dark, a few hours before dawn, and find Bertha. He'll be escorted by 261 Squadron.' She glanced over at the commander of the Spitsteam squadron. 'For all we know Bertha could be above our heads right now, so you'll stay with Squadron Leader Llewellyn until he determines whether there are any enemy aircraft in the area. Then, as soon as it is light enough to do so, you'll land and rewind in order to face the morning raid with 126 and 185 squadrons.' She met the eyes of the Harridan commanders briefly, giving them a nod, before looking around at the inner circle of Misfit Squadron pilots. 'As for us - we'll take off an hour before first light and climb to our maximum height over the island. Hopefully that will put us above Bertha and they won't see us until it's too late.'

She let the information sink in, then looked at Wendy. 'Tell us about your rockets. Will they melt through as much metal as the bombs? And how do they need to be targeted?'

Wendy grinned. 'They're quite comparable to the bombs for sheer destruction, although Bertha is much bigger than any ship and I can't guarantee that the acid will burn all the way from top to bottom. As for delivery, well, Strange and I figured that they were mostly going to hit something side on, rather than from above like the bombs, so we developed armour-piercing heads for them and adjusted the shaped charge so that, after they've penetrated, the explosion will be mostly directed forwards afterwards. That way the acid will hopefully be spread as far as possible into the target before gravity does its work.'

'Good,' said Abby.

'But what good is that going to do? That thing's lost its propulsion before and didn't come out much the worse for wear. I don't think a few holes in the side are going to bother it too much.'

'The envelopes.' Gwen said. 'We have to put enough holes in them so that it falls out of the sky.'

Abby nodded. 'Sounds good, although to make sure we hit as many of the hulls as possible it would probably be best to fly over the top and drop meltbombs.'

Gwen shrugged. 'Then we take bombs *and* rockets. It'll make us very heavy, but Excalibur and the rest of our aircraft can probably cope and the Spitsteams can always jettison the bombs if they have to. We launch the rockets at the fans from a distance, knock as many of those out as possible, then go in for a run on the envelopes with the bombs.'

Bruce chuckled. 'You make it sound so simple, Gwen. Are you forgetting that thing has as many guns at the Javelins did?'

Gwen shook her head. 'I'm not. We go in high enough to fly over Bertha and fire the rockets at a downward angle at the fans. That way we can offload everything in just one run, reducing the risk.'

Gwen looked to Abby. Having examined Drake's sketches of Bertha, she knew that her plan was solid and would work, but it would be her wingmate's call as to how the attack would be made.

The rest of the pilots followed Gwen's example and waited for Abby to make her decision, but before she could the air raid warning sounded and the opportunity was lost in the race for the door.

It wasn't until they were in the air and climbing hard to meet the incoming raid that Abby came over the general frequency and finally gave her answer. 'We'll do it Gwen's way. First thing tomorrow, we're going to put Bertha in the drink.'

The Coalition mounted two more raids that day and the British fighters met them each time, suffering losses amongst the Harridan and Spitsteam squadrons, but the Nelson remained silent and protected in their bunkers.

After flying was over for the day, the Misfits trudged up the road to the house at Birzebbuga, forced to walk because the road had taken quite a few hits and the autocars couldn't get through. They were exhausted, emotionally, physically and mentally, and, apart from Bruce and Monty, who stayed up to play a couple of games of chess over a few drinks before retiring, they went directly to their bedrooms and fell on their beds.

Gwen couldn't sleep, though, and she lay face up listening to the gentle, and not so gentle, sounds of snoring coming from the surrounding rooms.

The morning's mission was going to be just as dangerous as the attack on the Javelins, if not more so because of the height that they were going to have to fly at and the loss of power and manoeuvrability that would mean. It wasn't that which was keeping her awake, though, because every time a pilot took to the skies in war there was *always* a very real chance they wouldn't come back. Rather it was the thought of what the destruction of Bertha could mean for the war as a whole. It wouldn't end the conflict, not in itself, but it might bring about a cascade of events that would bring it to a close in favour of the British and their allies far earlier than it otherwise would.

The immediate effect would be the return of air superiority over Malta to the British, meaning that more convoys with reinforcements could be brought in safely, the island held and the shipping lanes to North Africa controlled. That would limit the ability of the Coalition to reinforce their troops, while allowing the British to do so freely and the fight in Africa would then turn in the favour of the British. They would be able to push the enemy away from the borders of the weak Ottoman Empire, which protested neutrality while at the same time appeasing the encroaching Prussians by selling them its vast gas reserves for its huge war machine. The Prussian armies throughout Europe would find themselves suddenly without the hydrogen they needed for their machines, while Britain and a reassured Muscovy would have an excess. The Prussians would be forced back from the lands they had taken and the push for Berlin would begin from all sides.

The war could be over by Midwinter.

The Misfits would then be freed from their duties and disbanded, after the obligatory round of victory parades, celebrations, and dinners, and she would be freed to start her life with Kitty.

Gwen smiled and shifted happily at the thought.

There was a groan from her side and Kitty lifted her head to peer at her with bleary eyes.

'If you're going to keep us awake we might as well use the time constructively.'

Gwen's smile widened as she rolled into the waiting arms of her lover.

CHAPTER 21

By the time the Misfits rolled out of bed, Owen had been in the air for half an hour. It was still dark when they left the house to begin the walk to the airfield and there was no way that they would have been able to see Bloodhound, but that didn't stop most of the pilots from peering up into the starry sky anyway.

The pilots hurried, not because they were late, but because they were eager to hear Owen's report, to know whether they had a mission to look forward to or just another gruelling day of facing wave after wave of enemy aircraft. They made it to the gates of the air base in record time. They were waved through the barrier by a Military Guard, who grinned and wished them luck as they passed - it seemed that the news of the mission had gotten around, even though Dorothy Campbell had insisted on keeping a lid on it, just in case.

The underground hangar was a hive of activity. Brightly lit, it was full of fitters and mechanics, all working frantically. The Misfit aircraft had carried rockets and bombs before, so the necessary hard points were already in place on them and it hadn't taken too long to fit them, but it seemed that the men and women had continued working all night, making absolutely sure that the machines were in tiptop condition. They had even polished them, bringing them to a high shine in the harsh overhead working lights, something that many pilots swore gave them a touch of extra speed.

While Abby went to get Dorothy Campbell, the other pilots made their way to the mess for breakfast. The few times they'd been in the mess at that time of the morning, the room had been deserted apart from a few sleepy cooks and the occasional group of servicemen and women coming off duty, but that day it was filled almost to capacity. However, nobody was doing much in the way of eating. They were just nursing mugs of tea or idly picking at toast. They didn't do a very good job of pretending not to watch the Misfits either, but the Misfits didn't mind and presented a confident front as they went about their business.

Wendy was already at the base, having gotten up early to see Owen off, and she joined them at their table after a few minutes.

'Everything's ready. You've all got a full complement of rockets and bombs and I've had release buttons for the meltbomb pods added to the weapons panel as well, so now you can jettison the pods before getting into a dogfight. Try not to unless you really have to, please; they were a bugger to make.'

Bruce leaned across the table and met her eyes seriously. 'When you say full complement you mean we each have six meltbombs and eight *Bertha Busters*, right?' He put special emphasis on his name for the rockets, glancing sideways at Monty as he did so.

Wendy shook her head. 'These rockets are bigger and heavier than the ones we've used before so you only get two, one under each wing.'

'Oh.' Bruce blinked, surprised and not a little disappointed. 'Which brings me to my next question - what exactly is a full complement of meltbombs and Bertha Busters on Dreadnought?'

Wendy grinned sheepishly. 'Sixty bombs and forty rockets.'

The Misfits laughed, but at that moment, the mess door opened and Abby and Dorothy Campbell appeared at the end of the short path through the bushes.

The room had been quiet before, with voices being kept down out of respect for the Misfits, but when the two officers came in all noise faded until the only sound was the faint chirping of the birds flitting through the trees.

The silence continued as everyone in the room watched the two women grab plates of food before making their way over to the Misfits' table. Abby immediately slipped into a seat and began munching on a bacon sandwich, giving nothing away, but a stone-faced Campbell remained standing, looking down at the pilots, who looked back at her expectantly.

Suddenly, she grinned. 'Owen has Bertha on his scopes. The mission's on!'

A silent crowd of men and women, both British and Maltese, gathered by the side of the airfield in the moonlight. Knowing that the mission could well determine the fate of the island, they had wanted to be there to watch the Misfits take off.

Dreadnought was the first to go, her six powerful engines deafening in the quiet of the early morning as they fought to pull the huge aircraft into the air. It was the first time she had flown over Malta and the islanders had never seen the like - even the Italian Grand Eagle bombers didn't come close. The RAC personnel were equally awestruck; they had heard of Dreadnought - everybody who had picked up a newspaper in the last nine months or so knew of her - but the reality was far more impressive than what could possibly be put down in black and white.

The sound of the massive machine's engines took several minutes to die away completely and then it was the turn of the single-engined fighters. They were far quieter than Dreadnought, but no less impressive, as they accelerated down the airfield in their flights and leapt into the air with an agility that was breathtaking, even fully laden.

In moments they too had disappeared into the darkness and along with them the buzzing of their airscrews. The men and women remained, though, gazing up into the sky as Father Bugelli led the islanders in a hymn of hope which many of the British joined in with.

Owen had found Bertha as soon as he'd switched on his radar equipment. The airship was sitting at thirty-five thousand feet, two-thirds of the way along the direct flightpath between Malta and Sicily. That was higher than they'd hoped for and the Misfits' job was going to be tough, but at least they didn't have to worry about the airship being out of range, or any anti-aircraft fire from the ground.

Campbell had ordered radio silence after Owen's report on the position of Bertha, in case the Prussians were listening, so the Misfits climbed in silence, each of the pilots left with their own thoughts. While most contemplated the coming battle and how they would face it, Gwen was more interested in the physics of flying so high and, as she divided her attention between the red-lit instruments on the panel in front of her and the barely visible shadow of Dragon on her wing, she tried to calculate what effect the weight of the weapons would have on the service ceilings of Excalibur and the other Misfit aircraft. In the end she was forced to admit that she had no real idea and resigned herself to finding out when the time came, which was something she never liked to do.

After fifteen minutes of steady climbing, with the sky to the east growing steadily brighter, the Misfits reached thirty-five thousand feet and pushed onwards and upwards. At thirty-seven thousand feet, the Spitsteams began to lag behind and just before thirty-eight thousand the cockpit lights of the four Spitsteams flashed on and off; the signal that they were as high as they were able to go. As had been agreed before takeoff, they descended a few hundred feet until they were comfortable again, while the rest of the aircraft continued to climb. At just over thirty-nine thousand feet it was the turn of Drake and Tanya to blink their lights and sink down slightly, but Wraith, Ghoul, Dragon and Excalibur were easily able to make it to forty thousand feet, where they finally levelled off.

The Misfits had timed their takeoff and rate of climb so that they would reach their maximum height fifteen miles from Bertha, just as the world around them became bright enough for them to see their target, and Gwen slotted her most powerful lenses into place to scan the sky in front of them. She was sure that there would have to be a shadow or a telltale glint of light off metal to give away its presence, but she couldn't spot anything. She did however find Dreadnought a few miles ahead of the fighters and at least ten thousand feet below, far lower than she should have been given her rate of climb. She must have reached her ceiling already and unless the Misfits could quickly knock out a couple of envelopes and get Bertha to descend, it didn't look like the big machine and her devastating armament would be joining the fight.

'Badger Leader, this is Watcher, target is rising, they must have spotted you. Suggest you get a move on.'

After flying in silence for so long, Owen's voice was startling and unexpected and Gwen jumped, letting out an involuntary squeak.

With no more need for secrecy, Abby immediately replied. 'Thank you, Watcher. I still don't see it, are we on course?'

'Roger, Leader. Target is at eight miles directly ahead. Approaching thirty-six thousand feet.'

'Keep us updated, please, Watcher.'

'Roger, Leader.'

'All Badgers, three minutes to target, begin evasive manoeuvres. And make your shots count, please, because unfortunately it looks like we're not going to be able to rely on Dreadnought liberally spraying everything.'

Just as Gwen was acknowledging Abby's order and beginning what little manoeuvres she could with her heavy machine in the thin air, the first black cloud of flak burst next to her right wing. Milliseconds later there was a loud clatter like hail on a tin roof and a sharp crack as a fragment of sharp metal penetrated the glass of her canopy. Her head was thrown to the side and she screamed as something ripped across her forehead, but the pain was gone immediately as everything went black.

'Gwen! Are you alright? Gwen?'

Gwen was dragged slowly back to consciousness as Kitty's voice penetrated her awareness and she opened her eyes to look around, unsure where she was. The sight of Excalibur's cockpit instantly snapped her back into focus, though, and she instantly took in her situation.

She was in a lazy spiralling dive, the sea and sky revolving sickeningly round and round and up and down in front of her. Out of pure instinct, before she was even aware of what she was doing, her hands and feet worked the controls and brought her back level.

It was only then that she realised she couldn't see out of her right eye.

'Gwen!'

'I'm here, I'm alright.'

Gwen looked around, but there was no sign of Kitty or any of the other Misfits in her immediate vicinity and a glance at her altimeter told her why - she was at twenty-eight thousand feet. She had fallen more than two miles while she had been unconscious.

'Watcher here, Target at four miles, approximately thirty-seven thousand five hundred feet.'

Praying she wouldn't be too late for the attack, but just knowing that she would, she struggled to put a suddenly reluctant Excalibur back onto her previous heading before pushing the throttle through the stops to emergency unwind and pulling her nose up into a maximum rate climb. The aircraft balked a couple of turns, lurching in a disconcerting manner, but finally she seemed to settle down and Gwen was finally able to turn her gaze upwards.

Her hands and feet went rigid on the controls as she took in the violence of the anti-aircraft fire that was being brought to bear against the Misfits. The sky was black in a wide swathe around the tiny cross shapes that were her friends as dark flowers bloomed and blossomed, while red, green and orange tracer rounds slashed past, creating a seemingly impenetrable web around them. It was a wonder they could survive for even a moment and she watched, unable to breath, expecting at any moment one of them to fall from the sky. When several seconds had gone by without producing the disaster she feared, she raggedly drew in air and, after a last look at the Spitsteam she knew was Kitty's, tore her eyes away from them to follow the lines of tracer back to their origin.

Her jaw dropped when she got her first sight of the immensity of Bertha.

There was no real need for Owen to call out the distances anymore, because the airship was now clearly visible, wreathed in the smoke of the discharge of the dozens of anti-aircraft guns and lit up by their flashes.

The Misfits seemed so close to it that she wondered why they didn't open fire, but then she realised that her hazy mind hadn't taken into consideration that the monstrosity was more than two thousand feet long. The Misfits would have to close to about half that length before they could launch their rockets.

The huge explosions and the tiny aircraft they were chasing, as they weaved almost drunkenly across the sky, crept closer and closer to the airship, but still the Misfits didn't open fire.

'I'm hit!' Derek's cry came just as one of the Spitsteams started spinning out of control, falling from the sky. 'Bailing out!'

His shout was followed only seconds later by Drake's, reporting that he'd sustained damage to his wing and couldn't hold his altitude, then three more as the other Spitsteams reported that Bertha was now too high for them to attack.

As always, Abby was calm as she replied - in perfect control, even in the face of the burgeoning disaster. 'Three, Four, Five, Nine, get clear. Seven, Eight, Ten, spread out.'

Gwen was now close enough to clearly make out the battle without needing lenses and she watched as four fighters dived away, leaving only four to continue the attack. It seemed like the situation was hopeless, but if just a few of them made it to the airship and managed to do some damage, then Bertha might be forced to descend into range of the devastating assault of Dreadnought.

Even as she had the thought, the lead fighter was rocked by a near miss and slewed sideways.

'Bugger! I've been hit!' Abby's voice was strained as she fought for control of Dragon and a note of dismay had crept into it for the first time.

'Me too, Leader. I'm going down.' Tanya's voice was so emotionless and impassive that Gwen almost thought she was joking for some reason, but then a huge chunk of wing separated from one of the fighters and what was left began to spin lazily, describing a ballistic path as it tumbled from the sky.

Abby cursed. 'I can't stay. Retreat! All Badgers return to base.'

'No way, Boss! We're almost in range!' Bruce called out. He laughed. 'Come on, Monty what do you say?'

'I'm with you, Bruce, old boy.'

'Seven, no! It's not worth the risk!'

'I disagree, Abby,' said Monty seriously. 'Ask Derek when you pull his arse out of the sea, but for now, if you don't mind, clear the bloody air! We've got a job to do, right, Bruce?'

'Too right, Mate!'

There was silence for a moment, but then Abby came back over the air, her voice soft, almost a whisper. 'Happy hunting, Badgers.' Her wish was echoed by all of the Misfits and then everyone who could turned their eyes on the two aircraft to watch.

It seemed almost impossible that the two could survive the full fury of the barrage, but they did, and after what seemed like an impossibly long time, four brilliant lances shot from them, connecting them to the airship with a line of fire.

The explosions seemed pitifully small, but they were in exactly the right place at the root of one of the fans.

'Nice one, Monty! Now, come on, let's get our arses out of here!'

Bruce immediately began turning Wraith away, but Ghoul kept going.

'No, I can get this!'

Gwen watched as the grey machine closed the gap with the airship, the thousand yards seeming to take forever to cover. With the rockets gone the aircraft was a bit lighter and slightly more manoeuvrable and Monty was using every trick he knew from his time as a stunt pilot to outfox the gunners, rolling and swerving, using every bit of agility he could squeeze out of Ghoul to the utmost.

The tiny cross had almost converged with the huge airship and it seemed like, against all expectations, Monty was going to pull it off, but at the last moment Ghoul seemed almost to halt in the air and then she was diving.

A second later she plunged into the side of Bertha and disappeared in a flash of yellow light as the bombs detonated within their pod.

'Monty...' Bruce's stunned voice was soft and mournful and Gwen looked to him, hoping beyond hope that he wouldn't try to do something stupid to avenge his friend and long-time partner. He didn't have the chance, though; the guns which had killed Monty found him and his aircraft all but disintegrated, then began the long journey to the sea.

The sight of one of the fans breaking free from the huge machine and following him down was no compensation.

The civilians and servicemen and women had waited on the airfield for the Misfits to come back, and a great cheer when up when the sound of Dreadnought's engines was heard. It died out very quickly, though, when the other returning aircraft straggled into sight one by one and they saw that there were only six fighters, all still carrying the long thin tubes of the rockets beneath their wings.

Hopeful that there were going to be stragglers arriving, they continued to watch the skies, even as the first of the battered aircraft began to land but, when a servicewoman who worked in the communications room came back with the news of the losses the squadron had sustained, heads drooped and tears began to fall.

Abby climbed slowly out onto her wing and stood staring numbly at the scraps of twisted metal that were all that remained of the tail of her aircraft. She wasn't really seeing it, though, because all she could see were the faces of the friends she had led to their deaths that morning.

'Abby.'

Dorothy Campbell's voice coming from by her feet brought her back to herself somewhat and she glanced down to find the Sky Commodore looking up at her.

She hopped heavily down from the wing and leaned tiredly against Dragon's scarred fuselage.

'Dot... Tanya and Derek...'

Campbell reached out and put her hand on Abby's arm. 'I know, the naval launches are already on their way to get them, don't worry.'

Three of the small and fast naval boats had been standing by to pick up any pilot that had been forced to take to their glidewings. The two Misfits would know to head for them.

Abby nodded. 'Yes.' She looked around the airfield, taking in the glum crowd on the far side and the battered aircraft being wheeled down the ramp into the hangar. There was no sign of the pilots, though, they had already gone, not waiting for the commanding officer who had gotten two more of their friends killed. 'It's over, Dot, we can't...'

'It's not over!' Campbell hissed, the hand on Abby's arm turning hard and pulling the dejected woman around to face her. 'This isn't the first time pilots have been lost in war and it won't be the last. It probably won't even be the last time *you* lose pilots either and if you give up you just make a mockery of their sacrifice, so bloody well pull yourself together! Yes, today's fight didn't go our way, but that doesn't mean the war is over, it doesn't even mean this *battle* is over and the people who are left need you.'

Abby stared at Campbell for long seconds, but then she swallowed and nodded. 'You're right, sorry.' She looked around the airfield again with new, assessing eyes, seeing the Harridans and Spitsteams lined up, ready for takeoff, their pilots on their way out to them. 'Is there a raid incoming?'

Campbell nodded. 'Yes, Owen reported it taking off five minutes ago.' She grinned. 'Looks like we've got an early warning system again.'

Abby grunted. 'And he won't be as vulnerable as Charles.'

'He won't, but we'll keep an eye out for him anyway.' Campbell slipped her arm around Abby's shoulders and began pulling her away. 'Come on, let's leave the fitters to get repairs started and go have some tea.'

The grin plastered on his face was starting to make the muscles in his cheeks and jaw ache more than they did when he was trying to look like he was having fun, while one of the vapid starlets he was forced to act with in Hollywoodland fouled up take after take. He wasn't able to stop himself, though; the memory of how the guns of his airship had ripped apart the Misfits was just too delightful. It was a pity he couldn't ask for trophies from the downed aircraft - that would have really rubbed his victory in the Misfits' noses. Especially since all Bertha had suffered in return was the loss of a single fan and wouldn't even have to set down to make repairs.

His butler was kneeling in front of him, doing up the laces of his flight boots. When the man finished he stood and took the gloves from their place on the stand next to his helmet, then held them out one at a time.

Gruber slipped his hands into the thin, armoured gloves, the best that Herr Gerber in Berlin had ever produced, and looked at the man while he made sure that his fingers were seated properly.

'You seem particularly dour today, Lang, what's the matter? Are we out of starch for my collars?' Gruber chuckled, but didn't expect or wait for an answer, he just stalked from his private ready room and went through the pressure room into the hangar where Hölle was waiting for him.

The Misfits had blundered, just as he'd known they would. They were weakened and would be licking their wounds, feeling sorry for themselves.

There was no need to keep playing games with them; they were ripe for the picking.

CHAPTER 22

Gwen was barely able to get back to Malta. Excalibur had sustained more damage than she'd realised and was proving more and more difficult to control with every passing moment, a difficulty which her injuries were only compounding - her right eye was gummed shut with blood, which no amount of wiping with the back of her glove would clear, the left was blurred with tears which wouldn't stop coming, her head was throbbing fit to burst, and she was fairly sure that she was slipping briefly in and out of consciousness every so often.

She made it back to Malta safely enough, but there were a few moments during her landing when she thought she was going to give the airfield repair crews another hole to fill in. Both she and Excalibur survived intact, though, which was good enough for her under the circumstances.

She came to a halt well away from the entrance to the hangar. Her fitters would have to push the aircraft further to get it to the ramp, but she really didn't want to try to taxi into her place in the flight line only to black out again and plough through a crowd of people. It was the work of moments to shut the spring down and secure it and only then did she allow herself to relax, close her eyes and lean back against her headrest.

The next thing she knew, she was on her back and being lifted into the air. She opened her eye and found herself on a stretcher, being carried towards the ramp, with Kitty peering down at her, a panicked look on her face. She frowned.

'What's wrong?'

Kitty stared at her. 'What's wrong?!? Gwen, you were unconscious in your cockpit and you're covered in blood!'

Gwen tried to shake her head, but found that it had been restrained. 'It's just a flesh wound.'

'We'll be the judge of that, ma'am,' the burly-looking female medical orderly holding the stretcher at her head smiled down at her, 'but from where I'm standing it looks like you've been very lucky. Although you're probably going to need a new helmet and lenses.'

'My lenses!' Gwen automatically tried to reach up to pull her helmet off, but found her arms had been strapped down as well. She looked imploringly at Kitty. 'How bad is it?'

Kitty grimaced. 'I didn't want to say anything, but... it's bad. Sorry.'

Scarlet appeared in Gwen's vision on the other side of the stretcher to Kitty. 'Hey! What's...?' Her eyes widened as she looked down at Gwen and she turned slightly green. 'Oh wow, that's a lot of blood.'

'She insists she's fine,' said Kitty, deadpan.

'But I'm going to wait until I get an expert opinion,' said Gwen, with a quick glance up at the orderly, who smiled and nodded.

Scarlet pulled her hip flask from the thigh pocket of her work coveralls and sloshed it back and forth a couple of times. 'If you need anything for the pain, just let me know.' She grinned at the medical orderly's disapproving look. 'Medicinal brandy. Honest.' She winked, not very subtly, at Gwen. 'Oh, and we've just got word that Derek and Tanya have been picked up by the Biscuit Bangers. They're bringing them back now. There's still two launches out there, though, you know, just in case...'

Gwen shook her head. 'I really don't think they're going to find anything.'

'You never know.' Scarlet and Kitty had to back away from the side of the stretcher as it was carried down the relatively narrow personnel entrance to the bunker, but they returned when the orderlies took Gwen around the corner and into the emergency station. The station was small, though, and there was no room for them, so they left, promising to come back when they could, which meant they weren't there to see Gwen almost passing out again when her helmet was removed.

It didn't take long for the orderlies to find out that, apart from a mild concussion and moderate blood loss, Gwen was in fact almost as fine as she insisted she was. The piece of flak that had come in through her canopy should by all rights have killed her, but it had hit the mounting of her lenses at her right temple and the brass mechanism had deflected the shard of metal enough to save her life. The impact had still been enough to knock her out and a fairly deep furrow had been sliced across her forehead, but there was no lasting damage and the orderlies assured her that if it did leave a scar it would be almost invisible.

Gwen was more worried about her lenses than her health, though, and, as soon as they gave their verdict, she thanked them, then pulled her helmet towards her - they had insisted that she stay under observation for an hour and she intended to use the time dismantling the lenses.

The mounting on her right temple had been destroyed, but that was easy enough to repair, especially because the intricate controls, like a miniature switchboard, were on the left side of the helmet and had been touched. The eight wafer-thin lenses were another matter, though, and she became more and more dismayed as she removed one scratched, cracked or shattered piece of glass after another. In the end she found only a single one of the lenses intact and she wrapped it in a piece of cloth that the sympathetic orderly gave her and put it inside her bloodstained helmet for safe keeping.

The hour was soon up and she went to the ready room to shower and clean her flightsuit before changing into her day uniform and going in search of the rest of the squadron.

She found them sitting at a table in the mess. Predictably, they were all looking rather down in the dumps, although when Kitty caught sight of her she scowled.

'I told that orderly to come and get me when you were ready to leave!'

'I didn't need you to come; I told you - I'm fine!'

'I know that! I just wanted to be there to help you in the shower.' The American grinned and the mood around the table lightened a little at the reminder that, even though they had lost a lot that day, life still went on.

'My flightsuit needs some care, you can help me with that instead.'

'That's not what I meant and you know it.' Kitty pouted.

'I know.' Gwen took the seat next to her and gave her a long kiss. 'I'll make it up to you later.' She looked around. 'Where's Abby?'

'She went to Luqa with Dot,' said Scarlet, without looking up from her glass of what looked suspiciously like whisky. 'The bigwigs are having a meeting to work out what the hell we're going to do next.'

'I would have thought it was obvious what we do - we bunker down like Campbell said.'

'If that's all we need to do, then why did we just throw away our friends' lives trying to bloody destroy Bertha?' asked Scarlet, a note of bitterness in her voice.

Before Gwen could answer there was an influx of men and women, the pilots from the other squadrons.

The Misfits watched as they queued up at the buffet table. The contrast between them and the Misfits in that moment couldn't have been more profound, despite the fact that they had lost far more pilots - while they weren't exactly laughing and joking, they were in good spirits, jostling for position and stealing choice pieces of food from each other's plates. They were also describing the dogfights they had just taken part in and more than once the Misfits caught the word "Baron". Tellingly, though, the word wasn't uttered in the hushed and fearful tones that it used to be; it seemed that the elite Prussian squadron was no longer held in so much awe by the RAC's pilots.

Scarlet turned away from them and sighed as she pushed her drink away. 'I'm sorry, I just feel so helpless. I have the whole time we've been here.'

'Tell me about it,' grumbled Wendy.

The Misfits fell silent as the pilots from the other squadrons began taking seats around them within earshot. Quite a few called out greetings, but there weren't any remarks about Monty and Bruce; it just wasn't done.

Gwen stole a slice of cold toast from Kitty's plate and took a bite, then waved it as she spoke with her mouth full. 'So, are we going up with the next raid or are we waiting for Abby to get back?'

'Abby said to wait,' said Kitty. 'None of our aircraft are completely fit to fly anyway and there aren't any spare Spits or Harrys for us to borrow while they're repaired.'

'Oh. Alright.' Gwen shoved the remains of the toast into her mouth then grabbed another slice as she stood. 'Well, I'm going to go and see how Excalibur is anyway.'

'I'll come with you.' Kitty pushed her chair back and accompanied Gwen out into the hangar.

The Misfit aircraft were swarming with fitters and those Navy mechanics whose ships had been destroyed and had volunteered to stay on at Hal Far. None of the aircraft had escaped damage, not even the Spitsteams which had retreated from the fight early - they were all liberally peppered with small holes from the ack-ack fire, some of which had penetrated and damaged the wiring inside, requiring them to be at least partially dismantled. Dragon was the worst off, though, and it was a wonder Abby had been able to bring her home with most of her tail gone, including three-quarters of the vertical stabiliser and the left-side elevator.

Gwen barely spared a glance for the other machines; her focus was firmly on Excalibur. There were multiple holes of various sizes in her right wing and fuselage from the explosion of flak which had almost killed her and the flap on that side had been knocked off its mountings and was hanging uselessly, which explained her problems controlling the machine on landing. She had been extremely lucky.

After she'd inspected her aircraft and had a word with Giuseppe and his team about repairs, Gwen went to stores, where she was issued with a set of RAC lenses. They were rudimentary at best, with only three thick, poor quality lenses - two for magnification and a smoked one to reduce glare - but they were better than nothing and it wouldn't take long for her to repair the mechanism on her helmet and attach them.

Campbell and Abby returned in the mid-afternoon, bringing with them not only Tanya and Derek, but also some very welcome news - Bruce had been found by one of the naval launches. He'd been knocked unconscious when his aircraft had fallen apart around him and only just woken in time to deploy his glidewings to arrest his fall, which was why nobody had seen him do so. He'd been liberally peppered by shrapnel, losing a fair amount of blood as a result, and was suffering from exposure, but he was alive in the hospital at Valletta and was expected to make a full recovery eventually.

The senior officers had come to a decision about how best to proceed with the battle, but the Harridan and Spitsteam squadrons were up in the air, intercepting another raid, so Campbell had to wait until they came back down to inform the pilots of what it was.

In the meantime, the Misfits went to their ready room and got themselves tea and biscuits.

The pilots said nothing as they sat in the sofas, they just looked to Abby. They knew full well that there was going to be a briefing shortly, but they also knew they wouldn't have the chance to discuss whatever Campbell had to tell them in such a formal setting.

Abby stared at the coffee table while she sipped her drink and for a few seconds the pilots thought that she wasn't going to say anything, that they were going to have to draw the news from her, but then she looked up and stared directly at Derek.

'Before anything else, I want to know why Monty said to ask you why it was worth him risking his life.'

'He did, did he?' Derek smiled sadly. 'Well, that's because he and I had a very long and very enjoyable conversation back in England after we heard about Bertha. To cut a long story short, we came to the conclusion that if we managed to destroy her it would probably set in motion a chain of events leading to a Prussian defeat in the not so far future. We also theorised that if she were left unchecked then there would be no way that defeat would ever come about.'

Gwen nodded. 'I was up most of last night thinking about it...'

Kitty grinned. 'I can corroborate that, although she did take a rather enjoyable couple of breaks from thinking during the course of the night.'

Gwen blushed as the other pilots laughed, but forged on bravely. 'But that was the conclusion I came to as well.'

Derek raised an eyebrow at her. 'In one night while trying to get to sleep?'

When Gwen nodded he laughed. 'It took us almost a week and several reams of paper.'

Gwen shrugged. 'Maybe I was oversimplifying it.'

Scarlet chuckled. 'Or maybe they were over-drinking while they were over-thinking.'

'Probably.' Derek agreed, giving her a grin. 'Whatever the reason for us taking so long, it was the inevitable conclusion. So yes, in my eyes that justifies us risking our lives this morning. I also *fully* believe that if we get the chance we should try again.'

'I agree,' Gwen said nodding emphatically.

Abby looked from Derek to Gwen and back again, then sighed. 'Dot has been trying to tell me exactly that all morning, but I thought she was just trying to console me and I hadn't wanted to believe it until now. Unfortunately, it looks like we're not going to get another chance any time soon; Owen reports that Bertha has been pulled back over Sicily and is now holding steady at forty thousand feet. Gruber's taken his airship out of reach, as we knew he would.'

'Well, that's that,' said Derek with a shrug.

'Yes. Unless something changes,' replied Abby. 'Which brings me to the news an undersea boat brought from Alexandria this morning.' She took a deep breath to steel herself before delivering another blow to her pilots' already low morale. 'Greece fell at the end of April. Bertha dropped thousands of glidewing troopers behind our army and they were forced to surrender after taking heavy losses. The Prussians then went on to assault Crete and the island is expected to fall soon since most of the men and women that had been stationed there had been sent to reinforce Greece.'

The pilots murmured, expressing their dismay, and she let them finish before continuing. 'All along we've been assuming that an attack would come by sea, like in Britain last summer, and that we would be able to stop it like we did then, by using our undersea boats and aircraft. It seems that the Prussians have circumvented the need for a seaborne invasion with the glidewing troopers, though, and our army just doesn't have a big enough presence on Malta to defeat the kind of numbers that were reported in Greece.'

'So, what you're saying is we're in serious trouble.' Drake said.

'That's one way of putting it, yes.'

'I think Bruce will find a far more colourful way of putting it when we tell him.' Scarlet said with a grin.

'I'm sure he will.' Abby said, smiling for the first time. 'But we're not lost yet. We know what the Prussians are going to try so they don't have surprise on their side and with Owen in the air we'll see them coming. Also, Bertha is going to have to get close enough to drop the troops and we have a significant amount of anti-aircraft batteries around the island to make that difficult. Those troops then have to make it to the ground alive...' She hesitated, knowing that her pilots weren't going to like what she was going to say next. 'And that is where we come in - our job will be to shoot as many of them out of the sky as possible.'

To her surprise, though, nobody seemed to baulk at the idea and Scarlet even smiled and rubbed her hands together gleefully.

'At last! Something I can do!'

Abby looked around the table. 'You don't mind?'

'They're not pilots who've bailed out, they're shock troops,' Kitty said, 'it's the same as shooting them on the ground. Besides, after what Gruber did to Gwen how can they expect us not to?'

Abby nodded in understanding; Gruber had shot Gwen down in Muscovy, then tried to kill her when she was hanging helplessly from her glidewings.

'In the meantime we're doing what Campbell said - we're not going to carry out any bombing raids, or attack any convoys that aren't coming here, we're going to restrict ourselves to meeting the raids that come over, because they might just decide to send over a few transport aircraft filled with soldiers while we're not looking.'

Derek frowned. 'At the rate we're losing fighters, we're not going to be able to do that very effectively for long and what's to stop the Prussians from just sending Bertha now, with one of the raids, and brute forcing their way through?'

'Dot did ask the same thing in the meeting. The only thing we could come up with was that, if they were able to, they would have done so already, before they showed their hand with Bertha. Maybe the troops aren't ready yet, or they want to be sure they have air superiority before they try to land them, we just don't know.' Abby shrugged. 'Whatever the reason, though, all we have to do is hold out for another week; there is a convoy on the way and this ones all for us. The War Minister, in his infinite wisdom, has finally decided that Malta might be important after all and, as well as sending enough supplies and troops to hold the island indefinitely, he has diverted two of our newest carriers from the Atlantic. When they get here, they will have an immediate effect on, not just the air battle over Malta, but the balance of power in the whole Mediterranean.'

Since they were grounded, the Misfits had some time on their hands and they used it to go to the hospital in Valletta to see Bruce, timing the journey between enemy raids.

The Australian had lost so much blood that he'd had to have an emergency transfusion on the boat that had picked him up, but the naval medics hadn't been able to stop the bleeding and they'd run out of supplies on the way back to the island. They had only been able to keep him alive long enough to get him to the hospital by taking blood directly from a string of volunteers. His wounds had been patched up easily enough by the doctors using the proper facilities at the hospital, but he was still so weak that he wasn't even able to sit up to greet them. He didn't smile very much, either, but none of them were sure whether that was because he couldn't summon the energy, or the will, after the death of his best friend and wingmate.

They stayed for an hour, keeping him company, but in the end he asked them to leave, pleading tiredness. Even though it was obvious he was lying and just wanted to be alone with his misery, they said nothing and obeyed his wishes, knowing that he just needed time.

They went back to Hal Far to lend moral support to the pilots going up to confront the bombers, but there was very little they could actually do and it was demoralising seeing the numbers of men and women coming back dwindling slowly with each sortie and not being able to do anything about it.

Eventually, darkness came, the Coalition air raids finished for the day, and Father Bugelli arrived to collect photographs of the day's fallen pilots to take to the cathedral. The Misfits gave him Monty's photograph, then left to go back to the house.

With Bruce in the hospital and Owen and Wendy up in Bloodhound keeping a twenty-four hour watch on Bertha, it didn't feel right to drink to Monty's memory yet, so the Misfits wearily went straight to bed, determined to get a good night's sleep and be rested in order to give the Prussians and Italians a good seeing to the next day.

CHAPTER 23

The Misfits were woken an hour before dawn by the sound of honking horns coming from right outside.

Gwen was absolutely exhausted after not having slept the previous night and then being injured, but she came instantly awake as two MG's burst in through the front door of the house, shouting for them to stand to. She immediately knew what it signified and cursed. 'They're coming. We're not ready.'

Kitty looked up at her sleepily and snorted. 'When are we ever?'

'Report, Sergeant!'

Abby's bawled order over the banisters carried to every corner of the house, as did the sergeant's answer.

'Commodore Campbell has put all aircraft on two-minute readiness, ma'am. All pilots are to go to their aircraft immediately, please.'

'Right you are, Sergeant, we'll be down directly.' Abby looked up from the man to find every one of her pilots peering at her, either from their doorways or over the banister of the landing above. She frowned. 'Well? You heard the man! Chop bloody chop!'

The Misfits raced for their clothes, putting on the bare minimum for decency, knowing that they would be changing into their flightsuits as soon as they got to the airfield, then ran down the stairs and into the dark of the night where two of the fastest of the base's autocars were waiting for them.

A hair-raising minute and a half later the autocars bounced onto the airfield and raced directly across, past the long lines of aircraft already waiting for their pilots, and almost literally flew down the ramp into the hangar. They came screeching to a halt in front of the ready room and they ran through the door, held open for them by another MG, and sprinted to the changing room.

'What's going on?' Farrier asked, as she shrugged into her dark blue naval flightsuit.

Abby shrugged, using the movement to seat her suit properly. 'I would assume the attack that we thought wasn't going to take place for a while is in fact taking place.'

As soon as each of the pilots was ready they grabbed sandwiches from the tray by the door and stuffed them in their mouths as they ran back out, then up the ramp, where they were waved to their aircraft by the ground coordinator.

The fitters had worked through the night, as they had so often before, and the Misfits' aircraft were, if not spotless, at least serviceable, although Dragon's missing tail sections looked like they had been replaced by those of an MU9 from the graveyard - it was actually a fairly close match, design-wise.

Two-minute readiness meant, very simply, that the pilots had to be ready to be in the air within two minutes of the call to scramble coming. This required their fully-wound aircraft to be on the airfield and for them to be strapped in and ready to flick the switches which released their spring tensions. Pilots were only ever brought to two minute readiness if a raid was imminent or expected imminently because it was extremely stressful for them to be kept in a constant state of tension, not to mention uncomfortable if the weather was hot, like it had been over the summer in England. However, the Misfits had only been in their cockpits for five minutes before the order for them to take off came and they immediately accelerated onto the field, leaving the Harridan and Spitsteam squadrons waiting patiently behind them for their turn.

No sooner were they airborne and climbing towards what seemed like a million stars than Campbell's voice came over the radio. 'Badger Leader, this is Haven. Watcher reports contacts heading this way. Possibly fighters.'

'Only possibly, Haven?'

'Roger, Badger Leader. There are ten plus medium-sized contacts which read as either light bombers or twin-springed fighters. They are currently at angels fifty, though, hence the uncertainty.'

'Say again, please, Haven... Fifty? Five zero?'

'Roger, Badger Leader. Angels five zero.'

'And what on earth are you expecting us to do about them, Haven?'

'Nothing directly, Badger Leader. At that altitude it is likely that they are intending to threaten Watcher. He has been sent west thirty miles. If they alter course towards him we will know he is their target, in which case he will be ordered to descend. This might be a prelude to an attack, though, so we *have* to keep him up for as long as possible. He'll make angels ten over the island and you are to position above him to cover. Understood?'

'Roger, Haven.'

The Misfits flew on in silence, climbing west towards Owen and Wendy in Bloodhound, waiting for further instructions. 'Badger Leader, be advised that contacts are changing course towards Watcher.'

'Well, bloody well get him down, then, Haven!'

'Roger, Badger Leader, the order has already been given.' There was a chiding note in Campbell's voice as she replied, letting Abby know that her outburst was unnecessary, but there was no real reprimand in it; it was obvious that the Misfits' leader would be worried about her people. 'Watcher is descending through angels twenty-five, fifteen miles due west of you.'

Gwen peered into the gloom, searching for any sign of the large aircraft. At that distance she should easily have been able to make it out, glinting in the light of the rising sun, but found that her new RAC lenses were completely inadequate for the job.

'Three here. I see him, Leader. He's slightly above and to the right of us.'

'I don't... Alright, got him. Thank you, Three. Badger Leader to Watcher, we have you in sight.'

'Roger, Badger Leader, and thank you.'

The Misfits waited until Bloodhound had descended past them, then turned to take up positions over her.

'Herr Gruber,' the communications officer came to a halt in front of his two senior officers and saluted. 'Seraph Squadron reports the spy aircraft has descended to ten thousand feet and is being shepherded by the Misfits.'

'Good.' Gruber grinned and rubbed his hands as he turned to the admiral. 'You have your instructions, Admiral. Launch the attack.'

The admiral seethed as he watched Gruber leave the bridge, going to join his squadron for the assault on Malta. The man was strutting around giving the orders as if it was his plan, but it wasn't. He hadn't even come up with the solution to the main obstacle to the plan, namely how to force away Owen Llewellyn's aircraft so that the operation would be able to proceed unobserved. It had been the Crimson Barons' engineer, Walter Blume, who had actually come up with the solution to that problem - a squadron of specially-designed high-altitude fighters - and he'd had to approach the admiral directly with it after Gruber had refused to listen to him.

The imbecile would probably end up taking the credit for the day's work anyway, just as he had for the innovation of the glidewing troopers, even though it had taken the daring escape of Lord Drake and his friends for anyone to realise the possibility of dropping troops from Bertha - ironically, the British peer had handed them the victory in Greece on a platter and would now give them Malta as well.

Not for the first time, the admiral wished that someone would shoot the arrogant popinjay down. Not only would life be a lot less stressful for so many people, but Gruber's death would actually make the war so much easier to win.

It was not the moment for such thoughts, though, and he thrust them aside to concentrate on the delicate coordination of the operation. He turned to the communications officer. 'Tell Seraph Squadron to hold their position and send codeword *Caesar* to all forces.'

'Aye aye, sir.'

As the man walked to the bank of radios, the admiral looked to his first officer. 'Turn Bertha towards Malta and ready the fans for full thrust, then inform Oberst Kühn that we will be over the objective in two hours and that he should ready his troops for drop.'

'Aye aye, Admiral.'

As the man hurried off to the wheel to carry out his orders, the admiral walked to the observation window in the floor and peered down through the plate glass. It was the work of a couple of seconds to get the correct angle through one of the metre-square magnifying lenses embedded in it and find what he was looking for - the fleet of ships outside Catania, almost forty kilometres to the north. As he watched, they received his order and the white lines of their wakes began to extend behind them as they set sail.

He smiled; it felt good to have a proper naval command again.

'Haven, this is Watcher. I'm seeing a major raid taking off.'

'Roger, Watcher. Waiting for details.'

It took almost a minute for Owen and his four-person crew to sort through the various radar returns coming from Sicily; the relatively low altitude that Bloodhound was flying at complicating matters and when his voice came back on, there was an incredulous note in it.

'Three... make that *four* hundred plus aircraft total. Advance group of one hundred plus fighters coming in fast at angels ten. Estimate arrival of the fighters in ten minutes.'

'Understood, Watcher.' There was a brief pause as Campbell considered the situation, but then she made the only decision she could. 'Land immediately, Watcher.'

'But...'

'That's an order, Watcher.'

'Roger, Haven, landing now.'

'Badger Leader, make angels twenty and move to intercept bandits. Gladiator, Soldier and Warrior Squadrons are scrambling now. Gladiator will join you when they can, while Soldier and Warrior will intercept the bombers.'

'Rodger, Haven. Badger Squadron moving to intercept.'

Abby replied calmly and matter-of-factly, but she had just acknowledged an order for eight fighters to try to hold off more than a hundred until the other RAC squadrons could arrive. What was left unsaid was why it was necessary - it would take Owen in the slow-moving Bloodhound ten minutes to land and at least another couple to be taken down into the safety of the hangar. He would be a sitting duck if the enemy were left unchecked and the British would be left without any kind of surveillance whatsoever, right when they needed it the most.

Gwen glanced around, as the Misfits raced to meet the incoming fighters, taking in what had become of the squadron since leaving Britain.

What had once been A and B flight were now unrecognisable; only Dragon and Excalibur remained of the aircraft which had travelled to the island and, of the four which had been built since, only Lion survived. Everybody else was flying a Spitsteam, most of which had been hastily assembled and lacked even a splash of colour to mark them as Misfits.

The pilots had changed almost as much as the aircraft, with almost as many new faces as old and she idly wondered at what point they would cease to be Misfit Squadron. Would it be when they were all flying mass-produced aircraft? Or would Abby be the keystone without which the whole thing collapsed? She suspected the latter, but hoped her theory never had to be put to the test.

As it was, Misfit Squadron was going to have a hard time surviving the War Minister if they ever made it home; after disobeying the order to rebuild, the King was probably going to have a hard time keeping them from being turned into a normal squadron, or even disbanded completely and spread around the RAC.

A future without the Misfits bringing hope to the British people and confounding the enemy wherever it was most needed wasn't a particularly pleasant one, but before she could get too depressed by the thought, her radio crackled and Abby's voice broke in, dragging her back to the present and the more immediate threat to the squadron's continued existence.

'Alright, Badgers, we've done this before, no need to get nervous.'

'Who's nervous, Leader?' Drake laughed, apparently feeling that he had to take over the job of making the fight less serious in Bruce's absence. 'I'm seeing nines, double h one-nineties and those new Italian machines, but no Barons. This'll be a piece of cake! We just need to keep bouncing them until they run home crying to their mothers.'

While the enemy had greater numbers, the Misfits had been in the air already and had the height advantage over them. That would usually mean that they could dictate the terms of the fight, but unfortunately, they had other concerns apart from just shooting down as many aircraft as they could and Abby silenced any chuckles that Drake's comments had given rise to by pointing them out.

'It's not going to be that simple, Seven; we have to get as many of them interested in us as possible to keep them off Owen. So we're only going to do one pass on the lead group before getting into the mix.'

'Sounds like fun, Leader.'

'I'm sure it will be, Seven. Alright, Badgers, stay in your pairs, watch out for each other and happy hunting.'

After the chorus of replies, Gwen heard her radio click as Abby turned to their private frequency. 'Check in, Two.'

'Excalibur's fine, Leader.' Despite the damage Excalibur had taken the day before she was handling well. The only quibble Gwen could possibly have was a vibration in her canopy and a freezing cold draft which was making her cheeks ache - the glass panel that had replaced the one which had been shattered in the attack on Bertha had been cut in a hurry and wasn't a particularly snug fit.

'I'm glad to hear that, we're going to need her in tip-top condition. Dragon's a bit twitchy today, though; she doesn't like this new tail one bit, so I might have to ask you to take the lead at some point.'

'Understood, Leader.'

'Good. Right then, we're going for the group of one-nineties in the middle at the front. Diving in ten seconds.'

Gwen peered over Excalibur's nose at the huge group of fighters in a roughly square formation, several thousand feet below them. Strangely, the fighters weren't even trying to climb towards the Misfits, instead they seemed to be ignoring them, a tactic which was tantamount to suicide. Gwen wondered what they could be thinking of, but then felt a chill when she realised they were probably under orders to make directly for Owen, which would make the job of distracting them that much harder. It also meant that he was in real danger.

More determined than ever to shoot down as many of the enemy as possible, she searched the incoming aircraft for the Hock-Hund 190's. It should have been easy, due to their having a shorter, stubbier silhouette than the other fighters, but the RAC lenses just weren't up to the job and she cursed them again as she squinted down at the mass formation. She found them right as Abby did a neat roll into a steep dive and kept her focus on them as she followed her down. Abby hadn't been exaggerating, Dragon was twitching and moving extremely erratically and she had to keep making small adjustments to stay on her wing. It was going to take some neat piloting for her hit anything, but if anyone could it was Abigail Lennox.

Abby always went for the lead aircraft with her first pass, so Gwen set her sights on the leader of the second pair. The gap closed incredibly fast and she opened fired, just as flashes in the corner of her eye told her that her wingmate was doing the same, but then she was too busy to take any more notice of Abby. She gave her first target a half-second burst, then touched her controls to give his wingman the same treatment. The aircraft were so densely-packed that she even had time to fire on a third aircraft as it swam lazily across her nose, but then she was through the formation and underneath it.

'Damn, these guys are either the most disciplined pilots I've ever seen or the dumbest.'

Once again Drake's comment was worthy of Bruce and Gwen found herself chuckling, but was cut off almost immediately when intense G forces took her breath away as she followed Abby into a tight loop.

The stress lessened as Excalibur's nose came above the horizon and when she was more or less vertical she was able to peer up at the enemy fighters.

The accepted tactics when being dived on were either to turn into the attack or scatter, but the enemy fighters had done neither, which had just made the Misfits' job easier and meant they suffered much higher losses than the needed to. More than a dozen of the aircraft had fallen out of the formation, either stricken and turning for home or falling towards the sea below. However, it was the group of forty or so fighters which had left it voluntarily which caught her attention.

'Looks like you spoke too soon, Digger.' Gwen said.

'Looks like, Goosy.' Drake replied, his grin audible.

'They're still not very clever, though,' said Abby. 'They're doing our job for us and taken themselves out of the fight. Ignore them, concentrate on the others.'

The group of fighters had been able to turn tighter than the speeding Misfits and had already reversed course towards them, but the Misfits' manoeuvre allowed them to regain their height advantage and they were able to simple fly over them. A few of the Fleas pointed their noses skywards, trying to bring their guns to bear, but they were out of range and their desperate firing did nothing more than waste ammunition.

The Misfits had more than enough speed to catch up with the first group of fighters and they began to pick them off, putting burst after burst into them. It was a duck shoot and they were knocked out of the sky one by one, but they continued to press on stubbornly towards Malta, now less than a dozen miles away, making only the barest of efforts to evade the incoming fire.

When they caught sight of the other British squadrons rising up to meet them something snapped, though, and their determination evaporated. They spun and banked in all directions, turning to confront the aircraft which had been dogging them, seeking to destroy them before the reinforcements arrived, and the Misfits suddenly found themselves swarmed, caught between the two enemy fighter forces and fighting for their lives.

'Seraph Squadron report that the spy aircraft has just landed, Admiral.' The communications officer called out from the other side of the room. 'They can no longer see us.'

'Excellent.' The admiral left the observation window and stalked over to his first officer. 'Full thrust. Take us to the objective.'

'Aye aye, sir.' The man nodded at the sailor standing ready by the wheel. 'Full speed ahead.'

'Full speed ahead, aye, sir.' The sailor grinned and turned to the ship-style engine order telegraph. A bell rang as he pushed the lever forwards, then backwards, then forwards again, as if he were on a ship, signalling in the engineer to adjust the engine speed. It was completely unnecessary on Berth because the fans were controlled by electrical circuits connected to the bridge and the telegraph increased and decreased their speed, but the admiral liked his men to act as if they were on board a proper vessel, after all, when the Kaiser eventually woke up to the fact that Bertha was just a huge waste of time and resources, they would all find themselves back where they belonged.

The admiral watched the pointer slowly make its way up to meet the selected fan speed as the springs in the bottom of the airship released their tension and felt the increasing vibrations below his feet. He grinned; despite how much he detested his posting, he had to admit there was a certain thrill in charging into battle on such a huge vessel.

Gwen struggled to stay with Abby as she carried out one impossible manoeuvre after another. Her job as the wingmate was to identify and guard her leader against incoming threats, but, with the sky and the ground constantly swapping places in a dizzying fashion and the sheer amount of enemy aircraft around them, it was nigh on impossible. However, that abundance of enemy fighters meant there was no shortage of targets to take potshots at and a quick glance at the dial on her instrument panel told her that she'd used almost half of her ammunition in the short time since the Misfits had first dived on the enemy.

Her head was starting to throb painfully with the physical and mental strain, though, and she didn't know how much longer she could keep up the same intensity. A single slip could well be fatal, for her or for her wingmate, so it was a relief when an unfamiliar voice came over the general frequency.

'Badger Leader this is Gladiator Leader, would you mind if we joined in the fun?'

'Not at all, Gladiator Leader, be my guest.'

'Thank you, Badger Leader, attacking now.'

If the Coalition forces had been uncoordinated before, they were thrown into absolute chaos when an extended line of twelve Spitsteams swept across them, cannon blazing. Most of the Misfits pilots immediately found a distracted enemy aircraft in their sights and didn't let the opportunity pass them by.

A pair of the dark red and gold Italian machines wandered lazily across Gwen's nose and she squeezed her trigger, giving them a quick squirt each. She was rewarded with the sight of a big chunk of wing coming off of one, but she didn't see if she'd hit the second, because Abby changed direction and took her away from them.

A new voice came over the radio, providing a fresh distraction.

'Badger Leader, this is Warrior Leader. The bombers have some of your old friends with them. Whenever you get a chance you should come up and say hello.'

Finding herself with a moment to catch her breath, Gwen scanned the sky overhead, looking for the bombers, wondering what the woman was referring to. She found what she was looking for almost immediately, even with the awful RAC lenses - bright red fighters mixed in with the large machines, tussling with the Harridans.

'Haven to Badger Leader, Watcher is safe and sound. Feel free to take Warrior Leader up on her invitation.'

'Badger Leader, this is Gladiator Leader, we can handle this lot, go have some fun.'

'Thank you, Gladiator Leader. All Badgers, disengage to the south and regroup. Let's go and say hello to Mr Gruber and his friends.'

Gruber banked Hölle behind an HO111, using it to block the incoming fire from the two Harridan fighters that were chasing him. The British pilots were hampered by the large machine and he continued the turn, intensifying it, using his aircraft's superior agility to come around behind them. He poured cannon rounds into the wingman and grinned in satisfaction when he saw huge holes appear in his wing, right next to the cockpit. He stabbed at his controls and switched his aim to the leader, but, before he could open fire, he caught a flash of yellow out of the corner of his eye. He immediately disengaged, rolling under the bomber formation and into clear sky; it was reasonably satisfying to kill inferior pilots in their useless Harridans, but it was nothing compared to the excitement of killing a Misfit.

Gwen peered anxiously up at the red machines of the Crimson Barons. Almost as soon as the Misfits had grouped together and begun their climb, the Barons had abandoned the bombers they were supposed to be protecting and had headed straight for them, forming up as they came. Abby's plan of climbing to the same level as the Prussian fighters before turning to face them was now impossible and the Misfits were at a severe disadvantage, just as the large group of Coalition fighters had been only a short while before.

'Looks like we're going to have to brave their guns or head for home, Badgers.'

'Why would we go home, Leader? We've got them right where we want them!'

'Yes, thank you, Seven, I'm trying to be serious here. There's twice as many of them as there are of us, we're tired, our aircraft are damaged, and we're running low on ammunition. Nobody would think the worse of us if we turned tail and ran this time and hopefully we'd draw them far enough away from the bombers for the Harridans to get a few.'

'Five here, Leader. The Barons have been doing all they could to avoid us, so if they're trying to engage us now they must have a reason. Maybe we *should* run.'

'Nah! Gruber probably just thinks we're easy prey, Derek,' Drake said. 'I think we should show him he's wrong.'

'So do I, Seven.' Abby said. 'Right, then, Badgers, we're going to stay on this heading and get as much height as we can until they dive on us. You all know the form - break off individually just before they get in range, but get back into your pairs as quickly as you can. Understood?'

Gwen acknowledged, then craned her head to look up and backwards at the Baron aircraft, just visible in the rear of her canopy. What Abby was proposing was incredibly risky, but it wasn't as if there were any better options, except for diving away for the cover of the anti-aircraft guns of Malta.

As the Barons got closer she was able to make out the individual aircraft. There were sixteen of them, a full squadron, so, either they hadn't lost any aircraft over Greece, or they had already rebuilt. Apart from Gruber, who seemed to have an almost pathological need to stand out from the crowd, the squadron all had identical aircraft, *Blutsaugers*, painstakingly-crafted machines that were superior to the mass-produced ones that were available to the rest of the Fleas, or the RAC. Like MU9's, Spitsteams and Harridans, the design of the Blutsaugers hadn't changed much since they had been seen over Britain the previous summer, but Gruber's aircraft was relatively new and vastly different from the one he'd flown over Britain. Then it had been *Flamme*, the distinctive triplane which had become synonymous with him at the start of the war. It had had incredible manoeuvrability and, with the latest in Prussian spring technology, decent speed, but technology had moved forward since he'd built it and it had become obsolete. He had built a new aircraft, Hölle, which was an amalgamation of the best parts of Dragonfly and Wasp, the aircraft that Abby and Gwen had been flying at the time and over Muscovy it had proven to be superior to any of the machines the Misfits had been flying. However, now the Misfits had Excalibur and Dragon and Gwen was sure that both aircraft would be more than a match for Hölle in a fair fight.

Whether Gruber would allow either of them to have a fair fight was debatable, though.

'Here they come, Leader.'

Kitty's sharp eyes immediately spotted the change in aspect as the elite Prussian squadron nosed over into a dive.

'Thank you Three. Alright, happy hunting, Badgers.'

The Misfits had been slowly drifting apart, making it harder for the Prussians to target them and giving each other room to manoeuvre.

Gwen had been watching the aircraft approaching and when she judged they were about five seconds away from being in range she began to push down on her right rudder pedal, making it look like she was beginning a turn while in fact Excalibur was just sideslipping. Her powerful airscrew quickly started to have an effect, though, and began pulling the aircraft in the direction she was pointing, but Gwen had judged it to a T and just as that started to happen she stomped her left foot down hard and slammed the stick hard over before pulling it into her lap, throwing Excalibur into a hard turn the other way.

Something impacted heavily on Excalibur, making her lurch and Gwen braced herself for more, but none came. She sharply reversed her turn to point her nose back at the Prussian machines, which were only just pulling out of their dives, and pushed the throttle forward to full unwind, sending Excalibur accelerating after them.

'Bloody hell, not again... Five, bailing out.'

Derek's voice was strained, but Gwen couldn't tell if it was due to pain or effort. She shot a glance to the side where his Spitsteam had been and saw it spiralling down, a third of one wing gone - it was the one defect of the wonderfully designed fighters; they were so delicately balanced that they couldn't take anything like the same punishment as a Harridan could and a few hits could knock one out of the sky.

She kept half an eye on the fighter as she chased after the Barons, but when she saw the small figure thrown clear she ignored it and turned her full attention on her prey.

Gruber grinned as he watched the holes appear in the wing of the Spitsteam. The Misfits' tactics had been basic, predictable, and all he'd had to do was throttle back and let his men get slightly in front of him so that he'd had time to react when the target he'd picked started its turn. It had then been an easy matter to put several cannon rounds into the machine, more than enough in his experience to knock one of the too-fragile British aircraft out of the sky.

For a moment he regretted shooting down one of the inferior Misfit pilots rather than his preferred targets - Abigail Lennox and Gwenevere Stone - but he had made a decision and he was going to stick with it. He would rip apart Misfit Squadron one by one until it was only those two arrogant women left. Until all their friends were dead. Until they realised just how mistaken they had been in thinking they were as good as him.

Then and only then would he kill them.

'Well, this is going to be fun,' said Drake.

Gwen glanced across Dragon's tail at Lion, tucked in on Abby's other wing, and found Drake looking back at her.

She grinned. 'What's the matter, Digger? Are you scared of a few boys just because they have prettier machines than you?'

'Actually, it's more the fact that there's sixteen of them and just three of us that concerns me.'

The Barons had tried to use the speed from their dive to climb back into the sky and regain their height advantage, but they hadn't banked on the power of Dragon, Lion and Excalibur, and when they turned to come back at the Misfits they found them nearly at the same height at them and fast approaching firing range. The Spitsteams hadn't been able to keep up, though, and were lagging about a mile behind, leaving the three aircraft to face the Barons alone, at least for a few seconds.

Gwen chuckled. 'Leader, I'm not sure that Badger Seven really has what it takes to be a Misfit; he doesn't seem to be revelling in the prospect of almost certain death.'

'That's enough chit-chat for now, please, children. Prepare to break.'

'Yes, ma'am!'

Gwen laughed as Drake pronounced the honorific with more "u" that he usually did, but she didn't have time to comment because the Barons were upon them.

She spun Excalibur away from Dragon just as pinpoints of light came into being on the wings of the red aircraft and as the bright tracers flashed past her canopy she squeezed her trigger and sent her own lancing back.

Most Fleas seemed to freeze like rabbits in the beam of a hunting lantern when the Misfits evaded their fire, but the Baron pilots were made of sterner stuff and reacted immediately, manoeuvring frantically to put off the aim of the British.

The aircraft Gwen had been aiming at rolled sharply onto its side and began banking away, but it was a split second too late and her cannons blasted a hole in its tail, the impact knocking it sideways and sending it spinning. Two more Blutsaugers, which had also unsuccessfully tried to target her, flitted by on either side of her, almost close enough to touch, but then she was through the red aircraft and into clear air again.

'Take that, you blighter!'

Gwen snorted with laughter at Drake's shout as she put Excalibur into a tight climbing turn, bleeding her speed off.

The Barons had scattered every which way, dividing into pairs, and she craned her head, fighting against the G forces to search for threats and targets.

Dragon was turning with her, but Excalibur was coming around quicker, so it was Gwen who first noticed that four of the red aircraft weren't turning with the others.

'Gruber's going after the Spits!'

'I see him, Two. There's nothing we can do about him right now, though,' Abby replied. 'Keep your mind on the fight, they can take care of themselves.'

'Roger, Leader.'

It was easier said than done to ignore the deadly threat to the Spitsteams and Kitty, but Gwen had no choice as she suddenly found herself fighting for her own survival, as the three Misfits spun and weaved their way among the twelve Blutsaugers.

The understanding Gwen had developed with Abby over hundreds, if not thousands of hours on her wing had the two of them instinctively leading pursuers under each other's guns, coordinating things with barely a word. Drake didn't have the same connection to either of them, but he was just as effective; Lion, like the Harridan, proving to be extremely adept in such close quarters fighting.

One after another of the Blutsaugers passed through the sights of the three Misfit aircraft and none of them came out the other side unscathed, but after more than a minute of fighting only three of them had been forced out of combat.

'They've done something to these damn things,' complained Abby, 'they're nowhere near as easy to knock down as they used to be.'

'They've probably stolen more of Gwen's ideas,' quipped Drake, his voice strained as he pulled a maximum rate turn, attempting to evade the fire of the two Blutsaugers that he had on his tail.

Gwen saw his difficulty and rolled towards him. For a brief second they were almost nose to nose, but then they flashed past, their tails missing each other by scant feet. She opened fire on his pursuers and grunted in satisfaction as holes appeared in the armoured glass canopy of one. She pointedly ignored what her very last cannon round had done to the man within, though. 'Whatever they've done, this is taking too long - my cannons are out and I'm down to a couple of seconds of machine guns.'

'Me too, Two, but I don't think we're going to have to do this for much longer; the bombers are going home and reinforcements are on their way.'

Gwen took the first opportunity she had to glance at the bombers. They had turned and were flying back north, their jobs done, still being harassed by the Harridan squadrons. The remains of the fighter flight had gone with them, but instead of pursuing, the Spitsteams of Gladiator squadron had turned back and were now grouped up and climbing to join the Misfits.

'The Barons aren't going to like being outnumbered, are they?' said Gwen. 'I wonder how much longer...' she grinned. 'Never mind, there they go.'

Even as she had spoken, the remaining Barons disengaged from the three Misfits and dived away, racing to join the rest of the Prussian aircraft. She watched them for a couple of seconds, but then something occurred to her and she inverted Excalibur and searched below her for Kitty and the rest of the Misfits.

She spotted Gruber and his flight easy enough as they raced after the retreating raid, their red aircraft standing out clearly out against the dusty landscape of the island below. She was pleased to see only three of them, but of the Misfit Spitsteams there was no sign.

'Haven, this is Badger Leader. Are you open for business?'

Abby's voice came over the general frequency and Dorothy Campbell replied from the command centre of Hal Far after only a couple of seconds.

'Badger Leader, this is Haven. By the time you get here we will be.'

'Thank you, Haven. On our way. Badgers, return to base.'

'Roger, Leader. Seven returning to base.'

Drake acknowledged immediately, but Gwen stayed silent, scanning the sky below for any sign of her friends, waiting to see if anyone else did. However, all she heard was the soft crackling of the occasional burst of static and finally she had no choice but to acknowledge the order herself, abandon her search and dive for the island.

A good morning's work, thought Gruber as he put Hölle into a gentle dive towards the island just over the horizon. All of the Misfit Spitsteams had been destroyed, leaving only the two women and that pest, Drake, to deal with.

He was fully aware that at least a couple of the pilots had survived, but that didn't matter; he would just keep shooting them down until they didn't get up again. Besides, the ease with which he had defeated them would weigh on their minds and they would cower from him in the future, which would only serve to further demoralise her true targets.

Gruber laughed to himself; the Misfits were already barely worth his attention anymore, but when Malta fell in a matter of days they would cease to exist entirely and the Barons would rule the skies again, as was their right.

And perhaps he would have a few of them as his guests for a while, as he rebuilt his labour force in the depths of Bertha.

CHAPTER 24

There was a single Spitsteam at Hal Far when Gwen flew over, but it was upside down, having apparently made a forced landing and hit one of the holes from the bombing. A gang of men and women were working to hook it up to a crane, while a medical vehicle was racing away from it, swerving around potholes. Gwen peered at the aircraft as it was lifted, but it was impossible to make out whose it was, or even whether it was a Misfit or Gladiator machine. She just hoped whoever it belonged to wasn't too badly hurt.

True to Campbell's promise, there was a big enough patch of the airfield repaired and marked with white cloths for the British aircraft to start landing when they arrived and the Misfits, having been up the longest, were lowest on tension and given clearance to land first. They were taken straight down into the hangar where they found Bloodhound tucked out of the way to one side, but no Misfit Spitsteams.

Gwen jumped out and gave her fitters the barest of greetings before running over to Dragon, arriving just as Owen and Scarlet did.

Abby held up a hand to forestall her before she could say anything. 'I know. Come on, let's go see Dot.'

Drake fell in with them before they were half way across the hangar. 'The Spit outside is one of Gladiator's. The pilot's a bit knocked about, but she's going to be fine.' He pointedly gazed around the hangar. 'So...'

Abby interrupted without looking at him or slowing her march. 'We're going to find out now.'

The five pilots went past the guards posted outside the door of the operations room, through the blast curtains and into the room.

The operations room at Hal Far was very similar to the ones the Misfits had seen in England. It was dominated by a huge map table in the centre of the room, which showed the five hundred miles around Malta, most of it blue. A dozen men and women stood around it with long poles, like snooker rests, waiting to push wooden markers around it when prompted by the operators serving the long desk of radio receivers sitting along one wall. A huge board, displaying the status of the fighter squadrons on the island, covered the far wall and lights on it showed the Misfits and 261 squadron as "rearm - rewind", but 126 and 185 squadrons as still being "engaged".

A small balcony, accessed via a short flight of stairs next to the door, overlooked the room and that was where they found Dorothy Campbell, frowning down at the map as she spoke into her headset. She looked up as they came in, but, as Abby started to mount the steps onto the balcony, she held up her hand to stop her, then handed a sheet of paper to the man sitting next to her, covering her microphone to say a few words to him. When she was done she gave Abby an apologetic smile, but then returned her attention to the map table and the markers being pushed around on it which represented the men and women in mortal combat high above.

The man, an aviator lieutenant with grey hair, stood and hurried down the stairs. He motioned for the Misfits to precede him from the room and, once the door was closed behind them, he nodded to Abby. 'Group Captain, the Sky Commodore apologises for not speaking to you in person, but she won't leave her post until our fighters are home. She told me to give you this and answer any questions you might have.'

He handed the piece of paper to Abby, who scanned it quickly. Her face fell and she slowly turned to look at Gwen.

'No...' said Gwen, recoiling, her eyes prickling. 'Please...'

'She's alive, Gwen, but she's hurt badly.'

'What happened?'

'I don't know.' Abby waved the paper. There were only a few short sentences on it, scribbled quickly by Campbell when she'd had a chance. 'It doesn't say.'

'I have to go to her.' Tears were now flooding Gwen's eyes and she turned to go, but, before she could take a step, Abby's hand caught her arm and pulled her to a halt.

'You can't, Gwen.' Abby said. 'You're needed here.'

'Kitty needs me too! I have to...' Gwen pulled at the hand, but Abby was unrelenting.

'No, Gwen! I'm sorry, but Kitty *doesn't* need you; she needs doctors and a safe hospital and you need to keep flying so we can stop the Prussians from taking that away.'

Gwen made one last effort to pull away from her, but it was half-hearted; while her heart desperately wanted her to run to Kitty's side, her head understood what Abby was saying and knew that the best way to help her was to stay and fight. She nodded reluctantly. 'Alright. But I need to know more.'

She looked at the man, who nodded. 'I'll do what I can to find out how whatever I can.'

'Thank you.'

'You're welcome.' The man nodded at her then looked at Abby. 'Commodore Campbell said you should go to fifteen minute readiness and asked me to tell you that she would come and find you when she could get away.'

'Good. Thank you.'

The man waited a beat, but when Abby didn't say anything more he gestured in the direction of the door behind him. 'If there's nothing else? I should get back to my post, ma'am.'

'Of course, please don't let us keep you, Lieutenant.'

'Thank you, ma'am.' The man hurried back into the command centre.

'Where are Tanya and the others, Abby?'

Gwen started; she had been so caught up in her worry for Kitty that she had completely forgotten about the rest of the squadron. She looked at Drake and found him staring at Abby with a strained expression, the tan he'd picked up during his months in the Mediterranean faded almost to yellow.

'Tanya ditched her Spit in the Grand Harbour - she's got a few bruises, but she's fine and bagged a Baron apparently. Derek landed his glidewings in one of the main streets in Valletta and is on his way here, but Farrier and Chastity are missing.'

Drake's expression softened slightly in relief at the news of his wife, but his worry didn't completely disappear. 'Missing? What does that mean? Surely they know more than that? I mean, we were fighting above the island, someone must have seen something, or heard their radio calls.'

Abby shrugged and waved the paper again. 'Sorry, you know as much as I do.' She looked around at the frantic activity in the hangar.

'There's no use waiting around here, I suggest we get some food, then go and see how our aircraft are.'

She began leading the way towards the ready room, but a shout from behind them had them turning back.

'Abby!' Campbell came out of the command centre and hurried towards them. Her hair had been hastily pinned back, she had black bags under her eyes and didn't even have the most rudimentary of makeup in place - she had obviously been turfed out of bed as unceremoniously as they had.

'Dot! Is there any news?'

Campbell looked at Gwen and nodded. 'I've just heard from Valletta hospital. Kitty made it there alive and is in the operating theatre now.'

'What happened to her?' asked Gwen.

'She bailed out and managed to deploy her glidewings, but then lost consciousness on the way down. The wind pushed her north, but one of the launches spotted her and followed her. They grabbed her as soon as she fell into the sea and rushed her back to Valletta.'

Gwen swallowed; it was just as well the glidewings were designed to come down on their own if a pilot lost consciousness, but Kitty could have drifted out to sea and never been seen again if it weren't for the Navy's rescue boats. 'How bad is she?'

Campbell hesitated and glanced at Abby who shrugged. 'She's going to worry all day anyway. You might as well tell her.'

Campbell gave her a small nod, then gave Gwen a sympathetic look. 'She got hit by a couple of machine gun rounds, one in the leg, one in the side. The one in her leg tore a pretty big hole in her thigh, but isn't serious, the one in her side is another matter. There are signs of internal bleeding and the doctors have to open her up to find out what's been damaged.'

'Oh, god.' The world seemed to fade away for a second as pictures of Kitty lying on an operating table, her skin peeled back and faceless men and women rooting around inside her flashed in front of her eyes.

'Excu...'

She covered her mouth, cutting herself off, and ran to the side, only just managing to reach the fire bucket she'd been going for before ridding herself of what she'd eaten before flying. It didn't take long and she wiped the back of her hand across her mouth before straightening. To her shame she found the others watching her, waiting until she was ready to continue the conversation.

Campbell looked at her with clear concern. 'I know the medics cleared you after your injury yesterday, Gwen, but are you sure you're alright to fly?'

Gwen nodded, then winced as that made her head swim. 'I'm fine. Nothing a bacon sarnie won't sort.'

Campbell frowned doubtfully, but nodded her acceptance. 'I can't say I believe you, but we need everyone in the air.' She looked at Abby and dropped her voice so that the noise in the hangar prevented any of the men and women hurrying about from hearing her. 'It's not even ten in the morning and we've lost about half our fighters. Most of the pilots have bailed out and will be ready to get back in the air as soon as they get here, but we don't have the aircraft for them. Too many raids like that and there won't be enough to repel a landing.'

Abby shook her head. 'There won't be any more raids like that. They lost too many aircraft themselves and for what? To put a few holes in the airfields that they know we can patch? No, there was something else behind today's raid.'

'They were after me, weren't they?' Owen said.

'Yes...' Abby said, unconvinced. 'But I don't think that was the main objective either.'

'Then what was?' asked Campbell.

'I wish I knew.'

The door to the command centre opened and the grey-haired aviator lieutenant from before appeared. 'Commodore! You're needed!'

He beckoned to her urgently and Campbell gave the Misfits a wry smile. 'I think we're about to find out.'

She rushed off and the door closed behind her.

The Misfits stared at the door as if willing it to open and disgorge information on the Prussian plans, but it didn't and eventually Abby turned to her pilots. 'Someone said something about a bacon sandwich...'

The Misfits barely had time to go to the bathroom then put their feet up before they were ordered to the briefing room, almost as brusquely as they had been woken only a couple of hours earlier.

The pilots of the other squadrons, many of whom had been in the medical centre, had also been summoned, along with the rest of the base's senior officers, but even so it was an all too small group of people that gathered at the front of the room to listen to what Campbell had to tell them.

The Sky Commodore's expression was grin when she entered the room and the pilots watched her come down the aisle in silence, not joking or catcalling as they usually did. She didn't bother climbing onto the platform, but just stood in front of them, leaning tiredly back against it. There was no preamble from her, or even a greeting, she just launched straight into her report.

'Half an hour ago, more than two thousand glidewing troops suddenly appeared over Gozo.' She jerked a thumb over her shoulder to the large map on one of the corkboards which showed the twenty-one islands which made up the archipelago of Malta. Gozo was the second largest of them, lying only three miles off the west of Malta. 'They penetrated our defences and made a landing and have begun consolidating a position at Mgarr, a fishing town with a harbour on the southeastern shore nearest to Malta. However, that is not the only threat we are facing right now. Navy scouts have also spotted a large group of ships steaming towards us. They will be here in less than four hours and will probably use the foothold created by the glidewing troops to occupy Mgarr harbour and land more forces.'

She wearily held her hand up to silence the dismayed muttering that naturally begun to swell up.

'I'm not going to lie to you - we're in trouble. It's going to be hard enough to get rid of just those troops with the limited forces we have, but if the ships bring in more then we're done for, so they have to be stopped.

'To that end, the Nelsons are even now loading torpedoes. They will take off as soon as they are ready to attack the ships and we will be flying escort on them. Once they're back you'll rearm and rewind if you need to, then fly to Gozo to strafe the Prussian troops. After you've done as much as you can at Mgarr, you'll return and rearm again. Then, depending on whether the enemy fleet is still coming or not, you'll either fly escort again or continue to attack the ground troops.

'It's going to be a very long day, so go and get some rest while you can. I'll send someone to let you know when we have an update on the readiness of the Nelsons. That's it. Dismissed.'

Without another word, she pushed herself away from the platform and trudged back up the aisle.

CHAPTER 25

While the Harridans of Warrior and Soldier Squadrons flew close cover on the Nelsons, the three Misfit aircraft, along with the eight remaining pilots of Gladiator Squadron, were given the job of high-level coverage and ascended to twenty-five thousand feet before following the bombers as they flew low over Valletta, then north out over the sea.

None of the fast-moving naval launches, nor the civilian spotters on the island could find any trace of enemy aircraft in the sky, but that didn't mean there weren't any and the bombers were too precious a resource to risk sending out on their own. Owen had offered to take Bloodhound up to take a look, but Campbell had refused to allow him; the mysterious high-altitude aircraft had disappeared into thin air in the chaos of that morning's fight and could still be lurking around, ready to pounce.

Gwen interrupted her scan of the sky to peer down at the sea. From so high up the enemy ships were clearly visible, even without the help of the awful RAC lenses, their wakes stretching out behind them, seemingly forever. They were almost half-way between Sicily and Malta and steaming at an estimated fifteen knots, which would put them off the north coast of Malta in only three hours.

The undersea boat which had spotted them leaving Catania, on the east coast of Sicily, and relayed their position to Malta was still shadowing them and several others had been called in from their positions around Sicily, but there were too few of them to make a difference, even if the screening ships allowed them to get close enough, and it was the bombers who would have to put the largest dent in the enemy fleet.

Gwen winced as she turned her gaze back upwards; the stress of the morning's fight and the worry over Kitty had made her headache a lot worse and every time she scanned the heavens, bright sparks flared in her eyes accompanied by a sharp pain. It took a moment, therefore, for her to realise that the flashes she was seeing high overhead weren't fruit of her mind playing tricks on her.

'Incoming fire!'

'I see it, Two.' Abby said. 'Trafalgar Leader, you have anti-aircraft fire incoming from Bertha.'

Abby's warning came just as the first dense black clouds of flack burst among the bomber formation.

The undersea boat had reported that the enemy fleet didn't include any dedicated anti-aircraft ships, like the Italian Javelins, so the bombers had expected only a moderate amount of fire from the war ships and were in a tight formation to protect themselves from any fighters that came. That only served to make them easy targets for the ferocious bombardment, though, and the first salvo sent three of them spiralling into the sea, sending huge cascades of water into the sky.

The Nelsons hastily spread apart, but it only prolonged their survival and the fire coming from the Prussian airship still found them.

One bomber disappeared into a huge black cloud and never re-emerged. A few others were torn apart and tumbled from the sky. A couple just dropped their nose or a wing and flew deceptively gently into the water. The lucky ones survived their damage, letting off great gouts of steam as their engines were hit, or shedding pieces of wing or tail, and turned to struggle home.

Gwen glanced across at Abby, wondering why she wasn't already ordering them to the attack, but the woman's distraught expression told her what she had known all along; there was absolutely nothing that could be done to help the men and women below, nothing they could do to protect them or prevent their destruction. With Bertha so high overhead there was not even anything they could do in reply.

They were still more than ten miles from the enemy fleet when the call came from Campbell to call off the attack.

Fully a third of the Nelsons had been destroyed in the few minutes that they had braved the bombardment in the struggle to reach the enemy fleet and now the remaining bombers had to endure it for an equal amount of time before they reached safety. More and more were destroyed, falling into the sea and dragging their crews down to the depths with them. After what seemed like a lifetime, though, they were out of range of the guns of the giant airship and, when the few survivors reached the Maltese coast, their escorts were finally freed to seek vengeance for their fallen brethren.

The glidewing troops had occupied Fort Chambray, a sprawling ruin dating back almost two hundred years on top of the hill overlooking the town and harbour of Mgarr. Despite the fact that it was not much more than a collection of walls and crumbling bastions it was a commanding position, easily defensible against a ground attack. It hadn't been designed to protect against enemies in the skies, though.

As the RAC fighters swooped down on them, small calibre machine gun fire reached up towards them from more than a dozen positions on the walls, but the few rounds that hit pattered off their metal fuselages and armoured windscreens like rain on a tin roof.

The return fire was far more effective.

A large group of soldiers had been caught by surprise, resting in the main courtyard, and the Harridans and Spitsteams went straight in to strafe them as they raced for cover. They could have just used their machine guns; they would have been more than enough to kill anyone touched by the metal, but that felt too much like mercy to the pilots who'd just watched hundreds of their colleagues die. They didn't just want as many of the enemy dead as possible, they wanted them punished and the survivors to know what fate awaited them.

The Misfits didn't participate in the slaughter. Instead, Gwen and Drake followed Abby as she took them to the end of the walls and began a run that would take them the length of the fortifications, allowing them to target the soldiers manning the guns from above, an angle from which the parapets would provide them no protection.

Unlike the other squadrons, they did have a reason to use their cannons; the heavy machine guns on the walls were the heaviest the Prussians had, the two anti-aircraft batteries that had been on the walls having been destroyed by the islanders who'd manned them before they had abandoned them. If they could be rendered useless then any British ground forces that were sent in would have a much easier time.

The first gun crew spotted them and struggled to swivel their gun around, but it was too late and they disappeared in a cloud of pulverised limestone as Abby opened fire on them.

Gwen swung wide to strafe the next section of wall, which had two gun emplacements on it. The men had seen the fate of their friends and faces contorted with terror turned towards her as she screamed down at them, but after all that had happened that morning, and the previous months, to herself, to Kitty, to her friends and fellows, she had no pity for them, and she unleashed her cannons without hesitation.

The Misfits made short work of the machine gun emplacements on the walls, the sand bags the Prussians had surrounded themselves with doing nothing to stop their heavy weapons, but when they turned their attention to the rest of the huge fort, looking for fresh targets, they found it deserted, aside from discarded equipment, bloodied remains, and the boldest of the carrion birds, already on the ground, working up their courage to feed.

Abby took them up to join the rest of the fighters circling overhead.

'Badger Leader here, where did the blighters go?'

'Gladiator Leader here, Badger Leader. There are tunnels and storage rooms underneath the fort. They started going down as soon as we showed up.'

'Dammit.'

Gwen peered over the lip of her cockpit as she followed Abby around the large circle they were describing above the fortifications. The buildings within the walls had long been in ruins, but that didn't mean that the basements, storage rooms and tunnels, which the Maltese seemed to delight in excavating in their islands, weren't intact and didn't provide excellent cover for the invading force.

'There's nothing else we can do here, then. Let's go home and see what Haven wants to do next.'

Gwen and Drake fell in beside Abby as she turned to the southeast and headed out over the short channel between Gozo and Malta, followed by the other squadrons.

'We must have gotten eighty or ninety in the courtyard before they scurried under the rocks like cockroaches, ma'am,' said the commander of Warrior Squadron.

The pilots were back in the briefing room with an increasingly worried-looking Campbell.

'We got about forty more,' added Abby. 'There were ten guns on the walls and four men working each of them. Not many got away'

'So, something like a hundred, maybe a hundred and fifty. Out of two thousand or so.' Campbell grimaced. 'I had hoped for better than that, but I'll take it for now. When the army goes in they'll have to stick their heads out and then you'll get the chance to really take the fight to them. But in the meantime we still have to do something about those ships.'

She lifted her eyes to look at the Misfits as she continued. 'Nineteen Nelsons survived the failed attack, five of which will need repairs before they can fly again, and there are forty-five ships in the enemy fleet. The numbers just don't add up, so I've already ordered the Misfit fitters to load Wendy's meltbombs onto the Misfit aircraft and I'm sending up Dreadnought as well.'

'Yes! About bloody time!' Wendy leaped off her seat, knocking it over and almost tipping Owen and Scarlet, sitting on either side of her, off theirs.

Most of the rest of the pilots jumped at the sudden noise coming from behind them and, despite the seriousness of the situation, there were a few laughs as she looked around sheepishly. 'Sorry!' She sat down heavily, Scarlet only just getting her chair standing again before she did so.

Campbell was the only one in the room who didn't at least smile and she continued on as if there had been no outburst. 'I'm informed by Rear Admiral Pritchard that this fleet represents a large part of the enemy presence in the Mediterranean - they are throwing everything they have at us. Therefore, if we destroy it we're not only going to be saving Malta, but we'll cripple the Coalition's ability to make war in this entire theatre.' She paused to let that sink in, then glanced at her antique aviator's chronograph and shook her head. 'Bloody hell, it's not even time for elevenses... Their fleet is still more than two hours away. We're going to wait until they're less than ten miles offshore before launching the attack. That's close enough that Bertha would be in range of our anti-aircraft batteries if it tried to pull the same trick as last time, so you're not going to be under nearly as much fire. However, they will probably launch aircraft to cover their final approach, so everyone else will fly cover - Soldier and Warrior at angels five for close support and Gladiator at angels fifteen.'

She turned back to Abby. 'Prioritise the merchant vessels, particularly those carrying troops if you can, please.'

Abby nodded. 'Will do.'

'Thank you.' Campbell looked around, meeting the eyes of her squadron leaders one by one. 'Any questions?' When there were none she nodded. 'Good. Take off is at twelve hundred hours. Dismissed.'

Abby came to a halt outside the briefing room and gazed around the huge hangar.

Nearest to her, Dreadnought's gun crews were giving their weapons a final check. The men and women who had volunteered to operate the big aircraft's weapons were universally a strange bunch. Of every possible physical type and social background, the only thing they seemed to have in common was a shared love of guns and explosions. That served to keep them together as a very close-knit bunch, though, so close, in fact, that they never really mixed with the rest of the squadron and preferred to be quartered away from everyone else, where they wouldn't disturb anybody with their experiments and "fun". The "Whizz Bangers", as they called themselves, had suffered losses, most notably during the attack on the Prussian-occupied ports during the summer, but there were always dozens more volunteers standing by to join them and Wendy was never short of crew.

Beyond Dreadnought were the aircraft of Warrior, Gladiator and Soldier Squadrons. Derek and Tanya were expected back at any moment and would be flying with the Gladiators for the mission and their Spitsteams were there, their fitters working on them to make sure they were up to their exacting standards. Beyond them, closest to the ramp, shut now, were the three Misfit aircraft. Hummingbird was with them, instead of in her place on the other side of the hangar with Bloodhound, and Abby frowned as she noticed unusual activity around the small gyrodyne. She sighed and picked her way across the cavernous space towards it.

Scarlet was bending down to peer underneath the fuselage of the aircraft while two of her fitters were lying on the floor beneath it, attaching meltbombs to a pod on its belly.

The diminutive Irishwoman looked up as Abby approached and stalked towards her. She planted herself firmly in front of Abby and scowled up at her. 'Before you say anything...'

'I want you with the bombers, you're the same speed as them. Use them as cover, then when they drop their torpedoes and turn for home make your run. By that time we'll have made ours and we'll cover you on the way back out. Understood?'

Scarlet blinked at her. 'Uh, yes. Uh, thank you.'

'Good.' Abby nodded, then smiled. 'Happy hunting.'

'You too!' Scarlet beamed happily, then spun and skipped back to her aircraft.

Gwen sat in a large wingback armchair in a corner of the ready room staring at the bacon sandwich, congealing in its own fat on the table in front of her. Without Kitty there to distract her, or remind her of the future that awaited after the war, she'd found her thoughts becoming increasingly morbid.

She had joined the Misfits ten months ago, in July of 1940. For six months of that time the squadron had seemed invincible, coming through pitched battles over Britain and overwhelming odds in Muscovy almost unscathed, where many other squadrons lost most of their pilots. That had changed drastically since their arrival in Malta, though and in less than five months they had not only lost almost all of their aircraft, but also several of their pilots. Mac, Monty and Chalky were all dead, as were Smith and Drummond, two of the three Navy pilots who had volunteered to join them. Chastity and the third of the Navy pilots, Farrier, were missing in action and, if there was no word from them soon, that meant they were probably dead too.

The Misfits had proven to be less than indestructible and she couldn't help but think that they only had themselves to blame; they had begun to believe in their own legend, to believe that they couldn't be killed and had thrown themselves into several fights they'd had no hope of winning. She also couldn't help but think that a large part of that blame was hers; with the improvements she'd made to the aircraft, making them far superior to those of the enemy, she had only fuelled those beliefs.

Which meant that it was at least partly her fault that her friends had died and that Kitty was in the hospital, barely alive.

Perhaps the Misfits would have been better off if she'd never joined them.

Lost in her dark thoughts, she didn't hear Rudy Drake call out to ask if she wanted some tea. She didn't see Derek and Tanya arrive, either, or look up when the pilots welcome back a bedraggled Farrier, who had been fished out of the sea by a small fishing boat which didn't have a radio to report the rescue, hence the doubt over her survival. Nor did she notice Abby come in and frown in her direction.

An hour later the pilots were called to the flight line. Gwen roused herself, went to the bathroom, then made her way out and up onto the airfield where the aircraft that were going to take part in the attack, including Hummingbird and Dreadnought, were waiting. She spotted Excalibur immediately and walked along the line to her. However, she didn't immediately climb into the cockpit, but stood staring at the myriad of scars that the once-pristine machine had picked up over the past months. Every one of the scratches, dents, or filled in holes had come from a near miss - a blast of ack-ack, a machine gun round, a cannon shell - and each and every one of them could have meant her death if it had been just a few feet, or in some cases a few inches, to one side.

She had been lucky, though. She had survived. Even when shrapnel had penetrated her cockpit and hit her in the head.

What made *her* special? What gave *her* the right...?

'Kitty's going to be fine, you know that, right?'

Gwen jumped and looked up at the sudden sound of Abby's voice from beside her. 'What? Oh. Yes... It's not that.' She shook her head, but then grimaced. 'Well, it's not *just* that. It's, I don't know, *this*.' She waved her hand vaguely, indicating the airfield and the five Misfit aircraft.

'What, you think you have something to blame for all *this*?' Abby mimicked Gwen's gesture with a smile, but then sighed when her wingmate's mood didn't lighten. 'Do you know how many times I've had that conversation with myself? And how many times I've had it with Dot? There are many people that we could blame for the situation we're in - the War Minister for sending us, the Ministry for not committing enough resources, or the Prussians for starting the whole damn shooting match. And yet, after Cece died, I laid in bed, night after night, blaming myself and trying to work out what I could have done differently. What I could have done *better*. Those thoughts went away for a while, but when Mac died they started up again and with every subsequent death - Drummond, Smith, Chalky, Monty, and now Chastity - they have only gotten worse. So, you're going to have those thoughts. It's only natural and it's *fine*. Like Dot told me, it means you haven't got to the point where you no longer care. But just remember that those thoughts aren't true, that there are plenty of people on whom to lay the blame for what's happened to the Misfits on this damn island but *you're not one of them*.' Abby punctuated her last words by poking Gwen in the chest, rocking her back. 'What you're feeling is called survivor's guilt and it has one cure - shaking hands with the Dark Scythesman. You just have to ignore it, like I'm trying to, and, for Darwin's sake, listen to what we've all told you *so many damn times* and learn to *live*!'

Her final words were almost drowned out by an immense hiss and then a cloud of steam rose from Dreadnought as the valves on her engines released excess pressure. The roar that followed as Wendy started her engines was enough to prevent any further conversation, so Abby just grinned, slapped Gwen on the shoulder, then went to Dragon.

Gwen smiled wryly as she watched her go, wondering how many times she would have to hear the same speech before she began to believe it. It wasn't as if she hadn't tried, but it was just her nature to overthink things - she liked to think that was part of what made her such a good designer.

She climbed up onto the trailing edge of Excalibur's wing, then walked up the narrow marked strip beside the fuselage to where Giuseppe was waiting patiently, ready to help with her straps. She gave him a nod, then clambered in and started doing her checks.

As ever, her worries dissipated, at least for a while, as she concentrated on the task at hand.

CHAPTER 26

'Campbell's cut it a bit fine, hasn't she?'

There was humour in Drake's voice, but his comment was understandable; the enemy fleet were clearly visible even as the Misfits flew at a thousand feet over the towers of St Paul's Cathedral in the centre of the island, where the photographs of their fallen comrades were still on display.

As expected, the enemy ships had sailed a slightly roundabout route so as to approach Gozo and Mgarr Harbour from the north, avoiding Malta and the sea defences grouped mostly around the Grand Harbour as much as possible.

Gwen hadn't seen them; she had been too busy peering over her right wing, watching the Nelsons at Ta'Kali taking off and forming up on Dreadnought and Hummingbird - there were so few of them it was hard to imagine them being able to do anything to stop the ships. She lifted her eyes now, though, and took in the sight of the Coalition task group. It was easy enough to pick out which ships Campbell had asked the Misfits to target; the fat and ungainly support vessels were clustered together in the centre of the formation like sheep, flanked by a couple of huge battleships, while the sleeker, far more nimble destroyers, frigates, and corvettes ranged around, hunting for undersea boats and other threats.

'Badgers. Go to full throttle.'

At Abby's command, Gwen pushed her lever to full unwind, then glanced at her Frobisher chronograph.

It was coming up to three minutes past twelve. According to Campbell's schedule the Misfits were due to make their run at five past, at the same time as the undersea boats. Then, at ten past, the bombers would make their attack, followed closely by Dreadnought and Hummingbird, the idea being that they would be covered somewhat by the chaos created by everyone else.

That was the plan at least, but, like most plans in war, it was unlikely to survive contact with the enemy.

'Haven, this is Gladiator Leader. I'm not seeing any enemy aircraft, over.'

'Haven here. They must be there, Gladiator Leader; they'd be foolish not to send some kind of escort. Keep looking, please.'

'Roger, Haven.'

Gwen spared a moment to glance up towards where the Spitsteams of Derek, Tanya, Farrier and the Gladiators had to be, even though there was no hope of spotting them. It was puzzling that the Prussians wouldn't send up at least their fighters to cover their ships during the approach to enemy territory; they must have known the British would send their remaining bombers back out. Perhaps they were planning a bombing raid themselves and they wanted the fighters to provide an escort, but even then, they had enough to send half to cover the ships.

She had no time to think through the reasoning behind the enemy decision because in that moment the first of the screening ships opened fire, closely followed by the rest, including the well-armed battleship.

Gwen pushed her stick forwards sharply, following Abby as she dived towards the sea. Blood rushed to her head, temporarily colouring her vision red and making her feel like her eyeballs were going to burst, but the pressure was just as quickly relieved as she pulled up again, levelling off a hundred feet above the waves and beginning to weave from side to side - the combined fire of the anti-aircraft batteries wasn't even a fraction of that of a single one of the Javelins, but it still had to be respected.

They were flying at top speed, though, so they didn't have to brave the fire for long and twenty seconds after the barrage had begun, Gwen swung Excalibur sharply around one of the huge battleships and lined up on the target she'd chosen, one of the larger merchant vessels, its decks packed with brown-clad soldiers sitting in regimented lines. Faces turned up to her in alarm and a few of the men tried to bring their rifles to bear on her, but it was far too late. She pressed the button to release the meltbombs then banked away.

Puffs of red smoke on the main deck showed that her aim had been good, but she didn't wait around to see what kind of panic she had created among the men; the Misfits had been tasked with causing as much chaos as they could, so she brought her guns to bear on the next troop ship.

Gwen had thought she was used to shooting at men on the ground, she had barely winced when she had attacked the gun positions on the walls of the fortress only an hour or so before, but this was an entirely different prospect. The soldiers were so tightly packed on the decks of the troop ships that every single one of her cannon rounds blasted through several of them, sending sprays of gore in all directions. The horror didn't end there, though, because the shots then ricocheted off the metal of the ship to cause even more destruction on the soft bodies.

She hardened her heart to it with an effort and continued from ship to ship, sending hundreds, perhaps thousands of the Prussian soldiers to meet the Dark Scythesman.

'Badger Leader, this is Trafalgar Leader, we are one minute out.'

'Roger, Trafalgar Leader. Badgers, time to give that battleship something to think about.'

Gwen banked Excalibur towards the battleship on the side of the formation nearest the Nelsons and saw both Abby and Drake do the same. The three of them converged on the huge ship from all directions, only a few yards above the sea.

Defensive fire came from the numerous guns mounted along the length of the ship, but it was completely ineffective against the fast-moving aircraft and only served to show the Misfits where their targets were.

'Incoming fire! Twelve o'clock high!'

Trafalgar Leader's shout contained a note of panic which startled Gwen, but she kept her mind on her job and her hand steady on the stick and completed her attack on an ack-ack gun, scattering and tossing the men serving it aside like rag dolls. Only after she had pulled up and gone over the battleship did she finally search the sky for the new threat.

It didn't take much effort to find it; Bertha was in the sky a couple of miles north of the convoy and raining fire down on the Nelsons.

'What in Shakespeare's name is that thing doing here?' Gwen asked. 'Doesn't Gruber know they're in range of our guns?'

'I'm sure he does,' Drake replied, 'but unless he's on board I'm not sure he really cares.'

The gunners on Malta, always vigilant, reacted extremely quickly to the apparition of the giant airship and the dozens of guns positioned along the north coasts of Malta and Gozo opened fire. The range was extreme and beyond that of the lighter anti-aircraft guns, but the 4.5 inch heavy cannon had no trouble and, after a few ranging shots, began to score direct hits on the stationary target.

Explosions began to blanket Bertha, but they were insignificant against its immensity and it seemed impossible that they would be able to bring the beast down.

The fire from the airship, on the other hand, was far more telling. The range was a lot shorter than it had been before and in quick succession, one after the other, the Nelsons were hit.

In desperation, the remaining bombers launched their torpedoes at long range and turned for home, but Bertha was relentless and sought them out until the last fell into the sea, tumbling over and over, spraying water and metal in all directions, before finally coming to a halt and sinking rapidly out of sight.

As the first black clouds blossomed amongst the Nelsons, Scarlet swerved Hummingbird away from the bombers and dropped to the wave tops. She was a tiny target, hard to hit and would be safe unless the Prussians got in an *extremely* lucky shot.

There was nothing Wendy could do to stop Dreadnought from being completely exposed, though. She could have turned for home, but chose not to and instead pushed her engines to their limits and raced for the convoy, thinking that the airship would have to cease fire when she was over them, for fear of hitting the ships. The ships were still a few miles off, though, and in the meantime her aircraft was struck over and over. Most hits were minor - flak bursts which did nothing more than scratch the inches-thick Duralumin - but a direct impact on her right wing put the outermost engine out of action and another on the middle of the fuselage knocked out a couple of her guns and killed the two Whizz Bangers at them.

The huge machine kept going, absorbing the damage without much complaint, but if she took too much more, then she would just fall from the sky.

Hölle swayed gently from side to side as an explosion rocked Bertha and Gruber looked up in alarm as the lights in the hangar flickered. He toggled his radio. 'Admiral! We're launching. Get the damn hangar door open, now!'

'Of course, Star Leader.'

Gruber waited impatiently as the giant slab of metal twenty metres in front of him began to swing outwards all too slowly. After the debacle in February when the mechanism controlling the door had been damaged and refused to open he had had it changed so that it rotated rather than sliding downwards. It had required enormously expensive structural modifications, but it was now almost impossible to damage and there were fail-safes in place to prevent aircraft being trapped again.

The incredibly thick, armoured door was finely balanced, but incredibly heavy, and the machinery had to work hard to overcome inertia, making it a slower process than before and dangerous to do quickly. However, there was another reason why Gruber had insisted that it be changed to open up and out instead of down and, as soon as he judged that there was enough sky showing at the bottom, he threw Hölle's throttle wide open and released the brakes.

The aircraft was nowhere near takeoff speed by the time the runway ended but it didn't matter; it had forty thousand feet of clear air below it and it just dropped, hurtling down towards the enemy aircraft far below.

'Shut down the feed to engine five!' Wendy shouted at Owen, her copilot for the mission, stabbing her finger at the control panel next to him.

'I know which one it is, Sweety.' Owen calmly reached out to flick the switch which cut the fuel to the stricken engine. His fingers danced over the complex panel as he sent fire suppression foam into it, making sure that the white-hot metal didn't start a blaze, then adjusted the flow of hydrogen to the other engines, compensating for the increased pressure to them now that the pumps were only supplying two instead of three.

Another explosion rocked Dreadnought and threw Owen forward. His straps brought him up before his head hit the panel, though, and he grimaced as the scars on his shoulder pulled painfully.

A light started flashing and he glanced at it. 'We've got a problem with the release mechanism for pod eight. The circuit's broken.'

Wendy swore. 'Call Strange, tell her to leave her gun and stand by the manual release levers.'

'Roger, Poochie.'

Owen grinned as she shot him an evil look; he refused to call her "skipper" like everyone else on the aircraft and instead, every time she let him copilot for her, he came prepared with a dozen or more pet names to tease her with.

He pressed the button to connect him with Georgina Strangeways. The woman had insisted on being on board for the mission, wanting to witness the weapons she'd helped design in use at least once. She'd been on Dreadnought for the mission against Bertha, but been frustrated when they hadn't been able to reach their target. This time it looked like she was going to get her wish, although at the moment she was manning one of the waist guns, replacing one of the two crew members who'd been killed in the opening moments of the bombardment, instead of being strapped into the navigator's seat in the cockpit, surrounded by armoured glass and with a good view, like she was supposed to be.

Once the woman had acknowledged the order, Owen scanned the instrument panels around him. Seeing no new life-threatening emergencies he glanced out of the windscreen at the ships. They were still a good few miles away.

'You know, I'd like you to call me skipper at least once before we die.'

Owen glanced at his wife, seeing the intense concentration on her face and the worry lines that had sprung into being in the last few months, many of them caused by him. 'I will,' he said softly.

She found a second to spare and looked at him expectantly. 'Well?'

He laughed. 'We're not going to die right now, my Rarebit!'

Wendy frowned and opened her mouth to berate him, but right that moment the barrage stopped.

His grin widened almost impossibly. 'See?'

Wendy rolled her eyes. 'One of these days, Llewellyn...'

Tanya watched as the fighters poured out of Bertha, magically appearing out of thin air. They dropped for several thousand feet before levelling out and forming up into their squadrons. Only then did they begin spiralling down towards their prey.

She was fairly sure the first dozen or so that had emerged were red, but she couldn't make out much detail with the awful lenses the British issued their pilots. Rudy was going to buy her a set when they got back to England, along with a proper flightsuit, although he'd said it probably wouldn't be a Petrov; due to the war there weren't many left outside of Muscovy. He was also going to get her an engagement ring to go with the wonderful but simple marriage bands he'd had made. Her first diamonds!

She grinned as she marvelled once more on the fates that had put a poor Russian girl in the path of a British Lord. It was like something out of a Dostoevsky novel.

She peered over the wing of her Spitsteam, her third, trying to spot Lion. It should have been easy with the ridiculous yellow and purple colour scheme Rudy had insisted on, but again the RAC lenses proved inadequate to the job.

She said a prayer for him, spared a smile for Derek, flying next to her, then returned her gaze towards what was now a swarm of more than a hundred fighters. Even though the Nelsons had all been destroyed, Dreadnought was still below, and the ugly aircraft was far too easy a target for the predators. Something had to be done to stop them.

Derek returned the Russian woman's smile with a quick salute, then turned his eyes skyward.

The big airship was wreathed in smoke and boiling black clouds. One of the three fans remaining after Monty's heroic charge seemed to have torn itself apart and there were gashes in the side of the gondola to show where pieces of the blades had ended up. That wasn't the worst of the damage, though, as there were also multiple jagged holes all over it which demonstrated very clearly the accuracy of the Maltese gunners and he thought he detected a slight list, indicating that at least one of the gas bags had been hit. It was beating a retreat now, though, having destroyed the bombers and delivered its load of fighters, although it would undoubtedly be moving a lot slower with only two fans.

He nodded in satisfaction. The formidable anti-aircraft batteries of Malta had done what the RAC hadn't been able to and dealt a blow to the most effective weapon the Prussians had. It remained to see whether they would be able to complete the job before it retreated out of range.

More than two dozen explosions had rocked the enemy ships, as the torpedoes from the Nelsons and undersea boats found targets, and over half of those were clearly sinking, but it wasn't nearly enough. The attack wasn't over, though, and Gwen completed her fourth run on the battleship just in time to witness the arrival of Dreadnought, raining down incandescent fire as she sped by.

'Form up, Badgers, let's give her an honour guard.'

Gwen broke off and joined the other two fighters as they accelerated away from the huge warship, leaving the majority of the Prussian gun crews broken and battered behind them.

Dreadnought's heavy cannon were having a devastating effect on the merchant vessels, ripping through their unarmoured sides as if they were paper and punching large holes in their hulls close to, and occasionally just below, the water line. The damage probably wouldn't sink many of them, if any, but Dreadnought was more than just a gun platform and meltbombs began tumbling from the oversized pods mounted on her belly. The dark objects struck one after another of the ships, sending up puffs of deceptively harmless red smoke, until eight of the ships were wreathed in it.

'That's my lot, Badger Leader. Want me to keep pounding them with my cannons?'

'Negative, Firepower, I don't want you staying around in case those fighters come down to play. Good job well done, now return to base and reload for the next sortie.'

'Roger, Leader.'

'Let's pave the way, Badgers.'

The three fighters surged ahead of Dreadnought as the big aircraft banked around towards Malta and dropped to the wave tops. The surviving gunners on the battleship saw them coming, but they had apparently had enough punishment for one day and dived away from their guns, taking cover wherever they could. The Misfits gave them a quick burst anyway, just to keep their heads down, but then they were past.

'You're on your own now, Firepower. Badgers, let's head up and give our boys and girls a hand.'

The meltbombs in the pod on Hummingbird's belly were long gone but Scarlet didn't really need a release mechanism like the other Misfits, who were locked into their flying sausages, and as she approached another of the merchant ships she just reached through her open window and grabbed a bomb from the rack bolted to the outside of her fuselage.

'Whee!' She laughed gleefully as she let go of it, then spun her agile machine through one hundred and eighty degrees and came back around to toss another.

This was the first time she'd been in combat in ages and, with no reconnaissance or sabotage missions to relieve the boredom, she was determined to make the most of the chance to play with the enemy for once.

Abby frowned at the battle raging overhead. At the first sign of the enemy fighters, the Harridans had climbed up to join the Spitsteams, but even with the squadrons combined, they were still vastly outnumbered. They were fighting valiantly even so, just as they had so many times before, and were shooting down more Prussians than they lost, but the enemy could afford the losses, they couldn't, and wouldn't be able to keep fighting for very long.

She glanced back down at Dreadnought, willing Wendy to get a move on. The big aircraft was well clear of the ships but still a good couple of minutes from the safety of Malta. Once she made it there, the remaining Harridans and Spitsteams would be able to disengage. If they lasted that long.

It was just as well help was at hand.

The fight had naturally descended as height was substituted for speed, meaning the Misfits didn't have far to climb to reach it and they fell on the enemy fighters, spreading destruction wherever they turned.

The last of the enemy fighters, the three Misfit aircraft, were finally engaged. It was time.

'Star Squadron, follow me.'

Gruber rolled Hölle onto its wing and let gravity take it. Fifteen bright red Blutsaugers followed him down, but they were unable to keep up as he pushed his aircraft to the limit. The airframe began to creak and protest, but he trusted in Blume's engineering and kept going, not wanting to lose the element of surprise, not wanting anyone to warn his target before he'd had a chance to shoot it from the sky.

He laughed, exhilarated, as the sea seemed to rush towards him, but he resisted the temptation to pull back on the stick and kept the nose down, pointed directly at the giant cruciform of the Misfits' heavy bomber, Dreadnought.

Georgina Strangeways fumbled the lenses on her borrowed flight helmet into place then bent down to peer through the armoured glass over the shoulder of Dreadnought's rear gunner. She grinned at the sight of the enemy fleet surrounded by red smoke - it looked like every single one of the merchant vessels had been hit at least a couple of times and most six or seven. She could imagine the panic aboard them as the men tried to wash away the acid and not only failed to stop its inexorable march but spread it further and caused more damage. She wished that she could stay around to watch the ships sink and make notes on which were the most effective placements for the bombs in which of the different classes of enemy vessels, but Dreadnought was an easy target for the Prussian fighters and had to race for safety.

Nervously, she leaned forward and squinted up through the glass at the fight taking place only a mile above. She could clearly make out each individual aircraft as they swooped and tumbled around each other like feeding swallows.

Dreadnought was far too vulnerable and they were far too close; the enemy could cover that kind of distance in a heartbeat.

She took one last look at the ships, intending to go back to her temporary post at the waist gun, but a flash in the sky over them caught her eye and she paused.

Her eyes widened and she fumbled with the wire of her headphones. She followed it to the jack and stabbed it at one of the sockets spread throughout the machine. On the third try it slipped in and she pressed the button. 'Incoming fighters! Six o'clock high!'

Gwen gave a 190 a quick squirt of her machine guns as it crossed in front of her nose. She missed by a couple of feet but the fright was enough to put the pilot off and he swerved away from the Harridan he'd been pursuing, allowing it to escape. Her own target couldn't get away from her, though, and she used a couple of her dwindling supply of cannon rounds to blast a big hole in its wing next to the fuselage and send it spinning away.

'This is Firepower, I have incoming fighters!'

Gwen didn't hesitate or even look, she just abandoned her search for a target, put Excalibur on her back and pulled the stick into her lap.

Gruber swore as his shots went wide - the guns of the immense aircraft had opened fire right before he had and he had flinched. It didn't matter; he would still say he hit it first and when the rest of his squadron shot it down the kill credit would still be his.

Hölle was out of her reach, but the rest of the Barons in their Blutsaugers were lagging behind him for some reason, apparently so focussed on trying to catch up with their wayward leader that they hadn't noticed her approach.

She slotted in behind a straggler and throttled back slightly so as not to overshoot, then opened fire, raking it with machine gun fire. The aircraft fell away and she put it out of her mind.

'Only fifteen to go...' A quick glance at her ammunition counter showed that there was no way she was going to be able to destroy all of the Barons, even if they lined up nicely for her.

A flash of purple off her wing told her that she didn't have to, though, and another of the Barons disintegrated in mid-air, the pieces scattering to the winds.

'Mind if I join the party, Goosy?'

'Not at all, dig in.'

'Very funny, Badger Two, now shift over a bit so I can have a clear shot as well.'

Drake laughed, but it was Abby's voice which filled Gwen's ears and she glanced in the mirror above her cockpit to find Dragon directly behind her. She gave her rudder a touch to swing out of the way and saw flashes come from beneath Abby's wings as she opened fire. Two more of the Barons tumbled away in quick succession.

'Show off.' Drake grumbled.

'It's not a competition, Three,' said Abby with a laugh.

'That's alright for you to say,' Gwen complained as she banked hard after a pair of red aircraft, 'you always shoot down more than anyone else.'

'I know. Maybe I should have said it's *no* competition.'

The rest of the Barons finally became aware of the threat bearing down on them and scattered. 'Goosy, go make sure Gruber stays away from Dreadnought. Digger and I have got the minions.'

'Roger, Leader.' Gwen continued her dive as Drake and Abby peeled off to follow the Blutsaugers. She blocked out their voices as they continued their banter and concentrated on Hölle.

For a moment, Gwen thought it was strange that Abby had sent her after Gruber instead of confronting him herself, but she quickly realised that, with Malta so close, he would only have time for one more run on Dreadnought before she made it to the safety of the coastal guns. There was no need for her to defeat him, or even drive him off, all she had to do was distract him for a minute. And if the room dedicated to her on Bertha was anything to go by, she was the one person who would be able to do that.

Gruber's full power dive had caused him to overshoot his target by a large margin and he was only just coming back around. He completed the turn quickly, though, and Gwen saw the nose of Hölle dip as he dived at Dreadnought. She put Excalibur on an intercept course, aiming for a point between the Baron and his prey. If things continued as they were she would have a very easy shot at him and he would have to fly through the combined fire of four cannons and six machine guns - she doubted he would survive.

He must have seen her and worked out that he couldn't continue his attack, because the profile of the aircraft changed as he pulled up. However, instead of banking away from her and retreating like she'd expected, Hölle's wings became thinner and the fuselage shorter and shorter, until he was pointed directly towards her.

Gwen couldn't believe that Gruber would have the nerve to try a head to head pass with her; it was completely uncharacteristic - he always ensured the odds were heavily stacked in his favour before taking on an enemy. Yes, he had a slight height advantage over her and was fresh into the fight, whereas she was tired and running low on ammunition, but that meant next to nothing in this situation.

In 1927 the Société Aéronautique had held its meeting in Japan. The hosts had put on an exhibition of Japanese culture, including such things as dance, music, automation and pottery, but there had been a couple of hours dedicated to the martial arts. While most of the members hadn't paid much attention to the displays of martial prowess, their interests being more technical or mechanical, Gwen had found it fascinating, especially the demonstration of swordplay by a group of masters, who had fought duels with bamboo swords coated with red paint; their focus and concentration before they moved and their speed when they finally did, had been captivating. It had quickly become apparent, though, that there was almost no way for either of the swordsmen to win cleanly, as both usually came out of the fight with red streaks on their white uniforms.

A head on pass between two fighters was very much like that - even if one of them did "win" it was very unlikely that they would come out of it unharmed, and by far the most likely outcome was that both aircraft would be destroyed and their pilots killed.

The two fighters were closing at almost eight hundred miles per hour and would be within effective range of each other for about a second. The part which came after that deadly second was just as dangerous, though, because the pilots had to then carry out some kind of manoeuvre to avoid a collision and hope against hope that the enemy didn't choose to do the same thing.

So many things could go wrong and not a lot could go right but Gwen was determined to go through with it and do what she could to make sure Gruber didn't survive, even if it meant her own life as well. Her death would be insignificant in the grand scheme of things, but so many of the Prussian hopes and so much of their morale, was dependent on the continued success and survival of the leader of the Crimson Barons.

She took a deep breath and settled herself into her seat, scooting down slightly to put herself just a little bit further behind the armour plate in front of her cockpit. She centred the dot of her deflector sight over the nosecone and the blurry circle of Hölle's airscrew, then covered the firing button on Excalibur's yoke with her thumb, tightening her grip at the same time, not wanting the vibrations of the guns to put off her aim.

Two miles. Ten seconds.

Steady Gwen.

The urge to turn away from the threat was almost overwhelming, but she forced herself to hold still and sent all of her awareness reaching out towards the red machine, feeling the path her bullets would have to take.

A mile.

Ready...

She blinked, surprised, as bright flowers bloomed on the enemy aircraft's wings and had to consciously stop herself from reflexively pressing the button and returning fire.

Far too early!

A couple of sharp bangs betrayed the fact that Excalibur had been hit, but the bullets were spent and didn't penetrate the Duralumin skin.

Hölle still wasn't in range when the points of light winked out and the aircraft pulled up sharply.

Gwen couldn't believe her luck, or Gruber's stupidity, but she wasn't going to look a gift horse in the mouth and she gently pulled back on her stick, leading the aircraft with the red dot of her sight.

Less than two seconds later she was in range and opened fire.

Excalibur juddered as her ten guns spouted lethal metal, but, after only a split second, first her cannons, then her machine guns fell silent.

Gwen glanced at her ammunition counters and found that every single one of them was showing nought.

She cursed, but instead of breaking off and returning home she grinned and throttled back a touch so that she could slot in behind the slower Hölle.

The sound of cannon fire didn't quite drown out Drake's laugh. 'One more! That's three!'

'Well done.' There was a slight pause, then Abby's voice returned. 'But I've got five.'

'Bloody hell!'

In spite of the ease with which the Misfits were shooting them down, the Barons were some of the best pilots the Prussians had to offer and they had quickly recovered from their surprise and regrouped, turning to push back at the two British pilots.

That only prolonged the inevitable, though, as Drake and Abby flew rings around them.

Eventually, elite pilots though they were, they'd had enough and, at some signal, they broke off and fled.

'Let them go, Digger.' Abby said, already turning away from them and towards Malta.

'Why? We've got them on the run!'

'Because I want to pick up another load of meltbombs before those ships reach Gozo.'

'Oh. Alright.'

The disappointment was clear in Drake's voice and she understood it perfectly, nevertheless it was the right thing to do and he fell in on her wing.

'Erm... What's Goosy doing? Three o'clock low.'

Abby peered over her right wing. A couple of miles away her wingmate was *playing* with Hölle, staying a couple of hundred yards behind Gruber, in an easy firing position, following him as he twisted and turned, frantically trying to get away from her.

'She's had half a dozen opportunities to kill him already.'

'More.' Abby clicked the selector on the radio panel next to her from Drake's number to the Misfit frequency. 'Two, this is Badger Leader. Check in, please.'

'I'm out of ammo, Leader.'

'Then what the hell are you doing still chasing Gruber?'

There was a moment of silence during which Abby saw Gwen's face turn up towards the two Misfit aircraft.

'I'm letting him know that he's not the best pilot in the world, but just a very naughty boy, Leader.'

'Jolly good. But he's going to realise something is up when you don't shoot him down soon. Break off and return to base, please.'

'Spoilsport... Returning to base.'

Abby gave the still-approaching ships a last, concerned glance, then turned her eyes upwards. The Spits and Harrys had lost quite a few aircraft, but seemed to be just about holding their own now. They didn't have to any longer, though.

'Badger Leader to all aircraft, Dreadnought is clear and so are we. Heading home. Suggest you do the same. Over.'

She pushed the throttle to the stops and put Dragon into a shallow dive towards Hal Far.

Even though the loss of the Nelsons had been tragic, the enemy ships had been dealt with and the few that would be left after the meltbombs had done their job would be easy prey for the Misfits.

'How many are left for us to sink? How many did our meltbombs destroy? And if you tell me I can't paint markings on Hummingbird, I'm going to be extremely annoyed, and you wouldn't like me when I'm annoyed.'

'None. None of the ships that were only hit by meltbombs were sunk.'

Scarlet's expectant grin faded at Campbell's answer and she stared at her in shock, open-mouthed.

The Misfits had gone to their ready room to rest for a few minutes while their fitters prepared their aircraft for another sortie and the Irishwoman had leapt out of her armchair as soon as Dorothy Campbell had entered and confronted her eagerly. That eagerness had vanished in the face of the news.

Abby leaned forward in her seat and stared at the Sky Commodore. 'None? None whatsoever?' When Campbell shook her head she turned to look at Wendy. 'How is that possible?'

The big woman sighed. 'I was afraid of this.'

'Of what?'

'Well, the Italians developed the acid in the bombs we're using, so it just stands to reason they would have developed a neutralising agent. They must have distributed it to the ships after we used it on them before. Sorry, I didn't think that they would work it out or distribute it so quickly.'

There were groans at the news and Wendy looked down at her tea, ashamed.

Owen put his arms around her and pulled her to him. 'It's not your fault, darling, it's not as if we could have done anything differently anyway. Isn't that right?' He looked up at Campbell defiantly. 'We had to try something.'

Campbell nodded. 'It was worth a shot, but now I'm afraid we're done here.'

'Done? What does that mean?'

'It means that for the rest of the day you and the rest of the fighters are going to attack the ships and do what you can to destroy their equipment and delay their unloading, but tonight we are evacuating.'

EPILOGUE

The British fighters carried out half a dozen more sorties during the day, strafing the Prussian forces as they unloaded their ships, but they had known the whole time that, no matter how many men they killed or vehicles they left smoking wrecks, it would make no difference; the British were leaving Malta that night.

The evacuation started after nightfall, under cover of darkness, and moved extremely quickly, the section heads having been briefed during the afternoon.

Whatever that was going, including Hummingbird, was packed into wagons and driven to the Grand Harbour, where it was loaded onto the Arturo and the two remaining destroyers. Everything else, including the remaining Spitsteams and Harridans, was destroyed to deny it to the Prussians, except for the food and medical supplies, which were given to the local communities. Once that was done, the men and women followed the wagons to Valletta, most of them walking the few miles.

As soon as the air bases were deserted, explosives were placed on the support columns of the bunkers and the mechanisms of the ramps by the RAC's demolitions experts. Clockwork fuses were set for mid-morning and, after the demolition experts were out, the personnel entrances were filled in with several tons of concrete and hidden under turf.

Wagons took the last few people to the harbour and at midnight the ships sailed. They turned east as soon as they left the harbour, then south, before finally turning west when they were out of sight of the island, describing a large circle in an attempt to avoid enemy detection.

Dreadnought and Bloodhound took off an hour later and flew south for twenty minutes before turning west. The large aircraft had enough range to make it to Gibraltar on their own, where they would be dismantled and packed into crates, ready for the Arturo to transport back to England.

The three Misfit fighters couldn't make it that far, so they were going to take off a couple of hours before dawn and would rendezvous with the Arturo when she was well clear of Malta. Radio silence had been imposed, though, so as not to give the game away, and the Misfits didn't know if the carrier would be waiting for them or not. There was a real possibility that it would be intercepted, sunk, or forced away and they might well be ditching into the Mediterranean, or landing in enemy occupied Africa a few hours after takeoff.

With the rest of the Misfits gone as passengers on Dreadnought, it was only Gwen, Drake and Abby left and they decided to spend the few hours they had before takeoff on the airfield with their aircraft instead of making their way to the empty house and back. They had brought cushions from the sofas of the ready room to lie on, blankets in case they were cold, some sandwiches, and a flask of tea each for the wait.

Abby immediately lay down and went to sleep, but Gwen couldn't and sat sipping tea, gazing into the night, towards Valletta.

The wounded and sick from the hospital had been among the first passengers taken on board the Arturo, but some had been too injured to be moved, Kitty among them. The American hadn't yet woken up and was still in a critical condition. The doctors wouldn't risk moving her and she was going to be left behind.

Gwen had been reassured that there was no danger of Kitty, the other patients or the doctors who had volunteered to stay behind, falling into the hands of the enemy. The underground facilities had been sealed off and the hospital building had been collapsed over it, as if it had been destroyed by bombing and there were concealed tunnels connecting the lowest levels with the sea, for when the time came to evacuate them. She couldn't help but be worried, though, not least of all because the doctors hadn't been able to assure her that Kitty would even survive her injuries.

'She'll be fine.'

She turned towards the sound of Rudy Drake's voice and found him propped up on his elbow, looking at her. The moon was almost full, something which had worried Campbell and Captain Hewer as they wouldn't have the cover of darkness, but, to everybody's relief, clouds had rolled in soon after dark and Rudy was little more than a shadow.

'How? We're leaving her on an island which is going to be crawling with enemy soldiers in a few hours. Even if she survives her wounds, she'll probably end up being handed over to Gruber and... and...'

She broke off and turned away from him to scrub the back of her hand across her eyes, grateful that the dark would hide her tears.

There was a rustle as Drake stood, then the cushions under her bent as he sat next to her. An arm went around her and she let him pull her close and rested her head on his shoulder.

'The Maltese know what they're doing. They've been smuggling stuff on and off this island for centuries and a few people aren't going to be a problem for them.'

'I hope you're right.'

'Of course I am! Now, come on, let's talk about something else. Um, did I ever tell you about the orientation flight they insisted on giving us in the University Air Squadron? No? Well, I took up the instructor, she was one of those old, stuck in the mud types, a bomber driver from the first show and she'd...'

Even though she could barely feel him through her greatcoat and flightsuit, somehow she found the contact comforting and that, combined with his soft, familiar voice, soon lulled her to sleep.

'Rise and shine, children, it's almost time to go.'

Gwen opened her eyes to find Abby grinning down at her. Like Kitty, it seemed that she was a disgustingly cheerful morning person and for a moment she wondered what the hell there was to smile about, but then something shifted behind her and her eyes widened as Drake's voice came from right by her ear.

'Do we have time for a cup of tea?'

Abby nodded with a smile. 'You've got time for a quick snack, but no more cuddling. Takeoff in ten minutes.'

'Righty-ho!' Drake said. He patted Gwen on the hip. 'Fancy a cuppa, Goosy?'

'Please.'

Gwen held perfectly still as Drake unfolded himself from around her and waited until he was up before sitting. He winked and gave her one of his cheekiest grins, then turned his attention to the tea, using a tiny clockwork lamp to see what he was doing.

Gwen scrubbed her face with her hands and groaned; as if it wasn't enough having to get by on a few hours' sleep, Rudy was probably going to be teasing her about dropping off in his arms for the whole flight.

A rustling noise caught her attention and she hissed to her companions as she leapt to her feet and peered into the darkness.

Abby and Drake stopped what they were doing and joined her.

They eventually made out a silent host swarming in through the twisted wreckage of the gates.

'Is it the Prussians?'

Before Abby could answer Gwen's question, a voice hailed them. 'My friends!'

Drake frowned. 'Father? Is that you?'

There was a laugh. 'Of course! Who did you think it was? The Prussians?'

Drake grinned at Gwen. 'No, of course not!'

The shadowy form of the priest, Father Bugelli, materialised out of the darkness, his black cassock serving to camouflage him fairly effectively until he was only a few paces away. The people accompanying him shuffled to a halt a few yards behind him and Gwen wasn't particularly surprised to see there were dozens, perhaps hundreds of them.

'You heard we were leaving then?' Abby asked.

The priest answered with a smile, even though the question was purely rhetorical. 'Yes, we did.'

'I'm sorry.'

Bugelli shook his head. 'Don't be, you need to go.'

'We will be back.'

'I know.' The priest nodded. 'The photographs of the men and women who have died protecting us have already been moved to a safe location and we will keep their memory alive until you return. The Prussians may occupy the land, but they will never conquer its people. Malta will be waiting and her people will be waiting.'

He made the sign of the cross in the air in front of him and there was a rustle as the people behind him did the same. 'Good speed and may we meet again under better circumstances.'

The Misfits took off ten minutes later, the three aircraft in their perfect formation waved off by the silent mass below.

As they banked away over the sea to the south, Gwen looked back and wondered if she would ever see Kitty again.

ABOUT THE AUTHOR

Simon Brading's interest in aviation began when he was very young and at thirteen he joined the RAF section of the Combined Cadet Forces of Dulwich College with the aim of becoming a pilot. However, when he was 18, had reached the rank of Flight Sergeant in the CCF and was trying to get into a University Air Squadron, he was told that his eyesight wasn't good enough to be a pilot, so he had to move onto plan B... something else.

He tried his hand at many things before it occurred to him that he might have a few stories to tell. He never lost his interest in flight, though, and hopes to add a PPL to his very basic and probably extremely expired glider license.

www.simonbrading.co.uk

For news of special offers, upcoming releases, exclusive content, competitions and events, please follow me on social media.

Instagram - @sibrading
Facebook - Simon Brading Author
Tiktok - @SimonBradingAuthor

In addition, souvenirs and merchandise, including T-shirts, badges, stickers and more, are available from the Misfit Squadron store on REDBUBBLE at
https://www.redbubble.com/people/misfitsquadron/shop

ALSO BY SIMON BRADING

The "Displacers" series - a young adult time travel adventure series for all ages.
The Time Traveller's Nephew
The Secret of the Ancients
The Whitechapel Plot
The Price of Greed
The Time for Vengeance

The "Misfit Squadron" Series - a Steampunk series set in an alternate World War 2.
The Battle Over Britain
The Russian Resistance
A Misfit Midwinter
The Lion and the Baron
The Maltese Defence
Tales From the Second Great War
The Siege of Gibraltar
The King's Mission
The Home Front

The Dismal Futures books - stand-alone science fiction tales suitable for adults.
Empath
The Lifeboat at the End of the Universe

The "Twin Ambitions" series - ballet books for children ages 7 and up.
Fight to Dance
Back to Basics

The "Ni Hon - The Two Books" Series - a young adult series set in a dystopian future Japan.
The Black Book

Others
Public Enemy